YOU'VE GOT TO BE KIDDING

YOU'VE GOT TO BE KIDDING

Brian O'Donnell

National Library of Australia Cataloguing-in-Publication

Creator: O'Donnell, Brian, author.

Title: You've got to be kidding / Brian O'Donnell.

ISBN: 9780648014621 (paperback)

     9780648014638 (ebook)

Subjects: Humorous stories. Short stories.

Cover and Typeset: Pickawoowoo Publishing Group

Printed & channel distribution:
Lightning Source | Ingram (USA/UK/EUROPE/AUS)

Table of Contents

PREFACE

THE TWENTIETH CENTURY

GOSH, DID ALL THIS HAPPEN IN A MERE 100YEARS?

We've gone from steam engines and cart horses to supersonic planes and Jumbo jets, which carry several hundred passengers around the world in a day.

We've gone from carthorses to computer-controlled tractors that use satellites to steer them around the paddocks. In the fields of medicine we have progressed from sawbones surgery to keyhole operations, even performed half a world away with television guidance.

Yes, of course it did, and much, much more. We have satellites and men in space. Men have walked on the moon and used telescopes to look at most of our universe. Organ transplants are an everyday event these days and with the help of plastic surgery we can, and do change the shape and appearance of the human form. Even our brains are frequently operated on to remove tumours and other abnormalities

Aeroplanes have changed the way we fight wars allowing the advent of the atomic bomb. Gas and germ warfare are now a reality as are other forms of hi-tech warfare designed to kill whole populations of people, without getting our hands dirty.

We now have vehicles that almost drive themselves with a host of magical gadgets for our comfort and entertainment as we travel along on bitumen roads. However the death toll and injury from traffic accidents is even more horrific than ever.

There are the massive ocean liners that cruise the world in supreme luxury and our homes are full of electronic wonders, made to make life easier and better for us.

We have worldwide communication networks to keep tabs on every one, with instant response times and minimal costs. Computers have become a necessary part of everyday living otherwise I would not be writing this article.

In spite of all this progress our daily lives are still full of incurable and deadly diseases. We are still faced with the common cold, influenza, malaria and many, many more illnesses. Even the more serious illnesses that, we thought we had eradicated, with the help of vaccination and immunisation are back with us today in many parts of the world, and those cure-all wonder drugs and antibiotics no longer work.

We fought our way through two world wars that we believed would end all wars, yet each night as we turn on the "telly", we hear of all the wars that are happening today on every continent and in almost every country of the world. Many of these wars are between various sections of people from the same race and country. The world is full of refugees who need to escape from their own kind. Most of these modern wars are fought in the name of one religion against another, or one ethnic race against another, within the same country.

Meanwhile, in spite of all our advances in agriculture and food production, better seed, better fertilisers, irrigation schemes and chemicals sprays that "kill all" and increase yields, half of the world's population is dying of starvation. More and more people need to be fed as populations increase alarmingly around the world. However most of the current production is being syphoned off to buy weapons and bullets whilst the children are left to starve and suffer in the most horrific circumstances.

Why is it, that in this modern hi-tech world so many greedy people, mainly men, are prepared to fight, rob, kill, usurp power, and inflict pain and suffering on others less fortunate than they, only to fatten their already overfull bellies, and over flowing coffers, with land that they do not need and cannot use, food that they cannot eat and goods that they cannot utilise? What are these people trying to prove? Why can't they be satisfied with what they have and live in peace with others? Why do they need to be the top dog and destroy those around them?

If all these resources, all this money and all

these assets, were put to good use, rather than warfare, no one would need to go hungry, and all the world's children would go to bed each night, with full bellies, in safe and secure homes.

There would, even be enough money left over, to fight, and maybe win some of the battles in health and medicine.

How is it that today, although we have all manner of electronic entertainments, so much mobility and education, many of our young people are turning to mind altering drugs, committing suicide and crimes, such as violence, and vandalism and murder. Our elderly citizens, who are no longer respected, are being robbed beaten and raped, even in their own homes.

However, we look forward to the future, in spite of GST, and hope that the next 100 years will see the world in much better shape, where we can all live together in harmony whilst sharing equally with our fellow men, regardless of colour, creed, race or religion.

Brian O'Donnell

ACKNOWLEDGMENTS

"YOU'VE Got To Be Kidding" is a collection of yarns and short stories about my life over the years. It would never have happened had not my youngest son, David, kept pestering me to write them down for posterity. He pointed out that once I departed this world they would be gone forever, which in hindsight may have been a good thing. However, I pointed out to David, that nothing in this world would induce me to sit around the house with a box of biros and many reams of paper just to please him.

He was "SO-O-o-o-H" determined to get me to write my stories that he turned up at our home one weekend with a metal box full of second hand bits and pieces then asked me, "Alright Dad, what's your excuse now?"

Dave worked in a computer store where he built up new computers to customer's orders.

He had a shed full of second hand parts that he had saved from scrap and obsolete machines which he proceeded to sort, evaluate and assemble into a metal box that eventually became a 486 computer. He only needed to ad a used keyboard, an old monitor and mouse then it was a short trip around to annoy hell out of his Dad. I was able to turn it on and off with a little tuition from my seven year old grandson. Dave located a very ancient Epsom tractor printer then painstakingly explained how it all worked.I joined a writers group organised by a dear friend who had shared part of my life in Hyden. Pat Clayton checked my stories and added them into a small magazine that she shared with a dozen or so of her friends who are scattered across WA. Pat and the other writers criticised my work and put me on the straight and narrow. I owe my thanks to Pat and her friends involved in her magazine "Magabout" for their undying enthusiasm for my efforts and their continual encouragement to continue.

As time went by I have upgraded my computers and associated equipment so that I can present a more professional version of my works. David is still a large part of my writing as he often has to respond to my urgent phone calls to sort out various technical problems that still occur and are sometimes beyond my ability to solve. David has also provided some of the material for a couple of my stories. I owe a debt of gratitude to Jim Drennan a dairy farmer from Waterloo in WA. who first challenged me to write a book after listening to some of my yarns whilst we enjoyed a cup of tea with his wife Jenny after cutting their lawns.

My stories are true stories from my life's experiences but I have changed a few names and added small amounts of materials to make them more readable.

I would like to thank all the crew at Pick-a-woo-woo publishing for all the assistance I received with formatting my books. without Pick-a-woo-woo there would be no books to publish. There dedication was legendary as they dragged me through my naivety with all the technicalities involved. Well done Pick-a-woo-woo.

Chapter 1

AIR RAID SIRENS AND TIME BOMBS

I was born in a small stone cottage in the County of Kent in 1940. The cottage had only two rooms. One room, the living room cum kitchen, was on the ground floor with a small bedroom above under the roof. It was a quaint old thatched cottage on a farm. The staircase to get to the bedroom wound around the chimney, which was built into the wall at one end. The floor in the living room consisted of stone flags laid on the bare ground. The staircase was so narrow and winding that it was impossible to get the bedroom furniture up there so it was necessary to completely remove the window and it's frame from the bedroom wall and winch all the furniture up the wall. The thatched roof was inhabited by many assorted spiders and some of them were so huge that mum used to get our cat to catch them for her.

The cottage was situated on the approaches to London from the east coast and was directly beneath the flight path of the German bombers that were heading for London and the docks on the river Thames. Only a narrow field away on the seaward side there was a large battery of anti aircraft guns set up to help protect London from the bombers

The second world war, had been raging for a whole year when my mother went into labour prior to my birth and the air raid sirens were screaming their warnings over the city. There were hundreds of Jerry bombers roaring through overhead and they were flying low, just above the barrage balloons over London. Virtually every bomber that was heading for London passed directly over our home.

One weekend shortly before my birth dad went into the town of Gravesend on the bus to shop for his family. On the way into town there was a loud crashing and tearing sound and some pieces of shrapnel and an adjustable nose cone from an anti aircraft shell crashed through the roof of the bus. The chap sitting in front of dad copped it on the head. Luckily for him he was an ARP. Warden and was wearing his hard hat and was unhurt except for a sore neck. Once the bits of shell were cool enough to handle dad picked up two bits of shrapnel about the size of tennis balls and the nose cone and took them home. He kept them in his home until he emigrated to Australia at the age of 80.

My father had to go down into an air raid shelter to register my birth because that's where the office of births and deaths was situated for the duration of the war.

When I was about one year old the Jerry bombers changed tactics and set about the total destruction of London using incendiary bombs to set it alight. The weekend that the German bombers set London on fire my dad decided to get the heck out of there and we evacuated first to a farm alongside the town of Selby on the river Humber then to rural Yorkshire where I grew up on a farm on the plain of York close to the start of the river Ouse near Boroughbridge. The river Ouse was formed when the river Ure joined the river Swale just east of the town.

We lived in the area where Herriot's Country of "All Creatures Great and Small" fame, merged with Heartbeat country of the television series of that name. From our home we could see the famous 'White Horse' that was carved on the limestone scarp of the Hambleton Hills

I cannot claim to have met that lovable old rogue Claude Greengrass nor even James Herriot but I grew up amongst many similar, quirky characters whom I hope to introduce to you in the following stories.

I feel sure that you will come to love them as much as I do, so please, just sit back and enjoy some of my tales.

Chapter 2

THE RED ROOSTER

My teenage years were so full of activity that there was never enough time to fit everything in. Oh no, we didn't have television, video recorders, computers, video games etc. like they have today. In spite of this severe lack of basic equipment needed for daily survival we had a ball. Every day was full of happy and humorous events that I'll remember to my dying day. Each day when the sun came up was a real bonus and still is today even though our lives haven't been all 'beer and skittles', so to speak and we've had our share of troubles and strife.

I spent most of my teenage weekends at a large farm, the home of a school friend, who was one of many children in a large family and they were all expected to pull their weight and help with all the many jobs that are needed to run a large family farm. They also ran a farm contracting business without too much outside labour because everyone had to "pitch in" to get the work done. Don't get me wrong, unlike our modern society, no one believed that there was anything wrong with this and in fact we would have been very upset had we not been allowed to join in and help. There were, of course many hilarious adventures from day to day that thrilled our young lives and gave us the entertainment better than television provides today and we were very fit, healthy and energetic as well.

On this farm the poultry were allowed to roam around all day at will and the stack yard was always a favourite haunt for them. Amongst them there was a huge Rhode Island Red cockerel, a magnificent creature who ruled the roost. He was big and proud and stood tall as he surveyed his flock of hens and his territory. When he crowed he pulled himself up to his full majestic height with his chest thrown forward in a fantastic display of his prowess, then let rip with a splendid rendition of his favourite call, warning all his competitors that he was lord and master of the stack yard and this flock of birds and woe betide any lesser bird who may be silly enough to enter his domain.

As a rule the rooster was pretty quiet and seldom bothered us mere humans although the occasional visitor could be at risk, especially if they showed any sign of temerity towards him during his initial inspection of them as a potential source of trouble. However, there were a couple of exceptions to this rule and one of those was David, the youngest of the farmer's sons, although not the youngest member of the family. For some unknown reason this lad was singled out as a whipping boy, so to speak, to appease the rooster's ill temper.

We were never sure whether the mighty rooster had any particular animosity towards David or whether it was just some sort of sordid game that he played. We thought that maybe the boy had shown some fear towards this mighty bird when first approached, and sensing his fear the rooster had capitalised on it to appease his frustrations due to lack of adversaries and rival suitors. The truth of the matter was that every time David appeared in the yard the rooster raised himself up to his full height and emitted a mighty crowing before attacking at great speed, thus terrifying the boy out of his wits and setting him off in a desperate attempt to reach safety. A large cockerel in full flight with his wings spread wide and his tail streaming out behind is a very daunting experience for anyone and terrifying for a small schoolboy. Maybe it was just the chase around the yard that pleased the cock-bird, who knows but he never missed the chance to have a go at David. The other exceptions to the rule were the farm dogs, who occasionally caught the mean side of his nature and ended up yelping around the yard at great speed as they tried to escape the wrath of this savage beast.

David often appealed to his father to kill the rooster and put him in the soup pot to relieve his suffering. However, we all felt that the farmer somewhat enjoyed the entertainment and was a little reluctant to put an end to it and destroy such a magnificent bird.

One day, Frank the farmer, weakened his

resolve and gave the fateful order allowing us to end this reign of terror and put the mighty bird in the pot.

As you can imagine this awful deed was easier said than done and I think the old farmer might have thought that we wouldn't win the day and catch that formidable brute, let alone get him into the pot, certainly not without some injury to ourselves, anyway.

Of course we realised the enormity of the battle that was to follow and there was a fair chance that one or more of us might be severely wounded before this day was over and at best some of our blood could well be mixed with the rooster's blood.

We boys, Eric, about my age, David and myself, realised that this was going to be a battle royale and needed very careful thought and strategies to minimise or better still eliminate any damage to ourselves.

The rooster was equipped with a very sharp beak and a formidable spur on each leg with which to attack us as well as to defend himself from us and others.

The best plan of attack was to wait until after

dark and then grab him off the perch in the hen house and hang on like mad until we could get him onto the chopping block to cut off his head. This idea had a lot of merit but the cunning rooster wasn't silly, he roosted right in the back corner of the shed and there was little or no chance of getting to him without disturbing all the hens and alerting him to the danger

I suppose this method of attack was the logical one but none of us mentioned it as an alternative to a direct assault in daylight.

Maybe we considered it to be a little cowardly and not a fitting end to so worthy a foe.

Possibly, we thought Frank might change his mind if left to think about it until evening. No, the deed had to be done and done sooner rather than later and to hell with the consequences.

So, the scene was set; we were going to round up that savage creature into one of the buildings to minimise the number of escape routes and then rush in and grab him, or so we planned.

We tried to entice him into a horse-box with his favourite foods and titbits but he seemed to be aware that we were up to something. Nothing was ever going to get him into that box of his own freewill, so it was back to the drawing board.

Then we decided to set up some wire and hurdles attached to the doorpost of the horse box to guide him in.

When we were ready we tried to herd him in with some of his favourite hens but once again he was ahead of us and at the last minute he jumped the fence and escaped.

What we needed was a strategy of war; a conference over a cup of tea and a few scones whilst we thought of a better plan of attack.

Eric thought that if we chased the bird like mad he might just forget where he was going and run into the horsebox flat out.

David thought this to be a splendid idea as he would get to chase that brute instead of it chasing him.

One of us, I won't say who, suggested that Dave could run around the yard until the rooster gave chase then all he had to do was run into the box whilst we closed the door behind them.

There were, obviously one or two flaws in this plan so we settled on the previous one much to Dave's delight.

Once we managed to get the rooster in full flight we blocked his track around the haystack and forced him into the alleyway which ran past the horsebox door.

The rooster was going so fast that he was in the box and the door shut before he realised what was happening.

We stood outside the door as we collected our wits and got our breath back.

Gosh! That was the easy bit, now what?

The next bit was never going to be easy as the box was about ten feet square with no partitions.

The ideas were coming thick and fast but none of them were even remotely possible.

The interior of the box was quite dark when the door was closed which might give us a slight advantage (we were going to need it.) However we didn't realise the importance of this fact and only when I bravely or foolishly tried to get into the box did it become obvious.

The bird didn't like being shut up in the dark and as I cracked open the door he rushed out in a vain attempt to escape. Instinctively I grabbed his neck just behind his head so that he couldn't peck my hand and hung on like crazy.

Then keeping him partly trapped in the door so that he couldn't strike with his feet I reached down toward those terrible spurs. I could see the venom in his terrified stare and feel the sheer brute power in his body. Could I hold onto this savage beast even if I managed to grasp those powerful legs?

After many tries I had both legs in one hand and the neck in the other; we had the brute at last, hurrah!

We ceremoniously escorted the rooster to the chopping block at the wood-pile and prepared to execute him.

Once at the block we admonished David and pleaded a reprieve for so noble a creature who, having fought so valiantly for his freedom, deserve to live.

David was having none of this so it was, "Off with his head".

Eric manned the axe as I held onto that powerful head and vicious spurs. I lowered the neck down onto the block and let go of the neck at the last moment lest I lost a finger or two in this final act.

Just as the axe struck the rooster's neck I let

go of the legs and, bugger me, the bird took off in a final act of defiance chasing David around the hay-stack with blood squirting freely from that terrible wound and David screaming his head off in horror.

Eventually Eric and I stopped laughing enough to prepare the rooster for the soup pot to round off an exciting mornings work and we had a fantastic tale to tell the others at lunchtime.

Many years later I returned to England after a spell of some thirteen years in Western Australia and I went to visit David and his young family in North Yorkshire.

After a good cuppa tea and snacks David took me proudly, and rightly so down into his garden to show me his wonderful collection of show-birds.

There were dozens of magnificent birds of many breeds and colours.

I was suitably impressed as they were a credit to his skill and judgement.

As we walked back to the house I made comment of my concerns about this wonderful array of poultry as there seemed to be a problem.

David turned towards me with a look of worry

and concern on his face, thinking, no doubt, that I had noticed something that he had missed, concerning the welfare of his flock. Laughingly, I pointed out to him that he didn't have any Rhode Island Reds in amongst them.

"No" he said with great vehemence, "And there's never any likely hood of that happening, although I have been offered plenty of top quality birds to add to my collection. Do you remember that great big brute that used to chase me at Firlands farm, Brian".

"How could I ever forget him, or his execution. You only had to say the word to save his life. He might even have changed his ways and grown to like you if we had let him go." I replied.

"Yea well I wasn't going to find out, was I?" Were his final words on that subject.

Chapter 3

THE CARRION CROW

Tim Barnaby was on a mission, he had a loaded, twelve gauge, shotgun and he was intent on murder. He was my dad's boss, a farmer, and there was a carrion crow nesting in the big beech tree in the shelterbelt around the farmhouse.

Carrion crows will attack almost anything, even pecking the eyes out of live sheep. This particular pair had a nest full of babies to feed and they were stealing eggs from around the farmyard and taking young chickens too so they had to go. They were extremely wary birds with great eyesight and they were hard to get a clear shot at.

Tim decided to shoot them on the nest high up in the beech tree. He was hoping to catch both birds at once and he needed to be very cunning to catch them off guard at all.

Dad was working in the barn repairing machinery and I was holding parts for him when he realised that Tim had been gone for a long time and we hadn't heard a shot as yet.

"Brian, you'd better go down there and see what's happening but be careful not to disturb him if he is still trying to get a shot." Dad said.

I crept close to where I expected him to be but I couldn't see him then I spotted his jacket at the base of a big beech tree. What the heck was he doing on the ground?

Feeling some urgency I began to hurry forward. Yes, there he was huddled up at the base of the tree. He'd slipped on the smooth, mossy roots of the tree where they lay above the ground. He was sitting very awkwardly and his finger was still in the trigger guard of the gun. Judging by the odd angle of the joints it seemed that he had broken it. The butt of the gun was on the ground and he was looking down both barrels. He was as white as a ghost and had a terrified look on his face, which was not at all surprising considering his predicament, and he said, "Get your dad Brian and be quick about it."

I ran back to the shed and shouted to dad.

"Come on, be quick. Mr. Barnaby's in trouble he needs your help. I think he's broken his finger and it's still in the trigger guard."

"Hell that gun has hair triggers. You only 'ave to blow on it to set it off, come on."

Dad had a careful look at Tim and the gun. Then he said.

"It's cocked, if I try to move it it'll go off and blow "is "ead off."

"Dad," I said, "Can you trip the lock and let the barrels drop without it going off."

Tim was sweating, he knew that if this went wrong he would be dead.

"Aye, go on Charlie, have a go but for god's sake be careful." He said.

"Nay, be buggered," my dad answered. "I don't like that idea at all. If it goes wrong I might be blamed as a murderer"

"Look 'ere," The boss said. We 'ave to do summat so 'ave a bloody go Charlie."

Dad slid one hand under the gun to take some of the weight and counter the push as he released the barrels. Steady, steady, steady, hardly daring to breath he put pressure on the lever to open the gun and remove the shells. Was this the end of the road for Tim? Let's hope not, the lever was moving sideways bit by bit but it had to go a fair way before it let go. Then suddenly, click, the mechanism let go and the barrels dropped on to Tim's chest. He was safe but dad forgot the gun had spring ejectors to remove the shells and he jumped back in fright as the shells smashed into his face. Tim breathed a huge sigh of relief and said, "By heck Charlie that was scary, you've just saved my life. I reckoned I was a gonner. Thanks for your help, and you too Brian. Well done."

Dad replied, "Aye well it were nowt really. You see, I haven't had me wages yet so I couldn't let you blow your 'ead off today, could I?"

Chapter 4

THE GYPSIES

At the junction of two roads, one a main road and the other merely a country lane, there was a small triangular field that had been created when the road alignment had been changed. The field, like a number of other strips and corner pieces had been endowed to the Anglican Church, who rented them out, mainly to small farmers or farm workers to help them to make a little extra income. This particular field was seldom rented because it was hedged on two sides only, and a small spring fed, stream meandered along the longer, side. The total area was too small to be much use and the cost of fencing it was not worth the return. There was an opening in the hedge close to the lane, wide enough to admit a horse drawn cart or small tractor, although it had never been used for years.

The hawthorn hedges had been sadly neglected and were so overgrown as to hide most of the field from the roads. As you may imagine, the field was a haven of delight for a small country lad to while away many happy hours of leisure time and it created a means of total escape from reality, especially when the hedges were in full leaf throughout spring and summer. Added to this there were the delights of the stream, bordered with huge weeping willows, which was alive with minnows, tadpoles and frogs hiding in the watercress that grew in abundance. The hedgerows provided shelter and nesting spots for the myriads of birds that called them home and the warbling of the birds added to the pleasures of this magical area. A young boy with plenty of imagination could play out all sorts of fantasies in an area like this.

One Saturday afternoon when I was about 8 years old, I approached the field and was about to cross the stream over a large log that acted as a bridge, when I realised that the field was occupied. There was a group of people setting up a campsite in the shelter of the hedges. They had three living vans or vardos as they were better known, and the horses were tethered nearby, enjoying a well-earned rest and a feed of succulent grasses after their efforts of pulling the family to the campsite. These people looked like the dreaded gypsies who often camped around the district in the warmer months of the year and they had taken over my favourite haunt.

One man was digging out a piece of turf to make a fireplace, and he surrounded it with stones carefully chosen from under the hedge.

The gypsies over-wintered in more comfortable climes than ours and when spring came around they moved back out into the farming areas to seek casual employment and to buy and sell horses.

Unfortunately the gypsies were a much, maligned group of people, generally hated and despised by all and sundry and distrusted by everyone. Maybe some, although very little of this notoriety was deserved, most of it was as a result of prejudice and ignorance.

The gypsies lived off the "fat of the land",

taking advantage of natures bounties and lived a free uninhibited lifestyle, without any need for lots of possessions and consumer goods. They paid no taxes or charges, rents or rates, and moved their living vans around from one piece of waste ground to another to suit the season and availability of work and feed for the horses. Because their needs were so simple they had no need to work at a permanent job or be tied down to one place. All this gave them the appearance of being thieves and troublemakers.

No one would doubt for a moment, that they would poach a certain amount of game, or dig up a feed of potatoes and a turnip or two, from a farmer's field, but they were not alone in these activities as many other people also indulged in these little 'sins'. In some respect the farmers deserved to be treated thus because they would employ the itinerants on a seasonal basis, and some of them would seriously under pay them, and sometimes not at all. This forced the seasonal workers to resort to more unusual means to even the score.

The gypsies were fantastic horsemen and

had "a good eye", for a quality animal, as they travelled around. They would often buy a troublesome horse from a farmer, take it home and quieten it down and train it ready for work, then sell it at a good profit at the horse fairs that were held each year throughout the area. These horse fairs were usually held late in the summer or early autumn, around harvest time and were a great spectacle.

Occasionally, some of the farmers would get quite upset to see a man profit from their own lack of skills, and inability to take advantage of the situation and make a profit from it. However, the more astute farmers would employ the gypsies to break and train their horses for them, rather than sell them on.

The gypsy women folk were gifted at handy-crafts, and would make clothes pegs from bits of willow, and they would strip the osier willow sticks to weave all manner of wicker baskets, which were eagerly sought after by the farmers wives and the villagers. The men folk would cut the willows, and carry them back to the camp ready for the stripping. The twigs were soaked in the stream until the bark could be peeled off quite easily hence the term, "stripping the willow". The whole family would sit around the campfire in the evenings and weave the willow twigs with magical dexterity and skill.

The women walked around the farmhouses and villages selling their handiwork. Although the quality of these goods was excellent, the gypsies were feared and despised by many of the locals. The village children were called inside their homes and all the doors were locked whenever the gypsies were in town. The children were taught to fear the gypsies in case they cast a spell on them or stole anything from them. Some parents even went so far as to threaten to send their children away with the gypsies if they didn't behave themselves

This attitude was due, in part to the gypsy's persistence when they were out selling their wares and the village people would often get very abusive in an attempt to get rid of them. The gypsies would sometimes retaliate to this abuse and threaten them with an evil curse for their trouble and rudeness. I can't recall any such curse ever working, or that they ever would, but the gypsies were well renowned for their psychic ability and would often tell people's fortunes for a silver coin.

Most of the vardos had a small cooking stove inside them for use in bad weather and to heat the van, but the gypsies mostly preferred to cook and eat out of doors and their meals were generally communal affairs around the camp fire whenever possible, with everyone pitching in together, and sharing life's bounties.

The men folk would spend any spare time foraging around the countryside setting traps and snares to provide game for the table, whilst the women and children would scour the hedgerows in search of nuts and berries which mother nature supplied in abundance throughout the summer months.

I, like all the other kids in the district, had been warned about the dangers of associating with the "gyppos" as they were generally called and I had always kept out of their way, but now the dreaded enemy were here camped in my favourite hideaway. Life was grossly unfair to saddle me with this dilemma. I would have to go through the whole summer without the pleasures of my secret hideout and even worse, if they liked this place they would return year after year.

I was sitting on the end of the log on their side of the stream where I was hidden behind an elderberry bush, and could watch their activities without being observed, or so I thought. I was admiring one of the horses, a beautiful mare with a blaze running down her forehead when a large hand grabbed me from behind and lifted me clear of the ground. A gruff voice said into my ear, "Now then young man, what have we got here, a spy or just a nosy parker?"

I was absolutely terrified, what was he going to do with me? Maybe I would end up in the large cooking pot on the fire?

I replied in a frightened, squeaky voice. "I was only watching you. This is my field. I always come here when I can. This is my favourite hideout. Please don't hurt me. I'll go back home and stay away from here if you let me go."

The man carried me into the centre of the camp and called out to the others. "Look what I've just found, a spy. What shall we do with him?"

One of the other men spoke up, saying, "I

suppose we could eat him for supper but he looks far too skinny, we'll have to fatten him up a bit first."

The first man, realising how terrified I was and being a nice family man said, "Naw, I reckon he might be alright and if he behaves himself, we might let him stay for tea if he helps out a bit. What do you reckon young man?"

"Please mister, I'll behave and I'll help out as well. What do I have to do?" I squawked out

"Aw, just help the young uns they'll show you what to do." He replied." You probably know where all the food is around here anyway."

I pitched in to help the gypsy kids. There were three boys, and a girl who was about my age. I showed them where to find a few items of food to add to their supply then I remembered about my snare run.

"Come on" I said, "We'll get a rabbit or two for the pot if we're lucky"

The oldest boy replied, "Oh! And how are we going to catch a rabbit then?"

"Just follow me over to that wood beyond the turnip field and you'll see, we might be lucky since it is almost dark." I said pointing to the woods some distance away.

I had, earlier, set a line of snares between the edge of the woods and the turnip crop where I knew the rabbits would come to feed on the young plants. The rabbits were already moving out of the woodland and two of them were trapped in the snares.

"Look, you three go into the edge of the wood and you'll find heaps of dry twigs and small logs for the fire whilst I reset these traps. Then we can all go back to camp and help out the others."

We all pitched in to set up the campsite, unpacked the cooking pots and other essentials ready to prepare the evening meal a little later on.

I gave the rabbits to Rom, saying, "I left my pocket knife at home so I couldn't gut them for you."

"You don't to need worry yourself about that young man we cook 'em as they are. We just wrap them in wet clay in the stream and cook 'em whole in the ashes and coals. You'll soon see what I mean once the fire is ready. Shouldn't you take these two home for your family? What will they say when you get home empty handed?"

"Oh that's ok we got some last night and the snares will all be full again by morning. Those woods are alive with rabbits and I'll sell them to the local butcher tomorrow." I replied confidently.

As evening approached I said, "I'd better get back home in time for my tea, or else I'll get into trouble, for being late."

The man who had grabbed me, Rom was his name, said, "Oh, we thought you'd stay and share our meal with us tonight. Do you have to go?"

"Yes." I replied, "Mum and Dad will be looking out for me if I don't get back in time, but I'll come again if that's okay." I answered.

"Sure, you can come anytime you feel like it it's your field after all," Said Rom with a huge grin on his face "And we won't eat you even if you do get fat enough."

In a highly excited mood I set off homewards across the fields to the cottage that we lived in. I had my head full of ideas that were going to take a lot of sorting out.

If these had been normal people I could have

just gone inside and made an announcement about my discovery, and the eventful afternoon, but they were strictly taboo, and I would be in big trouble for associating with them and forbidden to go near them again and that I didn't want.

Before going inside, I had to pick up enough kindling wood to start the fire the next morning and break up a bucket full of coal, to go with the hawthorn logs that were stacked in the shed.

Once inside the house I washed my hands and face ready for tea. In common with most people in the district, we were in the habit of having a hot meal in the middle of the day, and a much lighter meal in the evenings. This seemed far more acceptable than eating a huge meal in the evenings just before retiring to bed.

Television was still unheard of and any way we had no electricity, so apart from reading a good book the only entertainment was our old battery wireless, the battery for which I had to take three miles to the blacksmith's shop every week to be recharged. I decided to go outside again for a walk in the fields as the sun was sinking slowly from a cloudy sky, and of course I headed back towards the gypsy camp.

When I was standing on the log above the stream I called out to let the gypsies know that I was approaching and they called me in to join them. Their meal was almost ready, judging by the marvellous smells that wafted around us and they were all seated on the grass around the fire. Rom said as I approached them.

"I thought you might come back in time for a feed. Come on in and sit yourself down here next to me lad. I hope you're still hungry because there's plenty of grub for everyone."

"I've just had my tea thanks, mister, but the food smells great and I should be able to manage some of it."

"Right you are then, lets have it." And he picked a rabbit from the coals and began to break it open. The gypsies had wrapped the game in a ball of clay without doing any other preparation at all. The whole rabbit was encased in mud and laid in the coals to cook and simmer gently in it's own juices until tender. The clay had set quite hard but was easily broken open when cooked. As the clay was removed the skin and fur or feathers came away with it, leaving the succulent meat with the entrails still within the carcass. The meat was then lifted off the bones and carcass leaving the entrails untouched in the centre. The rabbit meat was fantastic, full of juices, moist and tender. The best restaurant in the world could do no better than this, and boy, I was hungry, now.

There were potatoes, turnips and Swedes, to follow and a large amount of black tea to wash it all down. Once every one had finished eating and washed their hands and faces, they settled down for an evening of music and fun.

The only light was from the fire, soft and mellow, setting the mood around the camp until a crescent moon arose a little later on, which added to the atmosphere as it dodged about through the scudding clouds.

The whole group were very musically inclined and were soon playing their favourite tunes on a range of instruments, which they had retrieved from the vans.

The leader of this family group, Rom, was a master of the fiddle and he could almost make it talk as he went through all those haunting airs as only a violin can. He was also an accomplished piano accordion player and swapped between the two, as the mood took him.

One of the other older men, called Marty, provided the beat with a small, battered drum, and he could produce music from any old collection of articles around the camp

The little girl, who was terribly shy, with a "foreigner" in the camp, played a number of sweet, haunting tunes on a recorder as everyone joined in the fun. I was also encouraged to join in with a screwdriver and some old pots and pans as my instruments. Oh! What marvellous people these were and what a wonderful evening we had together in the firelight.

Suddenly, I realised how late it was getting, and I would need a very good excuse to cover my tracks. I jumped up, and called out my farewells and thanks, as I headed off home at top speed, over the log and across the fields. The gypsy camp would certainly be taboo to my family and I would surely cop a severe belting for this nights work. However, I was able to redeem myself because on the way home across the fields, I checked the rabbit snares that I had set early in the day and managed to take home a couple of rabbits to stock the larder and avoid suspicion.

This turned out to be the first of many wonderful evenings with my gypsy friends in 'my' secret place. During the summer I learnt the art of peg making and basket making, beginning with stripping the willow and moving on to the actual weaving and decorating of the baskets I soon became an ardent admirer of these wonderful people, in spite, of their rough clothes and wild looks, and they welcomed me into the group without any reservations whatsoever.

During the days of spring and summer I walked for miles and miles with the gypsies, foraging in the fields and especially the hedgerows and woodlands, searching for game and fruits etc, to supplement the food stocks. There was an abundance of fresh eggs from coots, moorhens and ducks, if you were smart enough to find the nests early enough before hatching began.

I learned a wealth of knowledge from the gypsies, about surviving in the wild, finding foods and knowing what to eat and what not. I slowly got to know about their heritage and customs as well, and how to capture game and fish with a minimum of effort. This was a real life history and nature study, the results of which I would carry with me all my life and look back on with great pleasure.

I was enveloped in the most magnificent summer imaginable and was relishing every minute of it. I got into the habit of getting my chores done as quickly as possible to give me more time with the gypsies.

They say all good things come to an end eventually, and although I was always very careful to try and cover my tracks, there was always going to come the time when I would be caught out, and it did.

One weekend calamity struck with a vengeance, and I was in deep, deep, trouble unless I could talk my way out of it before my dad got home. My spiteful, bitchy sister had been into town on the bus and on her return as she alighted from the bus near the gypsy camp, she spotted me leaving the camp.

When I caught up with her she said, "You're going to get into trouble. You'll get a good belting when dad gets home. I saw you in the gypsy camp and I'm going to tell on you, so there."

I knew that if I pleaded with her not to tell it would only harden her resolve to tell, so I just said, "Alright then, if you feel like it, tell on me, but I'll get you back later on if you do."

"Oh you think you are so smart, but dad will belt the hide off you, you'll see." She said.

For some weeks now I had mentioned the gypsies to dad in a general way without letting on about my furtive activities. Dad had done a fair amount of contract crop hoeing with Rom and Marty throughout their stay, and I was hoping to broach the subject of my visits to their camp with him soon, because I hated all this deceit and subterfuge. This might be so but now it was all too late, I was in for it when dad came home from work.

We were all seated around the dining table at teatime when Joanne dropped her bombshell. She didn't have the guts to look across at me, she just looked down at her plate and played around with her food, then she burst out.

"Our Brian's been playing in the gypsies camp. I know because I saw him leaving when I got off the bus."

There was a deathly silence for a while and my mum gave me a pitying look and shrugged her shoulders, because she knew that she couldn't help me now. It was all too late to save me from a thorough thrashing.

My dad began to chuckle then laugh out loud and when he could speak he said, "Oh aye! I know all about that business, it's been going on all summer. I've spotted him many a time roaming around with Rom and Marty and that wild bunch of kids. He'll come to no harm there and he'll learn a hell of a lot as well. He's better off with them than he is with the likes of you young lady. Get yourself off to bed without any tea and I'll decide what to do with you before I set eyes on you in the morning. I never thought that one of mine would ever stoop so damned low, as to tell on her own brother. Bugger off to bed afore I give you a good clout."

Joanne burst into tears and ran upstairs out of the way and giving me an ugly glare as she left, as though it was all my fault that she was in trouble.

When she had gone dad began to talk about

my gypsy friends. He said that he had spoken to Rom the other day to make sure that I wasn't being a nuisance and he was assured that there were no problems there.

Once the gypsies knew that they could trust me they invited me into their caravans and showed me their belongings. I was absolutely amazed at what I saw there. The outsides of the vans were magnificent works of art. Each one was hand painted in fantastic patterns and colours and the inside was many times better. Every space was tastefully painted and patterned and all the glass doors were engraved and etched with the most magnificent art works that I had ever seen. There were many paintings and carvings of all manner of birds, animals, and flowers, each one perfect in shape and colour. Far from being dirty, as every one believed, the insides of the 'vardos' were immaculate and would have put even the most fastidious of housewives to shame. The local population scorned and despised these lovely nomads, yet, had they been aware or bothered to find out, they would have been put to shame themselves.

Meagan, as the little girl was called, soon came to accept my presence in the group and eventually began to teach me to play her beloved recorder. We were both about the same age and we got on well together after a very slow start. Meagan had never been to any school, other than the school of life in which she lived, but all the family were teaching her in their spare time and she was at least on a level with me. She was as bright as a button and I had to have my wits about me to keep up to her.

Once we were comfortable with each other, we began walking around the fields together and foraging in the hedgerows. We collected wild blackberries, strawberries, gooseberries and other fruits and berries.

As autumn approached, we collected many wild nuts that grew aplenty in the woods and hedgerows. There were hazel nuts, walnuts and beech nuts, to mention but a few and these were all stored away in the vans ready for winter.

Autumn that year was a mellow season, with the leaves slowly changing to soft pastel colours as they matured and began to fall from the trees and waft around blown by the playful winds into swirling eddies of colour and eventually heaped up in the corners of buildings and trees.

The grain harvest was over and all the sheaves of corn safely stacked away to await threshing day. The last of the apples had been picked and stored away on special airy shelves to keep through winter. This only left the hedges to be trimmed and the potatoes dug and stored and the season was over for the gypsies.

I was terribly upset at the thought of losing my friends but it was inevitable that they would soon be on their way south again, to find a sheltered spot to spend the winter. I was so used to having the gypsies around, especially Meagan, that I had put aside the inevitability of their departure, which I had ignored for months throughout this balmy summer.

On that final weekend I went over to the camp as usual to help my friends pack up their belongings and prepare to move away. The horses were all groomed and checked out, ready for work, likewise, the harness and tack was all cleaned and polished and thoroughly checked for possible faults. There was a very long journey ahead, lasting many days, and most of the hills were very steep as they made their way south.

All the wheels had to be removed from the vans, carefully cleaned and greased ready for the road ahead.

The latrines were filled in and the grass replaced in the fire-place.

Next morning the horses were impatient to be off, as they had a last feed of oats and were harnessed up to the vans. They knew what lay ahead of them in the following days just as the family knew.

The vans were pulled into line with Rom's in the lead and they were ready for off. Just time for a quick look around the site, and final goodbyes, and then they were off waving as they pulled out onto the main road.

I stood and watched their departure until they disappeared over the crest of the first hill and were gone until next year, maybe.

I walked slowly back into 'My' field, and it looked as though they had never ever been there at all, except for the flattened grass and the wheel-tracks leading out onto the road.

Later that day I went back to my field and sat on the edge of the log bridge. Some time later I was lost in a world of my own. I found myself standing in the middle of my field as night was falling and I could still hear the haunting music of my gypsy friends, especially the sweet notes of Meagan's recorder. I could still smell the smoke from the fire and that succulent meat cooking in the coals. All I had left were the thoughts of a long cold, Yorkshire, winter full of vicious frosts, snow, and biting winds, that creep right through my bones.

If only I could have gone south with the gypsies I would have been in heaven.

I often pondered on the fact that most of my young life to-date, I had been taught to hate and fear the gypsies. Like other youngsters of my time I had been threatened with being abducted by gypsies, or worse, sent away with them for not behaving, and now I could only hope and pray for it to happen, and soon, so that I could move down south and join them again.

I have no idea if the gypsies returned the following spring because, by then, dad had another job some distance away and we had to move house and change schools. I did actually ride my bike over to my field a couple of times, but it was empty and over grown as though it hadn't been used at all that summer.

Chapter 5

OLD JOHN

Old John had been a farmhand all his working life and for most of that time he had been working on the same farm, even though the ownership had changed a time or two over the years. John must have been at least 80 years old by the look of him but he was still very fit and capable of a sound day's work in the fields. Some of the locals thought that he was a bit, "soft in t'head," because he seldom made any useful conversation. In spite of this he was very good at his job. He was fantastic with the carthorses of which there were about a dozen. He seemed to have an uncanny knack of getting the best out of them and he could still plough a tidy furrow. Those great big shire horses thought the world of him and they would follow his every wish with only the slightest touch or murmur from the old man. He never had to raise his voice to them or growl at them.

As far as we knew, John's only pleasure apart from his pipe, was to visit the Black Bull pub in the nearby town, every Friday and Saturday evening, where he could still put away a good few pints of ale, especially when someone else was paying for it, which they often did in deference to his age and temperament.

The farm boss treated John with contempt, bordering on disgust, and the old man was often the target of insults and the object of ridicule. None of this seemed to bother the old fellow and he showed little or no reaction to any of it, and the farm men thought that he was just too stupid to realise that they were having a go at him. However, John lived in a two-roomed cottage just off the main road, about a mile from the farm where he worked. No one could work out how old he was but he should have retired years ago. He seemed to be a part of the landscape as though he had always been there. He was working there when James, the current owner, took over from his father and he just kept on riding to work on his old bike each day. He was never ill or late, in fact he was always the first to arrive. There was a large square stone block besides the blacksmith shop and each morning he would be sitting on it and smoking an ancient pipe as if he had been there all night. When the rest of the men arrived he would greet each one with a huge grin from ear to ear. He was a man of few words and just a nod of the head was his usual greeting. He must have been very easy going but some of this banter must have finally rubbed off and sunk into his old brain because he occasionally had a "bit of a go" at one of them.

It was at that time of year when the crops were all planted and growing well, that the old man finally retaliated to all the banter and insults that he had borne for years.

There were plenty of jobs that had been left aside whilst the more important job of seeding was under way. The first concern was to carefully check all the hedges and fences to make sure that the livestock would not escape from their pastures and get into the new crops.

One morning the boss told John to saddle up one of the carthorses and load up the cart with some tools needed to rebuild one of the wooden fences down near the stream whilst the rest of the men went down there and started pulling out the old posts and rails ready for some new ones that had been sawn during the last winter out of the old oak tree near the driveway.

When John arrived with the cart the boss shouted at him. "Now get away back to the yard and get us a load of them posts, and some railings, and look sharp about it, we don't want to be hanging around here all day waiting for the likes you."

John climbed back into the cart and carefully stoked and lit his pipe before setting off back to the yard. to load up again. Once his pipe seemed to be drawing satisfactorily he removed it from his mouth and studied the red glow with reverence and a measure of satisfaction at a job well done. By the time he got back to the field the men were nearly ready to put in the first of the posts and the boss was getting quite cross with the delay.

My dad was digging in the hard gravely soil and grizzling a fair bit about it when the cart pulled up alongside him and he called out, "By heck, old fellar, I wish we 'ad some of them, there, new fangled postholes, that we could put in here, it'uld save a lot of time and work."

The old man replied, "Aye, tha's right about that, but I heard they's 'ard to come by at this time of the year."

James the boss had overheard this conversation and he chipped in.

"Aye, get away into town and see if you can find about twenty of 'em John and look sharp about it."

John just gave them one of his beaming smiles and headed off back to the yard to load some more posts and railings. As he was driving along he thought of a bright idea, and resolved to turn this day around to his advantage for once.

The farm hands were hard at work as the day wore on when the boss suddenly realised that the old man had not returned with the fencing materials and he began to worry a bit. Finally he said to the others.

"Its been a long time since John went back to the yard, and I still can't see any sign of him.

I hope he's alright, at his age anything might 'ave 'appened to 'im.

"Oh he'll be right enough, nothing ever 'appens to 'im." Someone answered. "He's probably 'aving a quiet smoke somewhere since you all gave "im 'ell."

The boss answered back. "You needn't worry about upsetting the old sod, he's as thick as a plank of wood. It all just runs off him anyway."

The men were all sitting down enjoying their afternoon tea break, when dad looked up and said. "I reckon that's 'im coming now, I can see summat a'tween t'edges up near t' beck."

"I, 'appen your right an all, Charlie, there's summat coming." Said Jack the cowman.

"Well it's about time an all." Said the boss, "I'll 'ave plenty to say to yon old sod when he gets here. You mark my words".

The horse and cart rumbled along the rough cart track and pulled up near the men, and before the boss could give him a right earful the old man said, "By heck, that was a heck of a todo. I was beginning to think that I wouldn't get any after all, but I managed to get twenty four of them beggars at t'finish."

"Where the hell 'ave you been then, you daft old sod? What the 'ell 'ave you been looking for away? We were right worried about you, we thought you might 'ave gone and 'urt yourself or summat." The boss called out.

"Nay, you'd no need to worry about me and old Dolly 'ere," He replied, patting the horse's rump. We were all right weren't we old girl. You see we looked all ower t'town and nobody had any left, you sees, so I used me brain so I did. I went around to yon joiner fellow in Bright street, and he said there weren't any in town, but if I 'ad time, he'd make me a few since they were for you, and he knows 'ow particular you are. I was a bit hungry by then since I'd left me bit of dinner here in t'cart shed, so I went and saw me old pal Paul at the Black Bull, and he shouted me a sandwich or two and we 'ad a game or two of darts, 'til t'joiner feller telephoned up, to say they were ready. Then I hurried up and got 'em and I 'ustled old Dolly all t'way back, 'cause I knew you'd be waiting for 'em."

"You daft old beggar, what the 'ell are you on about, eh? It sounds like you 'ad a fair drop of bitter ale as well. What 'ave you got in t'cart then?" The boss demanded.

"Why, I've gotten you them postholes that you said you wanted, and this is all the thanks I get. I went to a lot of trouble to get 'em you know, and I got the joiner to book 'em to your account."

There was a deathly silence, as the men put all this together, they had never, ever, heard old John have so much to say, in fact it was normally difficult to get more than the odd word out of him. Then they all followed the boss over to the cart to inspect the postholes. As the old man said, there were, twenty four of them in the cart. It appeared that he'd gone straight to the joiner and asked him to make up some square boxes out of pine boards. They were just big enough to slip a square post inside and about the right length to end up flush with the ground, but he refused to let to the joiner know what they were for.

The boss exploded. "You stupid old fart, what the 'ell 'ave you gone and done, eh, and 'ow much is this all going to cost me then? Why don't you bugger off 'ome, and stay there? Don't you ever set foot on my land again"

As the men burst out laughing John said, "Some people you can never please. You reckoned I was too thick to help out and when I thought out a perfect answer to your problems and did exactly what you asked, you go and shout at me and now you've gone and sacked me as well."

As the old man walked away from the group, back to the yard, and home, he turned to dad, and with a happy grin on his face, gave him a friendly wink.

When dad and I went to see how he was at the weekend, he said, "Nay, Charlie don't be sad, I was ready to give it away anyroad, and I just wanted to see t'boss's face when he realised that old Johnny, 'ad 'ad t'last laugh, and in front of everyone, an' all. By, 'eck, I right enjoyed that. I've put up with a lot 'ower t'years from that smart arsed sod and 'e 'ad it coming."

He paused to have a few good deep drags on the ancient pipe and watch with pleasure the thick aromatic smoke drifting skywards before continuing, "I reckon I've enough to do around here anyways. As you know this is a right good bit of soil and I can put up a bit of a stall and sell enough vegetables to keep me in a bit o'bacca and t'odd pint or two. What does tha think about that idea Charlie? T'fellow in yon pub will take all t'eggs that I can spare as well you see."

"Well that's grand, John, I hope tha does al'right at it an'all." Dad said, "And we'll look in now and again and see 'ow you are, as we go past."

"Right you are then, I'll make sure t'kettles always on ready for a cuppa char, and we can 'ave a right old chinwag, when you 'ave the time. I'll be seeing you then, Charlie and you too youngun." The old man said as we prepared to leave him.

Chapter 6

MY GRANDAD

Grandad O'Donnell had always been old, or at least that was how it seemed to me his only grandson. After all he was 71 years old when I was born but he was still very active, and he had a couple of part time gardening jobs that still kept him busy, in between looking after his large vegetable garden and a yard full of poultry.

Although he was born in County Mayo, in Ireland, he had lived a large part of his life in rural Yorkshire and he loved every minute of it, despite the hard work, and low, and at times almost no wages. He had sired four children, two girls and two boys. The oldest boy, Walter, had joined the Duke of Wellington's regiment between the wars and gained the rank of sergeant whilst serving in the Punjab district in Northern India. During an assault on a hill in Italy in the Second World-war, he was leading his platoon up to a fortress when he was hit with a shell and killed. I was only a toddler at that time and never got to meet him at all.

At every opportunity, I stayed over with grandma and grandad at their home about twelve miles away from the farm where I lived. My dad, the other son, had fitted a small seat onto the cross bar of his bike so that he could take me with him and mum, on various trips around the country-side, and of course to granddad's home at the weekends. Before I started school I seldom went home with them, I just stayed with my grand parents until the next visit, and grandma always kept enough clothes in the cupboard, ready for me to wear should I decide to stay.

My grandmother had a very bad clubfoot but she had never allowed it to curtail her activities. Every year a large fair ground travelled the district and we were taken to visit it and enjoy the fun-fare, at each venue that it came to in our area. We always collected grandmother and took her with us, although I had no idea why this was necessary, because her clubfoot was quite an impediment on the rough grass fields where they held the carnival. Whenever she was with us we enjoyed free rides all night and didn't have to pay for toffee apples and fairy floss either.

I was about fifty-five years old before I managed to solve this mystery, after my father came to live with us at Harvey. One day when we were rambling in the forest near our home as we often did, and chatting about old times, I happened to mention this story and dad gave a little chuckle asking, "Do you 'ave any idea what that was all about then lad?"

"Well, no that's why I asked. I did think that it might be that she was somehow related to them, since she was born and lived in Hull City, which, as it happens is the over winter camping spot for the fair ground people."

"Aye well, I suppose that makes some sort of sense, but what you probably never knew was that your Granny was the local midwife for most of her adult working life, and she also laid out the bodies of the deceased as well. Whenever the fair ground people were around the area they used to come and get your granny to attend to any of their women who were 'expecting', and needing help. She often stayed with them right through the night or until the baby was born, and the mother had settled down afterwards. Plenty of people will tell you that the gypsies and fairground people are a bad lot, but they never forgot your granny, and they always came to see her as soon as they arrived nearby.

Because of her professional career, she was an old tyrant. She was as hard as nails, bossy, domineering and ultra fastidious in her ways. We grand kids, were afraid to sit properly on the chairs, especially in the sitting room, in case we disturbed any of the cushions. This used to come to a head when she took us, my sister and I, on the bus to York City to see a movie, usually a Walt Disney classic. Whenever I knew that she was coming, I would "accidentally" disappear or forget the time until long after the bus had gone and I could stay at home, even though I often received a good clip about the ears for my trouble. You see, I hated being pushed around and dragged along the crowded streets, and I had a bad habit of trailing my little hands along the wrought iron fences and other types of walls and windowsills which, of course, made them filthy dirty. As often happens, a small itch or two occurred about my face, and I had no option but to rub my face. It's funny how even today, if ever I get an itchy nose it always seems to be when my hands are dirty, and I can't scratch it. It took very little time at all for me to get my face all streaked with black soot, and gran always took offence. She would drag me into a side alley or rear entry, pull out her immaculately laundered and pressed hanky, spit on it and scrub my poor old face until it was sore. Oh God, how I hated that dammed city with all these people and all it's filth. I could play all day at home and not even get dirty enough to have to wash my hands for dinner!!!

On the other hand grandad was an old softy who loved the simple life. He was always pottering about in the garden where he grew all manner of vegetables and flowers. I loved to be outside with him, 'helping' him with the weeding etc. One of my favourite jobs was catching the snails, of which there was an endless supply, and feeding them to the poultry. They were so used to my feeding them that they went crazy, jumping up the wire fences to let me know that they would love another feed of snails whenever they saw me coming out of the house. Grandad often said, "Did you know boy, t'best flowers in any garden, is t'cauliflowers, cause after you've finished admiring them you get to eat 'em."

In spite of this he was very fond of roses and carnations, which he grew in abundance among the vegetables.

The garden was always full of wild birds such as robins, wrens and finches. It was often a kaleidoscope of flashing, colours as they darted around in the sun.

Throughout the winter months, he always put out strings of scraps for them, to help them survive the bleak winter weather. No matter how little they had for themselves he would always find oddments and left overs in the pantry such as, bread crusts, pieces of fat, and the odd nut or piece of fruit, which he threaded together on a length of string and tied high up in the apple tree, so that the small, and very agile birds, could get their share of the food, otherwise the bigger and more boisterous starlings and blackbirds would steal most of it from them. I spent so many happy hours in the winter watching the acrobatic antics of birds such as Blue Tits, Robins and Wrens, as they hung upside down on the string to reach their favourite foods.

Grandad was a very heavy pipe smoker and I loved the smell of his favourite "backy" both before he smoked it, and whilst he was smoking it. It had a soft mellow natural scent, unlike the commercial cigarettes of today, which are harsh, and bitter. He bought the tobacco in a solid lump from which he cut a few slices with his pocket knife and rubbed between his gnarled old hands before packing it into his ancient pipe. I loved to go with him to the little tobacconist's shop in the high street because, when you opened the door the heavenly scent of tobacco wafted out to meet you.

The old gentleman standing behind the counter was one the local characters. He always wore a city business suit with a waist coat beneath, and a spotted bow tie. There was always a pocket watch in the waist coat pocket with the chain swinging across his chest, and clipped into the button hole in the middle. He was a dapper gentleman, although he was only a little over five feet tall. He had a shock of tightly curled hair that any woman would be proud to wear, even though it was almost pure white, in deference to his age. He had a ready wit and knew all the latest gossip. He always had a store of the latest jokes that were circulating around, and he retold them with relish.

Beneath the counter he kept a large jar of assorted sweets, which he would pull out with great ceremony whenever a child entered his shop, unscrew the lid and encourage us to take our pick and maybe two or three if we had been extra good.

It is such a great pity that those type of shops have long since disappeared, only to be replaced with supermarkets, set in large characterless shopping centres.

We often went out on extensive walks around the country lanes near grandfather's home whenever the weather permitted. Grandad took me on long strolls in the country and we stopped frequently to admire a flower or look at some bird's nest that he had spotted. These weren't just walks, they were complete nature studies. He educated me in the ways of nature as we went along and this love of natural things has stayed with me all my life, and given me countless hours of pleasure. One of his favourite tricks was to pick a certain flower, maybe a humble dandelion or some other lowly blossom, then he would pick some type of foliage to go with it, but not it's own leaves. Then he would make them up into a posy for his buttonhole, and wear it proudly all day. Many of his friends and acquaintances, that we met along our way, would ask about the posy and try to guess what flower it was, the combination of leaves and flowers confusing them, somewhat.

He knew where to find the first flowers in the spring, and not a single white violet would escape his eagle eyes, nor yet, the early cowslip or buttercup. In late summer we collected mushrooms, nuts, and berries as we went along.

Our journey usually included a visit to the lovely village of Clifford, where he had once lived, in a tiny little thatched cottage adjoining the graveyard of the Catholic Church. We always called in at the convent school where he knew all the teaching Sisters. As we approached each of the classrooms one of the pupils would stand and open the door for us, and then the whole class stood up to greet him with a hearty, "Good morning mister O'Donnell."

After a chat with each teaching Sister, we went to the office of the Mother Superior for a chat by the fire. She always made a great fuss of me and gave me a glass of milk.

On one occasion when we arrived home, grandma asked me where we had been, and when told of the visit to the convent asked, "Did our Mother give you a nice drink as usual, then?"

"Yes grandma, she gave me a large glass of milk like she always does, thankyou."

"What about grandad, then, did he get a drink as well?" she continued.

"Yes, of course, he always gets a drink as well as me grandma." I replied.

"Did grandad have a drink of milk like you, then, or did he get something else?" she inquired.

"No grandma, grandad and Mother Superior had a drink from a bottle with a lovely white horse on the side." Was my earnest reply.

It was many years later that I realised that I had "dobbed" him in so to speak, when I learned that the white horse was a brand of whiskey.

"Yes I thought as much, they both like their little drop of tipple", she said.

Every Sunday, at lunch time, grandad used to wander over to the "Wheat sheaf" pub on the corner of the street and get the landlord to fill up his quart jug with a "drop of ale" to enjoy with his roast beef and Yorkshire pudding.

One such Sunday he happened to meet the local priest on his way home and the priest said, "Tut, Tut, Joseph tha' knows 'tis a sin to drink alcohol, especially on the Lord's day an' all."

"Aye well, you may be right about that Father, but the Lord knows it does me good." Grandad replied.

Don't you care about your immortal soul, and life after death, then, Joseph?" The priest continued.

"It's a funny thing that you should mention that father, as I've given it a lot of thought lately and I reckon that it won't matter either way. You see, I shall 'ave friends in both places, and anyway, I've met a heck of a lot of them 'sanctimonious' beggars as reckons they're going to 'eaven, and if they are all going there I don't think I want to be around there as well."

At that, grandad turned, and continued on his merry way, leaving the priest with a thoughtful look on his face, as he turned to walk home for his dinner.

One of the blackest times of my life, came when I was about ten years old. My fathers boss came puffing down to the cottage in a bit of a fluster to announce, "I don't know 'ow we're going to manage 'ere, without you Charlie, but we'll get by I suppose, it's just wrong time of t'year that's all do you see."

"What the heck are you talking about, has summat happened then? Why aren't I going to be 'ere?" Dad queried.

"Well that's it you see Charlie, we just 'ad a phone call from your sister in Boston. Your father 'as 'ad an accident. He was working at some big house or other, when a big pile of logs in the shed shifted and rolled down on top of him. He was trapped, and 'is legs broken. They've taken 'im to Leeds Infirmary. You'd better get there straight away." The boss stated.

"Aye well, now then, that's it then, we'll get a few things together and leave straight away, thanks for letting us know. I'll give you a ring when I know summat" Dad replied.

I went out to the shed where we kept our bikes, and got them out, one by one, checked all the tyres, and put a few drops of oil on all the bearings and chains. It was a hard twelve mile trip to Boston Spa with a good few hills to negotiate as well, and mam was the only one with gears on her bike. Most of the steeper hills were so steep that we would have to get off and walk to the top.

The rest of the family gathered enough clothes for a protracted stay at grandma's house, put our house in some sort of order, then we were on our way. We were fortunate that the day was fine and mild and we were able to push ahead quite well and hopefully arrive before dark, although we all had torch lamps mounted on our bikes they were not very good at lighting up the road, and we preferred not to have to use them as the batteries didn't last very long and were quite expensive.

We could always rely on grandma having the

kettle boiling when we arrived and very welcome it was too. We had a light meal as we discussed the days events, and the story from the hospital was somewhat gloomy, as the doctors felt that granddads leg had been trapped long enough to cut off the blood supply and he may need an amputation. It was a tired, motley, crew that crawled into makeshift beds after a quick bath, to face a worried restless night.

We all loved grandad dearly and we all felt his pain and suffering throughout the night and we were glad when daylight came, although it was to an overcast and leaden sky which promised rain before long. We all had a number of cups of strong tea but ate very little as no one was in the mood for solid food. It was going to be a long wait before we could ring the hospital for more news of granddad's leg.

All the adult members of the family put on their warmest clothing and prepared for a long, cold bus ride to the hospital in Leeds. I was totally devastated, as I couldn't accept the house without granddad's presence. Children weren't welcome in the hospitals in those days. We had to stay with my cousins. In spite of my sister's threats to tell on me, I put on a warm coat and heavy shoes then set off for a long walk to all our favourite haunts, to help to pass the long day.

I had no perception of time because the sun was hidden in the heavy clouds. I just wandered down to the riverbank and around the country lanes, hedgerows, and woodlands that I knew and loved so well and which I had shared with my old pal all these happy years.

Eventually, I found myself standing in a schoolyard. It must have been mid afternoon by then and it was still threatening to rain. I was glad that I had put my warm coat on because there was a stiff breeze tugging at my clothes and I was quite cold. I suddenly realised that fate had led me to this spot because I was standing in the yard of the convent school at Clifford where I had shared so much of my life with my dear old grandad. I was still standing near the school wall when a soft voice behind me asked me, "Now then young man, what are you doing standing here, shouldn't you be in school."

I turned towards the sound and said, "I wasn't doing anything bad, sister, I was just thinking about my grandad, you see, he's in hospital and I miss him so much."

As I lifted my head and looked up at the nun she seemed to recognise me. I hadn't seen her for a long time, because, after I started school I hadn't been for so many long walks with my grandad, and we hadn't been able to get to the school during term time. As I looked up at her I realised that I was talking to the Mother Superior and she continued,"Aren't you the young man that used to come and visit us with your grandfather, Joseph O'Donnell from Boston?"

"Yes that's right Mother I am Brian,." I replied.

"What's all this about your grandad then, you say he is in hospital? You'd better come inside and get warm you must be frozen out here, and then you can tell me all about it." She said.

We went inside to her study, she stoked the fire from a red glow to a roaring inferno and she made me a hot drink of cocoa before asking about grandad.

"Now, you sit down there close to the fire, and tell me what has been happening to you since last we met." She said. "What's all this about your grandad. Is he sick?"

"It's me grandad, see." I replied,. "I think he is going to die and I don't want him to go away. I still need him to look after me and take me for walks in the countryside."

She came and sat on the rug next to me and wrapped me up in her arms, saying, "Now come on lad tell me what has happened to him to make you think that he is going to die."

"Well you see, he got hurt when some logs fell on him and trapped him. His leg is broken and they took him away to Leeds hospital, and they say they might cut his leg off and if they do he'll die. He'll be so miserable with only one leg and we wont be able to come and see you again." I told her, with tears pouring down my cheeks.

"Now, now, come on cheer up, it probably isn't that bad and he might easily get better." She comforted.

"But I want to go and see him and stay with him until he is better. Why wont they take me to see him?" I asked her.

"Well, hospitals aren't nice places and they don't like children to visit there." She told me.

"Now look, you just drink your cocoa, and here are some biscuits as well, you must be hungry, and I'll try and ring the hospital and find out what is happening to your grandad, all right."

"Thanks sister you're always kind to me, can I always come to see you even without my grandad?" I asked.

"Yes of course you can dear." She said, as she gave me another big cuddle.

She went to the desk and picked up the telephone and dialled the Infirmary at Leeds. When they answered, she asked them about the condition of Mr. Joseph O'Donnell.

She went very quiet and kept her eyes looking down at the desk, with a very sad look on her face. I knew instinctively, that she was hearing bad news, and when she put the phone down she came back to me and took me in her arms again.

"The doctors have told your grandad that they can't save his leg, and they need to remove it immediately to save his life. If they don't take his leg off the poison will spread right through his body and kill him. You see he has a poison called gangrene, which happens when there is no blood flowing though the leg. Your grandad has refused to let the doctors remove his leg. He says that they should concentrate their efforts and money on much younger people instead of worrying about an old man like him. They are going to bring him home tomorrow, so you will be able to look after him and we will come and help you as well."

"See I told you he was going to die and leave me on my own. How long will it take, Sister?" I asked.

"I'm afraid it wont be very long at all, Brian. I am so sorry the news was so bad but we will come and see him and help you to care for him, and pray for God to help him." She said.

I finished my cocoa and prepared to leave but she stopped me by saying, "Come with me now, school is just coming out, and the Sisters will be free for a while."

She called all the Sisters together and told them the news, then we all walked over to the church next door where they prayed for grandad, fingered their Rosaries, and lit candles for him. I wasn't brought up as a catholic and I had very little knowledge of what went on but we spent a long time on our knees, chanting, and praying, for my grandad and it made me feel a lot better. I could feel all their love and care descending on my grandad and myself, but all this probably would not be enough to save him.

As I was setting out to walk back to the house the sisters offered to walk with me, but I assured them that I would be all right and it was only about a mile anyway, and I knew the road well. It was almost nightfall by the time I arrived and the adults were just getting home from the hospital They were all looking sad and worried and I suppose they were working out the best way to tell us kids about grandad when I blurted out. "Grandad is going to die isn't he? His leg is poisoned and it will spread all over him and kill him."

"Who told you that lad?" My dad asked, quite concerned. "Where the hell have you been? You were supposed to stay here with the girls until we got back."

"I went to the convent to see the Sisters and we prayed for my grandad and lit some candles. The Mother Superior rang the hospital and they told her all about it." I replied.

"Aye, all right then, as long as you know." He said bluntly, he was never one for showing his emotions, and would never have thought of giving me a hug or something "They'll bring him home in't morning and you can stay here till t'end. I 'ave to get back to work but I'll come back at weekends."

Next morning the ambulance brought grandad home and my dad had set up his bed in the front sitting room so he could be near us and it was easier to look after him there.

Shortly after we had gotten him settled, there was a light tap at the door and when I opened it to see who was calling I was surprised to see two of the sisters from the convent standing there. I asked them to come in and grandma took them into the sitting room to see grandad. From that moment until his death there were two of the sisters with him at all times, day and night. They took it in turns to mount a constant vigil over him. They just sat and prayed and fingered their Rosaries as they comforted him, but they were so unobtrusive that we hardly knew they were there. Every so often they swapped places with other Sisters as they each took their turn to sit with my Granddad.

One afternoon we were called in to be with grandad and he asked for my dad and me to sit close to his bed. Then he picked up his every day pocket watch, a very old chain driven affair, made in 1831, as I later discovered, and gave it to my dad to look after for him.

Then he turned to me and said, "Brian I have had a good life and a long one, and I have no regrets about any of it. I haven't much in the way of worldly goods to leave behind me, but I want you to be very brave, and look after this watch for me. It will last you for most of your life if you look after it."

Then he gave me his Sunday best watch, dated around 1841, which was also a chain driven pocket watch, which I had always admired. Then we hugged each other for a long time with tears pouring down our faces. I could feel how feeble he was and I knew the end was very near.

The next morning when I came downstairs they told me that he had died in his sleep, during the night. Grandma had "laid him out" ready for the undertaker to measure him up for his coffin.

The coffin was mounted on two trestles in the sitting room until the day of the funeral. Every one that knew him must have been there along with all his family and, of course some of the sisters from the convent.

Then my dad dropped a bombshell. He told me that a funeral was no place for a lad of my age, and I had to stay at home with my sister and my cousins, all girls.

I was absolutely smashed, this was my last chance to be with grandad and travel to Clifford with him. They were going to put him at the rear of the churchyard close to the old wall that separated his old home from the graveyard. They had decided to lay him to rest backwards. That is with his feet towards the wall so that he could look at his old home forever. Later on, about eight years later in fact, we laid my grandma by his side to share eternity together.

Grandma tried to console me by promising to take me to see the grave the next day, but that was no consolation to me, I wanted to be with him today. After my dad had given me a very stern talking to I was resolved to put up with this situation but then, when they had all gone and I had had time to reflect on it, I had a bright idea. I put on my good shoes and warm coat to go out for a walk. My sister gave me a hard time and she said, "I'll tell on you if you go outside. Dad said we all had to stay in here together. You'll get into awful trouble when they come home, if you go out."

I was determined to go anyway no matter what happened afterwards. I had had plenty of beltings in my short life and one more would be worth it to be with grandad at the end. I set off as fast as I could run and walk and it was not far to Clifford, when I arrived at the church I realised that I was too late for the service. I had hoped to sneak in when no one was looking and hide at the back of the church but the massive double doors were closed tightly. The doors were made of solid wood, with a huge cast iron latch, which had a large iron ring through it to lift it off the hasp. I wasn't sure that I could reach up far enough and turn the ring and I realised that even if I could open the huge door it was sure to disturb the ceremony and I was in enough trouble as it was. Badly disappointed, I went over and sat on the old, moss covered, stone, wall close to that awful hole in the ground. I was holding on to that huge pocket watch and fingering the ornamental chain that had once been grandma's necklace, before she had it converted to a watch chain for his new watch.

I was still sitting there with my head looking at the ground and tears rolling down my cheeks, when I heard a rustle of cloth and I felt a comforting arm around my shaking body. When I looked up, one of the convent sisters was holding me in a comforting embrace. We sat there hugging one another until they had lowered the coffin into the ground and the service was over. Then my dad came over and started to rant and rave at me, for being there, until he noticed the withering, angry, stares that he was receiving from the sisters and the priest. He walked away to comfort his younger sister Eileen, whilst grandma came over with my mum, to comfort me.

When the ceremony was all finished, they tried to get me to ride back to the house in the car, but I said,"Me and grandad, always used to walk back home together, after visiting the Sisters."

Grandma said. "Come love you can sit on my knee, it's not far, you don't have to walk, it looks like it might rain again. We don't want you to catch cold, do we."

My father, in a rare show of emotion said, "Come on then, we'll walk together, it'll do us good." So saying he took my hand and led me off down the road. With a strong breeze dragging at our coats and a weak, winterish, sun breaking through the heavy clouds, We walked together in silence, even the birds were quiet, except for an old carrion crow sitting on the top of a telephone post. I began to get the feeling that dad needed this time out to get control of his own emotions and not make a fool of himself by showing human weakness in front of all the others. He would have been devastated if he had shed a few tears in public.

The house was a sad old place, as we sat around the table, pretending to be enjoying our tea. I never got used to being in that house, ever again, and I was glad when the council relocated my grandma into a prefabricated cottage at the other end of the village. The cottage had once been one of the officer's homes, when the estate was a military camp for the Canadian air force during the second, world war, and it had a gas cooking stove and hot water system which made it easier for her.

When dad was about 65 he gave me granddad's other pocket watch, so that I would have one each to pass on to my two sons, David and Rodney, which I have already done, and both watches still go well and keep excellent time.

I sincerely hope that somewhere, there is a garden full of flowers, with plenty of roses and carnations, myriads of little birds, and maybe, the odd cauliflower or two, where my dear old grandad can walk in the sun and admire them, as he puffs away on his pipe forever more. I am really sorry that I only had those few precious years with grandad but all the things that he taught me have stayed with me right through my adult life, and I still adore gardening and interacting with wild life and nature in general. I still love walking around in the forest, that surrounds our home. Our garden is a "free for all" for all manner of wild creatures that wish to call it home, and frequently do so. We allow spiders of all types to range freely and set their webs to catch the bugs. We have the back patio walled with shade cloth and throughout the summer many small lizards live and hunt there. A large black skink and his family haunt the garden and the patio.

At night when we turn on the outside lighting the walls are alive with geckos. When I'm fossicking around the shed and garden I have to be very careful not to hurt the ground geckos and other small creatures that live with us in harmony. Poisons like snail killer and insect sprays are totally forbidden and I run the garden on a perma-culture system so that everything looks after itself and creates a suitable environment for the other species around it.

When we first moved here the walls and the inside of the shed were covered with large messy earthenware lumps which turned out to be those huge orange and black hornets that are quite prevalent around here. At first I was inclined to get rid of them then I realised that if left alone they were no threat to humans but deadly to an assortment of caterpillars so now we encourage them to live with us. Paper wasps however can be quite nasty so we only tolerate them when they decide to nest away from the house. Like the hornets they do a power of good in the garden and save spraying.

Author driving Case tractor aged about 6 years old collecting the sheaves at harvest time.

Grandad O'Donnell at aged about 80 years with his dog.

Chapter 7

THE VILLAGE BLACKSMITH

I grew up in a small farm cottage in Yorkshire that had no electricity or gas and relied on a wood and coal fired triplex range to provide heating, cooking and hot water. There was a boiler behind the fire to heat the water system and an oven beside the fire for cooking. Also there was a hob that swung round over the fire to sit a kettle or pan on to heat up and a hot plate across the top to warm the plates etc.

The range was quite efficient but it needed lots of fuel to keep it going. Coal was available but was very costly so we supplemented it with wood.

My father took on after hours work to get plenty of firewood. All the fields were surrounded by hedges, which sometimes became overgrown and needed rebuilding.

My father did the rebuilding work on contract. The work needed a lot of skill to end up with a stock proof barrier and dad was very good at this. The excess timber was cut out and sorted. The farmer often kept any millable timber and dad took the rest, which often amounted to a lot of firewood to be carted home.

There were no chainsaws around in those days so all the work was carried out by hand with two man crosscut saws and axes. We often had to use a large hammer and steel wedges to split the stumps and bigger pieces of wood to make them small enough to lift by hand on to the cart.

The old wedges that we had were almost worn out so dad decided to get some more made.

The local blacksmith was asked about them and he offered to forge some new wedges out of old plough axles of which he had a few on hand.

As we were nearing the middle of winter there was no hurry to get new wedges ready for the next hedging season, so dad asked Harold the blacksmith, to just do them when he had a bit of a slack moment.

The blacksmith worked until late on most evenings and in the winter the forge became the social centre of the village. The forge was always hot and most of the village lads had gotten into the habit of gathering there to keep warm and chat about the local girls and footy etc.

The atmosphere was very special with the heat, the smell of hot leather and white hot metal. All this, together, with the clanging of the smithies hammer on the anvil, the roar of the fire and the chattering of the boys made a cosy scene on many a winter evening.

Harold also had a ready wit and loved a good joke. He was well known around the district for his story telling and always seemed to have a few good yarns ready to entertain his customers and the village lads.

Old Harold kept a few pigs in the back yard, which he fattened for his own use. They were often fed on small waste potatoes, which he collected from the local farmers, sometimes in part payment for work carried out on farm machinery.

The spuds needed to be cooked to make

them digestible so there was a copper in the corner of the blacksmith's shop, which was fired with coals from the forge.

The small potatoes were very tasty and the boys were in the habit of helping themselves for their supper.

One Wednesday evening dad said he was going to the village to see if the wedges were ready and I asked to be allowed to go with him.

"Aye, of course you can, if your homework is finished, come on hurry up."

When we arrived at the forge Harold said, "By Charlie, I'm right sorry but I still have a fair bit to do on 'em yet. I've gotten most of 'em roughed out but they need tapering."

"Oh that's aw'right," dad replied, "There was nowt on t'radio tonight so I thought we might come for a ride to see 'ow you was getting on wi'em."

We stayed at the forge for a while listening to all the local gossip and Harold's yarns.

Eventually it was time to go so we went to say good night but Harold wanted us to stay a little while longer.

"Don't go yet Charlie," he said, "I've a little surprise for these lads and it should be a right good laugh."

"Aye, ok then, we can spare a few more minutes." Dad replied.

The boys were getting ready to head off to their homes and beds when Harold called out to them.

"Hey you lads," he called out, "Don't be going yet, I've gotten a little surprise here for you all, it'll warm you up for the walk home."

As the boys moved back in around the forge he said, "By heck I know how you lads like your taties, in fact some nights there's never 'nough left for me pigs so tonight I put some nice bits of meat in't copper for you as well. I 'ope you like a bit of meat, I'll just fish it out for you."

One of the older lads piped up and said, "Gee mister Swan that's real nice of you but you shouldn't have done that for us although we're sure to enjoy it just as you said."

Without more ado Harold slipped a multi-tined fork down into the copper and lifted out three lovely juicy rats. The boys reacted immediately with shouts of horror and repugnance. Then they all turned white and began to heave their hearts and stomachs out.

Harold got back all the taties that the boys had eaten that night along with most of their dinners as well.

The blacksmith burst out in a huge belly-rolling peal of laughter as the boys heaved their hearts out.

"Bugger me, Charlie," he said with a very straight face, "I thought they'd 'ave enjoyed that bit o' meat. I went to a lot o' trouble to make sure them rats was properly clean afore I cooked 'em. They should 'ave been nice, maybe I should 'ave gutted them an'all seeing as them lads is so fussy with their grub."

"Aye well, Harold, there no accounting for taste is there. I'll say goodnight now and we'll get going, this lad 'as school in't morning", my dad replied.

The sequel to this story came many years later because the girl that I married had trained as a nurse in Harrogate before emigrating to Western Australia for our wedding. Two of the girls that she had trained with lived on farms close to the same village as Harold Swan, the blacksmith and had married two of the boys involved in this story.

We had been living in W.A. for many years before we decided to make a trip back to Yorkshire to introduce our sons to their grand parents, and catch up with our family and friends around England.

Whilst in Yorkshire, we were invited to share a meal, and the evening, with Sandra's nursing friends, whom she had kept in contact with over the years. Little did we realise that the husbands came from Great Ouseburn, also.

I had forgotten about the gourmet supper incident, and I had no idea who had actually been there that night anyway.

After greeting the girls whom I had also known during their nursing days in Harrogate but not around the village where they came from we were introduced to their spouses by Christian names only.

We didn't recognise each other, as I was only about twelve when we left the district to live in the village where my wife lived and I also attended the grammar school not the comprehensive that the others attended. None of us were aware that we had ever known any of the others, in fact we weren't aware that we had ever met before let alone shared some of our lives around the same village.

They treated me as a total stranger, a foreigner in fact who had somehow stolen one of the local girls from under their very noses. By now my broad Yorkshire twang had softened somewhat, and mixed with a fair amount of "Aussie", it was not surprising that they thought I was a foreigner.

The evening was going very well until the ladies retired to the kitchen to finalise the dinner leaving me with their husbands.

I could hear the three women chattering and laughing as they went about their chores, but the men decide to treat me as a nuisance who had managed to get himself invited to dinner. For the most part they completely ignored me and made rude, terse remarks whenever I tried to join in the conversation.

However they were their own undoing because as they chatted away about mutual friends and their business dealings I was able to work out who they actually were and where they came from. As they were in the right age group I took a punt that they were participants in the infamous supper party.

What I didn't realise was that all the boys involved had sworn to a pact of silence and no one else was supposed to know of the their shame and misery.

One of the men had inherited the local carpenters shop and funeral business from his father.

Finally in desperation I decided to hit back.

I said, "I may be a bloody foreigner to you two snobs but I've never been reduced to eating stolen pig-taties and boiled rats for my supper in a blacksmiths shop."

Their reactions were astounding, if I had punched their noses I couldn't have wished for a better outcome. They had never even told their wives about that dreadful winter's evening and were stunned to think that an outsider knew of it.

They both began jabbering away at the same time and a bottle of fine malt whiskey suddenly appeared, at about the same time that their good old Yorkshire hospitality returned.

They begged me not to tell the girls about that night and I agreed to keep their embarrassing secret. However, in spite of all their urging I refused to let on where I fitted into the equation or how I came to know about their supper.

Chapter **8**

LAMBING TIME IN YORKSHIRE

Geordie Dodson was a very tall, thin and wiry farmer, whose property was situated along a country track at the back of Firlands farm. He was a very excitable sort of fellow with a high-pitched voice that went higher and higher whenever he got excited, and today he was extremely excited.

We were out looking for some runaway ewes which had escaped and were making their way along the back lane at a great rate of knots and they were already about two miles from home and still travelling fast even though they were heavily pregnant and carrying a lot of wool.

We asked Geordie if he had seen them in the lane and he replied.

"Oh, aye I seen 'em and I tried to stop 'em

and send 'em back to where they cum from, although I had no idea where the little beggars had come from. Were they yours then?" He said and then went on with his voice increasing in pitch and volume and his arms waving about in excitement. "Oh, aye they came, and they came, and they came, and they jumped, and they jumped, and they jumped. They jumped right over me 'ead they did and kept on going."

"Yea they're part of a mob that the old man bought cheap at the sale in Masham yesterday, the beggers are mad. They're highland sheep and used to roaming wild on the moors." Eric replied. "Does tha' know where they are now Geordie."

"They went straight down t'lane last I saw of 'em. Hey, look, t'lane bends round my boundary but if you look sharp and duck straight though my place past t'house you just might get ahead on 'em."

Thanking Geordie, we turned our bikes round, followed his directions and peddled like mad with our dogs chasing us down the farm track. We just got to the road ahead of the sheep and using our bikes as gates we managed to turn them round with the help of the dogs.

They still had plenty of life in them, although they were heavily pregnant and in full wool. However by the time we got them all back home they were blown out and a lot more docile.

When we got up that morning there were only nineteen of them in the field out of two hundred and fifty two that we put in there the day before. The fences were very good but being highland sheep they had just jumped over the top of them.

By the time that we returned home the rest of the family were busy raising the fence with some old wire netting whilst we rounded up the escapees. We reckoned that this mob were the last of them, but it was impossible to count them as they were so wild and timid. These tiny-framed ewes had somehow been mated to a great big Southdown ram or some similar breed and the lambing time was going to be difficult at best and probably nigh on impossible with almost certainly heavy losses of both ewes and lambs, hence the owner had rounded them up and sold them off.

The sheep were hard to handle since they were so wild and they were going to need a lot of handling to get the lambs out, hopefully alive.

When the first lambs started to arrive we realised that we would have to fold them in the farmyard so that they couldn't run away from us. The first few lambs were twins and popped out quite easily but then the men realised that they would have to separate the ewes as they dropped the lambs because they went crazy when we went near and were sure to trample the lambs to death.

There were plenty of empty, old stone buildings surrounding the yard and we had a big pile of pine hurdles that we tied together to make separate pens for each ewe and her lambs. Eric and I, had never been allowed to attend a lambing, or any other birth for that matter, boy oh boy, were we in for a great shock before this day was over.

This breed of ewe were mainly prone to bearing only single lambs which were always much bigger than twin lambs and therefore much harder to birth. Add to this the fact that they were Southdown cross, and we were in for a hard time.

When the first ewe to have trouble needed some help, the men each had a go at pulling the lamb out but it had to be turned as well and they had no hope of getting their great big rough farmer's hands into the birth canal. Old Frank, the farmer, so called because one of his many sons was also called Frank, or young Frank, said. "It's no good Charlie we'll never get 'em out. What we need is somebody with small hands."

"Aye your right there Frank," Dad replied, "But where the heck are we going to find a man with hands that small."

"Come ower 'ere, young un, he called out to me, give us a look at your 'ands, you and our Eric might get your 'ands in 'ere."

I climbed over the hurdles and he said, "Now listen carefully lad, thou 'as to get thee 'and in there and 'ave a feel round. T'ead and front legs 'ave to come out together and come out first, does tha' see, so thou'll 'ave to pull t'lamb around right way, so have a go."

I rolled up my sleeves and washed my hands and arms then rubbed in a mild antiseptic liquid and I was as ready as I was ever going to be. I worked my hand into the birth cannal and tried to push it up into the womb but it was too tight to go past the pelvic bones. After a good long struggle I pulled it out again and studied it carefully. I soon worked out that I could roll my hand up quite small if I really tried, so I practiced a little bit, out where I could see what was happening, and I was able to make my hand quite small in diameter by crossing my thumb over to the base of my little finger..

Dad said. "Come on you soft bugger, get your hand in there and get that bloody lamb out afore I belt your bloody lug holes for you."

Old Frank chipped in and said. "Shut your great gob and leave t'lad alone Charlie.If you don't behave you can bugger off and we'll get yon lamb out on our own."

Dad went into the sulks. He walked away lighting his pipe and calling out.

"You'm get that bugger out on your own seeing as you are so bloody clever I'll not be 'elping you."

By remembering how I had held my hand, I tried once more to fit it up into the womb, and low and behold, it slid in quite easily.

"Now then lad what can tha' feel in there then." Asked old Frank.

"Not much." I replied. "It feels like the middle of it's back. It's nowt like you reckoned. I can't feel no legs, nor a head. It just feels like woolly rug with a slimy cover ower it, that's all".
"Right then, what you 'ave to do is try and move it round until you can get hold of a leg. A'right?"

I reached to one side and dug my fingers in to the wool and pulled sideways. The lamb moved fairly easily and I felt a bony bit like a shoulder blade, or something like that. Then all hell broke out. The ewe on feeling the movement, decided to help out and gave a mighty heave, trapping my arm against the pelvic bone and it hurt like hell and I shouted out with the pain and tears began forming in the corner of my eyes.

"Don't worry lad you must 'ave moved it a bit, so try again each time she rests." Frank said. "Keep it up, and it'll come out, if we're lucky."

After a few movements that seemed like for ever, I could get hold of the nose and it was still alive so I vowed to try even harder for a live lamb at the end.

"Keep going 'til you can get hold of a leg, then try to turn the beggar over so that t'head and front legs come into 'ole, then you can pull 'im out.

As I took another grip and put some weight on, the ewe gave a massive heave and the lamb started to roll over, but this was pure agony and my arm hurt like mad. I could feel the tears starting to run down my cheeks. However, I managed to hang on, not that I could have pulled my arm out anyway. One of the legs was well tucked away from me and I had to push like crazy to get a grip on the elbow and slowly pull it around. At last the front feet and the nose moved into the birth canal. It was finally coming out.

The ewe knew that her ordeal was nearly over, and with renewed strength she pushed out a big ram lamb. She soon recovered and started to nuzzle the lamb, and what a lovely sight it was. As she started to clean it up the gangly looking creature attempted to stand up. It took very little time at all before the lamb was taking it's first suck of mum's milk. How the heck do they know what to do?

"By, I'm right capped young man." Said Frank tha' did a right good job and there are only about two hundred and fifty to go. Let's go up to t'house and get a cuppa tea, whilst she gets to know that little fellow.

As we walked towards the house, I was feeling very pleased with myself. I was hoping that the next one would be a long time because my arm was still throbbing madly.

Mrs. Tillet, the farmers wife, made us a nice pot of tea and found some cakes in the pantry whilst Frank told them about the lamb. Then she telephoned our schools and Eric and I got leave of absence for a couple of weeks, or until all the ewes had lambed.

It was necessary for us to check the ewes every hour or so, day and night, because it was necessary to separate any that had gone into labour and pen them in the sheds where we could handle them comfortably because even the days were cold and the nights were freezing.

Eric and I catnapped in the living room and took turns to walk down the yard to check the sheep. At night we took a torch because there was no electricity in the buildings and after a day or so the sheep got used to us and settled down a little bit.

Occasionally, for no apparent reason, I woke up in between normal visits and decided to go for a stroll down to the yard. Every time there was a lamb hanging out and needing help. I don't know how I knew but it never failed and later in my life I was heavily involved with pigs, and the same thing happened again.

There were a few sets of twins and triplets and these ewes coped quite well but they still had to be separated to protect the lambs. We only had a few dead lambs which we skinned so that we could tie the skins onto one of the triplets, to get the ewe who had lost own her lamb to accept the spare lamb and care for it.

By the time that they were all finished lambing we were both worn out and our hands and arms were a sorry state from all the wetting, washing and pain, but to see all those lambs romping around the field was medicine for our aching bodies.

Chapter 9

THE HAUNTED HOUSE

My parents were sick and tired of living in rented houses and worse still, tied cottages which were supplied by employers as part of a job situation where they were at the beck and call of the boss whenever it suited him and they were stuck with that job unless they could find alternate accommodation.

The house across the street from where we were living in a tied cottage was originally the manor house of the village and was built of solid sandstone two feet thick Years ago it had been divided into two separate houses and the elderly lady who owned half of it had put her half up for sale.

My parents went over and had a good look around the house and found it to be very sound indeed but lacking in modern amenities such as a bathroom, kitchen, hot water and a water closet. The existing toilet was an old thunder box at the far end of the yard. The house was going very cheaply because of this lack of facilities and the old lady just wanted to be rid of it.

Dad had heard from an old friend on the council that he would be able to get a low interest loan and a cash back subsidy from the local council to modernise the house provided that it was not for rental, so he and mam went into town and bought it, just in the nick of time, as two or thee others had heard about it by then.

One half of the house was still known as Manor House, whilst the half that we bought was known as Manor Cottage. It was a very old house with two stories plus cellars and attics. A repair job on the inside of the chimney in the attic was dated 1869.

The windows were the old-fashioned dormer type with the bottom half sliding up and down for ventilation.

This type of window has a cavity at both sides with heavy cast iron counter weights on ropes and pulleys at each side to take most of the weight of the window so that it could easily be moved up and down.

In the centre of the cellar floor there was a rectangular hole cut into the stone flags which was about three feet deep, and a beautiful stream of fresh spring water ran through the lower half providing a lovely water supply for the household. This stream also had, at one time, provided drinking water for the upper end of the village as well.

In the yard of the cottage next door, which was built on higher ground, we later found a disused well about ten feet deep with the steam running through the bottom.

One day when we were discussing this with the old gentleman who lived in the manor house attached to our place he took us down into his cellar to show us a hole in the floor similar to ours with the stream running through.

Then he suggested that we go for a short walk down the street towards a place near the village hall where he pointed to the stone wall alongside the road.

"I remember when I was a lad," He said, "The villagers used to get their water from a stone well set into the wall just about here. There was a cast iron pipe coming out of the wall and running into the trough. The water was as clear as crystal and icy cold.

That stream came out from under the manor house and it never stopped running, winter or summer. I reckon that it comes from the same stream because this area is much lower than our cellars and would naturally drain out at about this level. They must have buggered it up when they put in the deep sewerage system 'cause it don't run no more."

We had only been living in the old house for a short while when my sister started to complain about noises in the night. She was sleeping in the rear bedroom above the dining room and I was living away from home at the time because of my apprenticeship at Peterborough some, one hundred and forty miles away.

Jean said to my dad one day, "Will you come and have a look at my bedroom, please dad I think it must be haunted or something because I keep hearing scratching and squeaking noises in the night."

"Don't be so bloody daft," replied dad,

"There's no such bloody thing as ghosts, you must be going daft in t 'ead", I've never heard nowt so bloody daft in all me life, haunted, huh."

The next time that I went home for the weekend, Jean asked me. "Brian, how about you sleep in my room tonight and I'll sleep in yours, then we'll see if you hear the noises in the night and I can listen for them in your room then maybe some one will believe me."

"Did you know that there's a door leading out of your bedroom into the cottage next door, Jean," I said, "Maybe that has something to do with it."

"Like hell there is, it only has the one door from the main landing." She replied. "What the devil are you on about?"

"Come up stairs now and I'll show you where it is," I said.

We went up the stairs and into her room and I tapped along the adjoining wall until I had convinced her that there really was a door which used to give access to a small cottage built against the end wall. When we had first moved in we had boarded our side up with masonite sheeting on a wooden frame. Jean then said. "You may well be right but the noises are coming from over here near the window not on that wall at all."

"Hey! This wall is an outside wall and it is solid sandstone two feet thick." Was my response to that remark. "The only change in that wall is the fitting of the window and the window box under the actual window, maybe there's a secret trapdoor in the floor of the window box and a tunnel leading to the cellar and the scratching noise is the ghost trying to open it up."

"Damn you." She spat out as she left the room, you're a damn sight worse than my old man."

I had a jolly good laugh about it but agreed to swap rooms for the weekend anyway, just for fun. I was in the bedroom just as it was getting dark and, believe it or not I heard the noises just as she had described them. The agitated squeaking, sounded something like a mob of mice having a panic attack. I was getting ready to go out dancing and there was quite a lot of squeaking, scratching, and scrabbling about, and it seemed to be coming from the solid stonewall besides the window frame.

As we were about to go out for the evening, I decided to let the problem lapse until I had more time to check it out thoroughly and anyway this was no ghost. More than likely it was a bird or small animal such as a mouse.

I awoke early the next morning as usual and the day was just breaking, when I heard it again. There it was, squeak, squeak, squeak, scrabble, scrabble, scrabble.

What on earth can be making that noise I thought? It seems to be in the wall near the window, but how can that be.

I got dressed and put the kettle on for a cuppa then went outside to investigate. It was still quite dark outside and the window was too high up to see anything much. To make matters worse the back yard had been lowered to accommodate a new kitchen and bathroom. I was going to need to get out the extension ladder so I decided to have my cup of tea first.

Once the ladder was in place I was able to climb up and have a good look. There was a small piece of cement render missing alongside the window frame leaving a very small hole between the frame and the stone.

When I got close to the hole and tried to see into it the stink was awful, quite unbearable in fact and there were some small hairs and greasy rub marks all around the hole. That's when it became clear to me as to the reason for the noises, it was so obvious really. It could only be a colony of bats that had found the small hole and moved in. There was enough room in the side cavities where the counter weights ran for the colony to sleep undisturbed and it was only their exit and entry that gave away their secret. Sometime later the wall needed re-pointing and the poor bats were expelled and had to find a new home.

They duly found a small hole that gave them access to the sign outside the Royal Oak pub across the street, where they dwelt for many years prior to the sign being refurbished by the brewery.

When I last visited Yorkshire in the late nineteen eighties the next door neighbour who is keen on nature study, was lamenting the demise of this colony of short eared bats. He said that these bats were becoming very rare and he thought that the colony had died out because they had never been able to find any sign of them since.

One very wet afternoon I was at a loose end and I wandered into the old stone barn behind his house where he parked his Volvo motorcar. Just inside the door I spotted some "mouse" droppings spread around the base of the stonewall corner that formed one side of the doorway. As there was no suitable food for mice in the barn I began a diligent search for the reason for the droppings and their unusual placing right in the doorway. Eventually I discovered a small hole high up the wall where the huge oak beam that sat above the doorway was inset into the stonework. I felt that there must be a cavity in the wall around the beam big enough for a colony of tiny bats to sleep out the daylight hours, and that they had somehow found access to it.

I went into dad's shed and got out his stepladder to have a closer look and sure enough, there was a tiny hole between the stonework, and the oak beam leading into a cavity behind the beam. Just before dark that evening I rounded up my father who was also interested in wildlife, the next-door neighbour and his two little boys.

I said. "Come on, I have a lovely surprise for you in the barn, I hope."

I led them quietly into the barn as the daylight was fading fast to await the excitement. I was going to look a right idiot if the bats didn't show and I wasn't all that sure that I was right in thinking that they were in fact living in the wall.

We hadn't long to wait but we had great difficulty keeping everyone quiet, especially the boys, before the show began. I hadn't mentioned the bats as I wasn't at all sure that they were there, or that the droppings were from bats either.

My dad eventually asked. "What the bloody hell are we all standing in a cold old barn for when there's a good fire inside? What the bloody hell's going on?"

It was almost dark by then and I put my finger to my lips to silence him. After a few more seconds of silence dad heard a noise and began to realise what this charade was all about and maybe the cause of it. He mimed the question, whereabouts?

I grinned and pointed to the hole above the door. The bats were just waking up and were soon crawling out of their home and heading off on their nightly hunting trip. Once they had all gone dad asked, "How the hell did you find them little beggars, Brian, We've lived here all this time and couldn't find them anywhere."

I showed them the droppings and Allan, the neighbour said, "Well I'll be damned, I've seen droppings there many a time and just cleaned them up without giving it any thought about it. Them little sods were right here under our noses all the time. I thought that they were mouse droppings, not bats."

Then turning to his boys he said, "Well, what did you make of that then boys, was it worth the wait?"

"Aye, it was that," said the boys, "Thankyou for showing them to us Brian, we'll be able to tell the class tomorrow at school. They will come back, wont they?"

"Oh yes," I said "Just as it is getting light in the morning, if you can get up that early and keep very quiet you are sure to see them again."

Allan said, "Not on your life Brian, neither of

this pair has ever seen a day break before, and judging by the job I have to get them out it'll be time to go to school before we see either of them in the morning.

When I got up next morning and crept quietly into the shed both boys were sitting there waiting for the show to start and putting their fingers to their lips to keep me quiet.

Chapter **10**

WET ALL OVER

It had been a heavy night at the "Royal Oak' pub in our little village in north Yorkshire, and Harold had consumed his usual amount of best bitter in fine style, but now it was time to head for home. Harold lived at the far end of the village and he had to cross the beck, (stream), on the way home.

This should have been no great deal because the road ran over the top with a large diameter pipe to carry the stream below. There were strong stone walls on either side to guide the travellers and prevent them falling into the beck. However, Harold was having some difficulty navigating a straight course and he missed the bridge and fell down the bank into the water. He wasn't hurt at all but was very wet and cold.

Harold was sitting on the bank collecting his wits and crying his eyes out when another villager went to pass by. Seeing Harold very distressed sitting on the bank, he stopped to see if he could assist the old man.

"Now then Harold w'ats to do then, ave you 'urt yoursen?" He asked.

"Nay lad, I'm alright I just fell in t'beck, some daft bugger must 'ave shifted t'bridge cause it don't go ower t'beck no more." Harold replied.

"Well if'n you aren't 'urt, then, what's tha' crying about?" He asked.

"Well its like this see, I'm an old man now and this is first time I bin wet all ower at t'same bloody time you see." The old man answered.

Chapter 11

PIGEON PIE

The Verger of the church next door to our place had come looking for me. I hadn't long been in the village and he didn't know a lot about me except that I went to the local grammar school, but he had heard that I was a crack shot with my fourten shotgun.

"Now then young man," he said, "As he came into our yard. I'm Verger of yon church next door and I have to look after it and I need a bit of a hand and I wondered if you might be able to help."

"I'd love to if I can Mr.Turner." I replied. "What is it that you need?"

"Well I've heard that you're a good shot with a shotgun and I need to get rid of them pigeons in the belfry 'cause they're making a devil of a mess around the bells, and I thought you might like to 'ave a go at 'em for me."

"Aye, well, I already 'ave shot a few of them when they pinch the hen's food from our yard, but I was worried in case somebody owned 'em and might go mad at me." I answered.

"Nay thou's got nowt to worry about there, they're all feral pigeons and they've got to go." He said.

"Right you are then, I'll get stuck into 'em." I said, "But I need to get some more cartridges, first, when I get my pocket money on Friday I'll go into town and buy some."

"Don't you worry about that, I 'ave to go to town in t'morning, I'll get a box and leave it with your mother." He said. "If you can manage another bit of a job as well you'd better come and see me sometime. You see t'belfry is alus full of sticks and droppings because of them pigeons and t'jackdaws and I'm too old to get up there these days."

"Aye well," I replied. "I'll do that an' all so you needn't worry about it anymore."

I looked after the pigeons until I left home but they soon built up in numbers again after I went away, until one weekend I decided to go home for a day or two and catch up with family and friends. The next morning the verger came hurrying to see me about the birds because they were in plague proportions again.

"Well, I'm only here for the weekend but I'll see what I can do, Mr turner." I said. "There are a few cartridges left in the gun cabinet."

During the day I shot a few birds but then they got gun shy and I couldn't get near them. I was thinking of how I could get at them when I had a bit of a brain wave. I reckoned that I could have a go at them when they came home to roost after dark. The old church had a square tower up to the bell chamber, then it tapered into a very tall steeple where the pigeons nested and roosted on the stone ledges where the blocks overlapped on the inside, especially at the top. Now I reckoned that if I was game enough, I could go up and stand by the bells, angle my shotgun up and around the steeple and I might get few with the one shot as the balls rotated around the inside of the tower.

About nine o'clock I collected a hessian sack form dad's shed just in case I got lucky. I climbed up the spiral stairway into the bell chamber and stood alongside the bell frame. It was already pitch dark in there as I leaned my right shoulder against the wall and shone my torch up at an angle to the top. So far so good, there were pigeons camped everywhere up there and I was bound to get a few, but was it safe, where would all the stray pellets end up and how much noise would it make.

Well, it was now or never, so I loaded the gun cocked the trigger aimed up high and squeezed. There was an almighty explosion that must have been heard all over the village because I hadn't taken into account the built-in acoustics of the bell tower or expected the blaze of flame from the muzzle. Oh my God, what had I done. There would be hell to pay over this nights work, for sure. Just as the echoes were dying down there was more noise. I had frightened and dislodged all the pigeons and as it was pitch dark in there they flapped around everywhere and fell onto the bells as well. Oh dear God, this was pandemonium, what a racket. Soon there would be a rush of people up here to see what the heck had happened.

I began to calm down after a while and my

heartbeat slowed back to normal again and I realised that there were pigeons all over the place. Most of them were still alive and many unhurt, so with the aid of my torch I started rounding them up and stowing them in a hessian sack. By the time I finished I had nearly thirty in the bag and a good many were squabs (unfeathered) that would make a nice pie.

I crept quietly down the spiral stairway and out through the big door into the church porch. I was hoping that the huge amount of pigeons would appease the church council and get me out of too much of the trouble that I would surely encounter on the way out. I stepped out of the main door into the cool night air and all was quiet in the graveyard until, suddenly there was a loud screech that made me jump out of my skin. Don't tell me that I had upset the local ghosts. I had never heard about any ghosts in or around the church, or the church-yard for that matter but who knows?

The noise was only the resident barn owl out catching his supper. Amazingly there weren't any new ghost stories concerning the bright flash and deafening noises that followed.

Apparently no one had seen or heard a thing, but I was never game to try it again, in spite of the excellent results.

Chapter 12

THE GHOST

In the olden days before combine harvesters were invented, all the grain crops in England were harvested with a binder and tied into sheaves which were then stacked and stored so that they could be threshed later in the year to separate the grain from the straw and chaff. This task was usually carried out in winter when there was nothing much happening around the farm and there were extra men available on a casual basis to carry out the job. The farmers often assisted each other by sending their men to help the neighbour.

Threshing days were always great occasions with plenty of drama and humour. The stacks were full of rats and mice, which the boys chased and caught with the help of the farm dogs and cats. Between 8 and 10 men were needed to carry out the job of threshing and the farmer's men were supplemented with casual hands who travelled around with the threshing drum, which was owned and run by a contractor. Among these men there was always one or two wags and other interesting guys who, because they moved around a good deal, had access to all the latest gossip and yarns which generally led to an interesting day.

As it happened, one Saturday in November, all these guys were upstaged by a total stranger, a mere slip of a girl with a rough Scottish accent and homespun clothing.

On the day in question I had been asked by one of the local contractors to go to castle farm outside the town of Ripley to help with the threshing. They were short handed that day and needed some one to cut the strings around the sheaves to open them up for thrashing. I had done this job many times before and was quite proficient at the task although I was only about 15 years old. On this occasion the job was made much more difficult because the farmer wanted to re-use the strings, which meant that they had to be cut close to the knot and saved.

Castle farm was the home farm attached to a medieval castle, which, was still inhabited. The farmhouse and most of the buildings were of the same vintage as the castle and built of solid stone. Traditionally the farmer's wife provided the days meals for all the workers as part of the deal.

The morning's work had gone well and we all went to the farmhouse for lunch. Mrs. Turnbull had prepared a sumptuous meal for us and served it in the massive kitchen. There was a huge scrubbed pine table close to one wall, which was typical of such kitchens and around which we were amply seated. We had almost completed our lunch, in fact we were just enjoying a final cup of tea before returning to work when there was a quiet knock at the door. Everyone stopped talking and turned in quiet expectation since visitors were rare out on the farms, especially on threshing days when they were so busy.

John Turnbull, the farmer, a jovial man of solid build just like his farm buildings got up and answered the knock by opening the back door which led directly into the kitchen. He was surprised to see a total stranger standing there, a mere slip of a girl who spoke in an almost unintelligible language. She was dressed in homespun tweeds and had a very broad Scottish accent with many unusual colloquial terms which we didn't understand. She claimed to have travelled from the highlands of Scotland and none of us would have doubted that fact, and this was her first trip away from the croft where she lived with her family in almost total isolation. She went on to say that she had made this epic journey to see if she could help the Turnbull family with their problem.

"Problem, what bloody problem? What the hell are you on about? The only problem we have today is getting that bloody threshing done afore it rains". Said John Turnbull. "Aye and we 'ave no bloody time to spare with daft buggers like you." He continued, so tell me what the hell you're here for and then you can bugger off out of our way".

The girl was somewhat abashed as she handed John a badly worn piece of paper that had been torn from a newspaper. She claimed a distant relative had sent it to her. Knowing that she was an accomplished spiritualist medium she was sure to find it interesting, and maybe even be able to help the family with some advice as to the cause, and probable solution to the problem. The paper had been torn out of a copy of the Knaresborough Post, a local parochial rag from the next town. The story on that page was about a ghost in the farmhouse at castle farm near Ripley. It was a story about this very house and it's occupants in fact.

The occupiers, the Turnbull family, had told their story to the reporter of 'The Post'. They said that they frequently heard footsteps in the house in the evenings, especially at weekends, but they couldn't find any logical reasons for them.

John was very embarrassed by all this because he was a very earthy sort of bloke who wanted none of this rubbish and our presence was not helping him to deal with this unusual situation. The men were stunned into total silence and sat there at the table all ears pricked not to miss a single syllable of this enthralling saga.

In the middle of all this embarrassment and confusion, John Turnbull suddenly remembered his manners and in true Yorkshire style he invited her into the kitchen and offered her a cup of tea and a bite to eat after her long journey, which must have taken a couple of days at least. The woman gladly accepted the hospitality and entered the room; where she gazed slowly all around the kitchen as though she was expecting something to happen or was looking for someone. After a thorough inspection she promptly went into a trance, (or at least that's what we thought it was). She seemed to go all limp and closed her eyes as though she were asleep then suddenly looked up above the fireplace and asked.

"Excuse me mister Turnbull, where is the painting that was hanging over the mantle? It was a painting of a large stag set on a country hillside with trees and flowers and a wary old fox in the bottom left hand corner. The frame was a very ornate affair in a sort of brassy colour with lots of little knobs sticking out."

John was knocked for a six at this revelation and it was a little time before he managed to gather his composure, then in a quiet voice, he said, "Well it were after t'old man died a few years ago that we decided to redecorate the place. It needed brightening up and modernising so we gave t'kitchen a right going over. Anyway, what the bloody hell has it to do with you. This is our home and we'll do as we bloody well please. That old painting didn't fit in with t'new look so we took it down and put it up in t'attic, out of t'way."

Undaunted by the farmers manner and sharp words the lass turned round and pointed to the bare wall over the sink and asked about the two paintings that had hung there. Once again she was able to describe the paintings and their frames in great detail. She received the same terse reply from John who was now starting to lose some of his bluster and confidence.

Then turning in our direction, she surveyed the wall between the windows behind us. Once more she asked about the painting that used to hang there. This one she declared was a picture of a highland bull standing knee deep in water with the long shaggy coat dipping into the mountain stream. She added that there was a group of trees behind it, growing up the hillside. However, the frame was only very simple and not ornate like the others she stated. As you can imagine John was thoroughly rattled by all this and was rendered almost speechless until she asked if it was okay for her to have a look around the house.

John then blurted out, "You might as bloody well do as you please as it looks like you will do any road."

At that she walked out of a door near the sink and disappeared from view into a long hallway that ran the length of the house.

Everyone stayed at the table quietly waiting anxiously for the next chapter in this intriguing saga. Who the hell was this lass and what was she up to? What on earth was she was she going to come up with next?

We didn't have long to wait as we soon heard her footsteps returning along the stone flagged hallway before reappearing through the kitchen door only to drop another bombshell as she asked. "Mr. Turnbull, whatever happened to the grand father clock in the hallway. It used to stand opposite the side passage that leads to the cellar steps."

He replied, "Aye well, it's funny about that bloody clock, it was just like t'one in't ruddy song. It stopped dead about same time as t'old feller died and nowt would make it go again. I took it into Knaresborough to an old clockmaker there who's very good at t'job and he said there was nowt wrong with it but he had given it a good clean and oil and it was going well in t'shop. We brought it home again and put it back in t'hall and it went for a few minutes and stopped. I checked that it was perfectly level which it was, but nowt would make it go again. After a bit I took it back to the repair shop again and had a bit of a go at him."

Once again the old man checked it out, but could find no faults in it and it worked fine for him so we brought it back home.

Like before, that dammed clock refused to run no matter how we set it up, and when we returned it to the shop the old man said to leave it there and he would check it again, then bring it back himself and install it properly for us.

This was to be it's last chance and when it wouldn't go, not even for the clock mender, we put it down in the cellar among t'other junk and there it stayed."

Once again the woman stunned John and his wife as she said, "Now I can see your trouble." Pausing for effect she went on, "Every Saturday evening the old man used to listen to the seven o'clock time pips on the B.B.C. radio, then walk into the hall, set the clock to the correct time and wind it up."

You could have heard a pin drop in the kitchen we hardly dare breathe in case we missed a single word and the local gossips amongst the men were all agog with all this excitement. Boy, oh, boy, would they have a yarn to tell in the pub and around the district now?

The Scottish lass began again, "Now that you have taken the clock away he can't find it to wind it up on Saturday evenings, so he walks around the house looking for it and that's when you can hear his footsteps. If you put the clock back where it used to be in the hall he'll be able to wind it up each week and then he will leave you in peace again."

"Aye well that's alright but the damned thing won't go so what's the use of that?" John said.

She replied. "It won't matter whether it goes or not just so long as it is there for him to wind up on a Saturday night, then he'll be satisfied and leave you alone."

That should have been enough drama for one day or so we thought as the very irate farmer hurried us out of the house and back to work. We headed back to the stack yard to get back to the threshing again but the woman followed us outside and walked across the yard to where there was a sizeable stone outhouse that had once been a dairy and milk storage room but was now used as a grain feed store. She walked inside the building with the men crowding round her so as not to miss the next episode of the intriguing scenario. Once inside she looked up at the centre of the roof and pointed towards the oak beam running through the shed and said, "If you check the top of that beam you'll find that the top corners have been carefully rounded off and polished so that a rope will run freely over it. Also, if you clean off this slab beneath the beam you'll find a metal ring set into it You can tie one end of a rope through the ring, throw the other end over the beam, and you can heave on it to lift the slab up away from the floor. Under the slab is a cave in which there is an illegal whiskey still for distillation of spirits. The farmer used it to make his own whiskey out of sight of the excise men, down there in that cave. Also there's a tunnel leading out of the cave which runs down into the castle yard. It comes out behind a large boulder in a corner of the yard. This was the escape route in case the castle was ever under siege. The occupants could have obtained food etc. from the farm and take it through the tunnel into the castle grounds."

As you can imagine the men were eager to find a rope and lift the slab up so that we could check it out. However, John was having none of it, he'd had enough of this drama for one day and he had his mind set on the threshing not the cave, so he shouted out. "Come on out of there you buggers and get back to work. We've lost enough time already with that silly bitch and you can stay here until that bloody stack's finished even if it takes all night. There's rain coming soon and we had better be finished afore then or else there'll be hell to pay."

Once everyone was outside he snapped a large padlock on the door of the outhouse and walked off back to the stack yard with the men following reluctantly. This was a great day and none of the workers wanted it to end until all the avenues had been investigated thoroughly. The rest of the afternoon went according to plan and the men were left with plenty to talk about over a pint or two in the local pubs that evening.

There was a limestone quarry between the farmyard and the castle wall and a few months later, after blasting the face of the rock, the front-end loader moved in to load the lorries and it broke through the face of the rock and into a large cave. The driver backed out and jumped down for a look inside. He had to be very wary in case the blasting had weakened the roof and made the area unstable. Once he realised that he had broken into a tunnel he got a torch from the handlebars of his bike and carefully set off to investigate. He turned down hill first and walked along with his head bent down clear of the roof, until he came to a pile of rocks. There was light shining through the rocks so that he felt that the tunnel was about to come out into the open. He moved enough rocks to enable him to crawl through as the daylight flooded in. Once out in the open air he realised that he was standing in the castle yard and that the tunnel came out behind a huge boulder at the corner of the walls just the way the Scottish lass had said that it would.

After a good look around he went back up the tunnel, past the quarry and up the hill to the other end. There to his surprise he found himself in another cave with some bits of metal piping and a pile of rotten wood. It took a little while to realise that the contraption in the cave might possibly be a whisky still of some sort.

Whether the reader believes in ghosts and spiritualists or not, it would be hard to explain how a total stranger from a long way off, could possibly have any prior knowledge of the history of this area, let alone the specific details of the house, the family, and the old man's death. To say the least it provided a fascinating subject for talk and gossip for a long time to come.

Thinking about it all sometime later I began to wonder if the woman was some sort of ghost or apparition herself. No one could remember seeing her arrive at the farm. She would have had a long walk down the lane from the nearest bus stop, assuming that she came by bus to get to Ripley town. After travelling all morning she must have been quite thirsty yet she took no refreshment when it was offered. She had, if her storey was true, travelled hundreds of miles across the country to get there and would surely have had to change buses and maybe trains many times and stay somewhere over night on the road. Afterwards, she just seemed to disappear and none of the men could recall her departure from the yard, nor as far as we heard was she ever heard of again.

Chapter 13

SPARKS THE SPANIEL

Crowland is a very small town which is situated on the southern edge of the Fen district of Lincolnshire. The whole area has been reclaimed from the sea and Crowland had once been an island before the draining of the marshes. The town would still be an island today, were it not for a complicated system of ditches and dykes and sluice valves that keep the sea at bay as they do in Holland, hence this part of Lincolnshire is known Holland county.

I was working as an apprentice at the Perkins Engine factory in Peterborough, about seven miles away and I rented a bed sitter in Crowland from a lady who owned a small café in north street. I spent most of my spare time in and around Crowland where I soon got to know many of the natives who tended to be very reserved and close knit due to their isolation from the main stream.

Doris, the café owner was a huge woman with a soft, kindly nature and her husband, Burt, worked as an assembler at the Perkins diesel factory.

I had become very friendly with three local lads who had formed a skiffle band and they often played in the corner of the bar of the pub on Friday evenings. It was there that I met June Healy who was an orphan girl about my age. June was in the care of the council children's home and was out in service to a farmer's wife. She lived in at the farmhouse and mainly helped with household chores and also worked as house keeper for an American serviceman and his family who lived in the town It was through my spending time with June that she introduced me to mister and missus Allen, the farmers where she lived.

I got on very well with the Allens and their son John and they gave me shooting rights for game over all their land which had a plentiful supply of pheasants and hares to keep me interested, especially in the 'open season' for pheasants in return for my helping them on the farm. The farmer Dabby and his son John often accompanied me on Saturday afternoon hunting trips for pheasants, rabbits and hares.

My car at that time was an old Standard 12HP. sedan which I kept in an old barn, that a friend rented to me. Most Saturday afternoons until the start of the game season, were spent in the barn tinkering with my old car and keeping the old tub up to scratch.

One afternoon a very ancient dog arrived when I was working on the engine. It was a Golden Spaniel with a nametag on his collar that simply read 'SPARKS'. I never, ever found out if that was his name, or was it the name of the owner. Sparks, as I called him would spend the entire afternoon sitting nearby, half asleep but watching me through his watery old eyes as I worked on the car. When I left to go home he would get up and waddle out after me, then stop at the road verge and watch me walk away homeward.

He never made any attempt to follow me home; he just sat by the kerb until I disappeared from view.

I tried, out of curiosity, to see where he

went to, but he wouldn't show me where he lived. I asked all the locals whom I knew, but no one had heard of him or even a family by the name of Sparks.

On the first day of the game season in August, I walked down to the barn with my double barrel shotgun and a box of cartridges and Sparks was waiting for me as usual.

As I walked into the shed he hoisted himself up and waddled out to greet me with his tail wagging in anticipation. I was filled with amazement as he had hitherto shown little or no interest in me whatsoever. When I opened the rear door of the car to put the shotgun on the rear parcel shelf, Sparks pushed past me, climbed into the car, and lay down on the floor.

Whilst I was checking out my car I just ignored Sparks until I was ready to leave. Since I had no idea whose dog he was I decided to remove him before driving off. However, Sparks had other ideas, he was determined to come with me on the hunting trip and refused to get out. He even bared his teeth at me and growled ominously when I tried to reach his collar and pull him out so I decided that he had better come along with me anyway.

When I arrived at Allen's farm Dabby said, "Is this your dog, Brian? Is he any good at hunting?"

"No Dabby," I replied, "This is that old dog called Sparks that I asked you about. He's as old as the hills and can hardly waddle around so I doubt he'll be of any use to us I've no idea if he'll work but he was determined to come with me today. Once he saw the gun there was no stopping him so he must have been hunting in the past."

Dabby and John had a good look at the spaniel then they each declared, "I've never seen nor heard of him before but we'll soon see how good he is, we'll go down the four acres first, that will test him out."

Off we went out onto the fen where we stopped at the gate into a field of potatoes, the four acres as it was called, for obvious reasons. The potatoes were fully grown and there was a good crop of weeds in there as well so that it was impossible to see any game, even right under our feet. We were going to have to try and flush the birds out onto the wing to get a shot at them.

As soon as the door was opened Sparks

jumped out and set off at an amazing rate of knots for an old dog, I never even dreamt that he had it in him. Along one side of the field he went like a blood hound with his nose on the ground, and occasionally looking quickly over his shoulder as though to make sure that we were following.

The field that we were in was typical of all the fields in this area, since it had once been part of very large area of tidal marsh and, therefore contained no trees or hedges .The 'soil' was, in fact pure peat moss formed by the rotting vegetation over many centuries

These fields were not fenced either, instead they had a deep drainage ditch all the way round to control the water level with the aid of sluices and one way valves.

By late summer the banks of the drains were heavily over grown with grass and weeds, (no roundup in those days), so it was very hard to see any game.

The dog stopped about halfway along the crop looked down the bank of the drain into the water and set himself rigidly at 'The Point' thereby telling me that he had found some game, probably a pheasant.

There was only about four feet between the dog's nose and the water but the dog was adamant that there was something in the grass. However, we were just as sure that he was wrong so I called out to him, saying. "Come on you old fool there's nothing in there"

Sparks gave me a withering look and held his pose and then inched forward a little.

I, decided to cock the gun, pulling back the hammers, and put the butt up to my shoulder ready for a quick shot.

Once the dog was fairly sure that I was organized and ready he slid down the bank. Suddenly, there was a flurry in the grass and out shot a cock pheasant, with a loud whirring of wings and raucous calling as it took to the air. The dog kept on going down the bank into the water, up the other bank and out into the next field ready to catch the bird and bring it back to us

Unfortunately, because of my disbelief in the dog I pulled the shot and clean missed the prey without even ruffling a single feather. Sparks looked back at me from the next field and gave me a withering stare, as much as to say.

"Gee whiz what's a poor old dog supposed to do; I found the pheasant for you, got you organized, set up the bird, got soaking wet through (you've no idea what that icy cold water does to my rheumatism), ran out here to collect the bird and you miss the damned thing. If only God had given me arms like you I wouldn't need you at all and I wouldn't have missed."

I was totally humiliated by that rotten old dog and deservedly so, but I resolved to do better in the future. As a result I made up for my sins by not missing again that day and sparks found and set up a good many birds for me. He brought each one back to me and dropped it at my feet, but he wouldn't let either of the others pick it up, I had to hold it up first then pass it to John to carry.

Throughout the season Sparks went with us each time we went out and I was amazed at his energy and stamina as we walked for many miles each time and we found it hard to believe that this wreck of a dog could keep on going, and he was worth his weight in pheasants and much more.

I don't know to the this day any more about that old dog and he didn't show up the following year at all, much to my disappointment, so I assumed that he may have died, (or was he in fact, the ghost of some old dog in the past), and was now hunting game in some sort of doggy heaven full of pheasants. I really hope so for he deserved his retirement, and hopefully he has forgiven me for my ineptitude with a shotgun.

By the end of the season I had retrieved most of my dignity and we retired the best of friends. Once the season was finished and I no longer carried the gun, Sparks reverted to type and completely ignored me as I went about my chores and never attempted to get into my car again until one day he just didn't show up at all or ever again.

Chapter 14

DUCKS AND GEESE

Knowing that I was keen on hunting and game shooting, Paul called to see me on my section at work in the Perkins factor at Peterborough.

"Morning pal," He called out as he approached, "How'd you fancy a bit of goose shooting at the weekend? I haven't been out this season yet and I hear there are plenty about, do you reckon you can handle it?"

"Yep, sounds good to me pal. I'll get a box of heavy ammo tomorrow and I'm all set. When and where are going?" I replied. "I haven't been goose shooting since I was living in Yorkshire. It should be good fun and I just love roast goose."

"Okay then that's fine but you won't need any ammunition. I have everything we need, it's all sorted ready. All I need is you because we'll be using my guns"

Paul insisted that we would be setting off very early, and would pick me up at 2am. on Saturday morning.

I said, "Paul your kidding me aren't you, it'll be pitch black then, it won't even get daylight until after 6 at least."

"Oh yea I know that and we'll have to keep moving to be in place by then." He answered.

This all sounded a bit wacky but knowing Paul I wasn't all that surprised. If it was odd, unusual or downright crazy, Paul was in to it. Oh well we'll see on Saturday.

The weather forecast wasn't very promising at all. They were forecasting heavy fog, low cloud and drizzle for Saturday, but Paul seemed to think that it would be a great help.

This safari was sounding more and more bizarre by the minute. "Oh god, what was I letting myself into." My idea of goose shooting, was to sit behind a hedge on a Yorkshire hillside, and pick one or two off as they flew into the corn stubble in the evening.

It was two am. and it was bitterly cold and very damp and pitch black as the fog rolled around us. I still wasn't sure that I could fully trust Paul, but he was assuring me that all was well.

"Are you sure that you have all the gear that we need mate? I asked him.

"Relax, trust me pal, we're all set. Did you bring plenty of hot tea, coffee and a feed, it's going to be a while before we can sit down to a decent breakfast?"

"Yep, I have two thermos flasks full and a pack of sandwiches, that should do."

I still had no idea where we were headed but Paul was driving so I relaxed a little as we headed out towards Spalding and the open fen, (marshes). However it soon became a little clearer, we were headed for the 'Wash', which was a vast expanse of coastal, tidal mud flats running for miles out to sea off the Lincolnshire coast.

Eventually, Paul parked the car and we started to unload all the gear. He handed me a huge shotgun, far larger than any that I had ever seen. "That's a goose gun pal, eight gauge, of course." He said.

My god this thing was as big as a cannon and heavy as hell. I hoped we hadn't far to walk as he loaded me up with a folding shovel and an assortment of other gear and some huge cartridges.

He had brought full-length waterproof waders for us both, which we wriggled into and we were off. This expedition was looking even more, crazy as time went by. We set off out onto the marshes and were soon wading in cold water, at times over our knees, as we dropped down into the deeper channels. Paul had a compass of some sort and he kept checking our direction with the help of a small torch. I hoped to hell that it was a new battery and that he had a spare, but I wasn't game to ask him. I had heard of people getting lost and dying out here, so I prayed that he knew what he was doing.

All I wanted to do at that moment was to go home and crawl into a nice warm bed. Paul strode onwards and I was battling to keep up. What if I lost sight of him? It was still inky black and I could feel the cold, insidious, fog smothering me, and everything else. Why, Oh why, had I allowed someone as mad as Paul to talk me into this mess? I wasn't afraid of dying but wandering about on this horrible fen was too much.

"Where is Paul I've lost him?" I thought so I pressed on harder. Oh, there he is just ahead of me. I can see the glow of the little torch as he checked the compass again.

When we finally stopped Paul announced. "This should do, we must be about one and a half miles out.

"Is that all?" I asked, "It feels like ten miles to me."

"Okay, what now." I asked. "I need a mug of tea."

"Yea that's fine, then we have to dig our graves." He replied.

"I knew it, even he thinks this is the end, and we have to dig our own graves as well." I thought.

"You have to dig a hole about waist deep and heap the mud up on the seaward side to help screen us." He said.

"You've got to be kidding" I said, "Dig down in this awful mud and stand up to our waist in it. We are sure to die of cold even before we drown. Anyway, which way is seaward?"

We had been standing in the hole for about half an hour when Paul announced that they were coming. "Listen," he said, "can you hear them?"

"No," I replied, "Not yet what do they sound like?"

It was still as black as pitch, but there was a sort of lighter area further out to the east and seaward, as it was just about dawn, when he replied, "You can hear their wings squeaking as they fly and they call out to one another to keep in formation "

"Well, how am I going to see them to get a shot at them?" I asked.

"Just aim for the squeak, and if you are good enough, you should get one of them. They fly in a tight vee formation and in great big mobs." Was the reply.

Just then Paul fired off a mighty shot and a large goose landed nearby. "Got one." He called out, how are you going."

There was a loud squeaking coming in close to me so I lined it up, and squeezed the trigger. There was a hell of a bang, and I sank even deeper into the mire, then a large bird crashed down beside me.

In the next few minutes I shot two more

geese but no more went Paul's way.

"Ah, well, beginners, luck," He said. "Come on pal lets get out of here before the tide comes in. Just another point that he had forgotten to mention.

I was well pleased with my haul, and considered myself to be luckier than Paul, who had only managed to get one, for all his trouble.

As we set off back hopefully towards the shore, in the murky, grey, foggy dawn I realised that maybe he was the lucky one. Wild geese are wet and heavy and I had three of them plus all the gear, to carry back to the car. Also, the tide had already begun to come in and we were frequently wading waist deep, and at times almost swimming in the deeper parts.

Never again I vowed as we reached the car, never, ever. Once was enough for me even though the roast geese were fantastic.

It was about three weeks later that Paul caught up to me as I was clocking off work.

"Hiah pal, how's it going. Have you recovered yet?" He asked me. "Do you fancy a quiet bit of duck shooting at the weekend?"

"Not if you have anything to do with it I

replied, "I really do want to live a little bit longer yet, thank you."

"Look pal, I know you didn't really enjoy our last outing but you came out okay, didn't you? You got a nice haul of geese, and plenty of people who go out there come back empty handed as well as cold and wet." He said.

"Hell mate, are you telling me that there are other blokes so crazy, that they go out there regularly," I retorted.

"Oh heck yes, they go every weekend in the goose season and love every minute of it." He replied. "So what do you reckon about the ducks, I really need you to come with me."

"Well I can believe that. No one else would be so stupid as to go again. Where are you going this time anyway?" I asked.

"Well, one of my uncles has a farming property in Norfolk surrounded by the 'broads', {a waterway of shallow ponds, lakes and channels}. It's perfect for duck shooting and is a lot of fun as well, you'll love it," he said.

"My god, don't tell me that I'm stupid enough to even think of this crazy scheme," I thought.

"Then, will I get wet? Will I freeze to death?

Will I regret going with you again, Paul." I asked him.

"No pal, we'll have a fabulous weekend away. There's stacks of room at uncles place, and he has a really nice punt to cruise around in 'til we find some ducks. He and my aunt will be away in Spain so we have the place to ourselves." He declared.

"This all sounds too good to be true pal, are you sure that I won't get wet again? I queried.

"I can guarantee it pal, unless you fall out of the punt. So, what do you reckon then, are you coming or not? He asked.

"Yea, okay, God, I must be out of my mind to even think about another of your hair brained schemes." I said, "Lets do it, it can't be any worse than the last trip."

The trip down to the 'Norfolk, Broads,' a popular holiday place in summer, was lovely and the weather was perfect. We arrived at the old homestead and I was enchanted with it's scenic beauty, and rustic charm. This was all too good to be true, what is going to go wrong, there has to be a snag somewhere.

We cooked up a great feast and settled

down to a good night's sleep. We were up before daylight, (that sounds more like Paul), and enjoyed a good old fry up for breakfast and then we were off.

After a fair walk through delightful vistas as the dawn was breaking we arrived at an old shed. The air was filled with bird-song as the world came to life. Inside the shed there was a wooden punt ready to launch onto the water at the other end of the shed, which was open to the water.

"What do we do now, Paul, I thought you said there was a gun in here and all the other gear?" I queried.

"That's what I said, mate. Now stop whinging and give me a hand to get the punt into the water." Answered Paul.

So it was all hands to the task and we were soon floating out across the lake. We stopped by an island and pulled up some vegetation to stand in the front of the punt to act as a camouflage screen. When Paul was eventually satisfied we were off again.

As soon as we spotted a large flock of ducks on the water Paul tapped me on the shoulder and got me to kneel down in the middle of the punt and handed me a long piece of what looked like 2inch water pipe, and probably was. He whispered to me, "Lay this on your shoulder with this end butted down onto that cross member of the keel and hold it firmly against the timber. If it slips off it will go straight through the bottom of the punt and we'll sink. (I knew it, there had to be a snag somewhere).

He proceeded to load this monstrosity by tipping a couple of handfuls of black powder down the muzzle and packing it tight with a ramrod. Then in went a couple of handfuls of shot and we were all set.

Paul poled the punt as close to the mob of ducks as he dare with out scaring them, then he set the primer and stood up so that the sentinel duck saw him and sounded the alarm.

A large cloud of ducks took to the wing and Paul fired the primer. There was a terrifying roar that left my ears ringing for hours, a violent jar on the keel and the punt shot backwards at a great rate of knots due to the recoil of the explosion. I knew it, I should have stayed at home where I was safe, damn Paul and his crazy schemes.

Paul's aim was very good however, I lay down the monster gun so that I could help to retrieve the floating ducks. We spent a long time poling the punt around to collect all the ducks that he'd shot. Then it was back to the house to pluck and clean the birds and we prepared a couple to eat for lunch, stuffed with onions and herbs of course. I decided that duck shooting was better than goose shooting but only marginally.

Chapter 15

APRIL FOOL'S DAY

When television first started in England there was only one station available, the B.B.C., and they only had one transmitter in the London area. They then, as now were continually bombarded with phone calls and letters (no emails of course), from the viewing public complaining about the programs, the announcers, the reception and anything else that they could associate with television, There were even those who rang and complained about the weather, which they were sure had deteriorated significantly since the B.B.C. had started televising the daily forecasts.

The people at the B.B.C. became heartily sick of all this flak, and they decided to retaliate.

In those days, most people in Britain had only ever seen or heard of spaghetti when it was laced with tomato sauce and crammed into a tin can by a firm called Heinz. So the television company decided that it was time to educate these peasants in the ways of the world.

At some considerable expense they prepared a documentary, filmed in Spain, I believe. They showed extensive footage of women working in the orchards, cutting the spaghetti from trees that resembled grapefruit trees.

They gave their viewers a small clue. They said that it was quite amazing that all the strands of spaghetti were exactly the same length, just long enough, in fact, to fit into the boxes that were stacked ready to receive them.

Some one then asked the commentator, "Will the trees grow in England."

He replied, "The trees are very hardy indeed, and quite frost resistant, and yes, of course they'll thrive in the English soil and climate especially in the south."

The voice then said. "Is there a supplier of the trees in England, and how can we contact them?"

"As you well know we're not allowed to advertise on television, however if any of your viewers would like a tree they can ring up the B.B.C. and we'll give them the details of the suppliers."

Within minutes all hell broke loose, the whole London Telephone network, was inundated with phone calls and every exchange was jammed solid for hours by people wanting to obtain their spaghetti trees. The television station had to air a retraction and apology to stop people ringing in to order their trees.

This, of course proved the story that, April Fools pranks should only be played before midday, because they are likely to back fire on the perpetrator if played in the afternoon. You see there was no daytime television in those days and it went to air in the early evening.

Chapter 16

BUCCANEER'S BALL

Working in a very large, noisy, smelly, factory certainly has many problems concerning general health and welfare, but the amazing diversity of the people who worked therein, 7500 in all, provided a continual array of incidents and scenarios, ranging from humorous to downright dangerous and sometimes very embarrassing and painful.

I spent four years of my life there as a student apprentice and I can look back on it with a mixture of emotions. So much happened in those few years both in the factory where we built and tested fifteen hundred diesel engines every day, and socially in the town and surrounding hinterland. It was during the early days of Rock and Roll music with jiving, skiffle, calypso, jazz and ballroom dancing thrown in together at the time when bingo was taking over the cinemas and ballrooms around the country.

Teddy boys were waging their own, riotous, behaviour in the bigger towns and there were many very ugly scenes as a result. Then in the quieter moments some of my friends and I went to the magnificent Cathedrals, to witness all the pomp and ceremony of the symphony concerts rendered there by one or other of the great London orchestras.

The factory management were extremely safety conscious and far ahead of the times. We had our own, single bed hospital to look after anyone misfortunate enough to get hurt. There was also a fully equipped fire engine which was used as a back up to the town fire engine if needed as well as protecting the factory.

The Fire crew were employees like Rolly and myself, who were prepared to give up their Sunday mornings. Instead of playing sports or joining the many other social activities that the company offered, and they were many and varied. With such a large work force it became economically viable and necessary for the company to provide almost every sporting facility imaginable. We entered teams in most sports and were members of many of the local associations. We even had a sailplane, and gliding club, which I managed to find time to enjoy, mainly on Saturday and Sunday afternoons. The fire crew would assemble on the company's sports ground to train, and practice working together as a team so that when the call came, we would each know what to do to get the best result on the day. We even entered competitions with other brigades around the district, to further hone our skills and efficiency.

On one occasion, one of a row of terraced, thatched roofed houses, on the factory perimeter had a fire in the bedroom and we were there in a few minutes. We had an experimental fire pump that we were working on that was driven by a gas turbine engine. This three inch pump was truly awesome. It was started by hand like winding a cream separator. It only took a couple of turns on the handle to have the engine spinning up to ignition point of 13,000 revs, and then it ran up to 33,000 revs, at governor speed. The amount of water that came out was unbelievable.

We pulled up near the fire, one guy set up the hydrant to the mains, two more ran with the pump and placed it on the pavement opposite the house whilst another man ran out the hoses. When the pump started two men were holding the nozzle and directed it at the bedroom window which shattered immediately allowing the stream of water to flood the room. One man ran in the front door, pulled out the electrical fuses, and turned to run up the stairs to inspect the fire. As he was climbing the stair a stream of water rushed down on him and pushed him back out onto the street. The fire was already out and the other houses saved long before the town brigade arrived.

As part of our training we had to move around the factory and work in the various departments to help us to understand how each section worked, and how it all fitted together as a whole, to produce the end products. Because I had a broad Yorkshire accent the other workers called me Yorkey and most of the staff knew me only as Yorkey.

One day I was operating a huge machine called a broach, which machined the lower end of the connecting rods. Whilst the operator was enjoying a tea break, I took over the controls. When his tea was finished he came back up onto the platform and said, "Okay mate, you go and get a cup of tea now and I'll take over"

The machine was like two great lifts, one was rising up as the other descended, and they both stopped together at the end of the cycle, one up and the other down provided the machine was switched onto semi-automatic cycle, which it was always supposed to be. The broach bars were like huge files about 8 feet tall with cutting edges set in close knit rows all the way along them. John was loading his second components into the clamps when the electrical control box cross fused and the machine started off again with out warning. There was an emergency stop rail near the operator's knee which he activated, but before the machine stopped it had grabbed his left thumb and crushed it into the connecting rod. He screamed like mad and I ran to the foreman's office to raise the alarm. They had to call in the maintenance crew to work the machine whilst our own nursing team injected pain killers into his hand. It took one and a half hours to free the man because we had to wind the machine in reverse, by hand to release him. His thumb was so badly damaged that it had to be amputated at the local hospital. I was numb with shock at witnessing all this and the realisation that it was only seconds that decided which of the two of us lost a thumb that day.

I spent a fair amount of time in the prototype test shop, where all kinds of new ideas were tried out. We were always aware that almost any thing could and sometimes did happen. One day we were told to test run a small 4 cylinder engine that had a special cast iron crankshaft supplied by a new company who reckoned it would be able to supply them at greatly reduced cost. The engine ran very well all morning, then in the afternoon we started to give it a serious workout and it appeared to be fine. About 3pm.the engine gave a small shudder and sounded unusual so I went to hit the stop button and so did the test driver.

Our hands met on the stopper but before we could stop the engine it disintegrated and one of the connecting rods flew through between our heads and impaled itself in the wooden door behind us. There was very little left of the engine because the crankshaft had virtually exploded and the bits had smashed their way out of the casing. The two of us just stood still in stunned silence as the bits fell all around us.

Early in our days at Perkins, Rolly Griffen and myself, decided to start a teenage Rock and roll club in the works social club. We enlisted a girl called Val Badger who worked in the office at the apprentice training school. Val, like us was keen on pop and rock music and offered to help set up and run the club. The first night we only had our own collections of records, which we took along to get us started.

I was the only one who could jive, having been taught by Lisa Johns who was the lead dancer in the film "Rock Around The Clock" featuring Bill Hayley and the Comets.

I met Lisa at Butlin's holiday camp at Filey where she had been hired for the summer of 1977 to travel around the various Butlin's holiday camps and teach the campers how to jive and rock. Rolly was a bit of a bumble foot with size thirteen shoes but he eventually got the hang of it.

We only charged a few shillings entry and all of this was used to purchase the latest records each week. Val volunteered to be the disc jockey and look after the music as she couldn't dance. One evening I went onto the stage and Val was jiving very proficiently using the end of the key board of the piano as a partner. I tried to get her to come down onto the dance floor but she was too shy to give it a go and she lacked the confidence to try. I closed the curtains a little way took her hand, put my other arm around her waist and set her off jiving to "Rock Around The Clock". Val was quite competent at the dance but it took me a couple of weeks of secret dancing to convince her that she was as good as any of the others. Eventually I managed to coax her down onto the floor and she had a ball, we danced and danced until we almost fell in a heap.

The club went very well for a year or two then we heard about a concert at Nottingham, which was about 65 miles away. We used the club kitty to buy up a block of tickets to see Buddy Holly and the crickets in concert then set about selling them to our regulars to recoup our investment and they were eagerly taken. We hired an old Bedford coach to take us to Nottingham and it snowed lightly all the way there and we were frozen stiff when we arrived.

The concert was absolutely fantastic and we jived, rocked and clapped all though the night. At last we were warm again after our epic journey as we set off into the night to find a fish and chip shop for our supper where we enjoyed a feed of fish and chips before setting off home again. It was still snowing and it continued all the way home.

We got stuck in snowdrifts a few times and we all had to push and shove to get the coach going again. The return home was a nightmare but we felt better about it a year later when we heard that Buddy Holly had been tragically killed in a plane crash and would never be seen on stage again.

At regular intervals the Apprentice Association organised a fancy dress ball and many memories were created. The latest theme was to hold a Buccaneer's ball at one of the most prominent ballrooms in the town. Every one got dressed up and a small group of us who were familiar with an amateur dramatics group arranged for them to kit us out like real buccaneers, complete with greasepaint scars on our faces.

The department in which I was working at that time was in an old building that the company had just acquired and there was a fair amount of odds and ends still stored there including some very thin aluminium sheeting. I asked the section boss if I could buy some of it to make a couple of scimitars for the ball. He told me to take as much as I wanted before it went for scrap metal. I made up the swords and they looked quite realistic even though they were as light as paper.

So, it was off to the ball in all our splendour, and what a ripper of a night it was. Most of us consumed a fair quantity of beer and we were quite merry as we departed for home. The group that I was with had to cross the town's cobbled market place on our journey home and some idiot suggested that we should stage a sword fight to conclude the evening's festivities.

Peter Holly and myself each had a scimitar so we decided to entertain the rest with a bit of friendly rivalry. As we were settling down to a lively fun duel another couple of lads arrived and they were bearing real cavalry swords, which their parents had loaned them and they were still razor sharp. They decided to start another friendly duel and the whole scenario escalated into a noisy rabble as the others egged us on and shouted encouragement. We hadn't allowed for the fact that the shops surrounding the square were two story and the owners lived above their premises.

Some one rang the police and two "Black Marias" came roaring into the square with their bells clanging loudly and the four of us were arrested and charged with many offences including street duelling which was still an offence in those days and being drunk and disorderly.

At the police station we were duly processed and were about to be locked up when I called for a point of order. I asked the officer in charge, "How can you say that we are drunk without any medical tests being taken? When we get into court in the morning Mr. Johnson Q.C. will note that we are cold sober and your word against ours won't hold up will it?"

"Are you saying that you can afford a Q,C. to defend you then?" The officer asked.

"Mr, Johnson Q.C. is a family friend and yes he will attend us without any question." My friend relied.

"So you reckon that you can both pass a sobriety test do you" the officer asked us. We were quickly coming to our senses by now and we felt that it was worth the risk

"Yes, Officer I am quite ready to be tested. What do I have to do." I asked.

We were shown to a line joining two pieces of the floor and told to "walk the line"

I was having a little difficulty keeping the line still but I found that if I carefully placed one foot at a time on the brute it behaved it's self and didn't move too much.

Slowly but surely I walked the line and Peter followed my lead carefully, then the officer said. "Say this after me. Peter Piper picked a pick of peckled pethers." or something to that effect. He had a number of tries to get it right and only got worse and worse so I decided to help him out. I said.

"Are you trying to say, Peter piper picked a Peck of Pickled Peppers officer? The magistrate won't be very impressed to find that members of the police force were drunk on duty tonight"

"What do you mean, we haven't been drinking. What makes you say that we are drunk?" The sergeant demanded.

"Well if we hadn't been able to say 'Peter Piper Picked A Peck Of Pickled Peppers' correctly you would have pronounced us drunk as charged, therefore if you can't say it you must be drunk on duty." I replied.

"All right smart arse, so lets say you aren't drunk, that still leaves all the other charges".

"You charged us with carrying offensive weapons and our imitation swords are hardly that. If we hit the judge over the head with them he will laugh at us. Most kids toys would do more harm than our swords." I retorted. "And whilst we're on the subject of charges, why didn't you charge the onlookers with disturbing the peace instead of us. They were the ones that were making all the noise, and what about your police cars, your bells were clanging out all over town both towards the market place and back to the police station on the return trip. Any way, there was no emergency that called for the bells clanging in the dead of night, waking up half the town. It's not fair to blame us for all that noise as I am sure Mr. Johnson will point out to you in court tomorrow."

The Officer jumped up and shouted at us.

"Get out, get out of here, and damned well behave yourselves in future. You've caused enough trouble for one night and we need a bit of peace so get out."

We were off through the door and out into the street like rifle bullets and we didn't stop until we were nearly home. Peter said to me. "You could talk your way out of your own ruddy funeral"

"Well Pete, I would if the grave looked as uninviting as those bloody cells did." I answered.

PSYCHIC MEDIUM

One Friday evening, a group of us apprentices and some girls that we socialised with were at a loose end when someone suggested going for a short bus ride to a nearby village to visit a blind man. This man was well renowned throughout the region because he was exceptionally good at telling fortunes so we thought this would be a "great lark", and fine entertainment for the evening. Another point to be considered was the presence of a very fine pub called the Wheat Sheaf in the same village to complete the fun.

After a heated discussion we hopped on a double-decker bus and away we went. When we arrived we were a little surprised to see that the blind man was sitting behind a desk in almost total darkness, but of course he didn't need any light to "see" with. One of the girls opted to go in first but the old man refused to talk to her.

He would only say, "Young lady, this is a serious business. You and all your friends have only come here tonight for a bit of fun and that is not what this is all about. However, one day you will each return, probably together and when you are in a more serious frame of mind, then I will be able to help you."

One of our group said, "Who cares anyway, it's his loss not ours so lets get down to the Wheat Sheaf and sample their fine country ales until it's time for the last bus back to town."

We spent a memorable evening at the pub playing darts and all the latest hits on the jukebox. This was one of the first village pubs in the district to install a jukebox which jazzed up the fun no end.

It was probably six or seven weeks later that we were once again looking for an evenings entertainment and the blind man was mentioned. A couple of the girls were particularly interested in the experience so they talked us all in to going to see him.

The blind man spent quite a long time

with each of us and some of the predictions were very accurate with almost immediate results. Yvonne, my landlady's daughter was going out with a sailor who was stationed at Portsmouth at that time. The old man said to her, "You come from a very large family, I can see eight children."

Yvonne retorted, "Well you've got that wrong for a start since there are only seven of us, not eight."

The man replied, "I don't think so, you have forgotten the count the youngest one who's name begins with 'C' if my facts are correct."

"Well you've got that wrong as well. The youngest is Jeffery, and that doesn't begin with 'C' does it?" She asked

"Well let's not worry about it for now, you'll remember when you are on the way home on the bus, and you will see that I am correct." He replied.

Yvonne said, "There isn't any chance of that, Jeffery is the youngest, so there."

He went on to tell her, "You will marry your sailor boy but under false pretences. Unfortunately I can't see much beyond that time.

It's all blurry, but that's how it is sometimes."

Yvonne retorted. "My Lennie will marry me properly. He would never deceive me or do anything underhand so there." With that she got to her feet and stomped out indignantly.

When I went in he told me that when I qualified I would move away from the area, in fact a very long way. He said, "There is a long sea voyage and I can see the world is upside down, but the girl that you marry is one that you've grown up with. Unfortunately I can only see boys around you in the future."

"The world upside down", is a common way of referring to the southern hemisphere when you live in the northern hemisphere and I sailed out to Western Australia on the P. and O. liner, the Himalaya in nineteen sixty two. I intended to stay for a two year working holiday, living with my mother's sisters around Perth but I had never even considered it at the time of his predictions in 1958.

We set off home again after a few laughs and giggles regarding the predictions and we were about half way home when Yvonne shouted out.

"Oh my God, I forgot about Christopher, Brian. How could I not remember Christopher?"

Christopher was the latest arrival in our household and he was only a few days old at that time.

Yvonne was in raptures of delight when I arrived home after work one day. She was jumping around and waving a letter in front of my eyes. "Look at this Brian, my Lennie has proposed. We're going to get married. Oh! I can't wait. Look at this, he's going to sea shortly and will be away for six months. These are his sailing orders, look he's going to all these lovely places. I only wish that they could take their wives with them. I will miss him all the time. That old man was quite right he said we would get married."

I said, "Don't be fooled Yvonne that's an old sailors trick. They get one of their mates to type out the sailing orders to get their girls to make up their minds and say yes. The navy never releases details of the sailing dates and plans, (especially at the moment with this cold war going on with the Soviet Union). Even the Commander doesn't find out until he opens up his sealed orders at sea, after they've sailed."

"My Lennie wouldn't pull a stunt like that. Anyway I desperately want to marry him. I love Lennie dearly, this is the happiest day of my life and the old man can get lost, so there." Yvonne replied.

Yvonne married her sailor shortly afterwards but when I moved to other accommodation about six months later Lennie was still stationed at Portsmouth. I heard from my friends later on, that after Lennie went to sea Yvonne went out with any one wearing pants and the marriage failed miserably after a terrible break up when he returned home. Of course in my case the prediction turned out to be quite correct in most aspects although he did not manage to name the actual ship on which I sailed nor the name of my young lady who sailed out to join me in Western Australia. At the time of the prediction I was not even going out with Sandra. She was still going to school then but we had already met in the village where she grew up.

Chapter **18**

GOOD DAD, BAD DAD

When I was in my third year I experience one of the most embarrassing days of my whole life. The company decided to hold a parents and friends day for the apprentices. There were 250 of us in the plant at any one time and we were all encouraged to invite our families to visit on the Saturday afternoon. I had never really got on well with my dad. He was always trying to be a clever bugger and when that didn't work out he blamed me. I received lots of severe beltings throughout my young life often for little or nothing but sometimes because he managed to "loose face" in front of his friends. I suspected that he was very jealous because I passed all my school exams with flying colours where as he was a total failure at school. The only thing that the nuns managed to teach him was to write extremely well although he seldom put pen to paper. I walked into our home one evening and he was trying to explain to a workmate what a supercharger was. He was so far off the mark that I had little option but to correct him since I had completed three years training at the biggest diesel engine works in the world. Dad went completely berserk and it was only when I declared my intention to resign and come home to work for the mob that he was with (milling hen and pig food) that he calmed down.

My firm was to put on a special "open" afternoon and tea for all the families of the apprentices towards the end of my training. My family, Dad, Mum, and my sister Jean, travelled down from Yorkshire and my girl friend June came as well. When we arrived at the works we were all told to go first to the office foyer where we were to introduce our visitors to the company managers before escorting them on a tour of the works, followed by tea in the canteen. I assembled my party in the line waiting to be introduced when my father, who was always a clever dick, spotted an array of photographs depicting Perkins engines working in some of the various applications. Unnoticed by June and I, he led my sister away from the line and over to the photographs and started to show off his "knowledge" about them. Then he walked through into the main design drawing office next door which was strictly out of bounds even to us apprentices, and began showing off his knowledge in there.

Not realising that he had left us, I led my mother and June forward to be introduced, when I noticed that they had gone I asked June and Mum if she knew where they were and they pointed through the door into the drawing office. I had to pull out of the line at the last minute and with some difficulty, dragged dad and Jean out of the design room, then wait in turn at the rear of the line again. Dad was still protesting that it was Okay to go into the design section because we had been invited to come and have a look around the works. He refused to understand that certain areas had to remain closed even to family and friends or that certain protocols had to be observed and the formal introductions were a part of this procedure. He could not believe that there were secret projects going on that our competitors would love to know about.

Once the introductions were finished we went through into the main production area. I led our party to the beginning of the line where the raw cast iron blocks were machined and checked ready for assembly. My dad ignored all that I was saying, after all he knew it all, because we had been escorted on a quick tour around the works three years ago when I came for the job interview and he would never admit that I could possibly know more than him. I tolerated the awkward situation until we reach the machines that were used to harden and grind the crankshafts. Dad led my sister away from where I was explaining the operations to June and Mum, and began to tell her all about the machines. That was enough! I'd had more than enough humiliation for one day so I said to Mum. "You go over and join dad he knows all about this place and he can tell you a lot more than me. We'll go and get some afternoon tea and head off home."

"Nay lad don't do that, stay with us and show

us what you've learned." Mum replied.

"No way mum I'm not going to let him upset me any more. We're getting out of here, now. I'm so sorry I wanted this to be a very special day. I've looked forward to it for a long time and dad has thrown it all in my face and humiliated me in front of all my workmates and my bosses so I'll just say goodbye and leave him to it." I answered her. Then I turned away, before I burst into tears, took June's arm and walked away. I was totally devastated, but I should have known it would be like this. It always was and always would be. My old man was such a know all and smart arse and I was so inferior to him and always would be.

June and I made the most of the afternoon tea which was superb. The farming district nearby produced the most magnificent strawberries in all of England and there were heaps of them here and enough cream to drown them. My enjoyment was thoroughly spoiled by my old man but we ate our fill and left. We had planned to spend the evening with my family then show them around the district next morning, instead we went home put our glad rags on and went out dancing in the hope of shrugging off my humiliating day. At least I always excelled on the dance floor and my old man couldn't dance a single step.

It was never going to work but a few hours of rocking and rolling helped. I was reluctant to go home that night in case my father decided to come over and start a serious row so I stayed at June's place where they would not find me. June worked as housekeeper for an American Airman and his family and they were away for the weekend at his wife's family home in Buckinghamshire. Jerry had often told me to stay the night rather than drive home in the wee small hours after a fair amount drink so tonight it suited me well. I helped myself to a very large quantity of duty free spirits as instructed and wrote myself off. The next day I suffered desperately but I didn't need to see the old sod again for a long time. I didn't go "home" to Yorkshire for over a year after that terrible day. I might not have gone even then but my father telephoned the company to let them know that my grandmother was dying and asking to see me.

The drama of parents day was not over yet, though. On Monday morning my best friend and buddy, Rolly Griffen, looked me up and came to my section and gave me one heck of a bawling out in front of my workmates over the way I had treated my family. Rolly had visited my home in Yorkshire a few times and knew our family quite well.

Late in the afternoon of the parents day, Rolly was still showing his family around the factory and they were all down at the far end, where the engines were stored prior to dispatch, in huge racks right up to the roof. There were thousands of engines stored 4 and 5 high in row upon row of steel racks.

Rolly was ready to head out of the works and get a feed of those delicious strawberries when he bumped into my family. My mob were thoroughly lost. They had been trying to find their way out for ages and were going round and round the engine racks, which all looked the same to my dad. There was seemingly no way out of there. It was like a great big maze or labyrinth. Rolly took them along with his party and made sure that they got their share of food before they left the plant.

Rolly called me all kinds of names for neglecting my family and I had great difficulty getting a word in edgeways, but I did manage to tell him enough of my side of the story before storming off, to let him know that he may have had it all wrong. Later in the week after he had cooled down, he looked me up again but I told him to leave me alone as I had enough trouble with my family and I didn't need a, so called, friend who would stab me in the back without first hearing my side of the story. He did at least have the decency to let me tell him the truth of it before I walked off and left him standing. I was preoccupied with my girl June at that time so Rolly and I drifted apart socially from then on.

A month or so after parents day I heard that Rolly was about to leave the firm. He had decided to become a policeman. He was built for the job, had a very easy going attitude, was exceptionally patient with people and he became a very good copper being over 6ft tall with big bones and size 13 boots. Rolly was loving every minute of it and he was so proud of his position in the force.

Not long before I was due to leave Peterborough and sail for Australia, I accidentally bumped into my old pal Rolly outside the corn Exchange, one of the local dance halls in the town where he was on duty in an attempt to control the worst "Teddy boy" gang in the district. The previous Saturday, the gang had severely "beaten up" an American airman and his fiancée when they were leaving the hall at the interval to get a drink or two at a nearby pub. The gang were in the habit of beating up their victims with pieces of bike chain, flick knives and other weapons, without receiving any provocation at all and they had become a serious menace to everyone in the district.

When the interval was due, a huge man, an American airman from a nearby base wearing fatigues strutted onto the forecourt outside the hall and looked up the seven or eight steps leading down from a landing in front of the double doors of the hall. He positioned himself comfortably at ease and waited. When the gang came out of the hall and gathered on the landing prior to descending and moving off to the pub or indulging in their particular type of butchery near the hall, the airman called out "Hey You! You bastards. You, you, you, you, you, and you." (Pointing out each one in turn as he scanned the line), get your arses down here I'm going to belt the shit out of you buggers."

The gang members glanced at one another then the leader pulled out a long bike chain, let out a great roar and they rushed down the steps. The airman held his ground as he placed his fingers against his lips and let out a mighty whistle. Almost instantly a six, by six-wheeled drive troop carrier roared around the corner and as it slowed down about fifteen airmen jumped out ready for the fray.

The airmen picked up the gang members one by one and threw them into the rear of the lorry and the driver roared off across the market square and out of sight.

Once all the racket had subsided I turned to Rolly and asked him jokingly, "What are you going to do about that, pal, we can't have the Yanks abducting our good British citizens and taking them off to God knows where, can we?"

"What the heck are you on about, pal? What Yanks? I've no idea what you're worried about.

Have you gone loco or what?" Rolly replied.

I answered, "I mean the American airmen in that lorry. They grabbed those Teddy boys, threw them in the back of their lorry and drove off. You must have seen them. Don't you have to report them or something?"

"I can only report what "I" saw, not what you saw. "I" never saw no lorry nor any bloody Yankee airmen, so there that's it, let's hear no more about it." Rolly told me with a huge grin on his face."

Rolly must have been very relieved to be rid of that scum, after all what could he have done if they had started something, he didn't have a lorry full of mates to help him out, only his police whistle and his truncheon.

After about half an hour or so the Peterborough Memorial hospital received an anonymous phone call asking for a fleet of ambulances to be sent out to a remote spot in a country lane about five miles or so from town, to pick up some guys who had been in a severe accident of some sort.

When the ambulances arrived they found the gang members lying around in the edge of a wood. The airmen had broken everything that got in their way, arms, legs, heads, ribs etc and the men were a very sorry sight indeed. It's hard to reason why but we never saw, nor heard of any "Teddy boys" in our district from that day on thank goodness.

Chapter 19

RED TAPE AND BULLSHIT

At the time that I was preparing to pack up and leave for Australia I owned a powerful motorcycle which I used to travel back and forth to my home in Yorkshire as well as getting to work each day. The main A1 highway at that time was still only a two-lane road but there was a large improvement scheme underway called the Doncaster Bypass. Not only did this new road bypass Doncaster, which was a major town and traffic hazard it also bypassed the towns of Bawtry and Retford. The main road ran through the narrow, winding, central streets of these towns and at Doncaster there was a major highway crossing the A1 which was the only logical way to get from a huge industrial and residential area comprising of many large cities in the west, to their recreational playgrounds on the Yorkshire coast to the east. As you can well imagine, the traffic tying to get through Doncaster, especially on long weekends was horrific. I have measured up to seven miles of near stationary traffic on the A1, trying to get through a set of traffic lights where the east/west road intersected with the north/south, A1 highway.

On the last Easter weekend that I was living in England the new road was almost completed and it was due to be officially opened on the Tuesday after Easter. About six weeks prior to Easter I took a punt and turned off the old road and took the new one instead. I knew that the bridges had long been finished so I thought that I would be able to negotiate any obstacles on my motorbike. I had no difficulty whatsoever because the road was substantially finished and sealed, needing only kerbing, signs and landscaping to be done. I went along the new road each weekend prior to Easter because it was a good few miles shorter as well as having no traffic at all.

On the Thursday evening of Easter weekend

I was enjoying a cup of tea in a transport café at the southern end of the new road when a group of truckers who were sitting down beside me started talking about the benefits of the bypass when one of them said, "You would think that they could have timed the work a bit better and had it opened before Easter. Just imagine how much easier it would be this weekend if it was finished. I'm dreading going through Doncaster it'll take hours just to get through the traffic lights in the centre of town then there is Retford town to consider as well. I just want to get home to my family and enjoy a decent break."

I turned towards the lorry drivers and said, "But the new road "IS" finished. I've been using it for six or seven weeks now and there's no reason that it couldn't have been opened by now."

The truckers jumped up and asked, "Are you sure about that pal? You've actually driven along it then."

I said that I had and that I intended to go that way again tonight and unless they've closed it by parking their machinery across it to prevent anyone travelling along it I wouldn't expect any problems along the way.

Someone queried, "Are you saying that we could get our lorries through that way, now."

In reply I said, "You could have been using it for weeks if you'd known. They have barriers at each end and at the intersections along the way which I can get around but you lads will have to throw them out of your way, otherwise the road has been clear all the way through. The barriers are only light pine poles and easy to move"

"The rotten buggers," one guy said, "They could have opened it to avoid the traffic snarls this weekend at least. Look mate it's all right for you on your bike but are you sure we can get through. God help you if we get stuck half way and have to turn round and come back."

"Well, as I said, unless they've done something stupid with the machinery and blocked the road you should have no trouble, as a matter of fact the official opening is at 10 o'clock on Tuesday morning. The Prime Minister and all the bigwigs are coming up for the ceremony. The road must be ready now because no one will be working over the holiday. Any way you guys can decide for yourselves but I'm going that way, " I replied getting back to my tea.

The men were furious and they stamped off out of the café muttering and grumbling among themselves as they walked over to their lorries and headed off home. I left a few minutes later and drove past the trucks as the drivers were pulling down the barriers and the hessian covers off the road signs. They were going to use the road, rightly or wrongly, and they did so. Once the barriers were gone everyone turned into the new highway and headed both north and southwards. The lorry drivers removed all the barriers and sign covers in both directions so I kept ahead of them hoping to hell that there were no obstacles in the way, otherwise there would have been pandemonium further along the road. We had no trouble at all and there were only the barriers at the various intersections and the northern end to dismantle to allow the traffic to flow freely in both directions. The residents in the towns of Retford, Bawtry, and Doncaster must have heaved a sigh of relief that night as the flow of traffic suddenly stopped.

The authorities had to get the police to close the dual carriageway for about one hour on the

Tuesday morning so that they could have an "official" opening ceremony.

Shortly afterwards I sold my bike in preparation for sailing to Australia and I travelled home and back with a friend until my departure. My friend was a fairly new driver but he was very careful and I was more than happy to travel with him. When winter started to get a grip on the countryside we had to be extra careful because of the risk of frosts which made the roads treacherous, even for the most experienced drivers. One Sunday evening as we were returning to Peterborough I had an uncomfortable feeling. I felt that there was a black frost around which unlike a white or hoar frost was quite invisible, but from time to time, I spotted the glint on the hawthorn hedges alongside the road, which was worrying me a fair bit, to say the least. I said to Jeff, "You'd better be extra careful mate, I reckon there's a bit of black frost about."

Jeff replied, "Yes Brian, you may be right, there was a shine or two on the grass verge especially where it was shady. I'll slow down a bit and keep a good lookout from now on."

We had to pass through a shady area beneath some large trees where the road swerved round to run alongside a canal. There was a small humped back footbridge over the canal which led to a delightful cottage on the other side. We had often admired the cottage as we passed by and wondered what the interior looked like. We had heard that it was owned by a wealthy Dutch business man who imported bananas. As we went into the bend we hit a patch of black ice and began to skate along the road. Inexperienced though he was, Jeff did all the right things to counteract the skid but unfortunately we were in a Renault car with the engine in the rear and they were famous for rolling onto their roofs when the power was reduced to cope with a skid.

The little car flipped onto it's roof and stopped on the edge of the canal. The passenger door flew open and I fell out, banging my head on the door pillar as I went. I landed half way over the brink of the canal but, fortunately, I stayed on the grass. The water was almost frozen and would not have made for a pleasant swim.

I was only semi conscious but I was aware that

someone was helping me up. He supported me over the bridge into the cottage. When I came back to reality I found myself lying on the heavy pile carpet in the lounge room of that lovely cottage. I had a very bad gash on my head which was bleeding profusely, and Jeff had a broken collar bone. After wrapping my head in towels the occupiers told us that we were the fifth car to skid there that evening and three of the others had skidded into the hawthorn hedge and through into the field beyond.

They sent for the ambulance and we were taken to Stamford hospital where they set Jeff's collar bone and I had thirteen stitches in my head wound. We were kept at the hospital for a couple of days in case of concussion and my doctor refused to let me return to work for a while because I was working in the production drawing office and he reckoned that facing a large sheet of white paper all day would cause me some problems. During my rehabilitation I returned to Yorkshire for a while and one Saturday evening I bumped into one of the girls from our village whilst travelling on a bus into town. The girl was

Sandra Ingleby and we went out together until I went to Australia for my "holiday". I had intended to continue the relationship when I returned. I was offered a flight out to Australia just prior to Xmas but I delayed my departure so that we could all share one last Xmas with our families. Early in the new year I was offered a berth on the P. and O. liner "Himalaya" sailing late in late January which I accepted.

Chapter **20**

SAILING DAY

Having handed in my notice to quit my job I travelled to my home village in Yorkshire. I had just received my final technical qualifications and certificate of apprenticeship from Perkins Engines and Peterborough Technical College and was now a qualified Production Engineer. Hopefully these qualifications would set me up for a great career in Western Australia and I was about to find out. Because my mother was used to me departing directly from home every week I felt that it would pay to do so once more and also to save my family travelling to Tilbury docks to see me off. Very late on my last night at home, my father stuck his head into my bedroom and woke me up saying, "Here you are lad, there's a fiver for you. I won't see you around in't morning 'cause I going to Liverpool very early. Don't forget to write to your mam. So much for family, he had to escape to Liverpool rather than see me off to Australia. At least he could not lay his belt on me ever again. I left the his fiver on the bedside cabinet. On the way to London I spotted another chap who appeared to be travelling abroad, judging by his luggage with stickers all over it. There were so many people on the platform that I never got to speak to him. When I got off the train at King's Cross station in London I spotted the same chap again although there were hundreds of people between us. The ship was sailing from Tilbury Docks so we had to transfer to St. Pancras station to get the boat train to Tilbury. When I arrived at St. Pancras I found that I had quite a long wait so I went to the cafeteria for a light meal. As I was leaving the café the guy that I had seen earlier walked in and he spoke to me, saying, "By gum, this London's a big place ain't it."

I was a little surprised at this observation because London is one of the worlds largest cities with a population about equal to the whole of Australia so I replied, "What have you seen that brings you to that conclusion, you've only been here a very short while."

The Yorkshire man said, "Aye well, now then, you see, I got a taxi from Kings Cross station to St. Pancras station and it cost me twenty five bob for the fare." (In those days a labourer would have been earning about eight pounds per week, which is around six times the taxi fare).

I replied. "I think you had better come with me for a minute, I have something to show you."

We walked across the concourse of the station until we reached another entrance-way which was at right angles to the one through which he had entered. I pointed out a short flight of steps and said, 'Those steps lead straight up to Kings Cross station. You have just been done I'm afraid. If you ring up the taxi control board they'll refund your fare and give the driver a severe lecture, and if he has a history of this sort of thing they will fire him because they are very strict about customer relations."

"Nay, lad I've really nowt to complain about, yon driver showed me all around London. He took me to t'Houses of Parliament, Buckingham

Palace, St. Paul's Cathedral, Big Ben and lots more. I've never been 'ere afore you see and since I'm emigrating to Melbourne, I might never see it again so I'm not disappointed, it was money well spent."

We sailed down the river Thames in the late afternoon and there was a severe frost about by then. I spent the next three weeks in the lap of luxury as we sailed off to a new life. The voyage by sea was truly magnificent since, for obvious reasons, the "Himalaya" was known as the millionaire ship of the P and O line and she certainly lived up to all our expectations. She was fitted with stabilisers which smoothed out much of the movement that normally made passengers sea sick.

The cabin crew were mainly from Goa, a small state on the west coast of India, and they were fantastic. They fussed over their charges with great professionalism and zeal.

The quality of the meals could only be described as sensational We were supplied with a seven/eight course meals three times each day, and traditional English afternoon tea was laid out in the lounge for anyone who was still a little peckish. We found out by accident, due to the fact that our cabin backed onto the main dining room, that the kitchen staff prepared and served sandwiches and left over cakes at midnight. The sandwiches were assembled using up left over meats and other ingredients to save any waste. Possibly due to the sea air, and maybe all the activity, we were able to take full advantage of these feasts as we sailed across the seas. I had obtained a special pass to visit the engine rooms and Captain's bridge as we travelled through the Mediterranean sea. I arrived on the bridge around the time that a violent storm hit us. The captain ordered the stabilisers to be activated and the ship settled down to a steady pitch and roll action. Along side us a number of coastal trading ships were getting a heck of a beating, almost disappearing under some of the bigger rolling waves.

Entertainment on board was very special with extra shows being taken on at Port Said, in Egypt, and swapped over at Aden and Colombo. We stayed for seven or eight hours at each port for restocking of food, fresh water and refuelling the ship and shore trips were available at each port. Each time the ship docked the local traders provide us with a special form of entertainment as they plied their wares from tiny little boats that swarmed out to meet the ship as she anchored in the outer harbour. They created a kaleidoscope of colour and activity as they competed with each other for our money.

Halfway through the Suez canal we were hit with a gigantic sand stormed and had to stop and tie up for most of the day and all night. The next morning we awoke to find the ship was lying at a peculiar angle as she was listing sideways. The canal workers had tied her up to the lee side of the canal and the wind had blown us sideways until the keel had bottomed on the drift sand that had slid down into the edges of the water. The authorities had to send for a large tug-boat from Port Said, which, with the help of the ships own winches and donkey engines, finally refloated the old girl so that we could continue on our way to Aden and Colombo.

At Colombo we went ashore for the day to shop and sightsee. We had a splendid day ashore with tours up into the mountains and guided tours around a jewel factory. The owner then escorted us on a tour of the native sections of town where prices were much cheaper. Whole bolts of silk and other materials were next to nothing and clothing was so cheap. Radios, binoculars, radiograms, souvenirs etc were only a fraction of the prices in the tourist areas of town.

After we left Colombo in Celon, as it was called then, it was all plain sailing across the Indian Ocean to Western Australia. I said my final goodbyes to my shipmates who were going on to Melbourne where their relatives would be waiting for them and prepared to disembark into the brand new passenger terminal at Fremantle. My family were there waiting to meet me including two of my mother's sisters along with their husbands and children.

Chapter 21

A NEW HOME, A NEW LIFE

We arrived at Fremantle to the worst heat wave on record but not even that could deterred me, I was in love with this beautiful country from day one and after only three weeks had vowed to stay here and call this place home.

My relatives met me onboard ship as I prepared to disembark which caused a problem or two. My aunty Ethel had purchased a bag full of beautiful oranges on the way to the port and she had carried them on board with her but as we were heading back to shore over the gangplank she was stopped and her bag was checked for contraband by customs who spotted the oranges. They were going to have to confiscate the oranges because they were prohibited imports under the quarantine act. Aunt Ethel was furious and she raged at the poor official, "These are my oranges and they aren't imported, I bought them in town before we came aboard. Look here" she said, digging into the bag, "Here is the docket for them. See, I bought them just outside the port."

"That doesn't matter, madam, the law states that you aren't allowed to bring any fruit off the ship so I must confiscate them" The customs man stated. "I'm only doing my job."

"Oh yes, I know how it works," My aunt said, "You'll take them ashore and share them with your mates or take them home to your family so I won't give them up. I'll eat them before I let you have them."

That's fine lady, you and your friends are quite free to stand here and eat them but you cannot take them ashore."The official said.

In reply to that my aunt shared out the oranges between us all and, as there was one left over, she offered it to the customs officer as a peace offering and he took it gratefully and ate it thanking her for her generosity.

There was plenty of work around and having engineering qualifications I got a good job immediately.

I moved in with my aunty Jenny, who is one of my mother's sisters, in a gorgeous place called Glen Forest, where they still lived until they passed away recently. Because of the remote location of Glen Forest I needed a car to get to work and back because Glen Forest was quite remote in those days so I scoured the yards in Midland until I found a low mileage, Singer sports car which served me well for a number of years.

I found a job as a production engineer in Morley Park where we made lawn mower engines and refrigeration compressors. The work force was a fantastic group of people and I made a good many loving friends during the time that I was working there. The company dances and socials were not to be missed and were attended by most of the employees.

During the early sixties there were a series of serial killings being carried out around the Perth metropolitan area, which had the police completely baffled. We often discussed these killings in the canteen at work and various people amongst us were very vocal about what they reckoned they would do if they caught the culprit. The victims were young ladies and although the deaths seemed to be random, they appeared to be connected to the lunar cycles. One guy, Eric Edgar Cooke, who worked in the machine shop, was always very outspoken about the incidents although he was always very polite and friendly, often bringing in flowers and chocolates to share around on pay days.

One day an elderly couple were out collecting sprays of Geraldton Wax flowers on public land around Mount Pleasant and Applecross when they came upon a rifle hidden in the bushes. They had the good sense to leave it alone and notified the police who then staked out the area until the rifle was picked up by a man from Belmont.

The rifle was found to be the one that had been used in the murders of the women and the man who owned it was arrested and charged.

The story soon got around and we were flabbergasted to find out that the machinist, Eric Edgar Cooke had been the man detained. We all found it hard to believe that a guy who was so nice could possibly have carried out these horrendous crimes, and we were sure that the police had "cocked up" again and got the wrong man, but it was not to be. Eric Edgar Cooke was tried and eventually hanged at Fremantle gaol for carrying out so many murders and even today some other deaths are being attributed to this man who was the last person to be hanged in Western Australia at Fremantle Jail.

I soon bought a house in James street Bassendean, which I set about furnishing ready for the arrival of my bride. It took a year or so to convince Sandy's mother to allow her to emigrate, after all she was only seventeen, but the day finally arrived and oh boy what a day it was. I had arranged for Sandra to live with a lovely Irish couple and their two gorgeous little girls at Eden hill until we could be married. It was not the done thing to live in 'sin' in those days and we had to have a suitable address to meet the immigration requirements, anyway.

Sandra was sailing out on the S.S. Oriana, which was due to dock at Fremantle early on the 5th of June. When I got out of bed and looked out I was quite dismayed to see that there was a terrific gale blowing and it was pouring with rain. At seven am. I was waiting at the passenger terminal in time to hear the announcement that it was far too rough for the ship to dock so she had to wait out at sea. Later, at about nine am, the authorities broadcast another message to the waiting public.

"It was still considered unsafe for the ship to dock and they might even take her down the coast and berth her at Kwinana where it was more sheltered".

Unfortunately, Kwinana is only a commercial harbour and there were no facilities there to accommodate customs and immigration officials, let alone passengers and relatives therefore it would only be used as a last resort.

It was about ten am. that the authorities decided to risk docking at Fremantle. The main problem was the severe wind storm that was blowing from the northwest and could quite easily push the ship sideways onto the southern breakwater. The two largest steam tugs, the Yuna and Wilga, were called up and they moved in to position with their noses against the lee side of the ship so that they could counteract the wind and hold her steady as she moved into the harbour entrance. The ship lowered her port side anchors until they were trailing in the mud where they would help to hold her and be ready for a quick grab at the harbour bottom in case anything went wrong. Then it was steady, steady, steady as the tugs, oh how tiny they were in comparison to that 42 thousand tonne ship, nursed and nuzzled the old girl slowly into her berth, slipping out of the way only at the last minute as she slid safely alongside the wharf.

Still the storm raged and vented it's fury on all and sundry, what a welcome to Australia for all those migrants and visitors alike.

Eventually, with the formalities behind us we were together again, united in our love for one another. The drive home was awful with the wind and rain pounding on the windshield as though it was trying to destroy us and our love for each other. Thank goodness I had had the sense to borrow my friends big Ford Custonline sedan for the day since I only drove a small Singer roadster, a two seater sports car which wouldn't have coped with the weather or the amount of luggage anywhere near as well as the Customline.

My Irish friends, Dave and Pat Lovatt, soon took Sandra under their wings and together with the members of the Methodist church at Bassendean they made her welcome and she settled in to her new life.

After a couple of months we were married in the Methodist church at Bassendean by the Reverend Percy Danger, who was soon to be replaced by Reverend Derek Hope which was a good omen. Fortunately Sandra, in spite of her inhospitable welcome from the weather soon fell in love with Western Australia our gorgeous climate and friendly people.

By the time that Sandra arrived I was working at Hadfield's engineering works at Bassendean where we were involved in machining components for mining and heavy industries. I eventually got the job of machining axle support beams for the new rail trucks on the standard-gauge railway, which was being built to bring W.A. into line with the other states, and there were thousands of them.

Shortly after our wedding, Sandra became

pregnant and she had to be very careful because her blood group was 'O' negative which could cause problems for the baby.

However she kept quite well and her doctor assured us that all was well but he hadn't bothered to take blood samples for testing although he was aware of the potential for problems and the need for it to be done sooner rather than later. Both Sandra and I were very quiet people who didn't like to rock the boat, so to speak, so we left it to the doctor to do the right thing by us. By the time that Sandra was about six months pregnant it was becoming obvious that all was not well with her and her health was slowly deteriorating. Doctor Cherry assured us that all was still okay but she would need a little treatment from time to time Sandra started having severe abdominal pains, vomiting and diarrhoea so he was treating her for gastro enteritis.

One Wednesday evening I returned from work to find Sandra in dire distress. She was doubled up on the bed in severe agony so I carried her out to the car and drove the short distance to the doctors rooms. He was not in attendance because Wednesday was his golf day and he always took the afternoon off to play a round at a nearby course but there was a free telephone at the surgery door which was connected to his home for emergencies. I rang the phone and when I told the doctor who it was that was calling he said, "Oh it's you again, what do you want now?"

I told him how ill my wife was and how worried I was so he said, "Take her home, put her to bed and give her two aspros and I'll call to see her in the morning, (doctors still made regular house calls in those days).

I was far from satisfied with the instructions, but what could I do. In those days once you became pregnant you registered with "a" doctor who would then see you through to the birth for a fixed fee. This meant that unscrupulous doctors like doctor Cherry would try to get you through with a minimum of involvement.

The next day I went home for my lunch as usual and Sandra was still lying on the bed in agony and crying her eyes out. I asked her what the doctor had said and she told me that he hadn't been yet. I was very angry as you would imagine but all I could do was to make her as comfortable as possible with the full expectation that he would at least make the call as soon as morning surgery was finished. I returned to work with a heavy heart and I was seriously worried about Sandy but I managed to get through the afternoon. I asked the foreman, who was a close friend of ours, to excuse me from overtime that day because I was so worried about Sandra and I needed to get home as early as possible.

When I arrived home there was no change in the situation, it was much worse if anything and Sandra said that doctor Cherry still had not called. I wrapped Sandra in a blanket because she was shivering badly and carried her out to our little car. I drove round to the surgery of a doctor Richards, which was only two streets away from doctor Cherry's place. As I carried Sandra into the waiting room the doctor, whom we had never met before, came out of his room to get his next patient. Doctor Richards looked up at us stopped in his tracks, a very worried expression swept across his face and he pointed to us saying in a concerned voice, "Come this way please, I'll see you straight away."

As I was giving the doctor all the relevant details he picked up the telephone and began making a series of calls. He spoke to the local ambulance service to organise the ambulance to come to the surgery immediately. Then he called another number, which I thought was a hospital and booked Sandra a bed and a third call to what appeared to be another doctor. Turning to me he said, "Your wife is very ill Mr O'Donnell and needs urgent hospitalisation. I have arranged for her to be taken to Saint Anne's Hospital at Mount Lawley for treatment. I have booked her in as a clinic patient which means that there will be no charges whatsoever. If they do send you a bill by accident when this mess is all over, just bring it here to the surgery and I'll attend to it for you. I'll look into this lot at a later time but my first priority is to get your wife into the hospital as soon as possible. A doctor Connaughton will meet the ambulance and take care of your wife when she arrives." He is the best chance you've got.

As soon as the ambulance came they put

Sandra on a stretcher and loaded her into the van and left in a hurry. Doctor Richards was still sitting behind his desk with a furious look on his face. He was extremely angry and there would be plenty of repercussions before this scenario was over.

I followed the ambulance to the hospital where Sandra was taken to a private ward and put to bed. I was standing beside the bed when a nursing sister came in and asked me to go out to the visitors lounge whilst Mr Connaughton examined my wife. It turned out that this doctor and his partner Mr Pixley, were the very best that were available at that time so I knew that Sandra was in good hands, but could they possibly save her life and the baby's as well? Only time would give me the answer to that question so I settled in for a long wait.

When the doctor came out to see me he said, "You may have just got your wife to me in time, young man, but it will be touch and go. I have told the staff that Sandra must have total silence, even a loud noise could tip her over the edge, and there are to be no visitors except for yourself. When you are allowed to see her try to be happy and quietly cheerful and remember there must be total silence other than a quiet whisper, and no sign of worry or stress. Do you fully understand all that I have told you?"

"Yes thank you doctor and thank you for your kindness and help. Sandra is a Methodist and is very close to the minister at Bassendean so is it possible for him to visit her?" I queried.

"No definitely not. Your wife has chronic toxaemia of pregnancy and has been badly neglected by her doctor so you must do all in your power to keep her thoughts positive from now on, and with the help of the staff here, who are the best in the world we may yet pull her through, so put your faith in them and God." The doctor replied.

Although my visits were severely limited in number and length I went in everyday only to be disheartened by the lack of improvement in Sandra's condition. She hung on the brink for nearly two weeks and when I went in on the Saturday evening the sister in charge would not let me in. She said, "The doctor is with your wife at the moment Mr. O'Donnell so would you like to wait in the upstairs waiting room until I come to get you?"

"Of course I'll wait, thankyou Sister" I replied.

"Mr. O'Donnell, even if the bell goes at the end of visiting hour will you please stay upstairs and I'll let you in as soon as the doctor leaves, if that's okay?" The sister added.

I soon got bored to tears sitting up there in the visitor's lounge and I had already read all the magazines on previous visits. I was also getting more and more concerned for Sandra and the baby, especially with this late appearance of the doctor, until I could sit no more, so I went out into the corridor to get a little exercise and stretch my legs. I turned around at the end of the corridor and headed back towards the lounge when a man of about my size and build almost knocked me over. He began to berate me for still being upstairs after the bell had sounded but I managed to placate him by repeating the Sister's instructions and it was then that he realised who I was.

He asked. "Are you Mr. O'Donnell by any chance, is that why you are here?"

I replied, "Yes that's correct my name is O'Donnell and I am waiting to see my wife."

"I'm Pixley." He stated. "I need to talk to you, come into the lounge and you may be able to help me come to a decision."

Once in the lounge he said, "I have to make a decision immediately. You see, if I give your wife an injection right away it will give her, her best chance of recovery but I don't know if the baby will cope. She is still a long way too early and then we have to consider the effect of the toxin on both of them. However, if I delay starting her off for another week or two I don't fancy your wife's chances of survival either. We are in quite a dilemma and I can't be sure which is the best plan. What do you think about it."

"Well doctor, as you know all this is new to me but personally I feel that so long as Sandra survives we will probably have the chance to have another go, and with all this experience behind us, and you to guide us through it we may do better next time."

"That's exactly what I was hoping you would say, I'll give her the injection right away. Will you stay with your wife until we know what's happening?" The doctor asked.

"Yes certainly I will as long as I'm allowed to

stay up here." I answered but he had already gone into the room to administer the injection.

About twenty minutes later the injection began to work and my wife went into labour and I was allowed to sit with her for a while until I was sent home to await the outcome.

When I went back to the hospital the next day the Sister escorted me to the premature berth ward and showed me my son. I called him James Malcolm so that they could baptise him immediately. I had added the name Malcolm after Sandra's only brother in England. He was so small that he was lying across the humidity crib and not along it. They hadn't taken any time to weigh him but they were sure that he was less than two pounds. The baby appeared to be fine. I found it hard to believe that something so small could be so complete and so lovely. Of course, these days, babies this small are commonplace and many of them survive and thrive.

I was only allowed to stay for a few minutes that day and the next then it was back to the private ward to see Sandra. She was still very weak and needing constant care, which the sisters heaped on her day and night. Eventually they were able to tell me that she was over the worst and out of immediate danger but by then I had to tell her that the baby had only survived for two days before dying because the toxins had penetrated his tiny blood stream and the excess pressure that it caused was too much for the arteries to bear and one of them had burst internally.

Sandra took the news fairly well at first until an unthinking nurse told her that it was probably for the best because there may possibly be something wrong with him, and that other problems could develop later on. Sandra was too ill to be taken to see our baby boy and James was too delicate to be taken to her, so she never got to see her baby at all and later on as a result of the nurse's comments she began to wonder if there were any abnormalities with the child. Once Sandra told me of her concerns I was able to relieve her of her worries as I told her that the little one was absolutely perfect in every detail.

The day after the baby's death the doctors approached me to ask about the body. They said that very little was known about babies as small as our's, and they would like to carry out a full autopsy and many tests to try and amass more information to help them with future premature births. Because Sandra was still so sick and I had enough to worry about in that area, and had no desire to go through the formalities of a normal funeral, I gave my permission to the hospital management to try and extract as much as they could from that tiny body, which they then carried out after promising that, once they had learnt all they could, the baby would be given a respectful Christian burial.

Slowly but surely, under the guidance of doctor Pixley my wife recovered but her kidneys were damaged forever and she was to live with severe high blood pressure for the next thirty eight years. It was only after we discovered a product called 'Herbalife', for which we became distributors, did her blood pressure return to normal at last.

When we went to see the doctor for the final examination he told us that we were not to even consider trying for another baby for at least three years and then only after going to see doctor

Pixley again for a thorough check-up. It seemed like forever to wait that long but eventually we were given the 'all clear', and we were blessed with a lovely baby boy who we named Rodney Ian after two wonderful, lifelong friends, Rodney Riding and Sidney Ian Gibbins, with whom I shared many happy experiences over the years of our acquaintance.

During this time of waiting we went to Watheroo, a small farming community in the northern wheat belt to visit some friends who we had met when they were living in Belmont, an outer suburb of Perth city quite close to the airport. This was the couple who had happily loaned me their Ford Customline motorcar on the day of Sandra's arrival. We were invited to go back again for a holiday in the summer when they were in the middle of harvesting. Whilst we were there Doug and Marlene introduced us to a machinery dealer and general agent who lived and operated his business in the nearby township.

The dealer said that he urgently needed a mechanic to work in a new workshop that he was building and he offered me the job. Partly because of my farming background and partly because of my experiences at the Perkins diesel factory. I decided to accept the position and we moved to Watheroo.

We settled in well at first and met some very nice people, some of whom remained our dear friends for many years to come but it soon became obvious that my boss was the meanest man that I had ever met and also that he was a very devious character and an unscrupulous old rogue. There was a stock of assorted tyres in the showroom that were put there by the tyre dealership in a neighbouring town on a sale or return basis. When the sales representative for the tyre company arrived one day he told my boss that there was a front tractor tyre missing from the rack and he would supply a replacement and send out the bill for it. The boss got quite upset because he knew that he had not sold one of these tyres since the last visit of the rep. so he checked with his wife who also had no knowledge of the transaction. Finally it dawned on him that it must have been me that had sold the tyre and forgotten to book it out to a farmer.

However, I denied all knowledge of the tyre sale but he insisted that it must have been me so he would deduct the cost from my wages. That resulted in us having a ding-dong row about it and he decided to charge each and every customer on his books with the cost of the tyre. When he sent out his accounts at the end of that month, all 130 customers except for about 10 or 11 paid up without knowing that they had been robbed. The other few came in to pay him, deducted the price of the tyre from what they owed, vowing that they didn't even own any machinery that took that particular size tyre and that he could close their account since they would never come there again. My boss took all this quite casually and didn't seem to be upset about it at all.

A few days later a local shop owner, who also had a similar stock of tyres, came up the street when I was in the shop on my own and he was wheeling a front tractor tyre, which he gave to me to put back into stock. I asked him why he was bringing a new tyre to us and he told me that he'd had a sale for one a few weeks ago and he had borrowed ours because he had already sold his own. Of course I asked him who had served him and he said that it was the boss himself who had pulled it from the rack for him. When the boss returned I told him about the tyre and suggested that he would have to issue credits to the farmers who had been wrongly charged and to me to pay back my wages that had been confiscated but he informed me that, because they were so stupid and weren't aware of what had transpired, they deserved to get stung. I was so upset that I handed in my notice there and then and we moved on to greener pastures, I hoped.

After a short stay in Mullewa we settled down in a farming town called Three Springs, which is on the road to Geraldton.

This was a large farming centre and had a good range of shops and other facilities, including a well equipped hospital and a swimming pool. I had moved there to take up a position at Great Northern Motors who were machinery dealers and general automotive repairers. In those days the highway through the town was the only way of getting to Geraldton and other towns further north and that meant that we were always extremely busy and there was plenty of overtime to help out our family budget.

Sandra was pregnant again and eventually gave birth to Rodney. It was with the help of our friends in Perth that all this went off as well as it did. Thanks also to the magnificent staff at Saint Anne's Hospital in Mount Lawley.

Shortly after her return to Three Springs with the baby Sandra went into hospital because her feet were badly infected and I was left with the task of looking after our baby son as well as working at the garage during the day.

The wife of one of my bosses, Jean Pugsley was more than happy to look after the baby during the daytime which was just as well because he needed to be fed every 3 hours. Jean had never been able to have a baby of her own but we soon worked out a suitable roster and we were going fine until bath time on day one.

When I arrived at the Pugsley's house to take over, Jean had the bath on the table and was filling it with water. As I walked in she said, "I was going to bath the baby but I was scared in case the water wasn't at the right temperature.

Do you know how to tell when it is alright."

Full of confidence I said, "Oh, that's easy you just fill the bath and dump him in and if he turns red it's too hot and if he turns blue it's too cold."

Jean thought that I was serious and gave me a look of horror then said, "Oh dear I don't think that's the way you do it. I heard somewhere that you have to put your elbow in the water and you can tell if it's too hot."

I replied. "That sounds as good as any other way so lets try. If we get it wrong I'm sure he'll scream and let us know."

That method seemed to work well and the next night he was already bathed and enjoying a feed when I walked in.

After that we got along fine and managed until Sandra came home to take over. I have no idea if the baby awoke during the night for his 2 o'clock feed or not. Being a heavy sleeper, I fed and changed him just before jumping into bed at 10 o'clock and woke him up at 6 am. for breakfast. Rodney continued to thrive and he was always a very happy and contented baby.

Chapter **22**

PATRICIA

We had a small farm near Busselton when our boys were little and as it was very small we decided to augment our income by breeding and rearing pigs. There were a number of disused piggeries nearby as a result of the dairy farmers changing over to whole milk supply instead of cream, and therefore no longer had a supply of skimmed milk to dispose of to growing pigs.

I was able to lease two of these piggeries for a mere peppercorn rental and set about building up a breeding herd of top quality pigs with the aide of a pedigree Large White boar from Kulin called "Jillara Champion Turk."

Turk as we called him had a pedigree a mile long and was a magnificent animal. He was as big as a donkey and fortunately he was so quiet that our boys used to ride on his back.

We crossbred him with purebred Berkshire sows from Wyalkatchem to get true hybrid vigour and good quality porkers. These sows were almost jet black except for a few white spots.

The first litter of babies that he produced 12 in all were with a young female that the boys had called Rosemary. She was a Canadian Berkshire pig from an old friend in Kondinin. Our youngest, David, who was about four years old at that time was with me when I discovered her farrowing in the bush and he was astonished to see pure white piglets emerging from the rear end of a pure black sow.

David jumped up and ran all the way back to the house shouting at the top of his voice, "Mammy, mammy, mammy, rosemary is having babies and they're white not black." (Oh the shame of it.)

As we were building up our herd of breeders we needed to purchase weaners and slips to stabilise our output of top grade porkers to the local abattoir. This gave rise to a number of incidents involving their acquisition and transport home.

I noticed an advertisement in the local newspaper one day and replied by telephoning the farmer concerned.

His property was near Witchcliffe which meant a fairly long trip in my Dodge truck to inspect and collect them, provided they were the right quality and suitably priced.

Having arranged a suitable time to have a look at the piglets, 12 in all and from the same litter, I set off early one morning on the long drive south.

The journey to Witchcliffe was plain sailing and I soon located what appeared to be the entrance to the property as described over the phone. The block was a smallish hobby farm, mostly uncleared in heavy timber country, and I followed the track until I found a lovely cabin style house in the bushes with a small vegetable garden near one side.

The farmer came out at the sound of the truck and invited me into the house for a welcome cuppa after the long trip. He and his wife were very nice people and lived a fairly lonely life, as they were miles from anywhere, and they were glad to have someone to chat to for a while.

After the drink and a long chat we went out to see the piglets which were housed nearby.

The pig-pen was constructed of face cuts from a nearby timber mill. These face cuts were dug into the ground like fence posts and were over 5feet tall. The only other support was a horizontal rail bolted on about two thirds of the way up on the inside thus making a very secure yard with one corner roofed and enclosed as protection from the elements.

We opened the gate and entered the yard and the huge sow came up to us, grunting with pleasure whilst keeping a watchful eye on her babies.

The farmer said, "I haven't fed them yet I thought it would be easier if they were a bit hungry."

"That's a fine looking litter of pigs and a playful lot at that." I said. "They're just the sort of pigs that I'm looking for. They'll go on fine after such a good start"

The farmer replied, "We'd better agree on the price before we try to get them out of there."

"That's Ok with me but is there some sort of

problem with loading them."

"Oh yes, that's Patricia in there" he said.

"What difference does that make", I said. "She's very quiet and friendly and should be no trouble at all by the looks of her."

"You wait until the babies start to squeal then you'll see another side of Patricia, mate," he said.

We soon agreed on a fair price then discussed the loading problem.

"Reverse your truck up to the rear fence near to the shed. If you slide the tailgate open a bit we can pass them up over the fence one at a time. I'll get a bucket of grain and feed the old girl in that trough outside the yard then close the gate, that should give us time to load the little blighters."

Once Patricia was out of the yard we both went in and locked the gate securely then we fed the piglets to make them easier to catch.

As soon as we grabbed a piglet they started squealing their heads off and Patricia went mad outside the gate. Knowing that she couldn't get in we got stuck into the job of catching the little beggars and heaving them onboard the truck. We were going great guns and had most of them on board when the farmer shouted out in fear, "Hey!!! Look out mate, she's coming over the fence."

"We'll be right, I answered, "she'll never get over there, will she?"

When I looked round I wasn't so sure. The sow had her elbows on top of the fence and her huge head was well above the fence already. Her great gaping mouth, full of razor sharp, vicious teeth, was snapping in mid air on our side of the fence.

There were only two piglets left and the farmer grabbed one and shoved it into the truck and scrambled madly over the fence onto the stock crate and safety.

"Hell mate! Lookout," he screamed, as dear old Patricia pulled her massive body over the fence and landed nearby.

Grabbing the last piglet I heaved it onto the truck and followed it over the fence and through the sliding gate. I was still lying flat on my belly and scrabbling forward when she grabbed my foot, bit down hard and pulled back. Those great teeth had gone deep into my rubber gumboot but missed my foot. Patricia removed the boot and started to systematically destroy it chewing it to tiny pieces.

My farmer friend said, "By God that was close, are you all right, mate".

"Yes, I think so," I replied as I pulled off my sock to examine the damage. There was a scratch down the heel where the skin was broken and just starting to bleed. "I'm glad that I don't have to live with that bad tempered old bitch, how long will it take her to calm down."

"Oh! You needn't worry about that it's all over already. You can walk in there and scratch her ears now. She's only savage when her babies are squealing."

With great trepidation I went back into the pen with him and sure enough Patricia was her old self again, snuffling around as she cleaned up the last of the food in the trough. She turned around looking for a scratch behind her ears.

"I don't know what we'll do next time," he said, "she gets worse each time."

"Well you can do me a great favour mate, see if you can find some one else to buy the little beggars next time.'

"Are you telling me you wouldn't come again,

even for pigs as good as these."

"No mate, I'm only kidding I don't mind a bit of danger now and again.

"You'd better come back to the house now and have another cuppa to settle your nerves before you go, the kettles always on." He said.

Chapter 23

CYCLONE ALBY

One day in the summer school holidays I drove from Busselton to Katanning to a pig sale because, once again, I was short of small piglets. I took my boys with me and made it a day out. It was a long drive but worth the effort so long as there were enough weaners at the sale to fill my truck The day looked like being fairly hot but the promised early sea breeze should help as little pigs do not cope with too much heat.

The sale was well attended and there were lots of very nice weaners for sale. Whilst waiting for the sale to start I met a young pig farmer from Albany and got into a long conversation with him about his piggery.

The young man was John Bunn and the family had a farm at Redmond. To increase the family income John had set up a pig project. He said that he had 40 sows which he ran in open pens in the paddock but as he had no sheds to house the growing piglets he was forced to sell them at weaning time and he had a good many in the sale that particular day. We moved over to the sale pens so that John could show me his pigs and I was very impressed with the size and quality of them and knew that they would do well so long as the sale price was fair.

I asked John how it was all working out for him and he replied that the breeding cycle was going very well but he was at the mercy of the market forces at Katanning and that was not good. Sometimes the prices were okay but at others, especially around Xmas and summer holidays, like now, few people wanted to be bothered with a mob of weaners and prices were terrible. In fact they were so bad that he was thinking of giving the whole venture away.

I told John that I needed lots of weaners today so maybe today would be much better for him although he doubted that they would because there was such a large number available.

During the sale I had a bright idea, (it doesn't

happen very often), so I approached him after the sale with a proposition. I always needed good weaners and he often had plenty in Albany.

"Look John," I said, "I can use all the weaners you can produce and you need to find a better way of marketing yours".

"That's certainly very true Brian, what have you got in mind?" He replied.

"Well, what I was thinking of was that I could have a day out and drive to your place, say once a month and buy all your pigs direct. You see I hate having to buy pigs from the markets because of the risk of introducing disease into my piggery, and we would cut out the yarding fees and agent's commission costs which are eating into your profits."

"Would you be happy to travel all that way every time that I have a load ready to go," Brian.

"To get a constant supply of weaners as good as yours at the right price I certainly would, provided there was a reasonable load to spread the travel costs, and I could bring you a quantity of my weaner mix so that you could wean them onto my rations and minimise the stress on the babies when I get them home."

"That sounds great, Brian. Just what I need, you seem to have studied all aspects of the pig breeding and what problems to avoid if possible but what do we do about the prices so that we end up for a good deal for both of us?"

"Oh I think we can arrive at a fair and equitable price each time," I suggested, "Some where in the middle so that we'll both be better off. I suggest you go through your previous sales and work out an average net price as a starting point. Then give me a ring next time you have some ready to go and I'll check current prices in the various markets and see what happens. You can't afford to keep on getting ripped off here and if you decide to continue you need to know that you'll get a fair price to start with."

"Right, that sounds good to me, mate, give me your phone number and I'll be in touch." Said John. "I'll just have to run this idea past the family first though if that's okay with you. I don't think they'll have any objections as they aren't happy at the moment anyway."

This seemed like a great ending to a very successful day because I had managed to buy 80 pigs at a reasonable price and most of them were John's.

All I had to do now was walk them all to the ramp and load them onto the truck.

Strange pigs do not mix well and we had a very lively time before we got them penned ready to load. There were a number of sheep farmers watching this show and one or two 'helping' us. There were plenty of smart arsed remarks coming from that direction, believe me.

We drove most of the piglets onto the truck and closed the gate when there were still 5 or 6 left on the ramp. The sheep farmers were surprised at how many we crammed in and one said, "What're you going to do with the rest mate, eat 'em."

"Don't worry," I said, "They'll all fit in."

"Like bloody hell they will," He replied, "They're already too tight, you'll smother half of them before you get home."

"Never in a fit, mate," I answered, "They're not like sheep, they'll all cuddle in together to keep warm and they won't have room to run around and fight. By the time we get home they'll all smell the same and they'll be great friends. I'll just lift the rest over the gate and get cracking."

About half way home a strong sea breeze came up as forecast and the temperature dropped considerably. Shortly afterwards I looked into the big west-coaster mirror which gave me a limited view of the tray of the truck and it was empty, not a single pig in sight. Naturally I checked the other mirror only to see the empty tray there as well.

"My God," I shouted, "I must have forgotten to fasten the sliding gate, we've lost all the pigs."

Rodney replied, "Dad, I saw you put the pin through the gate and put the "R" pin in before we left Katanning and with the tail board up, there's not much room to escape any way."

"Yes mate' I think you're right, we'll stop and see what's happened." I answered him.

When we stopped I jumped out and looked in the back and burst out laughing with relief.

Rod said, "What are you laughing at dad, where are the pigs, are they alright?"

"Come and look, mate, they're all here, every last one." Was my relieved reply.

When the wind got cold the pigs on the outside had moved in closer and closer and they were all in a triangle with the cab breaking the wind. They were 2 and 3 deep with only their noses sticking up in the air. Who said they were overcrowded?

We arrived home safely, unloaded the pigs and bedded them down for the night none the worse for their ordeal. A good feed of grain soon got them squealing around and playing again.

A few weeks later I received a phone call from John and we arranged a suitable day for the trip to Albany.

I had friends who used to live in Hyden, who were now living at Crystal Springs near Walpole. Keith and Wendy were employed as National Park rangers down there, and we didn't get together very often these days so I decided to leave home the evening before, after feeding the pigs, and spend the night with them and their boys and leave for Albany early the next morning. A quick phone call to the Cuninghams was well received and all was arranged.

This broke up the journey quite nicely, and after a very pleasant night with my friends and their two boys, I arrived at Redmond about morning tea- time.

Once there I was introduced to John's

parents who are extremely lovely people, even though they are "Poms". They were pleased to see that the deals with John were working out well at last, and they invited me to stay for lunch to fortify me for the trip home with 70 baby pigs. They even thought that I may have paid a little over the odds compared to their previous dealings at Katanning, but I had done my homework well and I was sure that we had it pretty right, having been on the other end of the equation where I too was being ripped off. I knew that I could not get this quality for any less, most likely a fair amount more, anywhere else and not going near a saleyard was a definite bonus disease wise.

We followed this routine for a number of trips and everything went very well. I never lost a single pig, neither on the journey back, or later on at home.

All the pigs that I received from Albany were top quality and thrived in their new home. As a bonus we all became great friends and looked forward to the visits.

On one of my visits to Redmond we were relaxing after another of Mrs. Bunn's excellent meals just prior to setting out on the long journey home when Mrs. Bunn came in quite agitatedly and said.

"Brian, I am not trying to get rid of you, but I think you should leave straight away. There's just been a severe weather warning on the radio. They are expecting gale force winds and storms very soon and it seems to be streaming down from that big cyclone up north."

"Gee! Thanks Mrs. Bunn," I replied, "It's a good job you listen to the news and weather forecast everyday and heard about it, I'll get cracking straight away. Thanks for the lovely meal and I'll see you next time, I'll give you a ring when I get home to let you know that we're safe as I usually do."

Once outside there didn't seem to be any panic, all was quiet and not a single cloud in sight. The weather looked calm and serene as I set off homeward. However that situation soon began to change and about 15 miles from Mount Barker I ran into a solid wall of red dust. It blotted out the sun and rose high into the air almost up to the clouds which were now racing in from the north.

I groped my way slowly and carefully into the town and turned off onto the Muir Highway heading for Manjimup. The dust was not so thick now but the wind was already up to gale-force or more.

I had tied two light-weight tarps over the crate to keep the sun off the pigs but the wind soon tore them to shreds. The pigs, 72 of them, were hot and thirsty so I stopped besides a creek bed which had a handy pool of water close to the road, in the hope of being able to improve their comfort. However there was a problem, I didn't have a bucket or any other container to carry the water to the truck. I was just about to drive off in despair when I remembered my gumboots which were on the floor on the passenger side of the cab. They didn't make ideal buckets but after many trips back and forth I managed to soak the babies and the straw bedding to keep them a little bit cooler.

I had to repeat this operation at regular intervals along the road and I kept a good look out for handy pools of water in the creek beds where they ran under the road. Most of the water was quite salty but at least it was wet and cool. It was now blazing hot and the wind was violent. I struggled to keep the truck on the road, and at times the dust was thick and choking. The piglets seemed to be quite happy and comfortable and loved the water stops. They soon got used to the stops and squealed in anticipation of another bath of cool water as they ran around the truck and fought for the best positions.

As I neared Manjimup the road entered the Karri forest and this afforded some shelter from the wind and reduced the dust. About 25 miles from the town the wind, which had been blowing from the north, suddenly stopped and I drove along in almost dead calm for a few miles. I mistakenly, thought the worst was over at last. The sensation was quite eerie because there were no sounds whatsoever. Even the birds were silent and nothing moved, not even a leaf.

How wrong can you be? Just as I was starting to enjoy the drive again there was a mighty roar and I almost ended up in the bush as a massive gust of wind hit the truck from the opposite direction. What the heck is going on I thought?

Later on I realised that I had just driven right through the eye of cyclone Alby and this was only the beginning of the horrors to come.

As the wind rammed my truck again and again like a runaway bulldozer, the trees began to be uprooted and large branches were being torn off almost every tree. There were leaves, twigs and branches blowing around all over the place and the truck was battling to stay on its wheels.

As I continued into Manjimup, whole trees were being uprooted and thrown around onto the road. I couldn't decide whether to continue and try to reach the comparative 'safety' of town or find somewhere to hole up and wait out the storm. With speed reduced to a crawl I dodged the worst of the debris on the road and continued on carefully towards town. There was nowhere to park up and ride out the storm with any degree of safety. I was in a heavy forested area and although the trees would break the wind speed the danger of falling branches and trees was a constant worry. It was terrifying. The noise was deafening and the light fading out quickly as nightfall approached. My god could any one survive this devastation?

I had lost all sense of distance and nothing looked familiar to help me to judge how far away the town was. Then suddenly there it was, the first of the buildings in the industrial area on the outskirts of the town loomed ahead through the murk and I was soon in the comparative quiet, sheltered by the big sheds and factories. At least here there were fewer trees, less branches to tear off and the buildings afforded some protection from that savage gale force wind.

Once in town I looked for somewhere to park up safely and I needed to get hold of a tarpaulin in case we got some heavy rain. It was quite dark already and the power supply was down so there were no street lights to guide me.

Fortunately, I went first to the railway station to seek some local knowledge and hopefully a strong railway tarpaulin to cover the pigs.

The stationmaster was magnificent, and so helpful. He said that I could borrow a tarpaulin and could park my truck in the lee of the old goods shed. He reckoned that the shed was built of massive timbers and if the worst came to the worst it would be the last building standing this night.

He sent one of his men with me to locate a tarp and the chap stayed with me until I was "safely" parked and the massive tarpaulin securely tied in place.

The pigs soon settled down and went to sleep oblivious to the danger.

When I returned to the station buildings to check out the situation the stationmaster told me that I would have to stay the night because all the roads in and out of town were closed with fallen trees and or bush fires .The shire and forestry workers were all out trying to keep the town roads clear in case we all had to evacuate in a hurry.

There was a large fire rampaging towards the town from the north which had burnt a good many power poles. There was no chance of the power supply being reinstated for a few days at least. The phone box was not operating without power to work the coin parts so I called the operator to ask if I could reverse charges since I needed to call my wife

Sandra and my sons to let them know where I was holed up and that I was comparatively safe for the time being.

The operator put me through without charge and I had a long chat with Sandra and the boys, neglecting of course to tell them of the bushfires.

By the time I got back to the station the town was nearly as bright as day due to the fires which were very close now.

The railway ladies bless their hearts, had arrived with an impromptu meal for every-one who was gathered at the station. One lady had cooked up a large enamel basin full of minced meat and another lady arrived with a similar bowl of mashed spuds. Then another lady came in with a large box of buttered bread to mop up the juices. Even today I am amazed at the determination of those Ladies who put aside their own worries and fears to help us out. Maybe this was their way of coping with the situation and keeping busy was the antidote to all this horror and dread.

Believe it or not, but there was a mass of sweets to follow and buckets of tea to wash it all down. I'll remember those ladies and our impromptu meal for the rest of my days.

As we were finishing this magnificent banquet the south bound wood chip train crawled into the station and stopped alongside the platform. The crew were a terrified mess, and the poor old guard at the back of the train could hardly stand up. He said that when he looked forward the train was completely engulfed in a wall of flames and he could hardly breath. He thought they would all die and if the track failed to hold them they would surely have done just that. At one point he counted more than fifty consecutive sleepers alight beneath the wheels.

Nothing could be done about the fires and the police were turning every-one back into town.

They told us that the flying embers were lighting fires more than a mile ahead of the main front and they were afraid that the fire fighters would get trapped between the main front and the fresh fires ahead.

The dry cow pads were igniting and the wind stood them up on edge to roll them across the paddocks like Katherine wheels, spewing out sparks and flames as they went.

The noise from the fire was terrifyingly loud and increasing rapidly as the front roared towards us.

The flames were reaching high into the sky and lighting up the whole town, which had been in darkness since there was no power for the streetlights.

There was no hope the town would surely be razed with great loss of life. There was no way out of the town and the fire was roaring in so quickly that it would be impossible to out run the flames. The fire was upon us and was about to engulf us. Would any of us see the light of day? We all just stood there watching in horror, not knowing what, if anything, could be done to save ourselves.

All we could do was hope and pray for a miracle to save us because the fire was now right on the edge of town trying to get across the safety zone that had been created by the town's folk and the council. Everyone was watching out for the flying embers and stamping them out as they fell in the town area.

You can't believe what a fire that big is like. It

was horrendous, and we all thought we were done for. The noise was unbelievably loud and we could feel the searing heat. We found it was almost impossible to breath because the fire was robbing all the oxygen from the atmosphere. There were going to be a lot of dead people around town and very little town left by morning.

Just as we thought the town would burn the wind turned suddenly to the west and the humidity had built up so high that we could feel the wetness on our skin.

Rain would have been our salvation but that was not about to happen. However the humidity was so high that it was almost a heavy dew which together with the change in wind direction was enough to dampen the fire enough to control it along the flanks near the town so that we could stop it from encroaching further towards the town.

These two factors saved the town as the fire veered round to the east of the houses back into forest and farms to burn itself out.

Every-one breathed a sigh of relief and we all settled down again and gave thanks for our lucky escape. We were all hugging and kissing one another and thanking our good fortune that we were saved.

The stationmaster asked, "What are you going to do now mate. We have a spare bed on the veranda where you can kip down for the night if you like."

"Thanks all the same mate I really appreciate your hospitality but I must get back to my pigs to see if they are okay. The cab is big enough for me to stretch out and I have a blanket with me so I'll be right thankyou. You guys have done more than enough anyway. Please thank all your staff for their efforts and concern and I will say goodnight."

Back at the truck all was quiet so I settled down to try and get some sleep. I must have slept for a fair while but then something woke me. It was just after midnight by my watch as I lay there wondering what was afoot that had awakened me. I heard and felt the truck shaking and moving about and then the pigs grunting in displeasure. I jumped out to have a look and unfastened the rear of the tarpaulin to peer inside.

That's when my brain began to work again as I realised the tarp was stifling the pigs. They were too hot and needed fresh air to breath. I fastened the tarp again in such a way that the rear gate was left open to the cool night air. The pigs immediately settled down again and most were asleep by the time I got back into the cab.

The next time I awoke I sat up and listened to a fairly loud noise that seemed to be getting nearer and nearer. A glance at my watch told me that it was almost 7.30 am. The noise became clearer and I soon realised that a large truck was approaching from the north.

Suddenly I became aware of the fact that if a truck could get into town from Bridgetown then I could reverse the process and start my homeward journey.

First of all I had to remove the tarp and fold it up and then check the pigs. They seemed to be oblivious to all the drama but quickly let me know that they were hungry and thirsty. There was a tap nearby and my trusty gumboot sufficed once again to give them a drink but the food would have to wait awhile.

Having done my best to make the pigs

comfortable again I headed out of the silent town and hopefully, all the way home.

The sights that appeared before me were horrendous. Most of the farm homesteads had been well protected by firebreaks and I didn't see any that were burnt but miles of fencing had been destroyed along with hundreds of power poles. It would be many a day before these properties got the power back on again.

I was amazed at the work that had been carried out by the shire workers, foresters and everyone with a chain saw. They must have been out all night even when the trees were still falling around them, to cut enough branches off each tree to allow the traffic to pass. I had to drive slowly and very cautiously swerving from one side of the road to the other to get through. The men had removed the easiest branches from each tree to allow limited passage.

I passed through a small mill town where the sawmill had been burnt out but most buildings had survived. There were a few burnt and some dead sheep and cattle that had been trapped in the corners of the paddocks and against the fences.

When I got to Bridgetown I realised that I had a major decision to make. Was it possible to cut through the forest to Carlotta and Nannup as I usually did or was it safer to go the long way round via Bunbury rather than risk getting stuck somewhere in the forest?

I stopped the truck at the intersection near the river bridge and I was stretching my legs whilst trying to decide my next move when a massive log loader belonging to Palmer's roared into view. The driver stopped alongside of me and shouted out over the roar of the engine, "Are you alright mate? Can I help you at all."

"Yes mate, thanks for stopping, I was just wondering if this road was clear right through to Nannup."

"It bloody well will be by the time I get there and that's a fact mate," was his reply.

"Are you telling me that you are going right through to Nannup then."

"You bet I am and if you like to go first you can stop if you get to a tree or something and just wait for me to catch up and I'll shift it for you."

All went well until I was about halfway through and had to stop where three saplings were lying across the road. All the rest of the road had already been cleared in a similar method to the highway and I reckoned that I could probably bump my way over these obstacles, but there was a lady in a small sedan stopped at the other side. Her car was far too low to even think about getting over the trees.

"How long have you been here and where have you come from?" I asked.

"Only a minute or two," was her reply, "and I've come from Nannup."

"Oh that's great that means that when I get passed these trees I can get through to Nannup. Do you know what the road to Busselton is like by any chance?"

"You'll be okay after this but there are trees everywhere and you'll need to be very careful."

"I have some ropes under the seat so we should be able to move these logs around so that we can squeeze by. Hello! I think I can hear a vehicle coming we might get some help."

Sure enough a council utility came around the corner and two men got out and walked towards us.

"Got stuck did you guys? We'll soon have this cleared then you can go. We were clearing the road before and ran low on fuel for the saws after we cut up that big tree about half a mile back. We didn't know that we were almost through so we went back to town to get petrol, and grabbed a quick feed and some more coffee as well," One of the men said.

"I'll give you a hand, thanks for coming, you shire men have been wonderful. You can be very proud of your efforts, and thanks again" I replied.

From then on it was plain sailing all the way home but because the piggery was a few miles before my home I decided to unload the pigs, give them a feed and a drink on the way.

The piggery was on a dairy farm owned by a lovely family by the name of Torrent. These great people were of Spanish descent and were early pioneers of the district. I had a very close relationship with the Torrent family as I milked their dairy herd to give them a break from time to time as well as leasing the pig sheds.

When I pulled up by the house to open the gate Joe and his son Ron hurried out to greet me followed by their whole family. There were many hugs, kisses and hand shakes all round before Maude said, "I'll put the kettle on Brian. I bet you are dying for a cuppa, does Sandra know you're back yet?"

"No, not yet, I thought I'd better give these blokes a good feed and water as I was going past and get them settled first."

"Okay, I'll ring Sandra to tell her you're safe and our boys can help you unload, then you can tell us all about your travels over a nice cuppa tea.

We soon had the pigs unloaded and they were ravenous. I gave them a fairly small feed for the time being so as not to bloat them and showed them how to work the nipple drinkers for water. They soon got the hang of that although they had never seen one before.

As soon as the pigs were settled we went to the house for a cuppa and a sandwich whilst exchanging stories of the disaster. I cut the talk short as I needed to get home as soon as possible and I was glad to get there to check everything over and assess the damage, if any.

Sandra told me the story of their night of

horror with the boys chipping in from time to time. They said that the house had been rocking violently and would surely have gone had it not been for the concrete water tank.

We had escaped any material damage because there was a 12,000 gallon concrete water tank against the windward side of the house which had diverted the wind and taken the pressure off the walls and roof. One small tree had fallen on a fence and had to be cut up but all the stock were okay. We were without power for five days, which caused us plenty of problems as we relied on the power for water supply as well as lighting and refrigeration. We had bottled gas for cooking thank goodness. We were a lot better off than many others in the district and milking the poor old cows was a major concern without any electricity. All the farmers moved around from farm to farm to help each other through these difficult times.

There were many trees and fences to be sorted out quickly before the livestock went walk-about and many animals needed hand feeding and more often watering. Most of the farmers relied on the electricity to pump water for their animals as well as for their own domestic use.

Some dairy farmers could adapt a tractor to work the milking machines but others could not and this caused more problems that had to be fixed. All the milk had to be dumped as there was no electricity to cool it down but the poor old cows still had to be milked and quickly. All in all we managed to get through a pretty torrid experience by working as a group.

For some of the farmers it was a very long time before things got back to normal again. As for ourselves, we ended up well enough, and as usual the pigs thrived in spite of their ordeal

A friend that I got to know recently said that the kids were put to bed on a mattress laid on the floor beneath their pool table because they felt that the table would help to support the roof in case it fell in on them.

One man, a resident of Manjimup, was getting ready to go outside and attack some of the fallen trees around the town with his trusty chain saw when his son admonished him for not having a safety helmet. After a heated discussion the man agreed to wear his son's motorcycle helmet for protection against the danger of falling branches. As the guy walked along their garden path towards the road a large branch broke off the neighbour's tree and hit the chap on the head. Had it not been for the helmet he would have been seriously hurt, or worse still, killed.

Chapter 24

THE NEW AMBULANCE

Hyden town and general district was covered for ambulance services by the Kondinin and Kulin St. John's Ambulance Sub-centre which was based in Kondinin.

Because of the the 40 miles (60km) distance between Kondinin and Hyden every-one felt that there should be an ambulance stationed in Hyden as the time factor was critical in an emergency.

The committee, comprised of representatives from Hyden, Karlgarin, Kulin and Kondinin decided to raise funds for a new ambulance and a new garage in Kondinin thereby releasing one of the existing vans to be based in Hyden.

It was decided to raise funds quickly by way of a collection of wheat seconds from the farmers because the need was urgent. Each, town committee, was to organize a collection in their own surrounding district

Ray Herring and I were both active supporters of the ambulance service in Hyden so we held a short meeting to work out a suitable method of attack.

We each owned a tray type truck so on a Saturday afternoon, after closing our businesses we each set off in different directions, radiating out from town to ask the farmers for a donation of seconds of wheat. A local shearer. Bob Fraser offered to go with me and another townie, whose details I fail to recall, (probably Bob Baillie), went with Ray.

Since the farmers were still harvesting the grain was still scattered around the paddocks in open bags and typical of their type they donated freely to a good cause.

Boxer Lovering directed us to a freshly harvested stubble paddock just north of the Humps rocky outcrop which is a local land mark and tourist area, wherein there were a good many sacks of grain.

The Humps area is famous for the legend of a cross eyed aboriginal native called Mulka the terrible who had reputedly lived in a cave in the rock formation.

Boxer said, "You're welcome to take them all because I need to get the sheep into that stubble as quickly as possible. The only problem you have is how to get them out of there because the paddock is inundated with a large plague of sandflies."

Undaunted, but a little skeptical, we set off and soon realized that Boxer had not exaggerated at all. The stubble was so black with the flies that it seemed to have been burned. Wherever the bags were standing in twos and threes the space between them was so thick with insects that they could be shoveled up by the bucket full, and of course they bite like hell.

After a quick conference we decided that one of us would stand on the truck with a bag hook and lift whilst the other one stood on the ground to heave them up. Stitching the bags first was out of the question as it would have prolonged the agony so we just hauled them onto the tray as they were and propped them up against each other. This method worked as well as could be expected and as we were leaving the paddock I parked the old truck close to a large water storage tank so that we could jump from the head board into the water and wash off the sandflies. We reckond that it was worth the discomfort because we had collected about twenty five bags of grain, which was a good start for the day.

By the end of the day we had a full load of about 10 tons of grain and Ray had collected a similar amount.

The next problem was where to store the grain until transport and a buyer could be organized.

As there was no shed space available in Hyden we rang the Kondinin members who were flabbergasted. They hadn't even contemplated such a response and were somewhat embarrassed by the outcome. However, they agreed to turn out next morning and hopefully find a suitable shed to store the grain. Fortunately a local business man had a large shed that was empty and not needed for a while. Because both trucks were needed for work on Monday morning we had to get the loads off on Sunday morning.

The following weekend we went out again

in different directions until the whole district had been covered and two more truckloads of grain had been donated.

The Kondinin members decided to do it the easy way. They just rang the farmers in their area and asked them to donated some of their seconds of grain and bring their donations into town and they collected about 15 bags all told. The guys from Kulin had a similar responce

As a result of all this hard work, a new van was procured and the old dodge ambulance was earmarked for Hyden , much to the dismay of other centres who thought that they should have priority. However Hyden was another 40 miles away from civilization so we won the day.

All this activity surrounding the ambulance caused a couple of problems in Hyden. Firstly, there was the problem of a suitable building to house the van and even more importantly, who was capable of manning it when needed.

Duanes Country Service Centre had a lean-to shed on the main street which needed a new wall, and doors fitting to the front, along with a concrete floor which was to make an ideal home for the Dodge.

A busy-bee was soon organized and with most of the materials being donated the work was done one Saturday afternoon.

The local doctor agreed to help out by holding first aid classes in our C.W.A. rooms with the hope of training a suitable driver or two.

As it turned out, around 24 students presented themselves for training and most completed the course successfully although only a couple were ever likely to become ambulance drivers.

Whilst we were only about half way through the course the ambulance was needed urgently for a serious road accident at Marshes cross roads which is about 14 miles east of the town and in the opposite direction to the hospital. The accident was attended very successfully and competently by some of the first aid class members, and the patients were taken good care of, but that's another story in itself.

Chapter **25**

ROAD ACCIDENT

Our little town had at last received its first ambulance, an old but very serviceable Dodge 114, but unfortunately no one in the area had the necessary qualifications, i.e. a senior first aid certificate and a 'B' class licence to drive it.

The local doctor willingly agreed to travel out on a weekly basis from Kondinin to conduct first aid classes in our town, provided sufficient people were interested.

The notices were duly posted and the grape vine stirred into action and the word quickly got about. As a result, around about twenty-five eager citizens turned out each week and all of them stayed the course to proudly earn their certificates.

Unfortunately, no-one told a couple of contractors from Perth that we were not quite ready for them because we were only about half way through the lessons when they ran into a local farmer at an intersection some 14 miles east of town. As all three were badly injured the ambulance was needed urgently.

A local labourer raced the message into town and tried to get some one to help but due to the seriousness of the accident and their lack of training, the first people he approached declined to assist.

When Ray Herring was asked but he had to decline because he was ill himself with a bout of the measles of all things. However, Ray rang me and I agreed to take out the ambulance, trained or not, and do whatever I could to help.

We had a young fellow called Ted Smith working with us who had been a speedway driver, and could handle a vehicle at high speeds and on gravel roads, so naturally I grabbed him and set off to pick up the ambulance.

As we screamed out of the yard into the street we almost knocked over a local housewife who was standing nattering in the middle of the road, as housewives generally do.

Margaret Trant, the lady in particular had

been a hospital nurse for a number years and she agreed to come with us in case she could be of some assistance, even though she was hardly dressed for the occasion. It was a very hot day and Margaret was wearing only the skimpiest of clothing imaginable.

As it turned out she was of great assistance, but not so much for her nursing skills but for her command of the Italian language.

When we arrived at the scene of the smash it quickly became obvious to us that the situation was very serious.

A number of locals were gathered around, including some of our would-be first aiders who, fortuitously, had learned enough already to know not try to move the victims or try to pull them out of the cars. Also they were able to deter others from doing just that and making the injuries worse.

The vehicles were safely off the road and no danger to other traffic, nor were they likely to catch fire or cause further injury if they were left alone.

After listening to the first aiders I carefully, checked their stories and added to them as

I went over the patient's wounds etc. to try and get a full story on their condition and work out the best way to get them out of the vehicles and into the ambulance with out any further injuries.

I was certain that one chap had severe internal injuries, and was bleeding to death but due partly to the severe shock, he had reverted to his natural tongue, Italian, and I couldn't understand a word that he said.

Thanks to Margaret's prowess with Italian we were able to better understand his injuries, and reassure him that we could and would do our best to help him. I realised that we were going to have a mad dash on our hands to transport this young man about 230 miles to Royal Perth hospital before he ran out of blood.

His mate had a badly fractured pelvis and although I was unaware at that time, three cracked vertebrae in his lower spine due to the fact that he had been hit by a loose drum of fuel in the rear compartment. He gave us some warning of this latter injury as he was complaining of severe back pains, thereby warning us to take every precaution when we had to move him and settle him into the ambulance.

With the help of my motley crew and the locals I carefully extracted the patients and loaded them into the ambulance. In those days we didn't have the fancy lifting frames that the ambo's have nowadays so I used my left arm as a splint for their backbones as we lifted them out and lowered them onto the stretchers before setting off for the nearest hospital over fifty miles away.

With my friend Ted at the wheel and Margaret and myself in the rear, we negotiated the gravel section and were rapidly approaching Hyden townsite when a station sedan appeared suddenly travelling in the other direction.

A woman, who I had never met before was hanging far out from the rear window, at great risk to her life and limb waving her arms and trying to stop us.

Ted said "What shall I do Brian"

"You had better stop and see what she wants", I replied.

As soon as we were stopped the woman shouted out, "Do you want my help."

I shouted back, "No thank you we have everything under control."

Then, as we were about to take off again I had a sudden had a thought.

I shouted out "When you get back to Hyden," (about half a mile away), "could you please ring the hospital in Kondinin and tell them that we are on our way and that we have three seriously injured patients."

Whoops! It turned out that the lady was the matron of another country hospital some distance away, and was spending her days off with her family nearby. She was very peeved that I did not accept her offer of assistance and take her along with us.

Apparently, when she arrived back in town she whinged and complained to every body who would listen to her and told them what she thought of me and my stupid, arrogant ways. Due to her indignation, she forgot or deliberately failed to ring the hospital to warn them of our impending arrival.

As we were approaching Kondinin Ted was driving almost blindly because we were heading straight into the setting sun. A car sped past going like the clappers of hell in the opposite direction then suddenly turned around and chased after us although we were going flat out.

When the driver proceeded to flash his lights, Ted said. "What do you want me to do Brian?"

I looked out of the rear window and realised that it was probably the doctor's car that was following us.

"Pull up Ted," I said. "That looks like the doctor's car."

It was indeed the doctor, much to my surprise, and as he opened the rear door of the ambulance, I said.

"What are you doing here doctor. I expected you to be preparing your hospital ready for us."

"That's where I should be but I received a phone call from a lady who had been at the accident scene. She said that it was a sheer pandemonium and no one had a clue what they were doing. She was almost hysterical. She said that you were all running around like chooks with their heads cut off so I raced out to help you."

"Doctor," I said, "Didn't you get a phone call from Hyden, telling you that we were okay and on our way, and that we had three seriously injured patients on board?"

"Certainly not Brian. So tell me, what have you got in here for me."

"That man has a badly fractured pelvis, to say the least. I think he may also have other broken bones as well, maybe vertebrae," Doctor.

"I reckon that this chap has severe internal bleeding, and more serious injuries but I can't be certain. It may just be severe bruising and he is going into severe shock."

"The one on the top bunk is complaining of severe neck pain, so I put a collar on and handled him very carefully and supported his head with sand bags."

"Okay, let me have a look and see how much you've learned"

After examining the patients the doctor said.

"You, have done very well Brian, and I'm inclined to agree with your diagnoses at this stage. We can do nothing here so lets get cracking. Oh! Do you mind if sister Trayning comes with you."

"Of course not Doctor." I replied, "Margaret is

flat out acting as interpreter for one of the men as he can only speak and understand Italian."

"Yes, of course, that's a natural reaction to severe trauma, the patient reverts to his native language." He replied.

At the hospital the doctor asked. "Can you handle a trip to Royal Perth Brian, because that's where these two are going by the looks."

"I'll go and refuel whilst you prepare the patients Doctor, then we can leave as soon as you are ready."

"That's great then off you go. Oh! Margaret, can you go to Perth to act as interpreter for us please."

Margaret answered, "Certainly Doctor, I'll just ring home first to let them know where I am."

Whilst I was away refuelling and checking the van, the hospital nurses had arranged for Margaret to have a quick shower and a change of clothing to something more suitable for the occasion, as she was only scantily clad because it had been a very hot day. The staff managed to find a more suitable outfit for her to wear from their own wardrobes.

After checking the two men and cross

matching the blood, the doctor called me back in and announced that he had organised for the "Flying Squad;" a crack police escort, and a doctor, to meet us at the shell roadhouse in Brookton. They would have the necessary supply of blood with them for the transfusions.

As we were preparing to leave the telephone rang and the doctor said to me, "Brian, you'll have to manage without me as I am needed here but I'll send the sister with you so that you can concentrate on your driving whilst she attends the patients and Ted can get a lift home back home to Hyden. So, good luck mate, you have a long night ahead of you and well done so far."

All went well until we were about twenty miles from Brookton. The sister called out to me through the hatch between the cab and the rear section.

She said, "Can you please go any faster. I'm losing him. He's going blue?"

I answered, "Sorry sister, this old van will only do eighty five miles an hour and the speedo says almost ninety now."

Just about then we caught up to a landrover

travelling at about fifty miles per hour. It had N.S.W. plates on it and the elderly gent at the wheel wasn't at all concerned about me.

The road was a typical country road with only enough bitumen for one vehicle to travel on and to overtake was a tricky manoeuvre at best and downright dangerous at the speed at which I was travelling but I had to get past. The other driver had no intention of making way for me to pass even though I had the flashing lights going and the sirens blaring.

I had no alterative. I had to drive on the gravel shoulder to pass. Even though I blasted him with the Klaxon horns as well, the other driver never gave me an inch, he just continued to drive right in the middle of the narrow bitumen strip as I went past.

Once I was safely past the sister said, "Brian, he isn't going to make it to Brookton. How far is it now?"

I replied, "Only ten or twelve miles now so hang in there sister"

The flying squad had arrived just before us and the roadhouse was closing up for the night. I had to haggle with the owner of the service station to get him to leave his lights on for a few minutes whilst we set up the blood and saline drips. The mean old sod only wanted to get home quickly as it was closing time and be damned to any one else. Only when I reminded him that the ambulance often refuelled at his service station and that it would almost certainly never happen again if he didn't cooperate, did he back down and assist us.

Our patient had made the distance although he was in dire straights by then and would not have lasted much further without blood. We could only hope that the transfusion would buck him up for the remainder of the trip as we still had about eighty miles to go to the city hospital.

When the doctor decided that we were ready to go, I said, "Are we still in a hurry doctor?"

"We certainly are young man. Give it all you can please." Was his urgent reply.

Whilst we were stopped in Brookton our friend from N.S.W. had managed to get ahead of us again and when we caught up to him I thought that the police car would shift him off the road. How wrong can you be? That rotten old man did not give one iota, he just stayed put and we had to get past him as best we could. The road at that point was quite winding and hilly making overtaking almost impossible but the police car pulled along side the landrover and gave him hell on the horns but all to no avail. That pig headed driver refused to stop or give way to either the police car or the ambulance. Fortunately the road was very quiet at that time and we all got safely by.

I almost lost the ambulance descending Karagullen hill. I had miss judged the steepness and the sharpness of the bends as well as the heavy load and I felt that the right hand wheels lifting off the road. There was little I could do at that point except keep my boot hard on the throttle and hope for the best. Once we hit the metropolitan area we found that the police had closed off every major intersection right through to the hospital. I sat on the tail of the police car and we were travelling at eighty five miles per hour all the way along Albany Highway and up to the Causeway into the city centre and the hospital.

Once we arrived at the hospital I alerted the orderlies and we were unloading the patients and discussing their condition when the police driver approached me and said

"Did you get that bastards number, driver?"

"No mate, sorry, I was too busy staying on the road. All I can tell you is that he is from New South Wales."

"Never mind" said the cop "I'll send a couple of our blokes out on motor bikes to meet him, then we'll see if he knows how to stop."

"I had the same trouble with him about twenty miles before Brookton," I said

"Good job you told me, we'll hit him for failing to give way to the ambulance as well as failing to stop for a police car. The boys will have a field day, they'll go through that rig with a fine toothed comb and charge him with everything possible." said the policeman.

After a lovely hot roast dinner at midnight compliments of the nurses dining room at the hospital, I refuelled the van at the headquarters of the ambulance service in Wellington Street and headed for home 214 miles away.

We arrived back at Kondinin without further

incident, and dropped off the sister at the hospital, then Margaret and I set sail for Hyden in the wee small hours of the morning.

As we were travelling along I had a good look at the fuel gauge and realised that we were very low but I thought we would make it home. Not having made the Perth trip before we had no idea how far the ambulance would go on a tank full of petrol, but we were about to find out.

As we were climbing the last hill before the final downhill run into town the old girl spluttered, coughed and then stopped dead. Only another half mile and we could have freewheeled right into town.

I said, "Margaret, we had better push the van backwards onto the shoulder in case some-one comes along and runs into it while I walk into town for some fuel"

We both opened our doors got out and pushed against the doorposts, and I steered as well. Margaret became jammed between the open door and a handy sized prickle bush growing on the roadside. She seemed to be kicking up a heck of a fuss for so little a problem and it was many weeks later that Margaret explained what it was all about.

Apparently, when she had a shower and changed her clothes at the hospital she had somehow lost her own knickers and although she was happy enough to wear borrowed clothes it did not extend to knickers so she went without any. That naughty old prickle bush had had its wicked way with her tender, nether parts and there was very little that she could do about it.

As we walked the mile or so into town we found a tennis ball on the roadside and bounced it between us the rest of the way along the road. Once back in town I grabbed my utility and with Margaret at the wheel set off to rescue the ambulance. A jerry can of petrol made all the difference so I drove the van back to my shop to fill the fuel tank ready for the next trip. We then changed all the bedding checked and topped up all the medical supplies to prepare the van for the next trip before a welcome meal and shower. By then it was time for me to go straight to work for the day.

Chapter **26**

THE DAY OF THE STORM

In the early 1960,s I was working with a great guy called Syd Gibbins at an engineering works at Bassendean where I lived. Syd was very keen on spearfishing and went diving whenever possible and eventually talked me into giving it a go.

He was a member of the W.A. Undersea Club who organised regular outings to the various reefs around Rottnest Island. There weren't many boats available for hire in those days, especially one large enough to carry about 30 divers and all their gear, therefore, we had to take what we could get.

A salesman by the name of Rodney Riding was building a 36 foot boat on his front lawn in Inglewood and whilst that was in progress he took us out to sea once a month on a friends boat called Robina Dhu.

Robine, as we affectionately called her, was an absolute pig. Her owner had built her at home and she was all steel construction and as heavy as hell. When the hull was finished he bought and fitted a Parsons marine engine, which was little more than a Fordson tractor engine of about 50 hp. Had she had three of these engines fitted she would still have been under powered and she was capable of about 4 knots in a flat sea and much less in a lumpy sea. Robine was not built for comfort either and was very austere in her interior design and décor but she was all that we had so we gladly made do.

Unfortunately lack of power and speed were not her only vices because she was a brute to handle and wicked to ride in. She seemed to think that she should have been a submarine and often behaved like one. Even in a smooth sea, Robine would duck her bow to starboard, dip it down, swing it across to port and then rise up again, back over the top and down again. This mode of action is often referred to as corkscrewing, for obvious reasons, and is very uncomfortable to say the least. As a result of all these design faults all but the very best of crew members became violently seasick. Many an experienced sailor would succumb to her pleasure still swearing blindly that he never got seasick.

The skipper Rod, and myself, were two of the select few that were immune to her wickedness and loved every minute of it in spite of the lack of speed. However, we were all looking forward to the launch day of Rods new boat which was a 36 footer of New Zealand design with a fully flared bow and timber construction. The flare on the bow was so complete that the foredeck was semi-circular, making her a great sea boat, we hoped.

One day as we lay at anchor off the Roarers reefs which run southwards from the east end of Rottnest Island; out westwards of the stragglers reefs, Rod came up to chat with me about his new boat.

I was sitting on the cabin roof scanning the ocean with a powerful pair of binoculars as it was my turn to keep watch over the rest of the club members as they moved around the reefs.

As we talked Rod said, "Syd reckons you are a trained diesel engineer Brian, so I thought I might take the opportunity to pick your brains if that's okay."

"Sure it is "I replied, "I suppose this is about your new boat, Rod."

"Yes, I am a bit bogged down you see, I'm not very mechanically minded and I really need some help from now on. The hull is ready for the motor, transmission, and steering etc. but I don't know what to do first. The real problem is that I am running out of money and I have already mortgaged all we own and more so I can't pay for your services; all I can offer is unlimited use of the boat once it's ready. I can see you like fishing and I would love to show you all about deep sea line fishing if you're interested. I have plenty of fishing gear and I know this coast like the back of my hand so I can guarantee you plenty of good times."

"Rod," I replied, "I can never refuse a challenge and this is right up my alley. What say I come over next weekend and have a good look around the boat to see if we can work out a plan of attack?"

"That's great, mate, I'll give you my address and you can come over when you're ready."

"Hey, Rod, I am on permanent night shift at the moment so would it be alright if I wander over during the week whilst you are away so that I can spend some time aboard and get a feel for it first hand without any distractions."

"That's a really good idea, Brian. Feel free to come over anytime you like, I'll tell Margaret to expect you. You can bring Sandra over as well if that's ok."

So, the bait was cast and I became hooked forever. During the next week I spent a good many hours on the boat with tape measure and square etc… In fact I went there each day and finally on the Friday I set off on an expedition around town. I ended up in one of a number of wrecking yards searching for the parts that I might need.

My search did not yield what my heart desired, a fully equipped marine engine, but enough ideas to set my brain working on a solution. The yard specialised in wrecking heavy duty vehicles such as trucks and buses and contained a number of possibilities.

As Rod had returned from a country sales

trip on Friday evening, I went around to his home on Saturday with a few vague ideas and one interesting proposal.

Leaving Sandra with Margaret, to talk about cooking and domestic handicrafts like knitting and sewing, I took Rod to the outskirts of the city to where I had found the truck wrecking yard called Soltogio Bro's.

I introduced Rod to the man that I had been talking to the day before and explained my intentions to them both.

The only diesel motor in the yard that came anywhere near to my requirements was fitted in an old Perth transport commuter bus.

The engine, in fact, was a 6LW. Gardner and it was in an old wrecked MTT. Bus chassis.

The salesman assured us that the engine, at least, was in top condition and had been faithfully maintained right up to the demise of the vehicle.

He was able to produce some batteries to fire it up and test it out as best we could in the yard.

I said to Rod, "The motor runs very well with no sign of smoke and to start up like that, first pop, even though it has stood around for a very long time is a good sign. A handy feature of these Gardner engines is that they are fitted out with decompressors so that they can be hand cranked in an emergency, making it great for marine use."

"I think you might have come up with a winner here mate," said Rod "how much do they want for it?"

"Look," I said, "Before you get too excited we have a number of problems to sort out."

"I can't see too much to worry about with a motor as good as this, Brian," he said, "lets find out how much we can get it for and then we can start getting it out of the chassis and into the hull. You see I have to get the boat going very soon or the bank will be on my back,"

"It is nowhere near as simple as that, Rod, there are a number of things that we need to check out first."

"What could we possibly need to worry our heads about, it looks perfect to me," he said.

"Well, first of all we have to consider the sheer size of it in relation to the hull and, of course the weight. These Gardner motors are great but when we get it out of there you'll realise how big it is. I reckon that by the time we get it equipped it will weigh about 2 and a half ton and because of the depth of the sump it will need to go a long way forward to clear the keel. Also we need to consider how we can hook it to the drive shaft with fore and aft gears, convert the exhaust and fit an oil cooler and inter cooler. Apart from all that, how the hell are we going to get it home and up into the boat."

"Okay, then where do we go next, mate, I'm in your hands?"

"I suggest we have a long talk with these guys and see what happens after that Rod."

To cut a long story short, we managed to bargain a few fishing trips to get a good deal, with the wreckers happy to deliver the motor and lift it into the hull for us. They also offered us the use of the yard to find and modify whatever parts we needed to make up a marine type of gearbox and make the engine more suitable for use in the boat.

As a result of these talks we ended up with an old clutch and gearbox from a Fodern truck and converted it to give us a 1-1 reverse gear ratio as well as a forward one. The end result was a very large power unit of dubious value, but hopefully adequate for our needs, and certainly much more suitable than the one in Robine.

The engine was eventually installed and proved a great success in spite of it's size and it ran beautifully and very economically.

Once the motor was installed there was a frantic rush to build the rest of the engineering parts and the super-structure. Another trip to the wrecking yard yielded an old worm and wheel steering box out of a huge truck to connect the rudder to the helm. Finally we could see the end of the ordeal. Everyone pitched in with renewed vigour and thoughts of the happy days ahead.

One morning as I was working on the boat, Margaret, who was not very happy about the boat because the house was mortgaged to it, brought me some morning tea as she usually did. This day she gave me some toasted rolls with some vile, black stuff on them. They tasted awful, "yuck!"

When I got home I said to Sandra jokingly "I know Margaret doesn't approve of the boat but it's not fair to feed me rat poison for morning tea."

Sandra was aghast and she said "What? Margaret would never do anything like that, she thinks the world of you for helping out, are you sure?"

"All I know is that it tasted like hell and I threw it in the dust bin." I said.

That weekend Sandra asked Margaret, "What did you give Brian with his tea the other day, he said it tasted like rat poison."

Margaret was appalled at the very idea that she might harm me, or anyone else for that matter. Then she suddenly burst out laughing and said, "Does Brian like Vegemite, Sandra?"

"No, he certainly does not, is that what you gave him, Margaret."

"Well, I can't be sure but I may have done, I thought everyone loves it."

"No wonder he thought it was rat poison, he hates it." Sandra stated.

When the launch day arrived everyone was agog with the excitement and drama of the event.

We went for a trip to Bell Brothers the week before to arrange lifting and transporting. A crane and low loading semi trailer had arrived early in the morning as arranged and the drama began.

The assessor from Bell's had estimated the total weight at about 8 tons, and nothing would convince him that it weighed almost 12 tons, even though we showed him the designers plans.

The crane that he sent was only 10 ton and the driver set the drags and clutches to lift 8 ton as ordered.

When he applied the lift through a massive spreader bar to the cradle and slings around the hull, the clutches held and up she went.

He lifted it about a foot and stopped to check out the trim; BANG, down went the keel back onto the stumps as the winch brakes could not hold the extra weight.

The Driver jumped down and swore vehemently, "Who the hell worked out the weight of this bloody boat?" he shouted out.

We told him what had happened at the assessment and again we produced the plans, telling him that the motor alone weighed two and a half ton.

"So you guys reckon she weighs 12 ton do you. You bloody well should have told him, " said the driver.

"We did but he said we were off our rockers, and didn't know what we were talking about. What are we going to do now; get a bigger crane?"

"Like hell, the boss would go mad if I ring him. It would cost too much to bring another crane and it would have to come out of my wages. No all I can do now is screw up the brake and winch clutches to their maximum settings and hope for the best. After all it lifted the weight alright so I'll screw up the brakes to so that they'll hold the weight when I stop lifting, that should do it as they have a big overload factor built into these cranes."

Once the crane was fully adjusted it just managed the lift and the boat was slewed round onto the low loader with no further drama.

We took the boat, MARKSMAN, named after the designer, to the Raffles jetty at Como and prepared to launch her.

The jetty was solid concrete and ideal for the task, but would the crane handle it? The crane was attached and the ropes undone, we would soon know. The lift went fine and the boat was swung out and over the water but it was too close to the jetty and the crane had to lower its mast to get enough reach. This was a very dangerous manoeuvre because the crane cannot lift as much with the jib lowered as when it is higher up. The crane started to topple off the jetty and into the water causing the driver to panic. He pushed the levers forward and dropped the old girl into the drink with a huge splash and a bump as she hit the sand under the shallow end. The crane quickly righted it's self back onto the concrete

Rod and Margaret were on board to christen the boat and the spreader beam made of steel channels dropped onto the cabin roof narrowly missing them both.

It was a very shaky driver who checked out the area with some relief and began to pack up his gear. Meanwhile we set about checking the boat for damage and everything appeared okay. When the driver offered the delivery papers to be signed, I said to Rod, "Write on there that the boat was dropped twice during the operation then if there is a problem we have some evidence to substantiate a claim."

"That's a good idea mate, I will," Said Rod and he did so.

The driver said, "It's alright for you smart arses, it's me that'll get it in the neck when I get back to the depot."

"It wasn't your fault, you are only a driver not an assessor," We said, "And we'll back you up if there is any trouble."

Once in the water it was all plain sailing, or so we thought. There was no apparent damage and the boat was christened with a bottle of champagne as is the custom.

We set sail for our maiden voyage all agog with excitement and pride in our achievement.

All went well until we tried to change direction. When Rod swung the wheel we went the wrong way and hit the shallow mud bank for which the Swan river is well known. I went below to check the steering mechanism and found the lever on top of the rudder shaft at a peculiar angle.

Back on deck I said to Rod, "When you guys fitted the cabin and deck planks under the stern did you need to disconnect the rudder shaft."

"Yes" he replied, "we needed to fit some of the timbers under it and the easiest way was to remove the arm. Why are you asking. Is that the trouble ?"

"Yes" replied, "It's been fitted upside down and at 180deg. From where I had it"

"Art and old Tom did that, I remember them swearing a lot and calling you all kinds of rude names because it wouldn't line up, but eventually they got it working. What can we do to fix it, or will we manage for now."

It'll be very awkward to handle", I said, "Worse than old Robine ever was, but it's not like driving a car there's plenty of room out here."

This however, proved to be the understatement of the year, because it was almost impossible to get the direction right and we were all over the place with little hope of ever being able to dock the old girl.

Finally I said to Rod, "If we sail close to one of the shallow banks and let her drift onto it, one of you can put on a mask and snorkel and dive down below to hold up the rudder so that I can refit the lever. It'll sit on the lower bracket and not fall out or leak water whilst I reset the upper arm."

"A good job for Art, he stuffed it up," said Rod. "Hey, Art, get your arse up here we have a job for you."

When his brother appeared he said, "You stuffed up the rudder so get your mask and snorkel on, you just volunteered to hold up the rudder whilst Brian fixes the steering."

Art made a rude gesture at his brother and prepared to get wet. With Art holding up the rudder it was easy to change the arm over and fix the problem.

Once the steering was fixed all went well and that was the start of many fantastic years on the ocean, fishing every weekend, weather permitting.

Whilst we were building the boat we copped a great deal of flack from so-called experts; ("X", being the unknown quantity, and spurt being, merely a drip under pressure) about the way we were going about it.

Some said the glue that we used on the sheets was all wrong and that the sheets themselves were too thin. Others said that we hadn't put anywhere near enough nails in the joints. According to these, so called, experts even the nails were the wrong type. Gosh we were doomed to failure the first time that we ran a rough sea. The only place that we would end up was the bottom of the ocean.

In spite of all these negative vibes Marksman seemed to fulfil our every wish and she was a very comfortable ride, and a dream to handle. She relished a lively sea with a strong swell and rolled easily over the waves at a steady eight or nine knots. Even a following sea pushing on her stern didn't worry her and she never showed any sign of broaching sideways.

One weekend in October we were having lunch at sea whilst the fishing was a bit slow when Rod said to me, "You have heard me talking about Cervantes, Brian. The fishing up there is fantastic and I've been thinking about the long weekend next month. I reckon we can easily round up about 8 passengers to help pay for the fuel, and if you and Art want a part of it, we could leave on Friday and return on Monday. What do you think about that, eh?"

"That sounds great, I'm in for sure, are we

taking the dogs mate?" I asked him.

"You bet, we've tried leaving them before and they always end up coming. Midge reckons that he owns the bloody boat anyway."

"Have you any idea how long the run up will take," I asked.

"Yea well, it's about one hundred miles or so by sea so we should make it in about ten hours depending on the wind and sea. If we set off at the right time we'll, hopefully anyway, have a good strong sea breeze up our tail and that might save us a lot of time and fuel."

So, preparations were made, a full crew signed on and as soon as we were organised, we set sail for Cervantes on the Friday.

The weather was in fact perfect for the trip with a following sea and a brisk sou-wester helping us along our way and we were all ecstatic. The two dogs, Midge and Tiny were soon asleep at our feet, having run themselves ragged around the decks in sheer delight at being allowed to come.

When we arrived off Cervantes Rod explained the difficulties of negotiating the passage into the bay, which consisted of three dog-legs and the only way to tell where to change direction and pick a new course was to line up various features on the mainland and the islands in the bay.

The channel was difficult at best and impossible in a heavy, following sea or in darkness when, of course, the markers were not visible.

Once inside we anchored up in shallow water near the beach and after a meal we set out to catch baitfish to bait up our setline. We needed about seven dozen small fish to go on the setline but they were very slow and most of the crew went to bed leaving Art and myself to catch the remainder.

We were snacking on pieces of homemade meat pie supplied by Margaret who was a great cook and looked after us well. Our fishing lines were lying across our legs unattended when my line suddenly took off at a great rate of knots. I eventually subdued the fish and landed a good sized school shark on a tiny herring rig.

"I'm going to put out one of my heavy lines," I said to Art, "there are probably more of those sharks around."

"That's a good idea mate you never can tell," He replied.

I baited a heavy line and tied it lightly to the after cleat throwing the sinker out sideways and settled back down to catch more bait.

When we had sufficient bait for the next day we packed up to go to bed.

Art remembered the heavy line and said, "Did you pull in your big line mate or is it still out."

"Good job you thought about it Art, I'll need it tomorrow for sure," I said.

When I went to pull the line in it wouldn't move at all, and as I heaved away the boat swung round on the anchor. "I must have hooked a rock or something, Art" I said, "Its really stuck".

"Never in a fit," he replied, "there are no rocks around here, only sand."

"Maybe some-one has dropped an anchor or mooring out there," I replied.

"I suppose that's possible, do you need a hand? "he asked.

"Not yet, but I might before I get it in, Art. If the worst comes to the worst I'll tie it off and dive down tomorrow morning and unhook it, the water is only a few feet deep."

"Okay mate see how you go."

In desperation I put one foot up on the rail, took hold with both hands and heaved away like mad. The strain slowly swung the big boat around on the anchor line until the boat was in line with my hooks and I put on maximum pressure something had to give and give it did.

The brute on the end of my line shook it's great head and tried to swim out to sea.

After a battle royale which woke up all the crew, I pulled the monster along side the boat. Then the fun started to lift a huge fish aboard. It took six of us to heave the brute up onto the deck. It was a massive wobbegong shark about nine feet six inches long. This was the biggest fish that I have ever landed. When filleted and cut up the sale of the fillets paid the fuel bill for the weekend, which was a good start.

At daybreak we set off out to sea again to set about some serious deep-sea fishing on the rising face of the continental shelf, and later on the reefs nearby.

Rod hadn't exaggerated the fishing and we were soon very busy hauling in some very large Dhufish, pink snapper, kingies and queen snapper. It was a very tired and happy crew that settled onto the bunks, that night and the next one.

On the Monday morning we were out of bed before day break to enjoy a nice breakfast of fresh fish fillets ready for the long trip home.

The boat was made shipshape ready to leave at first light, as we had to pull up the set line, clean any fish and stow away the line before leaving the sheltered waters of the bay.

Once the line was aboard we set off for the passage out of the bay and I was still gathering up the set line into it's box as we entered the last leg of the passage. I was working on the fore deck and I could feel the swells starting to build up and, also, there was a stiff breeze tugging at my coat causing me some concern.

I went into the wheel-house and said, "Have you heard the latest forecasts Rod, there's a stiff breeze from the sou-west, not a nor-easter as forecast."

"Hell! Are you sure mate," He replied, "the forecast was for a lovely trip home with light nor-east winds and a flat sea."

"Yea, I know that, I just wondered if they had updated it."

"Take the wheel and hold this course whilst I check it out," he said.

Rod made his way onto the fore deck stood there for a few moments then came back inside with a worried look on his face.

"Hell mate," he said, "Your quite right, that's a strong blow and sou-westerly as well."

So saying, he went back into the cabin and asked the others if anyone still had the radio on.

"Yes, Rod some one answered what did you want."

"Have you heard a weather forecast lately?" Rod queried.

'It was on a few minutes ago and it was the same as before, low sea, low swell and winds light nor-nor easterly. Why are you asking." Someone called out.

"It's blowing like a bastard outside the bay, and it's a sou-westerly with the sea strong and lifting."

"What are we going to do, then?" Said another voice."

"I don't know yet, until we are surer, we'll have

to sail out further off shore to give us plenty of sea room and see what happens," said Rod.

"There was a strong sea breeze over night", Art called out, "Maybe it's hung on a bit longer than they reckoned and it might drop away now it is daylight."

"I hope to hell that you're right, but I don't think there's much chance of that happening," Rod replied, "There's too much power in the sea by the feel of it."

So there we were out at sea with no hope of turning back through the passage. There were only two serious options at this moment; try to reach Fremantle and home, or turn tail, and head for Dongara and Port Denison with the wind and sea on our tails and lay up there until the storm abated allowing us to sail home later in the week.

As we all had reliable jobs to get back to, the second choice was only ever going to be a desperation measure so we headed out to sea and turned the bow southward and home, if we were lucky.

As we were still pretty sure that the wind would die down soon and the forecast would prove to be correct, we moved out about fifteen miles off shore, instead of our usual five miles to give us plenty of sea room in case we needed it later and headed home.

We soon had to reduce speed to half engine revs. in an attempt to minimise the pounding of the waves on the hull. All the criticism that we had received about our boat building expertise was now coming back to us with a vengeance. Would the glue prove to be adequate and would the nails hold the sheets in place, and were the sheets strong enough? Eleven people's lives depended on us having got every one of those features correct. At least I had every faith in the Gardner motor to get us home safely so long as we stayed afloat long enough.

In fact, would the hull hold together at all if this sea lived up to it's awful promise, and was the boat good enough to stay upright no matter what the weather threw at it? We were already taking a battering on the starboard quarter and the waves were increasing rapidly.

Rod and myself took hourly turns on the wheel which was quite exhausting to say the least. It was almost impossible to hang onto the spokes at times and very hard to stand up. When we were not at the wheel we stepped out of the rear door in the lee of the after cabin and roped ourselves to the railings on the after deck. Standing behind the aft cabin was the only place to see if there was any shipping or other obstacles around us but it was very uncomfortable. Just standing up was almost impossible and there were tons of water cascading over us. By now there was so much green water flooding onto the windscreen that we had no visibility at all and could only rely on the compass for direction.

One of our main concerns was that the compass could only tell us the direction that the boat was heading but would not allow for the amount of drift into the shore due to the pushing of the waves and the gale force winds. It would be easy to drift onto the shore because we had no way of reckoning the amount of sideways movement or our actual position relative to the shoreline, which we couldn't see at all.

As we tipped over the tops of the waves the

propeller came out of the water and we hurtled head long down into the next trough. Oh god, was this the way it would end, straight down, nose first, to Davey's locker on the sea bed. Maybe the designer was used to these sort of seas around New Zealand because each time we came to a jarring halt at the bottom and banged our heads on the cabin roof as we started to lift again only to wonder if the Gardner had enough power to lift a twelve ton boat up that awful slope to the top of the next wave with only about half the revolutions needed.

At about 10.30 am. one of the passengers called out, "Hey, Rod, we have just gotten an update on the weather. They reckon that we are in for gale to hurricane force winds all day and they will be from the South West. The seas will be huge with swells and waves in the range of 30-40feet."

Rod said, "Cheer us up, why don't you? We already know all that, the waves are every bit as big as that and much more at times. That leaves us with the two choices as before. We can either run with the weather or battle onward for home. What do you guys think?

Even if we try to run with the sea we would likely take some of these massive waves on to the decks and be swamped."

After a long and hearty discussion it was decided that we had enough faith in the boat and our boating skills to get her home to Fremantle. The continuing problem was how to gauge our distance from the shoreline, and it was only going to be a wild guess at best, but that was all we had. Even from the after deck we could see nothing but huge waves of solid water and storm-racked sky, in fact we never saw anything at all to help us plot and steer a safe course home. All that we could do was to keep the compass setting at around southwest, instead of due South, which should allow for the sideways push of the elements and keep us away out of reach of those awful reefs that were awaiting us ashore. Just to hold any course at all was almost impossible because when the big rollers hit us the compass needle would swing off up to Ninety degrees before coming back on course again.

Art volunteered to man the water pump below in the cabin, and keep a wary eye on the hull whilst Rod and I nursed the old girl homeward. At least it was nice and warm in the cabins even though it was very rough. Most of the passengers appeared to be asleep on the bunks and seldom moved or even spoke, or maybe they were too busy praying to care. Fortunately, they like us, were all well seasoned seafarers and no one got sea sick all day

The waves were so enormous that most of the time we had to look vertically above our heads to see the sky and they would push us off course about 90° each time they ran into the fore end of the hull. They were so huge that as we rolled over the top the propeller would sit clear of the water and the motor would rev. it's head off until it bit the next wave. When we dropped into the hole between the waves all we could see were solid walls of water both fore and aft.

We all asked ourselves, is this the end? How will our families cope if we don't make it home. If only we had listened to others and put in the extra nails would it have made the difference? Will the old girl stand up to this terrible beating for hours and hours until we reach safety? Was there anything that we could have done to make her stronger? This was going to be a very long day because at this speed we were not making much headway at all and in fact, we might even be going backwards for all we knew.

We pounded away steadily all day but we had no idea where we were and we were not at all sure that we were making any headway. Our main concern was to maintain sufficient sea room between the boat and the shore and keep enough revs on the motor to make some headway and not be pushed back on to the shore reefs. It was impossible to know how fast we were actually travelling, let alone in which direction.

From in the wheelhouse we had no idea where we were so the observation point on the rear deck was critical. Between the bigger waves there was sometimes a lull, allowing us to see around, but all we ever saw, thank goodness, were the waves, water and spray, and the inky black storm clouds racing across the sky. It is impossible to describe the terrible roaring of the wind and waves making it necessary to shout at each other to be heard above it.

It was at about 3.30pm. that Art appeared from below. He called out to us, "Hey guys, the bulk head across the front of the fore cabin and the deck has parted. The bolts have all snapped and we are taking a lot of water through the gap. I've hooked up that big centrifugal pump that Brian set up the other day and the water level seems to be just holding. If the big pump can't hold the level we'll have to run with the sea."

"Yea, right, thanks Art," said Rod, "Keep in touch at all times and let us know how you're coping, O.k."

I called out to Art, "Hey, have a look in the big tool box there should be three or four heavy "G" clamps in there. Maybe we can clamp the two beams together and close the gap."

We found the clamps and fitted them to the beams which reduced the water flow but wasn't enough to stop it altogether. Arthur remembered that there was a quantity of oakum packing string stored beneath one of the bunks. I had to leave Rod on the wheel whilst Art and I rolled up the oakum and hammered some of it into the gap with a bolster (a large flat chisel). We never managed to stop the water entering but we managed to reduce it to a manageable flow, which the pumps could handle. We screwed up the 'G' clamps in sequence whenever possible. When we could do no more I went back topside to take over the wheel.

We held our course as best we could and it became dark very early that afternoon. The boat was coping well at about a third of the normal revolutions but the sea showed no sign of easing. By about 4 o'clock it was pitch black, further adding to our anxiety but we could not see anything outside anyway.

We should have been in Fremantle harbour by around 5.30pm. but we were still miles away and no one knew where we were or if we were safe. The wife of one of our passengers became so worried because we hadn't returned that she went to the harbour master to report that we were overdue. He told her not to worry too much yet, as we would certainly be very late returning because of the weather.

The lady pestered the harbour master to do something and finally insisted that he send someone out to find us.

"Look here, madam," He said, "If they are still out there they will have to look after themselves. It would be madness sending a boat out there now, we could pass within a few feet of each other and not know. We could even run straight into them and sink their boat."

"If they are not in by daylight we'll mount a sea and air search until we find them. They may even have found shelter somewhere and be curled up snug and warm in their beds waiting for daylight." He surmised.

"Look, Please remember this, it's very important. If they turn up or you hear from them, you must ring us immediately so that we know they're safe. I am very sorry but that is all the help I can offer at the moment. This storm is creating all sorts of problems for us as well as you, but if I could help I surely would, O.K." And that was his final words on the subject.

Rod had been taking his turn on the wheel and I moved back inside to take over from him at about 8o'clock and as I approached he pointed to the compass and said to me, "I've changed course, Brian. Those of us who are used to this coast at night have been studying the lights on shore. We think that the nearest lights are Scarborough, and that bright glow down south is Fremantle, so I've decided to head straight for them We are nearly home now so just stay on this course until we know for sure. At least now that it is dark we can see the lights on the coast"

At sometime during my shift on the wheel, I saw a monstrous wave roaring toward us and I turned the wheel to full lock to minimise the shock as it hit us. I must have over reacted because we burst through the wave and turned our nose out to sea. That's when I received the shock of my life.

A beam of light swept across the storm clouds on the horizon. I was still too far away to see the actual light only the sweep of the beam on the inky black sky, but as luck would have it I noted the approximate compass reading and was able to return and have another look. I looked at my watch to time the flashes and this could only be the centre light on Rottnest Island. We were only just close enough to see the beam so we still had a long way to go, about 30 or so miles at best maybe, and the lights on shore were more probably Yanchep not Scarborough.

I was so pleased that I wanted to walk over the water and kiss that blessed light. No wonder the ancient mariners thought so much of the light houses. It was just so good to know exactly where we were that I can't begin to describe the feelings of relief that flowed though my body and mind at that moment.

I stayed on a course straight for that blessed light until Rod came back to relieve me and I could sense the worry and stress slipping away from me. However it was not over yet. There was still a heck of a lot of water between us and safety and the storm hadn't eased at all. If the boat let us down even the strong swimmers amongst us would stand little chance of reaching safety. However we would soon be partly in the lee of the island and should get some protection. The good news was that we were about 15 miles off shore as planned with plenty of sea-room to manoeuvre.

When Rod took over the wheel he was about to admonish me for changing course when I pointed out at the light, grinning like a

Cheshire cat with several tails.

He stared at the light in total silence for some time then, as he threw his arms around me in a deathly hug, he said, "How the hell did you find that me old mate? That's the loveliest thing that I've seen for a hell of a long time. That's the centre light at Rotto we must have been heading straight for Eglington Rocks near Yanchep. Thank God and the guy who invented those bloody lights."

"We'll stay on this course until we can see Bathurst Point lighthouse. By then we'll be in the lee of the island and maybe get some degree of protection from this damned sea. From then on we'll be able to relax a bit and it should be possible to pick out the navigation lights of the Kwinana channel"

"Yea, that sounds good to me, I'll be so glad to get off this bloody ocean for a while, Rod. Hows Art going down below? I had better get down there and let him know about the light. They'll all be glad to know where we are."

When I told the crew about the light they each in turn, shook my hand and thanked me for saving their lives. I said, "Don't bother thanking me, I wasn't concerned with saving your lives only my own and it's still too early to crow about that. Anyway we still have some seven or eight hours to go at best before we get in."

On a later shift on the wheel I spotted the light at Bathurst Point only about three miles away and I could feel the waves easing as we sailed into the shelter of the island. The long row of red and green lights on the channel markers, showing the big ships the road into Fremantle and Kwinana were now coming into view.

When Rod took over the wheel again there was no longer any reason to stand watch on the after deck so I collapsed onto one of the bunks to get a short nap before we docked at Aquarama, the marina where the old girl normally lived between voyages. I awoke to a steady shaking of my shoulder and looked up into Rod's smiling face.

"Crikey mate, I thought you were never going to wake up," He said.

"Where are we," I said rising to a sitting position on the mattress. Is it my turn on the wheel again. Sorry mate but I just died?"

"No mate your far too slow for me, we're tied up in the pen mate, we're home." He replied.

As we left the boat and set off along the jetty we had a good laugh at the dogs. They were trying to walk ahead of us but the decking seemed to be moving around and they were in danger of wobbling off into the river. Midget spotted a mooring post and decided to relieve himself but he couldn't stand up on three legs and finally fell in a heap with a stunned look on his face.

Once ashore and after many hugs and kisses the women told us of the phone calls to the harbour authorities so we called them immediately. By then it was 2.30am. and the duty officer was amazed that we had returned safe and sound and his first words were "Where the hell have you guys come from, we expected you to have laid up somewhere, you must have had a hell of a trip. I'm glad you are back though as all the other boats are accounted for and now I can relax until the end of my shift. Well done guys that must be one hell of a boat. You must be very pleased with yourselves"

How right he was, and terra firma really felt

good even though we had a fair amount of strife standing up in the welcome, and well earned shower. The walls of that small bathroom at Rod's place just refused to stay still.

I have been asked several times if I have ever been tempted to go deep sea fishing since that awful day. The answer of course is, "NOT UNTIL THE NEXT WEEKEND BECAUSE WE HAD TO WORK ALL WEEK."

Chapter 27

LIVING ROUGH

Whilst I was working as a country mechanic, I spent a good deal of my time travelling around the farms in our area to service and repair farm machinery and tractors.

We had recently sold a new chamberlain tractor to a farmer whose property was very remote, in fact it was outside the vermin fence in the northern wheat belt and had none of the services which we townies take for granted, such as water, refrigeration and electric power, and he had to make do with more primitive facilities in his home.

The new tractor was now due for an after market service and it was my job to travel out there and attend to it but I was always a little reluctant to visit this farm because, although the farmer was very nice, the facilities left a lot to be desired.

The farmer was a single man and he lived alone in what was no more than a garden shed. When it rained he collected the water off the roof into a galvanised tank, and when that was empty he had to bring water from a soak which was about half a kilometre away so he used it very frugally and not much of it was used for washing, either himself or his dishes.

The wall at one end had been cut away so that he could build a crude fireplace on the outside with rocks from nearby paddocks. This fireplace provided his only source of hot water and was his only means of cooking and heating. The table had been built out of old pine boxes that had once contained machinery parts and stood on a bare dirt floor. There were saucers of water to stand the table legs in to slow the ants down but the flies had been allowed to roam free.

He was a very friendly chap and was always ready to share his meagre supplies and humble abode with anyone who happened to visit his property.

There was no refrigeration not even a

kerosene fridge and most of the food was left out for the benefit of the local ants, mice and flies etc., although he had built a sort of cave in a bank of dirt near the doorway which served quite well as a sort of cooler.

Never the less, a meal there was always a decided risk of stomach upsets and other more serious ailments. David must have had guts made of solid cast iron to cope with all this.

Whenever I received a call to visit David and service his machinery I always tried to time myself not to arrive near mealtimes to save the bother and embarrassment of refusing to join in to this form of Russian roulette.

On one occasion though, I was out on the road early and my boss rang through to a previous call and left a message for me to visit David whilst I was in the area and save time and money.

I had taken ample supplies of food with me, and a thermos of tea, so I decided that I would stop at the run through, (a sort of cattle grid) at the vermin fence for lunch. There I could eat a hearty meal in the bush, enjoy the fantastic scenery, flora, and wildlife and I would be too full to eat with David when I arrived at the farm.

As I expected, David invited me in to dine in splendour in his 'castle', so to speak, and he had just sat down to his humble lunch as I walked through the door.

His meals didn't vary very much and today was no exception, it was boiled leg of mutton wrapped in stale bread and generously dosed in tomato sauce. The mutton looked as though it was only a few days old and the remains of the leg were still on the table, even though it was very hot that day.

Naturally David asked me to take part in his simple meal but I pointed out that I had just eaten a good meal because I didn't know that I had to call at his place, where I knew I could get a nice feed.

He persisted with trying to tempt me to eat and I resisted quite firmly. The knuckle end of the joint was facing me and it was alive with blowfly maggots and I was trying hard not to let him see my concern but he noticed my steady gaze and twigged what the problem was and took immediate action.

He said. "Heck mate, you don't want to

worry about them little beggars, I'll fix them in a second."

So saying, he stabbed the joint with a large fork and carried it over to the fireplace and dunked it into a large pot of boiling water for a second or two before returning it to the plate.

"There you are mate, tuck in whilst the going's good." He said.

I pointed out to him once more, that I had eaten already, and he finally gave in, but then he said. "But you'll have a mug of tea with me in a minute won't you mate? I'll make a brew as soon as I finished this."

What could I say? Anyway, what could be safer than a scalding hot mug of tea, even though the mug was badly cracked as I was sure that it would be?

Once David had finished eating he set about the job of making the brew.

"Do you take it black or white, mate", he asked and my reply was

"White, thankyou, and a couple of sugars if you have any."

David then poured the boiling water into the pot and poured out two mugs of steaming hot tea then he dumped a dessertspoon full of powdered milk on top of mine to whiten it. After evicting most of the ants from the bag of sugar, he added the two spoons full that I had asked for.

As I about to take my first sip of this strange brew it suddenly dawned on me as to where he had gotten the boiling water to brew the tea. That's right, Straight out of the large pot on the fire that had been used to expel the maggots.

Somehow I managed to drink the tea so as not to offend him, and suffered no after shocks. I strengthened my resolve to time my visits more carefully in the future to avoid the risk of serious harm and I decided that I would train my taste buds to manage without milk, and maybe sugar, in my tea from then on.

Chapter 28

THE WINE FLAGON

I was working as a country mechanic far out in the southern wheatbelt, when I received a call to visit a farm a few miles away to check and repair an old 32volt lighting plant. This was a common occurrence because it played up frequently and the owner had no idea what to check to find even the simplest fault. More often than not it was only corrosion on one, or more, of the many battery terminals that was stopping the flow of current. The plant had 16x 2 volt batteries (32volts)

I had been there so many times that I knew most of it's tricks and could get it going quite quickly without too much drama.

It was mid afternoon when I arrived and it was extremely hot that day, about 114deg. fahrenheit. I always carried a couple of water bags on the utility to keep up the fluids, and prevent dehydration.

I was aware that these clients would scorn such basic fluids in favour of their usual amber fluid or something even stronger, but ice cold water from those old fashioned water bags was the best thirst quencher of all and it occasionally came in handy to top up the radiator of the vehicle.

I was able to sort out the trouble with the lighting plant with very little drama, and I decided to leave the single cylinder lister engine running to charge up the batteries, because they were dead flat.

I was about to leave when it occurred to me that I had better see if I could find Clarie or his offsider Bill and tell them that the plant was fixed and the engine left running. I went over to the old cement brick house and knocked and shouted but the place seemed empty. I decided to go in and leave a note on the table for when they returned. I called out again and walked into the kitchen, and blow me down, there they both were.

There was a large laminex table in the middle

of the room and Clarie was sitting on a chair at one end of the table with his head on his arms, apparently asleep. Bill was at the other end in a similar position, and there was a wine flagon right in the middle of the table with about 1 inch of, what looked like claret in the bottom of it. I gave Clarie a bit of a shake and called out, "Hey Clarie can you hear me? I've fix the lighting plant and I've left it running so don't forget about it, ok."

Clarie managed to grunt something unintelligible in reply so I started to leave. As I reached the kitchen door Clarie looked up with bleary eyes and said.

"Hey Brian, is that you? Don't go yet. Can you start that bloody flagon off again, the bloody thing escaped?"

It seemed that they had been sharing the pleasures of the flagon. One of them would take a swig and slide the flagon along the table to the other, who would also take a swig and return it.

However, eventually one of them had failed to give it a big enough shove, and the damned thing had escaped. It had stopped mid-way along the table where neither of them could reach it, so they had gone to sleep hoping that some kind soul would come and rescue them before they died of thirst or severe dehydration. I said to Clarie, "Hey mate have you ever thought of sitting at either side of the table instead of at each end then the rotten flagon would never get out of reach."

"Clarie looked up at me through his bleary eyes and agreed saying, "Heh, come on Bill shift you arse around didn't you hear what Brian just said. It might save us a lot of pain in the future."

Chapter **29**

THE ROOT RAKE

Bonzer, a local farmer, had just purchased another farm adjoining his own well established property for his son who had just left school. The new property was only partly developed, new land, and still had tons of mallee roots to be cleared away. A Pedrick root rake was needed to sweep them into windrows for collection after the plough had pulled them up, so Bonzer went into town to see the dealers in an attempt to find one of these excellent machines, which could no longer be purchased for the manufacturer because they had gone out of business. The firm that had manufactured these excellent rakes at Wagin had fallen on hard times and closed down, so Bonzer needed to locate a good second hand one if possible.

As it turned out, a farmer from Mount Walker, near Narembeen, who was selling his block had approached me only the previous day to ask if I could find a buyer for his rake, which he assured me was in excellent condition. I happened to be in the area later in the day and had a very good look at the rake and assured myself that it was little used and in excellent condition. Further more the price that he was asking was very fair for a rake of such good quality.

I told Bonzer about this machine and as he was very interested in it I arranged a meeting between the two parties for the next day.

I ought to have organized a margin for myself to cover my costs and make a modest profit from the deal but knowing Bonzer as I did I decided to keep right out of the deal, except for the initial introductions and this proved to be a very wise decision indeed.

Since the two farmers had never met each other, I arranged for them to meet at my shop where I introduced them to each other and stood back whilst they agreed on a deal.

Bonzer agreed to buy the machine and a very fair price was negotiated between the two parties.

Bonzer wrote out a cheque in full payment of the rake and the two men shook hands.

As neither of them had any form of receipts or docket books with them I agreed to write out an invoice, and a receipt for the cheque to finalise the deal.

After the other farmer had left, I assured Bonzer that he had pulled off the deal of a lifetime because I knew that the rake was in top condition and was very cheap at the agreed price.

The very next morning Bonzer came into town to see me about the rake deal.

He said "I've stopped the cheque to Dangelo because I've just found out that there's a root rake for sale in a farm clearing sale next Tuesday and I think it may go quite cheaply and save me a lot of money".

I said "Bonzer, are you going back on your deal with Dangelo? What sort of a bastard are you? Thank God I didn't get involved with the deal. My reputation is worth much more than that. You are just a rotten old rogue and I hope you live to regret this day. Hey!!! This other rake, is it the one in Garde and Andrew's sale at north Hyden, because if it is you are a damned fool? The rake in the clearing sale is a heap of junk. It is only fit for scrap metal as it's a B.H.B. rake and they weren't a patch on a Pedrick at best, and that particular rake has had a very long hard life with only the barest maintenance to keep it going. Apart from clearing their own property, they've used it on a contract basis all around the district and it is really stuffed."

Bonzer had the decency to look upset and casting his eyes around in some embarrassment he said, "I'll have to leave things as they are until after the sale now, and if that rake isn't any good I'll clear the cheque and drive up there and pick up my rake the next day."

"You do as you like" I said, "But you'll be sorry if you miss out on the Pedrick."

"No way," He said "He can't sell it to anybody else because we have a signed deal. That rake is mine."

"Don't come crying to me if it all blows up in your face." I said, "Because, once you stopped the cheque, the deal was off and the rake still belongs to Dangelo and he can do whatever he likes with it." and I walked away in disgust.

Bonzer went to the sale only to find out that my valuation and description of the B.H.B. rake was very accurate indeed. The rake had little more than scrap value at best and wouldn't even be worth the trouble to tow it home.

On his way home Bonzer called in at my shop and declared, "I've just phoned the bank and let the cheque go through," he said. "I'm going to pick up the Pedrick tomorrow.

"Good luck" I said "It'll serve you right if it's gone."

When Bonzer got to the farm at Mount Walker the next day the rake was gone but it had a left a very clear and distinctive set of wheel tracks in the sandy soil heading out to the east. Because the wheels of the Pedrick are steeply angled to the ground they leave tracks that are easily followed, so he set off in hot pursuit. After traveling a fair distance towards the east, the tracks turned south at a cross roads and soon turned into a farmer's paddock and headed up hill towards a ridge. The hillside below the ridge had all been windrowed and there was a mountain of mallee roots waiting to be picked up or burned. Apparently the farmer had been very busy with the Pedrick rake over the last few days and the results showed off the prowess of the rake.

An elderly Italian man was working near the ridge tidying up close to the track leading up the hill. Bonzer drove up to him, jumped out of his Landrover and shouting at the old man said, "Hey you, old man where the bloody hell is my rake".

"It's not your rake". Said the man. "When you stopped the cheque the deal was cancelled and mister Dangelo agreed to hire it to us to clear this paddock."

"It's my rake now I've cleared the cheque so I'll take it; where is it, anyway?"

"It's just over this ridge but we're still using it, you can have it when we're finished". Said the old man "Come back on Friday afternoon."

After a fierce argument Bonzer realized that he had been outfoxed and agreed to return on the Friday. He drove onto the ridge to turn round and got a huge shock. His rake was on the down slope in the middle of about 400 acres of heavy, mallee roots It was attached to the rear of a very large Fiat tractor and was traveling at great speed around the paddock, pushing a huge windrow of roots before it. It was obvious to Bonzer that the rake would be a sore and sorry apology of a machine by the time that he got it home, and it would need a thorough, and expensive overhaul before he could use it but he was powerless to do anything about it.

Chapter **30**

AMBULANCE DRIVER

"There goes that damn phone again, as though I'm not busy enough already. I wonder who it is this time," I thought as I walked over to answer it. It was Charlie Walker calling me and he was very upset and anxious by the sound of his voice. Charlie had a large farm about fifteen kilometres from town.

"Is that you Brian," he said, "old Phil has busted his leg, can you bring the ambulance please."

"Sure I can Charlie, I'll get cracking right away, should be there in about a quarter of an hour mate, where is Phil at the moment."

"In front of the shearing shed on the ground" Charlie replied.

"Okay mate, listen carefully. Don't give him anything to drink, just wet his face and lips with a towel or something if he's uncomfortable, and don't try to move him as you'll only make it worse. See if you can rig up some shade over him and keep him cool till I get there."

Knowing Phil and Charlie as I did, I was sure that they would have already consumed plenty of booze today and would probably be the worse for wear anyway, but I felt I had to do my duty and warn them not to give Phil any fluids until the doctor had seen him. They were the sort of guys who sank a couple of bottles of beer, and I don't mean stubbies, each morning, just to get the day started.

"Yea, okay, see you soon." Was the reply as Charlie put the phone down and rushed back outside to attend to his mate.

I drove the van out to the farm and parked beside a makeshift tent Using his cattle truck and a tarpaulin.As I checked my patient I asked him, "Phil, how did you do this? Your leg is definitely broken and pretty bad at that. I have to realign it to get you in the van, so hang on 'cause it might hurt a bit

Phil answered. "I was just walking around, mate and I forgot where I was."

"Oh! Where were you, exactly Phil? I asked.

"On the bloody roof of the shearing shed looking for a leaks and loose nails before we get any more rain." He replied

It appeared that the old bloke, as he said, had literally just stepped off the edge of the roof from where he had been carrying out some maintenance work without any thought for where he was. Hopefully the alcohol in his system was enough to dull the pain until I got him to hospital.

Chapter 31

GOVERNMENT WORKERS

There was a Toyota Hiace work van parked on the edge of the road alongside the street lawn of the farmhouse. It had number plates that showed, quite clearly, that it belonged to a state government department, in fact the public works department, which looked after water supplies and drainage.

Because the area around the town of Burekup was all set out for flood irrigated pastures there was a very deep drainage channel running parallel to the road and about half way between the road and the garden wall. The channel was surrounded by lawn along both sides of the banks and it was the responsibility of the public works department. All maintenance work on the channel and it's steep banks was the duty of the department of works and their employed workers to maintain it in good working order. At this point in time, mid summer, the grass and weeds had overgrown the vertical banks of the drain and would severely impede the water flow if it were not cleaned out. Therefore, a gang of 'workers' had been sent out to remedy the problem, five men in all who travelled around in the Toyota Hiace van nicely equipped for the men's comfort .

I had a contract to mow the lawns around the farmhouse and out to the street on a weekly basis. Although it was scorching hot that day the job still had to be done so I unloaded the mowers and set to work.

This lawn area was one of the largest on my round and it took a long time to cut all the grass and the owner was as fussy as hell. He always checked it after I finished and if every blade of grass was not lying correctly or cut to the correct length as specified he would have a go at me. Each run of the mower had to be the correct width and dead straight until it looked like a cricket ground with, even, dark and light green runs.

I was somewhat intrigued as to what the government employees were up to as there was only one of them outside the van. This one man was up to his shoulders in the channel using a spade to chop at the banks and cut off the weeds back to bare clay before throwing them up onto the bank top. The other men hadn't left the van since I had arrived.

After a fair amount of time the man in the channel climbed out, walked over to the Toyota and got inside it.

Meanwhile, one of the other men got out of the van, climbed down into the channel and took over from his mate. This raised the thought in my mind that the poor men were taking it in turns to have a bit of a dig at the banks whilst the rest of them relaxed in the van out of the heat to keep their strength up.

Sometime later the first man got back out of the van and swapped places with the one who was in the channel. Now this didn't seem like fair play. Why was the first man back in the ditch and not one of the others?

As I was just finishing the main lawn and checking that it was perfect, the same two men swapped places again and therefore raised my curiosity even further. There was sure to be a story here if I could just unearth the details.

After a long cool drink and a dunk in the nearby cattle trough to cool off a bit I started to cut the street lawn and it was when I did a long run alongside the van that I saw the solution to the mystery. The men were sitting in the van playing cards and it appeared that the loser always had to get out and dig the weeds.

I was amazed to find that these men could be so devious, but even more surprising was the fact that two of the men were so stupid, that they didn't realise that they were hopeless at cards and therefore refuse to play. I was quite shocked to realise that my income taxes were going to line the pockets of these devious layabouts. After a little thought I drove up to the public telephone box (no mobile phones then) next to the post office which I had to pass to leave the area anyway. I checked the number of the Office of Works and rang the office doing, as I thought, my public duty. The man who answered the phone informed me that it was a very hot day and maybe that was the best that they could manage in these conditions.

Chapter 32

SPAGHETTI AND MEAT BALLS

Our son, aged about three, had to go into hospital for an operation, and we were feeling a bit guilty about dumping him in there to be operated on, when we hadn't been able to explain fully all the reasons for this, and what was actually going to happen to him without scaring him to death.

We decided to take him out to posh restaurant in King's Park, for his favourite meal of spaghetti and meatballs prior to entering the hospital.

We had just settled at a table to await our meal when Rodney announced.

"I need to go to the toilet daddy."

"Okay, mate." I answered and taking his hand set off for the public toilets nearby.

I didn't realise that he had never been into a male toilet before, apparently he had always gone with Sandra to the ladies toilet and he had never seen a urinal. As he was finishing off, the automatic flush activated and he was amazed to see the waterfall running down the wall.

He jumped back, turned around and ran out of the building. He ran all the way back to the restaurant shouting loudly. When he arrived back at the restaurant he charged through the door shouting at the top of his voice.

"Mammy, mammy, mammy, we did wee-wee in the shower."

Sandra was appalled at this lack of decorum, but there was a dinner convention of eminent doctors at the next table, and one of them turned round with a huge grin on his face and said, "Don't worry about it dear we all have 'em. Bless 'em."

To add to this lack of manners, Rodney proceeded to pick up his spaghetti piece by piece in his fingers, hold it up high, and suck it down into his mouth with a big slurping sound. Sandra was inclined to try, and get him to eat properly, but I said not to worry for once as no one seemed to mind anyway, and they were actually enjoying the whole scenario immensely.

We went in to see Rodney the next morning after the operation and we were expecting him to be pretty sore and sorry for himself and peeved with us for dumping this on him. As we neared the door into the ward we could hear him shouting loudly, "Come on Sister, kick it again."

We were amazed to see that he and one of the nuns were playing football with a balloon in the ward.

Chapter **33**

DRIVE-IN THEATRE

Hyden townsite was so far from Perth that we had only limited access to television, and only the ABC at that, via the repeater station at Mawson tower near Quairading.

Even the nearest theatre, a drive-in, was forty miles away in the town of Kondinin, and up to twice that distance for some of the farmers of the district.

Although drive-in theatres were severely in decline at that time, due partly to the invention of videos, we felt that such an amenity would become a great asset to our little community.

Graham Ford from Merredin, who also owned drive-ins at Merredin and Bruce Rock, owned a defunct theatre at Beverley, about two hundred and thirty kilometres away from Hyden. Graham told us that if we bought his theatre, instead of any one of a number of others on offer at that time, he would be able to provide a constant supply of good films at the right price.

A theatre and films was only a small part of the deal, as we needed a suitable block of land, extensive earthworks and the cost of dismantling, transport and reassembly of the facility.

Then there was the cost of building a brick building for the projection room and toilet facilities with water, power, and drainage. All this began to slide into the 'too hard basket' and most communities would have walked away from the project, but this was Hyden that we were talking about, and this was no ordinary district. We had tackled and completed, successfully, other difficult and impossible tasks in the past and anything, short of a miracle was possible in Hyden and there were a couple of characters around here who would even tackle one of those if they given half a chance.

We knew from past experience that all of the non-technical work could be achieved with a series of busy bees and most of the equipment needed was owned by our local farmers. There were plenty of tractors, bulldozers, loaders, and tip trucks available, so all we needed was someone to organise everything.

There was some vacant land available which surrounded the Mobil roadhouse on the eastern outskirts of our little town and we thought that if the drive-in went there we could use the facilities at the roadhouse to provide snacks and refreshments, thus helping the roadhouse at the same time.

The block of land was very low lying and needed building up by about a metre or so before grading in the car ramps. A busy bee was called for one Saturday and a good number of farmers turned up with a motley assortment of tip trucks and front end loaders to attack the sand pit near Wave Rock, and shift a large amount of it down the hill onto the agreed site, which had been acquired by a nominal payment to council.

A local dam sinking contractor provided a bulldozer and a road grader to level the sand and create the ramps, as the trucks unloaded.

Since I was part owner of one of the local garages I provided free repair facilities during the day to keep this ancient fleet of vehicles on the move, and acted as relief driver to give the farmers a break for meals.

By nightfall the site was ready for the next phase of construction. The site now needed a thick layer of road gravel to stabilise it and make suitable for motorcars to drive on.

There was an adequate supply of gravel nearby so another busy bee was organised for the following Saturday. This was even better attended because the few dissenters could now see that the project just might be a goer, and with the same successful format as last week we soon had a sound gravel surface to work on.

The next phase was a trip to Beverley to dismantle the facility there and begin the colossal task of getting it Hyden and re-erecting it. The following Tuesday was nominated as 'the day'.

On Tuesday morning very early, a convoy of vehicles equipment and men set off for the long trip to Beverley. On arrival with very little organising, the men set to with a will, like an army of ants and started to dismantle almost everything in site. All the underground wiring and the speakers were dug up and the fence pulled down and loaded onto trucks for the long trip home. Fence posts were dug out of the ground and loaded onto trucks. As soon as a truck was fully loaded it set of for home with enough blokes on board to unload it prior to returning to Beverly for another load.

A huge crane arrived from Perth to hold onto the sections of the screen as they were cut away with oxy/acetylene torches, and lowered them onto trucks. The screen had to be cut vertically into three sections to fit legally on the road.

The screen support frames were bulldozed out of the ground along with their massive concrete bases, and laid onto a suitable low loader for the trip to Hyden. Meanwhile a large hole was bulldozed in front of the gatehouse, a wooden famed building set on a concrete base. A tip truck was reversed into the hole and the gatehouse was then slid onto the tip truck in one piece. By the time that the day was over there was only the brick ablution block and projection room left on site.

The crane followed us back to Hyden to help with the unloading and re-erection of the screen. This was by no means easy, as the holes had to line up exactly and a couple of men had to hang on as best they could, some 40feet above the ground ready to fit the bolts back in, whilst the supports were pulled and push around to get them to align properly. Then men with welding experience like Ben Mouritz and Brian O'Donnell had to sit up there with welding hand pieces and a supply of rods to weld the framework back together. Meanwhile other crews were laying cables, installing speakers and erecting the fence. Amazingly these operations all took place with little or no supervision or arguments. Everyone just got on with the job and picked out the next part as soon as they finished the current one. So after two very long days there was only a small amount of finishing off left for the following day.

As soon as the brick building was completed it was all systems "go" for the following weekend. Graham arrived with a large tin trunk full of films. It takes four or five large reels of film for each movie and therefore eight or ten for the whole show and they all have to be run through a re-winder to reverse the direction. As the film runs through the machine it has to be checked and repaired if there are any faults or cracks.

Two projectors are needed to run a film show and get a smooth change over from one reel to the next without the audience knowing about it.

The first weekend we ran two old family movies that are favourites everywhere, and every one loved them because very few of us had ever seen them before, and we had a great turn out.

Over the next few weeks Graham coached me how to run the show on my own, as he was needed at his other theatres. After he was sure that I could manage, he rang to say that the films were coming direct from Perth and I would be on my own for that weekend.

All went well on my solo run and for the next couple of weeks, then one Saturday Graham turned up at the last minute to watch me. He was quite happy with my prowess and he said, "I suppose you think you're very clever now, Brian, but you'll stuff up one night soon, you just wait and see. It'll probably be on a Thursday night when you're engrossed in an "R" movie".

He was correct of course, although it wasn't on a Thursday night that I stuffed up. It was on a Sunday night. I was so rapt in the movie that I forgot to light the next projector, let alone change over the film. It was only when the end of the film was flapping across the screen, and everyone sounding their horns and flashing their headlights that I realised that I had stuffed up. After a few minutes of bedlam, with me tearing around the projection room as though my backside was on fire, I got the third reel running through the projector. I was showing 5 reels of TOM and JERRY cartoons. Boy oh boy do I love "Tom And Jerry cartoons, I could watch them all night. I am afraid that I cannot stand most of the modern cartoons with Starwars themes etc. grotesque animals and vicious, senseless violence. I realise that there always was plenty of violence in Tom and Jerry cartoons; and remember road runner

and that poor old E Coyote, boy did he cop it.
The good guy always won in those cartoons.

Chapter **34**

A COUNTRY PUB AND A POWERHOUSE

The town powerhouse, only a tin shed really, was situated right next door to the local hotel. An absolute marvel in town planning because the single cylinder engines were extremely noisy and could clearly be heard thumping out their tunes all over town. They were a nightmare for any visitors staying the night, especially as we had to shut down the large engine at about eleven o'clock and start the small one to run through the night on light load. The change over procedure was very noisy indeed.

When the town grew and the S.E.C. reduced the price of power, one of the old engines was removed and a very large turbo-charged Volvo was installed to increase output to meet the new demands. The alternator however, had a bad habit of melting it's diode valves on days of high loads and I had to revert to the use of the old engines, even though they were somewhat inadequate by then.

Late in the morning on a very hot day that is exactly what happened and we ran out of power very suddenly. I raced to the shed on my little old Yamaha motorcycle and quickly started the smaller of the old engines and put it on line. The town circuits fortunately were split into three sections and I could only feed one at a time, but with some difficulty. I then tried to start the other motor to help out and it absolutely refused to perform. It was generally very easy to start but not this day. No matter what I tried it steadfastly refused to go, one of the start valves was slightly bent and not sealing properly. I rang the duty officer at the S.E.C. and he came straight away, only a 40 mile trip, and I explained that it appeared to be the diodes that had failed yet again.

He said "There are spare ones in the cupboard, I'll soon have them in whilst you try to get some more power."

I said, "I've looked everywhere for the spare diodes but they aren't in the shed. I was going to have everything ready for you to save time. I'll change to the other circuit now to help keep every-ones fridges cold."

"Right, I'll go and ring the supervisor and see if he knows where the diodes are," He said.

It was so hot in the shed that the sweat was already running freely even though we were wearing only shorts and boots.

"Hey, Brian," he said are those power gauges working okay on the small generator."

"Yep, I think so. Why is that Greg?" I replied.

"Hell it's severely overloaded. It will blow any minute at that rate," he said.

"No, it always runs like that, and anyway if we try to cut it back we wont be able to run any of the circuits at all, so let's keep our fingers crossed and hope for the best. It's been running like that for a couple of hours already anyway." I reassured him.

I tried to change over to the main street circuit but the load was so excessive that it wouldn't hold in and I needed to get the co-operation of the users to reduce their loads until I got it going. I had already alerted every one to cut back as much as possible.

The biggest user was the pub next door, so I went to see the manager/barman and asked him once again, to turn off the big air conditioners until we got back on to full power.

Jack said, "I can't do that, the blokes will go mad."

I said, "Look Jack, the only way that I can let you have some power is if you reduce the load and don't forget, hot drinkers will drink more beer than cold drinkers. You can have cold beer or cold people but not both."

Jack said, "We don't have to put up with this, I'll ring the S.E.C. and complain"

"That's a good idea Jack." I said, "And tell them to bring some bloody diodes with them, and to hurry up. They can work in that oven of a shed and put them in for us."

At that I turned off the air conditioners and left the pub. I soon had the power on and all was sweet, when suddenly a big power surge hit and threw the overloads. I had a fair idea what had happened and ran back into the bar just as the barman was about to turn off the switch to the air conditioners with a guilty look.

Jack said, "It wasn't me. As soon as the power came back on that mob, pointing to a group of drinkers, turned it on again."

"Pull out the plug and tell them not to turn it on again, okay" I said, and left quickly before I was tempted to tell them what I really thought of their selfish attitude.

Once more I switched the circuit and after a few minutes the overload hit again so I went back to the hotel and pulled out the fuses and put them in my pocket. By now the inspector was back and he said, "Guess where the diodes are, Brian."

"Lake Grace would be my first guess," I replied.

"Yep, that's exactly where they are," He said, "The tech. reckoned that the plant had settled down now and we wouldn't need them again."

"That's great "I said, "What do we do now."

"I told him to bring them over here and to hurry up." He replied. "He complained that today is a public holiday, so I read him the riot act. He'll be on his way by now I hope, or else he'll be looking for another job."

"I'm gasping for a drink, I'll go next door and get one for us." I said.

As I set off I realised that the barman probably wouldn't serve me in the bar because I wasn't wearing a shirt so I went around to the beer garden, which fortunately was unoccupied, stuck my head through a small serving hatch and called out to the barman.

"Excuse me Jack" I said "its boiling hot in the powerhouse, please can I get a couple of big bottles and some glasses before we die of thirst. I'll fix you up when we've finished, if that's okay"

"Yea mate of course you're doing a great job, sorry about the air cons, please hurry up and get the power back on these guys are really giving me a hard time" He said.

There were two shearers, straight from the shearing shed sitting at the bar quite near to where I was standing. They were wearing their dirty old black singlets, trousers and shearing boots and I could smell them from the beer garden; it smelt like somewhere between the bottom of a shearing shed and the drafting pens on rainy day, Oh yuk, it was enough to make you sick.

Just as Jack was bringing the beer one of the shearers spoke up.

"Hey Jack, you can't serve him he hasn't got a shirt on,"

"Yea but he's outside." Jack retorted.

"You know the rules Jack, no shirt, no beer."

Jack turned to me and said, "Sorry mate you heard what they said. That's the way it is around here"

"It's a pity that I don't stink like a bloody shearer," I replied. "Then you, would be happy to serve me without any worries."

Absolutely fuming, I went back to the power shed and the supervisor said, "Can we do anything to get that main circuit running, its not fair that the other users have to suffer because of a pig headed barman."

"Yes, we certainly can just watch this, I'll show you how." I said as I reached in behind the open door of the shed.

I pulled out an extending wooden pole with a brass slot at one end and walked out side. Each building has a special fuse, called a pole fuse; high up on the power pole next to the supply line, to protect it in the event of a serious short. The pole in the shed was specially made to remove and install these fuses and I did just that. I removed the one supplying the hotel.

"You can't do that can you? " the supervisor said, as I successfully turned on the power to the rest of the town.

"Of course I can and I just did didn't I. Look, just throw the pole fuse on the floor next to the pole then if anyone kicks up we can just walk outside , find and replace the damned thing." I replied as the engine settled down to handle the bigger load and puffed away happily.

"Yes, but if someone reports it we'll get into trouble." He replied.

"When there is a major short on a building that's what we have to do until it's repaired isn't it? We have to disconnect each circuit in turn until we find the faulty one then get the others running again quickly, whilst we locate the short if possible." I said.

"That's true enough but there isn't a short is there?" He replied.

"There's only you and me and I say there might be. A short is only a heavy overload and that's what we have here, So outcomes the fuse until we find the fault that's causing the overload. I won't tell on you will I. It's your job to find the fault not mine. If you have any better ideas you'd better sing out now." I answered.

In spite of the heat we carried on and after about half an hour the barman came out and said, "Brian, have you any idea when the power will come on because we're getting desperate."

"No Jack, sorry, its too hot to work in here now so we're about to knock off until it cools down. Maybe the Albany Doctor, (a very strong wind from the south), will come in early and cool it down, if not it won't be much before midnight before we get back to it. We're all gasping for a drink and we're likely to die of dehydration if we carry on, as you can see the sweats pouring out of us."

"Hey I'll fetch you some drinks if that'll help to get the power back on," he said and he disappeared back to the bar.

Jack soon came back with a tray on which there were three bottles of beer and three glasses.

"Thanks Jack," I said," how much do we owe you."

"Nothing at all mate, your smelly mates paid for it but I just forgot to tell them"

"That's great Jack, but some cheese and pickle sandwiches would have finished it off nicely." I said, jokingly. "After all, it's going too be a long day before we get any lunch.

"Would you like some sandwiches, mate?" he asked.

"It's already past lunch time and we still have a long way to go Jack. That would be great if you can manage it so that we can stay here over lunchtime and carry on with the repairs." I replied.

Jack soon returned with a large tray of sandwiches and as he handed them over said, "There's plenty more eats and drinks if you need them guys, just send up a smoke signal, okay.

Shortly after the tech. arrived with the diodes, which we quickly soldered into place, and then it was all systems go. We fired up the big Volvo and it soon took the full load so that we were able to replace the pole fuse to the pub.

Chapter 35

GHOST IN THE BEDROOM

It was two thirty in the morning when the telephone cut loose, awakening my wife, Sandra, who is a very light sleeper at the best of times, and she jumped out of bed to answer it.

"Hello, whose there," she said.

"It's me Mam. Get dad quick. I have to talk to him now." Said our youngest son, David, who was about twenty and in a rare old state of agitation by the sound of his voice.

"Dad's sound asleep. What do you want that's so urgent, at this time of the day, anyway." Sandy retorted. "Can't you just tell me?"

"No, no Mum, I can't. I have to talk to dad, he'll understand." David replied.

Considering how close Dave was to his mother, this was a bit surprising. It must be something pretty awful if he felt that she wouldn't understand.

Sandy ran to our bedroom and shaking me by the shoulder shouted, "Brian, Brian, wake up quick. It's David on the phone. He's in a rare old state about something. He wants to talk to you, now. He won't talk to me about what ever it is. He's really upset. Come on quick and find out what's upsetting him."

I jumped out of bed, ran into the living room and picked up the phone. "What the hell's happened, mate? What have you done this time? I asked him. "Are you in big trouble or is it Becky (his girl)?"

Dave replied, "No dad it's nothing like that at all."

"Well, it had better be good then. It's two thirty and I start work at six"' I spat out at the phone.

"Do you remember telling me all about those psychic experiences that you witnessed in England, years ago? Well this is something like that, but worse, I don't know what to do."

"Well, you'd better start, by telling me what you saw and what you felt, then I'll see if I can help you." I answered.

David was working in Perth as a photocopier technician and was required to live close to the business area of the city so as to be available when required.

Dave and his fiancé were living in a recently renovated duplex house in Victoria Park, an older suburb of Perth, Western Australia. Victoria Park is located close to the centre of Perth city on the eastern side of the river, not far from Burswood Casino.

At this point I will let David tell the tale in his own words so that the details fall into place as they happened.

The first few weeks were uneventful as myself, and my partner, settled into our home. After about four weeks, I awoke at around 2AM. in a cold sweat. I was unable to move and was essentially paralysed.

I distinctly heard a voice say "The back door's been moved!"

After what seemed like an hour, but was probably only a few seconds, I was released and was able to sit up. I was under the impression that the house had been broken into, and had images in my head of intruders, missing furniture, and items thrown everywhere. I got up and with my partners help, we searched the house from top to bottom but were unable to find any evidence of intruders. Feeling a little uneasy, and apprehensive, we returned to bed and the rest of the night passed uneventfully.

I went to work the next day feeling a little odd, and confused, but by about lunchtime I had forgotten the events of the previous night and just settled down to busy afternoon's work around town.

The following night I had another 'visitation'. Again in the early hours of the morning, I awoke and was able to 'see' a large man, standing in the doorway of the bedroom. It was obvious from the posture and the facial expressions, that the figure was emanating waves of anger at me for some unknown reason. The man had me very confused because he had a distinct resemblance to my older brother, who I didn't have any time for, in both size and manner.

By this time my partner had awoken and she said in a concerned voice, "What is it love? What's the matter? You're all tensed up, what can you see? Is it the same man again? I can't see anything wrong."

I was about to answer when she touched my arm as if to soothe my nerves and when she touched me she let out a gasp of dismay, and then a terrified scream. She could now see the figure standing in the bedroom doorway.

At the sounds of her screams the figure promptly disappeared, and as soon as we gathered our wits again, I said to her, "Please get out of bed, dear, go to the lounge room and write down everything that you have just witnessed, but please don't say a word to me about it beforehand."

Once Rebecca had left the room I wrote down all the details that I could remember about the visitation. I wrote, 'I saw a naked, male figure (man), who looked distinctly like my older brother, Rodney, standing in the bedroom doorway. He gave me the impression that he had just left the shower and glared angrily at me, as if he wanted to kill me.'

When we compared notes, Rebecca had written, 'A large man with a beer gut, and wearing only a towel around his waist was glaring angrily at us from the doorway.

After reading this I panicked, and rang the first person I could think of who might possibly understand, 'My Dad.'

After talking to Dad for a while I hung up and the two of us returned to bed, but we slept the rest of the night with a small bedside lamp left on. Interestingly enough, the light was not on during the visitation and the room was in total darkness.

The next morning I was really spooked. My nerves were all jangling, and I was finding it difficult to concentrate on anything sensible.

I went outside and collected the morning paper, and after a quick perusal, to make sure that the world was still round and rotating, I turned to the classified adverts at the back. It was there that I found an advert for a clairvoyant and rang the lady in question. After listening to my stories of the previous nights she instructed me to contact the 'Psychic Development Association' in Perth and see if they could help us to interpret this weird phenomenon, and see if we could avoid any further incidents of a similar nature in the future.

I called the association and was put through to the president, a Mr Willie Moore who suggested I visit him at an address in Hay Street West, to talk to him. That afternoon I went to the address and found a little, run down, old house. It was the only, old style, house left in Hay Street, because every other building had been converted to modern, high-rise, apartment style construction.

I had a talk to Willie, who as it turned out made a living from "ghost busting", {exorcising} and he assured me that I was most certainly not an isolated case. That particular locale in the Vic Park area was becoming notorious for these types of events. He suggested that he should come and spend a night at the house with us, if that was okay. He duly arrived at about 9pm that night and settled down for an all night vigil.

That night our sleep was uninterrupted, however, the next morning, Willie informed me that we had definitely had a problem, but that he had dealt with it and we should have no more trouble on that score. He also informed me that there might be other issues with the house but he wasn't sure. From that night on we never had any more trouble with the older male figure.

It was several days later and I was sitting in the back room when I realised that the window sill was brick and sloped as if it had been an outside window and after a bit more thought, I realised that the back room was originally a back verandah, and had been walled in to make a 'sleep-out,' or extra bedroom. The layout of the house had changed considerably during the upgrade, and what used to be the back door, was now an adjoining door between the kitchen, the sleep out, and the laundry. The voice had been correct, and it occurred to me that I might have found out why the 'figure' was upset. As it turned out I was miles away from the truth.

I began to research the house and it's history. I spent hours and hours, scouring the archives in the Vic Park Library until I eventually found what I was looking for. I found a story set about 40 years ago.

It was a story about a young family that had been murdered in the Street by the father, before killing himself. There was the father, his wife and their small son who was about 6. Apparently the father had killed his wife and child and then committed suicide. There was a picture of the man, and he bore a strong resemblance to the figure we had seen.

I then, approached the landlord of the house and asked him if there had been anything strange reported to him from his previous tenants. His immediate reply was

"Oh no! Not you too!"

I found out that the property had a bad rental history with tenants leaving after only a few weeks.

The final episode regarding the house as far as we were involved anyway, concerned a little boy of about 6 years old.

We had some friends staying with us who used to party in the city till the early hours most weekends and they were in the habit of ringing me to go into town and pick them up from the night club at closing time. Invariably when they rang, I was wide awake drinking a cup coffee in the lounge room waiting for the phone to ring. What nobody knew was that each time, shortly before they rang, I was awakened by a little boy. He never spoke but was always standing by the side of the bed with a sad, little face watching me. As soon as I got out of bed he would disappear. I then had time to make a coffee and sit in the lounge waiting for the phone to ring.

There was another incident in my life a couple of years earlier concerning a visit I received from a "friend" and it wasn't until a few years later that I was able to put the pieces together on what had happened but that is another story I will tell you about it some other time.

David O'Donnell.

Well there you have it, David's story, and what an amazing tale it is and all the more remarkable for being true. Did someone say there are no such things a ghosts. David's tale really makes one wonder. Unfortunately I cannot put David's voice tone and inflections into words without it sounding bizarre Only someone who had listened to the telephone call between David and myself could possibly begin to understand all that went on that night.

Chapter **36**

THE MILK FACTORY

Colin Duffy owned a very large dairy farm near Wonnerup, in Western Australia. Colin was a forward thinking person and he was into all the latest innovations, modern gadgets and technology in an attempt to maximise his profit levels and reduce labour costs. To these ends he bought and installed a rotary milking platform in the days when this technology was in it's infancy, to reduce milking times and therefore reduce his massive power bill and the wages of the staff.

There were a number of hiccups with the machinery, initially, but these were overcome with time. The dairy was equipped to milk 28 cows at the same time and they walked on and off when the platform stopped at each station. We were milking 350 cows at that time and until cyclone Alby changed the routine.

The cyclone destroyed an older style dairy on a nearby farm, also owned by Colin. That dairy was milking 200 cows at the time and the only way that we could milk them was to move them up to the rotary dairy to join the others already being milked there. The cows had to be split into two mobs to fit into the yards, but that aside, it all seemed to run along quite efficiently although it was a massive effort.

I ran the operation at the weekends to relieve the regular workers for a well earned break but we saw very little of Colin, who considered himself to be an entrepreneur, and vowed never to spend his valuable time pulling tits and shovelling shit, to make a living.

One Saturday afternoon Colin rang me at home to confess his sins, or at least the latest one. Colin said somewhat apologetically, "I'm afraid that I've had to drop you in the deep end, mate. I hope you and Loraine will be able to manage. You see, I've arranged for a party of students from the University and Tafe colleges in Perth to visit tomorrow morning, Sunday and I hoped to be there to show them round the farm and dairy. However, I've just received an urgent call to an appointment in the city and I will be tied up until late tomorrow so I was hoping that you could show them around the dairy during milking, and then around the farm whilst Loraine starts the cleaning up and hosing down the yards. I know this is a big ask mate, but I really must get to this convention and I can think of no other solution. So what do you reckon, Brian, can you manage to help me out? I promise that I will make it up to you later."

"Yes Colin," I replied. "We'll manage somehow, but it'll cost you dearly over time, okay."

"Yes, that's right, hit a man when he's down. Okay, I'll see you next week and thanks Brian, I won't forget this," Colin answered.

The weather forecast did not look good for the next morning as this was the depth of winter and we were expecting heavy rain, but the job still had to be done. I wasn't expecting the bus full on students to arrive early, since they weren't used to rising in the middle of the night and had a three hour trip to get down from the city, so I set about the job as usual and it was at about 8.30am that I heard the bus arrive. I greeted the students and welcomed their visit, and set about the task of showing them round, explaining how it all worked, and keeping a wary eye on Loraine and the machinery at the same time.

The whole visit was a total waste of time because the students had no interest in the dairy, except for the abominable smell of cow manure that we never even noticed, but which was really bothering our visitors almost to the point of nausea.

Poor darlings, they had been dragged out of their lovely warm beds in the city at some ungodly hour only to be brought down to this awful place and forced to stay here until decency allowed them to depart.

However, there was one bright young lady who had no worries about the smell and who wanted to know, and understand, just what this huge contraption did, and why.

After a while this young lady, probably around twenty years of age, approached me and asked, "How come you need all this wonderful equipment to milk so few cows, surely the capital outlay can't be justified, can it?"

"How many cows do you think we're milking here, and what brings you to your conclusions that the outfit is not economic? How many cows do you think we need to put though a dairy like this to make it a viable operation?" I countered.

"Well, I've been counting up the cows and I reckon there are about 35 in the yard plus these 28 on the table, so that means about 60 or 70 altogether." She stated.

"Follow me and I'll show you the ones that you've missed. When you've counted them all you'll have a total a little bit closer to the truth and better understand it." I said to her.

I then led her up into the rotary yard where the cows waited prior to milking. This yard alone held about 400 cows when full, not just the thirty five or so that were in it now. We crossed the yard amongst the cows which caused her some concern, then climbed the far fence which gave us a panoramic view of a large part of the farm sweeping down away from us into the valley below and more especially, a full view of the raceway leading out from the dairy. There was a sea of black and white backsides moving away from us towards the pasture that had been allocated for the day.

"Goodness me," she cried out in surprise. "How many cows have you got here altogether then?"

"We're milking around 550 at the moment," I answered her question. "Now does it all make sense to you? Does it fit nicely into your mathematical equation?

"Well yes, but are you saying that you've already milked all those in the roadway?" Was her amazed reaction.

"Oh yes, we were nearly finished when you arrived. I was beginning to think that you would be too late for the milking." I said.

"My goodness me," she began, "What on earth time did you start milking?"

"I was out collecting the cows very early, ready to start milking at 5.00 clock sharp. Loraine was setting up the machinery ready for the first cows to arrive." Was my reply."

"We had to get up at about that time this morning to catch the bus to come down here and it was pouring down in Perth then and it rained all the way down here in the bus." She replied. She then, asked. "How often do you need to do this, then Brian?"

"You mean milk the cows. Twice a day, every day, of course, no matter what the weather, and believe me it was pouring down here as well this morning, so it was on with the waterproofs and onto the motor bike." I stated as we walked back into the dairy.

My young lady friend then wandered off into the milk room whilst we finished off and made ready to flush out the stainless steel pipes.

Once the milking was over I had to remove the milk pipe from the large refrigerated vat full of milk prior to flushing the pipes with cleaning and sterilising fluids. It was then that She raised the questions.

"I've been doing it again, adding up etc, and I can't make sense of it. It just doesn't add up. How many people are there living around here and how much milk can they drink? There must be more than enough milk in these vats to satisfy a town like Busselton, and more. I was led to believe that there is an extensive dairy farming area down here and this is only one of many dairy farms around the area. Is that not so then?"

"You seem to have lost the plot somewhere," I answered. "What you are saying is true enough, but what about the rest of the state? Where do you think your 'pinta,' on the doorstep, each day, comes from? Surely, God has better things to do than make sure you have milk for your breakfast and coffee each day?"

"Are you trying to make me believe that some of 'this milk' ends up in my coffee in Perth each day, Brian." She retorted.

My answer was, "Where the hell else are you going to get milk from when you live in a city?"

Standing up to her full height and eyeballing me indignantly, she spat out, "Don't you know there are two milk factories in Perth these days? Only a couple of weeks ago we went on a visit to the one in Bentley. We saw them filling the bottles and cartons with a big machine then packing them into crates ready for despatch. The milk had to be pasteurised first then homogenised, whatever that is before bottling ready for sale. Everything was done in Perth, in Bentley to be exact"

Totally nonplussed I said, "On the way down here this morning, did you happen to see any big silver tankers heading towards the city?"

"Well as a matter of fact we did and we were all trying to guess what it was that they were carting. Oh, my god! Are you going to tell that it was bulk milk, your milk, from this dairy?"

"No not all of it came from here that tanker travels around the various farms to collect the milk before transporting it to Perth for you to play with."

"Anyway, where else do you think the milk comes from? They don't make it in the factory, only treat it and put it into cartons for your convenience, as you noticed." Was my amazed reaction to her ignorance. Surely even preschool kids could tell her that milk comes from cows, bacon comes from pigs and wool from sheep.

If the average student in our tertiary education system is only as bright as this girl, and please remember that she was the brightest of the bunch, why the heck don't we send them to a kindergarten instead?

Chapter **37**

THE SHOPLIFTER

My partner and I owned and operated a motor garage, machinery agency and hardware store in the Hyden townsite. All the local people were hard working and as honest as the day was long. We often went away for the weekend, leaving the house unlocked whilst we were away. I was in the habit of saying that if I was silly enough to leave our shop unlocked one of the locals would find me and tell me about it, or make it secure somehow.

In those days hardly anyone in the district locked their doors as it all seemed so unnecessary.

One public holiday Monday, I spent most of the morning working in the office catching up with a mountain of bookwork that seemed to pile up from nowhere and threatened to swamp the office. My partner Keith came around during the morning to give his car a good service and check over before it fell to pieces.

I had unlocked the front door of the shop to gain access and I unlocked the rear doors so that Keith could drive his car in to the workshop. After some time I looked at the clock and realised that I was feeling hungry because it was past my lunch time, so I drove home on my little Yamaha motorcycle leaving the front door open, but secure in the knowledge that Keith was working in the rear and would know if any one entered.

I had finished my lunch and was having a bit of a snooze before returning to the office when a local farmer called Russel Mouritz knocked on the front door.

"Hello Brian," He said. "I thought I had better call around at your house to let you know that the front door of your shop is wide open and so is the workshop. I drove in to town in the hope that you would be around because I need a full set of filters for my Super 70 tractor. I went into the shop and called out but there was no answer. I managed to find the parts that I needed and I wrote the details on the order pad on the counter so that you would know what to charge me for. I hope you don't mind. It was as I was leaving, that I thought you may not realise that you have left the doors open, so I decided to call around here to let you know."

"Gee thanks Russel, it was good of you to care and take the time to come around to our house to let us know." I replied. It was okay though. I left the door open because Keith is working in the workshop. He is servicing his Cortina."

"The Cortina is in the workshop as you say, and the bonnet is up, as though someone is working on it, but I can assure you that Keith is not in the shop. I had a good look around and called out a few times but no one answered." He said.

"Well what can I say, thanks once again mate and thanks for your concern, Keith must have gone home to lunch at the same time as me, not realising that I had gone home too.

I had been back in the shop for about half an hour when Keith wandered in through the rear doors and came into the office for a bit of a chat. When I told him what had happened Keith said, "You have always reckoned that is what would happen Brian, and it seems you were right. We need to be a bit more careful in the future though, as you never know who is about these days with the tourist industry building up like it is.

Chapter 38

THE CYCLONE SHED

Clarrie, one of my bosses at a country garage and agency, called me in to answer the telephone and as he thought that this was a private call he was quite sharp with me.

The call was from a mate, George Thompson, a local farmer who lived about twelve miles from town.

"Gooday mate," he said, "I have a question for you. What do you get when you cross a cyclone shed with a chamberlain tractor?"

"I haven't the slightest idea, George," I answered. "Is this leading up to something serious because I am at work as you know and Clarrie is watching me like a hawk. We have heaps of work in at the moment and he doesn't like us wasting good time with personal calls, in fact he will probably charge you workshop rates for my time if we aren't careful."

"Yea, that 'ud be right, the tight fisted old fart." George spat back at me, "And he can do that if he likes because this is work. I need you to come out here straight away and check out my tractor, okay."

"Tell me what's wrong with it mate and I'll see what can be done," I replied.

"Like I told you, I caught it mating with the shed so I switched it off. and now it wont go at all. I think the starter's buggered."

"Right you are then, George, I'll just round up some tools and come out." I concluded. "This is the champion 9g that your talking about"

"Yea that's the one alright and as you know it's my main tractor and I am lost without it. I need it to feed the sheep and cattle this afternoon. OK."

I turned to my boss and asked, "Did I see a champion starter motor in the storeroom Clarrie, I might need it for George .He wants me to go out there straight away and I'll take it with me just in case. Is that alright?"

"We have plenty for you to do here Brian, but I would love to sell that starter. It's been here in the store for years. It was part of the original stock from Chamberlains that they reckoned we would need to keep in store for emergencies. The damned thing cost us a fortune plus the interest to hold on to it so you had better go but don't hang about. Get back here as soon as you can."

When I arrived at George's place, he took me down to the machinery shed to show me his tractor. They had been using jumper leads directly onto the starter connections to start their truck, and left the insulator off the lead by mistake, and the lead was a little loose. It was loose enough that during the night the heavy lead had moved and touched the other terminal and activated the starter motor. The engine had started easily and the electrical short kept the starter engaged with the flywheel until it disintegrated. Unfortunately the tractor was in first gear and it ran forward into the shed pole. Because the motor had enough revs on it, it kept running.

The rear wheels spun on the gravel floor until they dug two big holes and lowered the drawbar onto the ground. It looked as though it was trying to mate with the shed post when George found it in the morning, hence his unusual question when he rang up. I asked George if he had the tractor insured because the starter motor would cost him a fortune, if not, but I could put in a claim for insurance if he had." George replied, "It will cost a hell of a lot more if we don't get it going today."

Whilst I was removing the old starter I was able to assure him that providing the flywheel ring gear was ok and no bits and pieces had fallen inside I would get it going which I did.

Chapter 39

HELL BENT ON MURDER

It was a quiet day on the farm, the birds were calling and the world was at peace, but then, the phone started to ring insistently over and over. Pam was out in the yard hanging out yet another load of washing. Where the heck do all these dirty clothes come from she was thinking.

With her husband Ron, and two school age girls from her previous marriage to look after and helping around the farm as well, she led a very busy life. Even shopping was a big job involving a forty mile round trip two or three times a week, to collect the mail and papers as well as buy stores because no one had freezers on the farms, only kerosene fridges if they were lucky.

The general store in Henden had a good

cool-room and limited freezer space to enable them to carry most basic food lines needed by the little community.

However, the phone was still ringing as she hurried indoors but it stopped just as she entered the room. "Damn, I wonder who that was, I hope it wasn't urgent." She said to herself. "I suppose it will ring again if it was urgent. Maybe if I put the kettle on and wait a minute it will ring again."

As she was filling the kettle the phone started to ring again, who could it be at this time of the day. They didn't receive many phone calls during the daytime.

It was the sergeant of police from nearby, town, "Had something happened to one of her girls, or maybe her dear old mother in Perth."

"Is that you, Mrs. Hadley," a stern voice asked, in a very official manner.

"Yes, sergeant that's right, how can I help you?" She replied.

"Is Ron around by any chance Pam, I have an urgent message for you both." He said.

"He's in the shed fixing the tractor, I'll give him a shout. He'll be here in a second. Will you hang on, or I'll call you back."

"I'd better hang on, but you hurry up and get him now please. It is very urgent"

Pam put down the phone and ran out to the shed shouting loudly to Ron, "Come quick love, it's the police they want to speak to us urgently."

"My god, are the girls in trouble at school, or is it something else. Why the hell couldn't they tell you what it's about," Ron retorted.

"I don't know but we'd better run and find out." She replied.

"Ron ran into the house and picked up the phone, saying, "Are you still there, sergeant. What's all the fuss about? What the heck do you need that's so urgent."

"He's coming Ron. He's on his way. You'd better get away from the house straight away? He left Dumbleyoung a fair while ago. He's managed to get hold of an ex-army .303 rifle and some ammo." The sergeant said.

"Are you talking about Chris Morton, Is he really heading this way? How long have we got?" Ron asked the sergeant in rising panic.

"If he gets through, no more than an hour so you'll have to hurry mate. We're setting up road blocks already so which ever way he comes we'll get him, but we don't want to take any risks so you get out and pick up the girls from school as you go. We need to know where you'll be, so have you anywhere in mind?" queried the sergeant.

"We'll go straight out to the Clapton's place north of Henden. We'll be safe enough there and they'll take us in gladly so we'll grab a few things and head off straight away, now." Ron stated.

"Okay mate, you hurry up and we'll take care of things from this end." He replied and put down the phone.

My god, how naive can you get. The bloke lived around here for months and worked close to town whilst he was here. He was very familiar with every road in the area including all the back tracks as well. He could find his way here blindfolded. He knew the area far better than the police.

Ron and Pam grabbed handfuls of clothes, mainly for their little girls and set off quickly for town.

Only a short distance from home they passed a pale green, EH Holden station wagon travelling eastwards very fast.

"My god that's him already," Pam said.

"He must have come the back way along commonwealth road to get this far by now. Oh Ron, put your foot down and get to the girls quickly"

"Thank god we bought a new car after harvest and he didn't recognise us." Ron answered.

As soon as they hit town they called the police to let them know where Chris was, grabbed the girls from school, and headed north to the Clapton's place which was about four miles out of town.

Chris had lived in Henden for a while and formed an attachment to Pam, when she was the district nurse. Chris got seasonal work with a local farmer and often spent his evenings in town with Pam, rather than in the lonely old farmhouse on the property.

Chris and Pam, eventually split up and Chris left the district and took a job at the local hotel in Dumbleyung town.

After Chris left, Pam took up a relationship with Ron, they got married and lived on Ron's farm way out east. When Chris heard about the marriage he was consumed with jealousy and vowed to get even, when the opportunity occurred.

When Chris got to the farm and found the place deserted, he found a can of petrol in the shed, poured some in middle of each room, and set the place alight.

I ran the local bush fire truck in Henden and the police called me from the house to ask for assistance to put the fire out because they had to follow Chris and try to catch him in case he knew, or guessed, where the family would go to hide.

It was a long way out to the farm and the old model 'A' Bedford fire truck was very slow indeed. I thought this would be a totally fruitless mission because the house would be little more than a pile of ashes long before we got there, unless some of the neighbours got there first.

When we pulled up close to the burning home, we realised that we were the first unit to arrive, despite our slowness. Amazingly the fire had been very slow to take hold and even now was not burning very fiercely at all. About half of the house was beyond help, other than to extinguish the flames, however the living room end was still only slightly damaged and, in fact the family were able to camp in that part until the bedrooms were rebuilt. My crew had the pumps running as we entered the gate ready to attack the flames as soon as I got the truck close enough for the hoses to reach the fire. We quickly attacked the flames and controlled the fire. About that time some of the neighbours arrived to help us mop up and they stayed at the house to make sure that there were no flare-ups. There was fortunately, a well stocked farm dam close to the building to replenish our meagre water capacity.

Once we were sure that the property was safe we left it in the hands of the locals and returned to town.

The police were looking for me as I parked the fire truck and a local constable who I was friendly with asked me if I could get hold of any powerful firearms, quickly.

Apparently the villain had gone through town a little while ago with a senior police officer chasing him in his private car. He was headed straight towards the Clapton's property where he obviously thought his quarry would be holed up. A couple of miles out of town Chris had somehow managed to fire a .303 calibre bullet at the officer's car whilst still racing north. Luckily the bullet fell short, ricocheted off the bitumen road and made a hole in the metal shield around the front bumper of the sergeant's car.

My friendly constable said, "I don't mind some bloody madman firing .303 bullets at me so long as I have a similar weapon to return the fire."

The constable knew of course, that I held the local firearm dealer's license and would be sure to know where I could lay my hands on some suitable weapons.

"You can take my .303 rifle, mate," I said, "And Byron Dunway has a .303/25 rifle. Hang on, Roger Fisher has a .303/25 as well and they're both nearby in town. That should equal the equation a bit, but for god's sake be careful, that guy is a maniac and he won't hesitate to shoot you if you get in his way."

"Yea, tell me about it mate, but someone has to try and stop him. Thanks for your help" he replied and headed of with my rifle tucked safely under his arm.

Shortly after shooting at the police, the

fugitive abandoned his car in the middle of the road at the place where the floodway overspill from the lake crosses the road, and then headed westwards through heavy mallee scrub and salt lake country.

The police called in an aboriginal native tracker to try and follow the tracks through the scrub. Meanwhile they were setting up roadblocks at all the intersections to try and keep Chris isolated in this area of bush. This was going to be a very long night, unless we got lucky soon. The aboriginal tracker was very good but he finally lost the tracks in heavy scrub.

My friendly copper came back to see me to see if I would use my utility to ferry drinks and meals out to the officers manning the roadblocks around the area.

"Yes, mate I'll help out on one condition," I replied.

"What's the condition, mate, tell me about it." He said.

"Well, can I carry my other rifle for protection, loaded of course," I said.

"I wouldn't expect you to go unarmed,

although the commissioner might not be amused, but for Christ's sake be careful and only shoot if you are seriously threatened." Was his stern reply.

Later in the evening the police came to see me once more. They had gotten bogged down, partly because it was now dark and tracking impossible, and partly through lack of local knowledge.

They said that although they often came this way on official business they had gained little knowledge of the surrounding terrain, including even the settled areas.

When they came this way it was for specific reasons and they had some knowledge of the properties that they had dealings with, but nothing of others nearby.

The sergeant asked if there was a derelict farm homestead or some other, out of the way buildings that Chris might hole up in, for the night, at least.

At first nothing useful came to mind, but as we were heading out, passed the place that the villain had abandoned his car, to take a meal out to the police, I had a bit of an idea.

When we returned to town I caught up with one of the senior policemen and suggested that he come for a drive with me in my utility as I had a bit of an idea as to where the man might be holed up.

I drove out northwards to the roadblock, then turned left for about a mile or so then turned left again. We drove through salt lake country for a while then the road started to climb on to higher ground. There was mallee scrub and bush to the left and on the right it opened out into farmland where we stopped at a farm gateway that was little used. I pointed down through the gate and said, "There's a track running along that fence line, then it turns left at the first cross fence and runs along it to a set of farm buildings then an old farmhouse. We used to rent the house when we first came to the district, it belongs to an Italian family from Harvey, down on the coast south of Perth."

"The family live in another house when they're here, and have no use for this one. Also, the farm is leased to their son-in law who lives down south of here on his own farm, so this house is usually empty. The interesting thing is that our man used to work for the son-in-law and he camped in this house when he was working on this farm so he knows it well. Hop back in I have more to show you."

Then we drove out onto the main road and soon stopped in a gateway. There was a farm driveway leading away from the gate and dropping down hill onto the flat below. "Look down there just beyond the second fence line, you can just see the outline of a house with a dam bank in front of it. That's the one that I told you about back there on the hill."

Driving on again I turned a long bend in the road before straightening up and going due west. The second fence line which ran in front of the house connected with the boundary fence by the road after we straightened up and that's where we stopped again.

"The track running along this fence also leads into the homestead." I pointed out. "So, he has three exits to escape plus any one, of many tracks leading out through the lake country at the rear of the property."

"Well, this sounds like the place we're looking for, and he was headed this way, you might have the answer, mate." The policeman said. "Well done. I'll get some of the blokes to stake it out until morning then we'll check it out"

Next morning we were asked if the ambulance was available in case it was needed, so Roger Fisher and I headed out to the main gateway of the farm with the ambulance.

When we arrived the police told us that they had seen flickering lights in the house during the night and they were pretty sure that he was holed up in there.

There were many more police here now because the TRG had arrived during the night with sharp shooters carrying thirty calibre rifles. The media were on hand to record all the gory details, if there were any, for posterity.

In a news bulletin on the radio they related the details to date, and mentioned the shot that had been fired at the police yesterday.

The farm telephone was working so the police could talk to the fugitive. Chris denied that he had fired the shot at the police and demanded that they clear his name in the next bulletin before he would give himself up to them.

Although it was not true, the police arranged for the newsreader to say that the previous report was incorrect and no shot had been fired at the police car, nor at any of the police officers. Chris told the police that as soon as he heard the retraction on the news he would give himself up and come out.

The radio stations catch cry was, 'News every hour, on the hour,' so we all waited with baited breath for the hour to arrive. Then there it was, being read out for all to hear. As the sound of the news was dying away, there was a loud report from the house then total silence. The police tried to talk to Chris on the phone but there was no answer.

The senior policeman then said. "It looks like it's all over, he may have done the world a favour and shot himself."

Then he sent in the TRG to make sure that it was now safe. They soon reported that the man was dead.

The police asked us to collect the body for removal to the hospital morgue in a nearby town. When we took the ambulance down to the house we found that he had placed the muzzle of the rifle in his mouth and pulled the trigger.

Roger and I, then had the grizzly job of cleaning up the mess and taking the body to the local morgue to be certified.

All that was left now was for the family to rebuild their home and their shattered lives, which they certainly did.

Chapter 40

WRONGLY ACCUSED

When I first arrived in Western Australia I lived with my mother's sister Aunty Jenny, in Glen Forrest. Glen Forrest is situated at the top of Greenmount hill to the east of Perth city, and adjacent to Great Eastern Highway running out to Kalgoorlie. The area around there is very rugged and mostly untouched virgin Jarrah forest and bushland resulting in one of Western Australia's earliest national parks being established on the north side of the highway.

The park of course, is "The John Forrest National Park" and our family used it extensively for recreation and leisure activities. There is a creek running through the park which has been dammed in two places. The lower dam provides a delightful swimming pool with a steady stream of fresh water running through it in the early part of the summer until the creek dries up. The upstream dam contains a back-up water supply which is used to flush the lower dam and keep the water safe to swim in and enables the rangers to clean out the pool from time to time.

As you can imagine, the stream is a constant source of pleasure for all the little children who manage to find it. Being situated in a deep winding gorge running up through the park with an overhanging canopy of native trees and scrub makes it ideal for recreation activities. It creates all manner of situations for junior, worldwide adventurers to whet their imaginations and pit their skills and daring against the awful unknowns of this world.

Pirates, buccaneers, bush rangers, etc. all slotted nicely into this secret place and many were the fierce battles fought between them over the years.

We spent many happy hours in the company of my cousins exploring every nook and cranny of the area in and around the stream and pools. Even on the hottest of days the climate in the forest was quite pleasant and the water added that magical ingredient to make it superb. A permanent water feature of this nature naturally had its own ecology of plants, animals, birds and insects, which gave us many hours of entertainment and lots of surprises.

Although there were no exotic animals like the duck-billed platypus there were myriads of parrots and lots of robins, wrens, wagtails etc. and, as you might expect, kingfishers and kookaburras. Dragonflies were everywhere along the stream, darting and flitting around in the dappled sunlight shining through the trees. In the water there were plenty of minnows and other small native fish, which the boys spent many hours trying to catch in old jam jars with string tied to them. Of course, there was always the constant danger from sharks, crocodiles and pirhannah fish to worry about.

One Sunday afternoon we spotted a yabbie, a type of freshwater crayfish, in the water and this opened up another avenue for our hunting skills A few weeks later aunt Jenny suggested spending the afternoon in the park with a barbeque picnic near the swimming pool to finish off the day. Of course the boys were delighted but insisted in travelling with me rather than with their parents since, at the time, I was driving around in my Singer sports car with the hood down and the wind in their hair, whilst their car was a lowly old ford prefect sedan.

The boys were so excited that aunt Jenny and uncle Les were left to gather together the picnic things and the boys grabbed their jam jars and climbed aboard the Singer. As soon as we arrived the boys set to work to catch some minnows and hopefully some yabbies. When they had caught a few fish and a yabbie or two they looked around for other things to amuse them. The adults had just arrived so the boys gave aunt Jenny, after serious warnings about the penalty for failure, the responsible job of looking after the jam jars and their contents whilst we 'men' set off to explore the jungle up stream.

When we returned we were amazed to see a man in uniform, a park ranger as it turned out, giving Aunt Jenny a hard time. He had caught her with fish and crayfish which had been illegally captured in a national park and she was trying to convince him that she was not alone. She claimed to have some small boys with her who had conveniently disappeared, and that the fish were not hers, she was only guarding them for the boys. Aunt Jen admitted that she did not realise it was illegal to hunt and take fish in the park because the boys had been doing it for years. The boys admitted their guilt and the ranger eventually left with a stern warning not to hunt or fish in any national park ever again. Much to the boy's displeasure he made them return the fish to the stream.

We all enjoyed a lovely picnic beside the pool and by the time I got the boys home after a long tour around the district in the sports car as a consolation they were quite happy again.

Chapter 41

THE BUSH FIRE

The area around Hyden townsite contained some sort of geological feature, I have no idea what, that seemed to make it prone to thunder and lightening storms of great ferocity. One very dark night with the rain pouring down in torrents, I was driving along Chalkhill Road only a few miles south east of the town in my Austin eighteen hundred utility when a blinding flash of light caused me to skid to a sudden halt. I sat quietly, totally stunned and badly shocked. It felt like a massive bomb had exploded just in front of the car. I was blinded by the brilliance of the flash and had to wait quite a long time before I could see enough to start off again and resume my journey.

The Chalkhill Road was aptly, named because it rose up and over a huge expanse of limestone, or chalk as it is sometimes known, before dropping down onto the sand plain on the other side.

Afterwards, I decided that what I had witnessed was a lightening bolt and had I been a second or two earlier I would, almost certainly not be here to write this story.

We often had lightening storms, sometimes every night for weeks on end. I loved to watch these storms and witness the awesome power and might of them. After dark I would quite often sit on the front veranda of our home in Hyden, and watch the fireworks display. Sandra hated these fierce displays of nature's power.

Hyden is situated in a basin with a heavy clay soil type and therefore beneath a large stand of massive salmon gum trees which stood out against the backdrop of the surrounding hills, and they jumped out like ghosts when silhouetted with every flash.

These storms were a real worry as they were seldom accompanied by rain, and the lightening could easily start a grass or bush fire throughout the dry summer months.

The boundary of farming operations was

alongside the vermin fence, about 40 miles east of the town and east of that line was a huge almost undisturbed mallee forest some 120 miles wide and 150miles long. It stretched all the way to Norseman in the east, and from Ravensthorpe in the south, almost to Southern Cross in the north. This area was totally uninhabited in the years that we lived there, but after a large deposit of nickel was located it became a very busy place.

Late one afternoon, a powerful thunderstorm started a serious fire out in the mallee forest but since it was situated well away from the vermin fence it was allowed to run its own course. It burned for over two weeks, blotting out the sun and dropping tons of ash over the district whenever the east wind was blowing during the day.

As the wind changed from strong easterlies during daylight hours, to south westerlies at night, when the Albany Doctor (a strong S.W. sea breeze) took over, the fire zigzagged back and forth, finding new ground to burn each day, but coming ever closer to the fence as it did so. Generally, the farming population although worried about it, assumed that it would eventually double back on itself and go out without causing any damage.

However, during the day on Sunday it came perilously close to the vermin fence and the fire control officer of the district called for all the bush fire brigades to attend in case it did jump over the fence into farming territory. I got the old model 'A' Bedford out and gave it a final check then set off on the long journey, about 30 miles out to the fence.

There is a well graded track along both sides of the fence, for maintenance and routine checks, thus, making access very easy, and also affording a safe area to back burn from so that we could run another fire out to meet the main fire, rob it of it's fuel and so burn it out.

When I arrived, the fire control officer was extremely worried. He had not had to control, or try to control a fire of this magnitude before. Another problem was that the fire was on crown land and he wasn't sure whether this area came within his jurisdiction, and what would happen if he got it wrong. In later years this area lies within the jurisdiction of a government department called CALM, which stands for Conservation and Land management and they are totally responsible for anything that happens out there.

After a while, I, and others became impatient to attack the fire, or go back home, if that was not going to happen. The fire truck that I was driving, belonged in the town, to protect it, and there would be some awkward questions to be answered if a fire broke out in or near the town and the fire truck wasn't available to attend The news on the radio was not good either, as the weather bureau was forecasting temperatures well in excess of 100 degrees and strong easterly winds, which added together meant that we were in for a hell of a day anyway.

In spite of our heckling, the officer could not decide what to do, so I pointed out that I would have to leave him to it and return to town with the truck. Finally he agreed, and told me to leave, as he thought that the fire was moving away again, and when the wind changed in the evening, which it was almost certain to do, it would blow the fire back onto itself.

I reluctantly left them to sort it out themselves,

but I felt sure that if we had lit up the far side of the fence, the sea breeze would make sure that the whole area would burn out and stop any further risk of it jumping the fence.

It was early on Tuesday morning that I next got involved again. A local farmer drove into town, because the town phones did not open until 9 o'clock, to say.

"Hey Brian! Quick! Can you take the fire truck out to the fence again, the fire jumped over during the night and it's roaring through the scrub toward the farming areas. It's still in the scrub and there's a fair amount of buffer if we hurry."

"Yea, right you are I'm on my way. Have we got any other help at all, Ken?" I asked.

"All the little units have been called in, and there's Ben's grader working up from the south. He started at the east/west road and he's working his way northward, but it's a hell of a long way, and in heavy mallee it'll be slow going."

"Okay, that means I'd better start at the north end, probably at Meeking's place and work south and hope that we meet up somewhere in the middle. I'll just slip around and get Ray out of bed and see if he can bring his big tanker out and keep ferrying water to us so that we can stay on the fire line all the time."

Right you are then mate I'll get straight back to Frank's place and meet you there with enough crew to man your team. How many men do you need?"

"I reckon about 5 for a start, one to light up, two on the truck and two with knapsacks mopping up behind." I replied then added, "If you guys need to have a raging bushfire you could at least pick a better day, they are forecasting 114 degrees again to day, and strong to gale force north-easterly winds. That damned fire could be in town here before this day's over. We'd better pray for an early Albany Doctor, and a very strong one at that, if we're to get through this day safely."

"You're not wrong, mate, it's going to be hell out there alright, so lets all keep our fingers crossed, eh. I'll see you soon then."

With that, Ken jumped into his utility and took off like a bat out of hell, heading back east to face God only knows what. Lets hope that he, God that is, would be on our side this day, as we were going to need all the help that we could muster and a fair bit of luck as well.

The ancient Bedford, moaned and groaned and rattled as we made our way out east.

The sky was already thick with smoke, which was blowing right over the town, and the smell of burning bush was getting stronger and stronger as I approached the fire.

When I got to Frank's place there were vehicles everywhere. It seemed that the farmers had been gathering here since day-break and they were ready to go.

Although I couldn't see them, the farmer's wives were there, as well, in their guise as C.W.A. members and, as usual, they were hard at work preparing sandwiches and tea in sufficient quantities to feed the army of men that would pass here before this day ended. Where they managed to obtain sufficient supplies was a total mystery to me, as the nearest small shop was about twenty miles away, and the closest supermarket over 100 miles away at Merredin. But, whenever these fantastic ladies were needed in an emergency, they would just drop everything, and still do, bundle up the kids and head off to anywhere in the district where they were needed. They could be relied upon to empty their larders and store cupboards, load it all into the cars and set off ready and willing to give their all, to help their men folk, and anyone else, who needed them.

I have no idea who began this tremendous organization, although I am sure that it is well documented somewhere, or where it all began, but we country folk owe them a great deal of thanks and gratitude, although they never looked for any, nor expected any. When the show was all over, they would, and still do, just return home to their families and pick up their lives again, as though nothing had happened.

If heaven is full of old C.W.A. members, there will never be any need for angels.

As I was getting out of the truck, Frank Meeking came over and said, "Thanks for coming Brian, we're going to need you, and the truck shortly. Look, slip up to the house, the girls have got the billie on and there's a ton of tucker there as well, you'd better eat as much as you can now, as you may not get any later on and this is going to be a long day."

"Okay mate, just sing out when you need me." I replied, and headed off over to the house, where the back veranda was loaded up with food and the huge teapot was steaming full of hot strong tea. All the ladies were old friends and they chatted happily away with me about their concerns relating to the fire and the impending weather conditions. One lady quizzed me about my plans for the day and I pointed out to her that, any plan of action, was not my worry directly, although it would end up on my plate to some degree before nightfall. I pointed out that ultimately the local fire control officer had that responsibility, but that he would be supported by the rest of us, and the chief fire officer of the shire, who was not in attendance at that time, but could probably be reached by telephone if need be.

By about 9 o'clock the smoke had thickened dramatically and if we were to gain the upper hand we had to attack the fire soon. I went over to the fire control officer to discuss the situation, which was rapidly becoming very serious. He said.

"Brian I'm very worried about this fire but I

can't see how we can attack it. It's nothing like a grass or crop fire and I don't know how to deal with it. Where do we start"

I answered. "Like I said on Sunday, you have my full support, but I have other responsibilities as well. I have to think about the town and I have a business to run. I don't mind helping out and neglecting the business so long as we are doing something constructive, not standing around waiting till it's too late. Look, mate I'm going over to get a quick snack and another cuppa and then I have to make a decision about what to do, okay."

"Yes, okay that sounds fine for now, thanks for your support anyway, I know I can rely on you." He replied.

When I walked back to the truck after my snacks the fire officer approached me and said in a very concerned voice. "Hey, Brian, do you want this fire?"

"Are you asking me to take over from you and take full control? I queried.

"Yes, that's what I'd like you to do, I can't manage this one it's too far out of my experience."

"Okay, I'll do that for you although I don't have any more experience than you do, and it's a big responsibility, especially if something goes wrong."

With that, I proceeded to gather my crew, together by calling out for volunteers, to man the truck, and I went over to the house again to see the ladies.

I said. "We are off now to start a back burn and we'll need supplies, probably for the rest of the day, as we'll be out of contact from now on." (There were no two-way radios available out there in those days), and we would be on our own, in uninhabited bush all day. "Can we get food and water enough for six of us please, then we are on our way?"

"We have boxes of sandwiches here, and there are a few spare water bags that you can take. Good luck and take care of yourselves, okay." They answered.

I checked my crew and started the old truck ready for the fray, and we were off.

There was a rear gate in the back fence leading into the crown land and scrub country, which led us off in the right direction. I noticed a kangaroo track heading off in the direction that I thought we needed to go but we had no idea where the fire actually was or how fast it was travelling. I arranged for the fire lighter to go on ahead of the truck and light up the side of the track nearest to the main fire, so that we could follow at some distance to let the back burn get a hold. We then, set off with one wheel on that narrowest of tracks and the other in the scrub alongside and carefully extinguished any burning debris and hot spots on the side of the track away from the fire. Two of the crew took it in turns with the men on the hoses to walk behind at a distance and ensure that the fire was on one side of the track only and there was no chance of it sneaking up on us from behind and trapping us. One of our biggest worries was trying to find the smoothest track to minimise the risk of punctures. The men on the hoses called out after a time to let me know that we were almost out of water, so I said, "Okay, we'll stop on that ridge ahead and have a drink. Hopefully, Ray will have followed, and he'll soon show up. I'll give him a few blasts on the horn to let him know that we need him." Oh boy, wouldn't it have been nice to have two-way radios, to keep in touch with each other.

Looking back from the ridge, we could see Ray carefully following in our wheel tracks to minimise punctures as well. With about 10 ton of water on board he had to be very careful where he went in this wild virgin country. Once Ray came up alongside we soon started his pumps and transferred some water to our, much smaller tanks. Ray said, "It looks as though you'll get about 3 or 4 fills before I have to leave you and go back to King rocks to refill."

"Yes, we only hold a few hundred gallons but the further we go, the longer it'll take you to return with a refill. Thanks Ray we'll press on and lets hope we don't need too many refills."

Once more we were on our way, with still no idea where we were, or where the fire was. We weren't even sure that, what we were doing was effective or not, let alone if it would stop the blaze, but we had to try. The whole crew were magnificent and a pleasure to work with. They had the worst of it, out in that impossible heat and smoke, carrying a heavy knapsack full of water, and walking in rough terrain, whilst

I sat in the truck carefully negotiating my way through the mallee. They kept up a cheerful banter and swapped places frequently to reduce the fatigue. When I offered to swap with one of them they refused, saying, that I could have it all on my own. None of them wanted the responsibility of the truck and every ones lives as well. One mistake and we would have a long walk to get out of there and back to civilisation.

Around midday, we stopped once more for water and decided to eat some of the delicious food before the heat made it unfit for consumption. Ray joined in the picnic and we all had a good old natter about the situation. None of us were any the wiser about what was going on around us so we decided to carry on whilst Ray returned for more water, as his tank was nearly empty.

It was about 3.30 or 4.00pm when, the guy who was lighting up ahead reached a bigger crest from where he could survey quite a long way ahead. We were coming into an area of sand plain country, which meant a sudden change in the vegetation. The mallee bush cut out along the ridge and changed to a much lower sand-plain bush land where the scrub was only a couple of feet high, and we had a far better idea of what was happening around us, although we still couldn't see the fire.

When the fire lighter reached the ridge and looked around, and ahead, he spotted something on the distant ridge up ahead of us. He put out his lighter and trotted back towards the truck, waving and shouting to us. When he got close enough he said, "Hey, we did it. There's a grader coming to meet us from the south. It must be Mick. They said he was working this way and we're dead in line with him."

"How far away is he and can you see the fire at all?" I asked.

"There was no sign of the fire but the smoke is as black as hell. Mick is just on the next ridge and heading straight for us."

"Hey, that means that he's still a long way off. Probably still a mile or two away yet. What the heck are you doing back here, we have a lot of burning to do yet, One of you had better get back out there and keep going, until we meet up with the grader.

If that fire comes over the other ridge on our

left with this wind behind it, it'll be over the top of us in a flash, come on let's get cracking."

One man grabbed the fire lighter and set of at a fast trot up to the ridge and we were off again. Soon we could see everything up ahead. The terrain dropped away into a large valley and apart from the low scrub the only feature of note was a fairly large clump of very tall salmon gums which were growing in a patch of heavy clay soil down in the lowest part of the valley and furthest away from the direction of the fire.

We were progressing steadily down the slope towards the grader when we noticed a tractor and plough coming out from behind the salmon gums. It turned out to be Peter Padovan who was desperately trying to create a diversion so the fire would sweep around to the north and south and so miss his property which was directly in it's path. The tractor kept appearing and disappearing in and out of the salmon gums and smoke as Peter worked back and forth in a desperate attempt to increase the width of the break and he could have no idea that we or the grader were so close.

Then, suddenly, we could hear it, roaring through the scrub as it burst into view away over to our left and came rampaging down the valley towards us. Oh my God, there was a massive front roaring down towards us with that hot savage north east wind up it's bum. We had no hope of putting it out unless we could get far enough ahead of it to give the back burn a chance to work. Maybe there was still time. It had a fair way to come at us, so we veered away from it to our right, in a desperate attempt to gain more time. This route brought us in line with the salmon gums where Peter was working and there was a lot less ground fuel around the gum trees. We could no longer see the grader since it was screened behind the trees. We swung around to the west side of the gums but the fire was roaring down at us and we could see that we were fighting a losing battle. If only we had started an hour or two earlier it would have been okay. Just then the tractor and plough appeared right in front of us as Peter made another desperate run through the scrub. He was surrounded by fire, and kept disappearing from sight in the thick smoke and flames. Then he was gone as the intensity of the fire increased dramatically, where was he, was he still okay. Then suddenly, there he was over to our right, coming out of a belt of thick smoke beside the salmon gums. He was alright; thank god for that. Peter had a lovely wife and a small family to provide for and they were battling out here, in this virgin farmland, which he was trying hard to conquer and civilise. Peter was a trained schoolteacher before embarking on this farming venture.

By now the grader had reached the trees, maybe we would hold it yet as we were alongside the gums also, we were so near. We had to stop it getting into the trees then we would still have a chance to control and extinguish it. At that moment there was a savage roar and the Albany Doctor, a strong cold wind off the south coast came in like a tornado, stopping the north- easterly in it's tracks and pushing it out of the way. As the two winds met they created a massive whirlwind, which picked up the fire and threw it into the trees right up to the top of the canopy. The noise was unbelievable and the heat so fierce that all we could do was run for our lives as I drove the old truck out through the smoke into a clear area west of the gums. Peter pulled in alongside us as the grader moved around into view on the other side. At least we were all safe for the moment as we once more counted numbers to make sure no one had been left behind.

All we could do was to look on as the windstorm swirled the flames higher and higher up into the tops of the trees and much higher, right up to the sky. The roar was deafening now and the heat so intense that we cowered before it and covered our faces as we moved even further away.

The "Doctor" however, was dragging massive volumes of cold air in behind it and was sucking the inferno into an ever tightening swirl, leaving a cleared area behind it and around to our side of the gums. That's when we realised that all was not lost yet. There were only a few wisps of fire that were still outside the cleared area, so braving the heat and still choking in the smoke we drove around the trees and extinguished the burning debris running away from the gums and, whoopee, we had won through after all provided that burning embers were not carried ahead of us to start another fire.

We had a good look all around to make sure that there would be no flare-ups and with the "doctor" in charge, we knew that the fire could only burn itself out before morning.

As the fire was dying down Peter showed us a quick way to get out of there and over to his farm homestead for a quick clean up and a very welcome cuppa. From there, we were able to telephone Frank Meeking's place to let them know that we were all safe, and that the drama was over, so that they could all relax again and get a good night's sleep.

I still had a long slow trip back to town in the Bedford, but the old girl had served us well once again and never given me the slightest concern throughout this dreadful day, not even a puncture.

Before I could relax in a nice hot shower the old truck had to be checked over and serviced. The fuel and water tanks needed refilling ready for the next trip.

Chapter 42

MALLEE ROOTS

The mallee tree is more of a shrub than a real tree and there are untold millions of them throughout the wheat-belt of Western Australia and parts of Victoria. The common mallee was the bane of the poor old farmers who were trying to clear their land and make a living. The mallee bush has many upright 'trunks' growing from a single root ball. The trunks are only a few inches in diameter rather than one large trunk and they only grow to about eighteen or twenty feet tall. There are a number of different species of them, often depending on the type of soil where they grow. They are generally so dense that it is impossible to drive between them and they are the main species found abundantly on most farms throughout Western Australia, and indeed most of the southern states.

The early farmers hated the mallee as they were difficult to remove, due to the fact that they grow from a common root ball, the 'mallee root', and some of them were quite huge. The upright stems were tough and hard to chop, and if they were burnt in the natural state the stumps that were left, were perfectly shaped to spear through even the toughest tractor or plough tyres.

The roots themselves are very hard to dig out of the ground, and some of them are absolutely huge. One day a nearby farmer came in to see me to ask if I had any ideas on how to salvage his chisel plough. He had hooked onto a massive mallee root and heaved it out of the ground but as it stood up, it lifted the plough into the air, until it was well clear of the ground, and there it stayed. He had tried a number of ways to clear the stump but all to no avail.

I had an ancient sort of homemade tow truck which we hoped might be strong enough to lift the plough away from the root, but we needed to tow the root out from under the plough whilst I held it clear. The farmer only had one tractor so I took the weight of the plough, so that he could knock out the drawbar pin and release the tractor to pull the stump out of the way once it was clear of the stump.

A nearby resident, a farm labourer was in the habit of drinking more of the local ale than was good for him and his vehicle. On the way home one night the road suddenly seemed to disappear causing him to run into a large mallee tree near his gate way, which he hit with enough force to topple it over and flatten it and so pivoting the root up out of the ground and standing it on end.

The first that I knew about it was when his wife called at the workshop the following morning and asked me to go out and retrieve his 1 ton utility and tow it back to town and repair it.

When we got to the site of the smash we were surprised to see that the utility was actually parked on top of the mallee root. The force of the impact had flattened the tree and the root had emerge beneath the vehicle and jacked all four wheels clear of the ground. We spent most of the morning lifting and dragging it clear of the root ball before we could finally tow it away. Amazingly the only damage was a broken pinion shaft in the differential

These roots were are constant menace to the farmers when they were trying to get a wheat crop in the ground, and they were also a constant menace during harvesting, since many of them stayed partly in the ground and stuck up in the air to damage the harvesters. However, the mallee roots had one valuable asset in that they were an excellent source of firewood, every bit as good as coal and much cleaner, also they were readily available, and free. In later years, some inventive people in the city of Perth, found another use for them. They realised that when cut into slabs with a diamond saw they became a valuable raw material for craftsmen to make clocks and other household ornaments, because they polish up so beautifully and exhibit an astonishing grain structure.

Getting mallee roots small enough to fit into the, ever famous, metters wood stove, and various hot water heaters, was quite difficult and needed a fair amount of skill and a lot of persistence, since they are extremely hard and cannot be chopped with an ordinary axe. They had to be broken up with the axe, rather than cut. They needed to be studied to work out which way they would break along the grain, which criss-crossed back and forth at all angles.

One of the local farmers came up with an innovative way of breaking them up, without too much effort on his part. Matt, made a habit of stacking the roots on a large flattish outcrop of granite near which he had built his house. Whenever his wife complained of the lack of fuel for the house, Matt would start up his old bulldozer and drive it back and forth across the top of the heap until enough bits broke off, for his wife to collect.

Occasionally when breaking up mallee roots a small sliver would break off and spin through the air at a great rate of knots, screaming like a ricocheting bullet, and god help anyone who got in the way, as you will see.

It had been raining hard for a number of days, and although we needed the rain to establish a crop and water the homes and animals, enough was enough and we were heartily sick of it. All the creeks and flood-ways were running flat out and had mostly, broken their banks and were inundating the low-lying country around the district making travel very difficult and often impossible. It was cold and wet and not one bit pleasant but it was wintertime, and the rain was essential out in the farming areas.

I was glad to get home this night and get out of the rain and wind, have a lovely hot soaking bath to warm my bones, followed by a comforting meal of boiling hot soup with a hot, roast dinner as well, before settling down for a quiet night, and hoping that none of the farmers would break down during the night, and drag me from a warm cosy bed. Just as I was preparing to retire the phone cut loose with its insistent ringing. Oh no, I thought, not this early, at least let me have a few hours kip before dragging me out into the cold wet night.

It was the sister in charge of our Silver Chain Nursing Post, who answered when I reluctantly picked up the handset. I was instantly alert, this was no ordinary call from a farmer, this was something much more serious. She asked, "Brian are you available for an ambulance trip to Princess Margaret Hospital."

"Yes, certainly, sister," I replied, "just give me a few minutes to put on some warm clothes and I will be right there".

I knew that this was going to be a long cold night, because the hospital was in Perth city, some 220 miles (350km) away, and the ambulance was not fitted with a heater system.

When I arrived at the Silver Chain Post, where the ambulance was housed, I saw that the roller door was open, and the sister had the rear doors of the van open, ready for loading the patient, it was obvious that we were in a hurry to get away.

"Hello sister, sorry to take so long but I was ready for bed, what's happened?" I queried.

"We have a severe eye injury that needs urgent surgery at the children's hospital in Perth". She replied

"The patient must be a child is it? Who is it, and what happened" I asked as I scribbled the beginning of my report.

"Come inside quickly and I'll tell you about it, but you have to call Princess Margaret before you do anything else. I have a nice hot cuppa ready for you and I reckon that you're going to need it before this night's over." She told me.

As I was gulping down the scalding hot tea, she picked up the phone and dialled the hospital, and asked for the eye specialist with whom she had spoken earlier.

"I have Dr.----- on the line now Brian, he is insisting that he speaks with you before you leave town." She stated.

"Thanks sister I'll take it now." Then into the phone, "Yes doctor, what is it that I need to know about my patient's transport."

"Are you the actual driver of the ambulance?" He asked me.

"Yes that's correct doctor," I answered.

"Fine, now I want you to listen very carefully to what I have to say. It is vitally important that you do exactly as I say. How far away are you at the moment?"

"About two hundred and twenty miles away, doctor." I replied.

"Okay, now according to me, it's 8.45 pm., and I don't want to see you at my hospital before 4.00-4.30 even 5.00 am. in the morning at the very earliest. If you get here any earlier I will personally crucify you. Do you understand?" He spat out. "That little boy's eye is your responsibility. You must get it here, to me in an operable condition. You must drive slowly, no more than 30 miles per hour all the way, and it's vital that you do not hit even the smallest bump on the way. Do you fully understand what I am telling you, driver?" He asked.

"Yes sir, I certainly do understand and I will do my very best to get him to you in one piece, even if it takes all night. I'll see you for breakfast in the morning, cheerio for now." I stated.

"Do you know how to support and transport an injury such as this? He queried.

"This is the first time for me doctor, but yes I have been well tutored in the technique and I can certainly manage that part of it, thank you for asking." I answered. "Goodbye for now."

The sister had time to explain, that the boy's father, had come home from the seeding work, only to be told by his wife, that, they were out of firewood, so could he please oblige and chop some mallee roots whilst she finished off preparing his meal. He asked his eldest son about 9 year old to shine a torch onto the wood to enable him to see to chop it and a small chip flew off, hitting the boy in the eye and bursting a blood vessel in his eyeball.

So, there you have it, except for a few small details. Our town, like most in the wheat belt, was built in a hollow. I have been told by an expert that the railway line is the main reason for this habit. They have to have a reasonably level area to facilitate shunting of the rail cars, and in most areas this is in a hollow or valley between two hills.

These valleys, and ours was no exception, often become waterways in times of heavy rain, and raging torrents at times. The little towns were often flooded in the winter. Our town had always been prone to this problem, as it lay between two fairly steep hills and was in the water-course which began many miles away near the 'Ironcaps', which are two large hills on the way to Norseman.

After the last serious flood, a few years ago, our local bulldozing contractor had cut a deep gully to the west of the town, with solid levee banks each side to make sure that it would never occur again. Then, a solid floodway had been constructed to give access to the town, with some large concrete pipes running under the road to allow the water to flow beneath the road surface. However, the road crossing was made wide and flat so that any excess water could flow above the bitumen, but be shallow enough for cars to cross.

At the moment though, this crossing was still headlamp deep, even in a big vehicle like the ambulance, and had been for a few weeks. There was a distinct possibility that there were also holes in the bitumen surface where the water had undermined the surface and caused potholes.

As this was the only way out of town, we set off with a fair amount of trepidation. I eased the big ambulance down the levee bank and started to crawl across to the other side. As I expected, the headlamps went below the surface of the water and darkness prevailed. However, I had taken the precaution of arranging for one of our neighbours to come along to the crossing, and shine his headlamps across to the other side to guide me on my way. I felt a great weight lifting off my shoulders as we rose up on the far side without any problems. It seemed that the road surface was holding together quite well at the moment.

It was a great relief to be on solid ground again but there were at least three more flood-ways to negotiate before we got to the next town 40 miles away but none of them was as bad as this one as they were shallower and wider.

Driving an ambulance through the night is not much of a drama when you are in a hurry because the adrenalin keeps the driver alert and the journey is much shorter in time. Having to drive slowly and carefully was a positive nightmare. Every change in the road surface looked like a bump, even where the bitumen just changed colour slightly. The concentration was a terrific strain on every fibre of my body as well as my eyes and brain. Seven or even eight hours of this sort of driving was going to test every part of me to the limit.

I was extremely pleased to see the Brookton roadhouse, although I still had 80 or so miles to go, but everything had gone well to date. How I wished that the café was open, as I could have killed for a cup of hot tea, or a bowl of hot soup.

In spite of my precautions, I was frozen stiff and my feet were numb from the cold. All that I could do was press on to the city, where at least, the traffic would be very light at this early hour. I had to drive right across the city to get to the children's hospital at Subiaco.

When we were in a hurry, we were escorted by the flying squad, a crack arm of the police force who negotiated a smooth passage through the traffic but on a slow trip we were on our own.

Then, there it was, I was descending into the metropolitan area at last and I could pick out the streetlights in the distance. There was still a long way to go yet, though, and although there were no flood-ways, the city streets had their own problems, including railway crossings.

It was with an immense feeling of relief that I reversed into the ambulance bay at the hospital and a waiting orderly took over from me.

After unloading my patient, I went up to the ward to see the surgeon, and check on the boy.

The surgeon, who was the doctor that I had spoken to earlier, (it seemed like days ago, not hours) congratulated me on my driving. It was almost five o'clock, and he thanked me for getting the boy there in good condition, and he was able to assure me that the eye would soon be on the mend.

As a rule, the city hospitals were very good to us country ambulance drivers, but this was my first visit to this hospital and I wasn't aware of the protocol, so I enquired of the attending sister about how I could obtain some urgent refreshments. Knowing that at 5am. I had no chance of getting anything around the town, and it was imperative that I received some sustenance at the hospital ready for the long drive home.

The starchy old sister gave me terse instructions to find my way to a self help machine, which was situated miles away on another floor in the day clinic. She made it quite obvious to an ignorant country ambulance driver like me that it was way below her dignity to worry about refreshments at a time like this.

The surgeon, who was still examining the eye picked up the vibes that all was not well with me and turned around to ask, "Do you have a problem of some kind driver?"

"Oh no, not really," sir I replied, "I was stupid enough to think that I had, probably, earned a nice cup of tea for my nights work, and as I have no chance to buy one around town at this time of day, I was silly enough to think that the hospital might oblige me and supply one, but it appears that I was wrong."

The doctor got off the bed, where he had been sitting chatting to his patient, and pulling himself up to his full height he said, "We will have a tray now sister, if you don't mind, thankyou."

Giving me a withering look, the sister stormed out of the ward and returned some little time later with a tray of sandwiches, cake, tea and coffee. As she put it down the surgeon said, "That will be all now, thank you sister."

We made ourselves comfortable on the patient's bed and began to enjoy our little picnic.

All that was required of me now, was to refuel at the ambulance base in Wellington Street, and face a 5 hour trip home for breakfast and another day at the office.

Chapter 43

THE DAM BUSTERS

It was a cold wet winter's night and we had had many like it in recent days. It seemed as though it was never going to stop raining again, and although we were glad of the rain, we were getting sick of it this winter. All seeding work on the farms had been halted because the tractors were forever getting bogged, and that was making a mess of the paddocks, as well as causing tempers to flare. Even a drive into the town, to obtain supplies, and maybe, a quick visit to the local watering hole to check that the amber fluid was still flowing efficiently was a trial. The roads were quagmires of slippery mud and even on the bitumen we had to watch out for the flood-ways because the creeks were "running a banker", and threatening to overflow out on to any flat land around them

One positive thought that came to mind was the distinct possibility of a massive crop of mushrooms for many weeks to come The fairways of the golf course could always be relied on to fill the pantries of the townies, and the farmers would bring in buckets full each time they braved the conditions to drive 30 or 40 miles to get to the town.

I had heaps of repair work to keep me busy, because the farmers were using this lull in procedures to catch up with repairs, ready for the "big push" as soon as it was dry enough to travel again.

Late one evening, it was pitch dark and raining like mad again and I was working at one of my benches, which looked out across the residential street, and between the two nearest houses. I had a clear view of the north road running out of town.

There was a glow appearing in the far distance as though someone was coming along the road into town, in spite of the late hour and the terrible conditions. The glow quickly materialised as the headlamps of a vehicle and by the look of it the driver was going flat out.

This was looking like a serious emergency and I quickly rubbed my hands clean on a piece of rag. I was one of the only two people willing to man the ambulance at all, and this was looking like I might be needed. Oh God, not on a night like this, please. I was nearly ready to go home and crawl into bed after a nice cuppa tea and a long hot shower, and the thought of driving the ambulance around all night wasn't my favourite dream.

As I watched the vehicle, getting close now, it was obvious that, whoever was driving it was in a serious hurry, and it finally roared into town and braked hard, before sliding sideways around the corner into our street and heading this way. The driver was probably expecting me to be at work as usual, at this time of the evening and had spotted the lights in the window.

I was always ready and willing to attend the ambulance when it was needed, after-all, I might need it myself one day, but tonight I was definitely averse to the idea of a long cold journey to get medical assistance for one of our residents.

Much to my relief, the vehicle, which I could now see clearly, was a white Holden utility belonging to one of our nearby farmers. Ben, the owner, was also an earthmoving contractor whose main bulldozer driver lived across the street. The utility slid into the driveway and Ben was jumping out long before it stopped. As his feet touched the wet ground he started running up to the front door of the house and began pounding on the door, and shouting out, "Mick, come quick. Open up and get your boots on, I need you now".

Mick who had been relaxing ready for bed after a long hard day working a large caterpillar bulldozer, opened the door to see what the heck was going on.

"Come on inside out of the rain and tell me what's going on, Ben", he said.

"No, I 'aven't time for that. Get your boots on quick and come with me. I need you to drive your dozer. Hurry up, we 'aven't much time."

With that Ben was running back to the utility ready to take off again, as soon as Mick ran out of the house still pulling at his boots. Mick was hardly in the seat when Ben slammed the utility into reverse and took off with the door still swinging free, and swung the wheel into full lock as he hit the street. With the tyres spinning as they tried to get a grip on the wet gravel, they took off out of town heading north towards Ben's farm and home.

Upstream and behind Ben's house, there was an earth dam, which had served as their water supply for many years but it was finding all this rain too much to bear. The earth walls were about to collapse and the stream of water in the creek was already running dangerously close to the house in which Ben lived with his wife and about ten assorted kids. Earlier, realising the danger, Ben had started up his brand new Caterpillar D7E dozer and began to remove the bank farthest from the house to let the water out of the dam. He had ventured too far along the bank and the lower side of the bank gave way beneath the bulldozer's tracks. The machine sank down quickly until one track was completely under water and the footplate was awash right up to the driver's seat before it found a bit of reasonably firm ground. Ben didn't fancy loosing his brand new and very expensive machine, but he was too scared to move it again without some sort of safeguard.

He needed help, and fast, very fast unless he was to loose the D7. That's when he took off into town to get Mick. Fortunately the farm was no more than 5 miles out of the town, and when they returned the dozer was still parked at a crazy angle, but stable for the time being.

Mick jumped aboard the D6C that he usually drove, and which, fortunately, was parked in the farmyard and not miles away on a job as it would normally be. He fired up the motor and roared over to the main shed where Ben had picked up one end of a long heavy chain ready to hook it onto the draw bar of the D6. They dragged the chain over to the side of the dam close to the other dozer and Ben hooked the free end around the arm of the dozer whilst Mick screwed his machine around with it's rear end pointing at the D7. Once the chain was securely attached, Mick took up the slack, then put a fair amount of strain on it with the D6 until the tracks were just beginning to slip. At that point Ben was satisfied that the D7 was fairly safe, so he jumped aboard and fired up that huge engine. As soon as the engine was purring happily he put the transmission into reverse, lifted the blade and signalled to Mick to increase the drag on the chain. Using the D6 as an anchor, the D7 swung around like a pendulum on the end of the chain as it moved slowly backwards to the safety of dry land. The sunken dozer had opened up the bank enough to ease the pressure on the dam for the night and the house would be safe until daylight, when a further appraisal of the situation would be required. The relieved men, retired to the warmth of the massive farm house kitchen, to warm up, dry off, and attack a well earned cup of tea before driving Mick home again.

Chapter **44**

THE EASTER STORM

Easter-time is always a great bonus to serious fishermen like us. It means, weather permitting, four full days of fun on the ocean with heavy lines hanging over the side deep-sea fishing. It isn't easy to explain life at sea to anyone not familiar with the experience. We often hear tales of seasickness, engine trouble, and other forms of disasters, involving small boats and the ocean, and I have no wish to diminish the discomfort, sometimes pain and suffering of any one unfortunate enough to be so afflicted. I have personally been involved in a few such experiences much to my displeasure at the time, but I have spent countless hours at sea in a number of different boats, which afforded me great pleasure that I will look back on for evermore.

After the original motor in my mates boat died of old age, we had to fit a new Perkins marine motor and gearbox. The company representative who arranged the supply of the new motor had no knowledge of life at sea, and he was having some difficulty coming to terms with our enthusiasm and urgent desire to get back on the water, so we invited him to come with us, once the refit was complete.

Andrew, a Scots laddie was quite eager to come to sea with us, once he had thought about it and he gladly accepted our invitation. Because Andrew had never ever been fishing in his life, Rod suggested that I take him, under my wing as they say, and show him the ropes. We started off in very deep water on the edge of the continental shelf looking for snapper and other similar fish. Because the water was so deep we needed to have 250 to 300 yards of line out in the water with 3lbs of lead on the end of it which meant a long haul in with a fish or as often as not just to check and re-bait the hooks. After an hour or so with no results Andrew was getting a little bit sick and tired of hauling in the line and letting it go again just to check the bait and he began to whinge and complain about it saying, "Och man, dee I have to keep hauling in this bloody line when I aren't catching anything? It's alright for you, you've caught three or four of the damned fishes, but I haven't even had a bite yet."

"Oh, don't worry any minute now you'll get one then you'll see how good it gets." I replied.

"That's okay, but my arms are aching like mad, and my back and legs hurt as well." He answered.

"Yea well, that's because you sit around in your cosy office all day, eyeing off all the girls, you're just soft, that's all. You need a bit of toughening up. A good stiff walk through the Scottish highlands will do you a lot of good." I told him.

I had no sooner finished talking than his line went tight and he began the fight of his life. He had probably, more by good luck than good management I should say, hooked a large fish, probably a snapper by the performance that it was putting up.

The battle was on in earnest and I coached him carefully to make sure that the line went safely on the deck, and none of it got around his arms or legs where it might do him some serious harm if things went wrong. When the fish was almost up to the surface I pretended to push him aside and take over so that he could rest his sore hands and aching arms but he would have none of it saying, "What dee yee think I am, A bloody bairn or something that I cannay pull up a wee fishy on my own, then? I'm a lot bigger than you and I can manage this wee ane."

Eventually he landed the fish, a very large pink snapper and he held it up high with pride to have a good look at it and asked, "Why dee they call them snappers?"

Just then the boat rolled and the fish swung in close to him and snapped a bit of skin off his bare elbow. "I think you have your answer, Andrew" I replied once he finished swearing.

Easter was almost upon us and we were preparing for a hard weekend, Rod, Art, Andrew, who was by now a seasoned and ardent fisherman, and myself. One of our main concerns was always the weather, which governed all things at sea. We were always listening to the reports from the weather bureau, although we felt that they couldn't be relied on to be very accurate, and they had got us into serious trouble on one or two previous occasions. However, it was the best that was available to help us make our decisions as to which direction, and how far we went, and of course, whether to go at all on that particular day.

As I was working in a country town some 200miles away, the run up to Easter had to be carefully planned. The arrangement with Rod was that if I showed at the marina before 11.30 pm I was going fishing, but if I was any later they were not to wait for me and I would miss one days fishing.

We had the travel arrangements down to a fine art. Sandy would have everything ready for my return home after work at 5.00 o'clock. I would hit the shower whilst she packed the car, then we were off like the clappers in our Morris 1100, there were no maximum speed limits on the open road at that time so it was full throttle most of the way to Perth.

We ate the sandwiches that Sandy had prepared, as we hurtled along the highway. We only needed to make one quick stop, at New Norcia, to re-inflate the tubeless tyres on the front wheels. As the 1100, was a front wheel drive, I was able to corner much faster than a rear wheel drive and this appeared to roll the tubeless tyres on the rims and allow tiny quantities of air to escape and reduce the pressure. Other 1100 drivers confirmed this as a definite possibility, so we eventually fitted tube type Michelin tyres, which fixed the problem. If ever I was running late, I would flash the headlamps at the top of the hill on Preston Point Road before descending the cliff to the marina. The guys could see me from there and would wait until I arrived. I did have one near miss, but the guys were delayed any way and I arrived in the nick of time.

One Tuesday, one of our regular customers, Jack Payne, called in to tell us that his near new Pontiac Parisienne was playing up.

He said, "I took it into City Motors in Perth for it's regular check up and service, but on the way home I couldn't get above 92mph on the Marchagee Straights, so they must have got the timing wrong or something. Can you have a look at it for me?"

I answered, "There can't be much wrong with

it if you can get a huge car that size up to 92 mph, most of the systems would have to be okay and City Motors are the state distributors for this model. We have very little information on the Pontiac range and that is only basic lube statistics. If you're game enough to trust me with your pride and joy I'll give it the once over and see what happens."

"Look mate," Jack replied, "This car usually does 110mph along the Marchagee straights without any bother so I know there is something wrong, okay. I know it's in safe hands with you so just do your best. If you can find the fault it'll save me a wasted trip to Perth. "

I was a bit surprised to find out that this quiet gentleman, now in his late 60's, was a bit of a speed hog and I thought he owned this beautiful motor car for the sheer pleasure and comfort of driving long distances with ease. The marchagee straights was the only decent stretch of straight road within miles and I was forced to ask him, "How the heck will I know if it is fixed, I don't have time to drive it to Marchagee, and there's nowhere around here that I would want to drive this great tank anywhere near that speed?"

"Just take it for a burst up the road to Three Springs, you'll soon know if it's okay. It's not just the top speed, you can feel it in the other gears. It just doesn't perform at all, like it should." Were his final words as he walked off home.

I had never even seen under the bonnet of a Pontiac, in fact, this was the only one that I had ever set eyes on from close range. I lifted the hood and looked in the engine bay. It contained a huge V8 motor with a big 4 barrel carburettor that was nearly as big as the engine in my little Morris. I checked out all the basic setting and all was fine so that left me with that awful carburettor. I disconnected all the pipes and other fittings, carefully marking every item so that I would be able to refit it correctly, providing of course that it was fitted correctly to start with. I undid the nuts that were holding it on to the manifold and lifted it out onto the workbench. There was no obvious way of splitting it apart so I decided to upend the brute to see what the under side revealed. As I turned it over there was a solid clunk and a counter weight swung around and hit my thumb. The weight was attached to one of the four throttle spindles running through the body of the carburettor and I felt that it should not have been free to turn on it's own. Maybe I've just got lucky, this is where the fault might be.

Deeply set into the base, were the heads of 4 screws, which held the whole thing together. When I lifted the base away I could see what may be the problem. Because the screws were underneath the carburettor, it had to be upside down to fit them, and this meant that the counter weight was upside down, causing the spindle to turn and putting the butterfly valves at 90 degrees to their normal position, where it fouled the main butterfly valve above it, preventing it from opening fully. I soon realised that it was necessary to rotate and hold the counter weight with my thumb until the base plate was in it's place, and the screws started.

With hope in my heart, I reassembled the motor, and with a fair amount of trepidation I hit the starter. I was dreading the distinct possibility of having to tell Jack that his beloved engine was wrecked, but it fired up beautifully and began to purr contentedly like a massive pussy cat. So far, so good. Now, out onto the road for a quick trip to the next town and back. There was very little straight road, but as I approached the best bit, I kicked the throttle down hard and slammed my back into the sumptuous upholstery, as the massive car surged forward and hurtled along the road, as any good Pontiac should. I saw the speedo needle hit 98mph before I realised that the next corner was very close and I was forced to brake hard and reduce the speed to a steady 65mph or go bush.

I returned to the workshop, delighted with my mornings work, and rang Jack to let him know that all was well with his car When Jack came to collect the car I said to him, "I could only get it up to 98mph on the Three Springs road mate so you'll have to wait till you go to Perth again, to find out if I've fixed it."

"Hell Brian, I'm glad I wasn't with you, I wouldn't be game to go that fast along there. It's a wonder you didn't end up in the bush or someone's paddock. I can't wait until the weekend though, as we're going south again to Busselton, since it's Easter weekend. Will we see you on the road? I suppose you're going fishing again."

"Yes that's the way it is Jack but I hope we don't see you on the road because you generally leave early, and I don't finish here until 5o'clock, you should be in the city by then unless I've stuffed up with your carburettor." I replied.

By this time I had the Michelin tyres fitted, and I was running on a 25% methyl benzene mixture that took the speedo "off the clock", on the longer straights. On Thursday afternoon we set off shortly after 5 o'clock and drove hard and fast towards the city.

This was one weekend that I didn't want to miss out on. South of Moora we were dismayed to find ourselves running into very dense smoke from a bush fire in heavy forest country. There were big trees over-hanging the road on both sides, completely shading out the late sun, which would normally make for pleasant driving, as we didn't have the modern luxury of air conditioning in those days, but with a rampant bush fire around this could be a nightmare. We could easily be trapped and burned to death. We considered turning back to Moora and going down the main highway instead but this tactic would have made us very late. We had seen no sign of the fire, just huge amounts of dense choking smoke. Had we decided to return we could easily find that it had closed in behind us and it might be better to continue onwards. I had been forced to slowdown as the smoke thickened up, but still there was no sign of flames and the smoke was so spread out over a vast area pointing, hopefully, to the fact that the main fire was still a long way off. Eventually the smoke began to thin out as we approached Bindoon Hotel, and then cleared away altogether, so we breathed a sigh of relief as we speeded up. It was about then that I realised that in the hurry to leave home, I had forgotten to refuel the car, but no worry, I could get methyl benzene at the shell service station at Upper Swan.

I was just finishing off refuelling when I glanced aside and spotted a familiar Pontiac pulling in at the other bowsers behind us. I couldn't help myself, I walked over and said to his back, "Gooday Jack, running a bit late are we."

"How the hell did you get here before us,

what time did you get away?" he asked.

"Like I said mate I had to work till 5 o'clock. So what's your excuse?" I replied.

"That's crazy, how could you have left after 5 o'clock and still got here ahead of us. You must have got away early. What did you think of the bush fires? They were quite spectacular and pretty scary, eh. I was beginning to think we might be held up all night." Jack asked me.

"Bush fires?" I queried. "What bush fires? We never saw any fires at all, just a hell of a lot of smoke."

"Come on, mate you must have seen them. The main road was closed for nearly two hours as the main front roared through. I thought that truck was a goner. He only just backed off in time. My god, I've seen plenty of bush fires, but nothing like that. How close were you when it went through? You must have been behind us. We left town about 3 o'clock, and we were sitting on 110mph along the Marchagee straights, so you must have been a fair way back behind us. I know that little rocket of yours almost flies but you couldn't have passed us without us knowing." Jack told us.

I laughed and said, "Look mate I've got to go or I'll miss the boat, come and see me on Tuesday and we'll see if we can sort this out. Your car must be okay if you were doing 110 mph. We must have been flying above the trees if we could only see the smoke."

Jack was waiting for me when I got to work on the Tuesday morning. "Now then, you can't run away so tell me, how the hell did you get ahead of us on Thursday? I've been chewing it over all weekend and I can't make any sense of it at all. If I hadn't seen you and spoken to you I wouldn't believe it was possible."

"Just get your map out and have a good look at it in the Moora region, you'll soon work it out. I thought we were in big trouble when we ran into the smoke and I thought we had made a bad mistake. As it turned out, we got it right, and you got it badly wrong." I stated.

"What the heck are you talking about, come on tell me before I get mad and flatten you." Jack retorted.

There's a short cut from Moora, straight down beside the railway line, which saves about 11miles, but it's a bit narrow and winding and a gravel surface. We always go that way instead of going down the main road. I really thought we were in big trouble this time though. If that fire had come right though it would have jumped that narrow road and we would have had it, for sure." I told him.

"Well I'll be damned, I've lived here all my life and I never knew about that road, I suppose it comes out near Bindoon hotel". He said.

"Yea, that's true, and now I've got work to do. I'm glad your cars fixed. I bet you have a few harsh words to say to City Motors this morning." I concluded.

"That's for sure, I'm going home to ring them up right now. I'll certainly give them a piece of my mind. Fancy a simple bush mechanic showing them city slickers the way round." Jack stated, with a huge grin as he got into the Pontiac and drove off.

After we left Jack at the service station we had a quiet run through the city, and arrived with a bit of time to spare. As I jumped aboard, Rod's brother Art cast off the mooring lines and Rod reversed the boat out into the current and we were away. The weather was perfect with only a slight sea breeze in our faces and a flat, calm sea, although the forecast had been less favourable with a storm threatening in the background.

I was relaxing on the foredeck after my long drive down from the country. My dog was asleep on my lap and midge, Rod's dog, on my feet as we approached the heads of the harbour groynes when I got the shock of my life. I found it hard to believe. This must be a hoax of some kind. I jumped up, spilling the dogs, and called out to Rod.

"Hey Mate, have a look at this, the storm warnings are up on the heads. Somebody's got to be joking don't they? There isn't a cloud in sight, stars everywhere and hardly a breath of wind. Surely it can't come up that quick, can it?" I asked him.

"Hardly think so would you. Maybe our friends in the bureau have knocked off for Easter and put up the storm warnings before they left, just in case they're needed." Rod called back, "Or maybe, they want the whole ocean to themselves, for the weekend."

"Well what are we going to do, ignore them,

or stay at home?" I queried.

"What say we sail over to Rottnest Island and have a look from there. If it does blow up it will be from the south west, so if we head out south west from Parker Point, instead of going to direction bank, {one of our favourite fishing spots, as long as the conditions were ok}, we can put it behind us and sail home in comfort." Rod suggested.

"That sounds okay to me." I answered. "I'd always trust your judgement ahead of the bureau's any day. What do you reckon Art, go or stay? Rods never been wrong before and my gut feeling is the same as his, that we have a magic day ahead of us, so do we go southwest? What do you say?"

"Southwest sounds fine to me mate, but I reckon it doesn't matter any way with conditions as good as this. If it blows up we'll have plenty of time to return safely." Art replied.

By about 1.00 am. we had turned away from the island and put Parker Point on our stern quarter. The sea was dead flat with only a hint of swell and a clear moon, shining down on us from a star filled sky. This was shear bliss, if heaven is this good I'll have no complaints. There was just a slight westerly breeze in our faces, and the big engine was purring happily below decks.

When I awoke it was just breaking day and the weather was still ideal. "Where do you reckon we are, Rod?" I asked.

"About 35miles due west of Mandurah, mate. We could just see the glow of the lights from Mandurah on the far horizon when it was still dark. Art has the kettle on and as soon as we have breakfast, we'll get down to some serious fishing. There's still enough breeze to give us a drift, so we should go quite well, once we find a nice bit of reef." Rod told me. "It's a great pity that Andrew had to pull out at the last minute, he's going to miss a beauty." Rod knew this coast like the back of his hand, and with the help of the Ferruno echo sounder, he would have no trouble putting us onto a nice bit of reef.

With a hearty breakfast inside our bellies we settled down to some serious fishing. The boat was drifting steadily and she was just rolling slightly as we settled onto the reef. It was only a few minutes before Rod had a good bite and he was soon hauling in his first fish of the day, a very nice Dhufish.

We were still enjoying our fishing until about mid morning when the wind died away altogether. It was really eerie, a completely new experience for me. There wasn't the tiniest breath of air, and the ocean settled down to become dead flat like a sheet of glass. There wasn't even the slightest ripple on the surface, nor was there the slightest sound except the occasional cry of a sea bird somewhere far away out of sight. Even God must have been holding his breath. It felt as though we ought not to speak to one another and disturb the stillness. It was like being in a church. After about a half hour, there came a sudden thump on the cabin wall on the opposite side to where we were fishing, and the dogs took off with a salvo of sharp barks as they ran around the foredeck to investigate. I went to see what had caused the noise and found a good sized flying fish lying stunned on the deck. Apparently it had been flying through the air and the boat had got in the way. This occurrence was repeated a number of times during the next few hours. The fish had stopped biting and the lines were just hanging limply over the side. I was starting to understand how the ancient mariners felt when they were becalmed. No wonder they went mad or did really crazy things. At least we could always start up the motor and go home. This was so eerie it was unbelievable and continued for about 5 or 6 hours, then suddenly Rod called out, "Did you guys feel that."

Art replied. "Do you mean that tiny puff of air on my face, Rod".

"Yea, that's what it felt like, it was ever so light. Hello, there it goes again look to your lines, with a sea breeze coming in the fish will soon wake up and we'll have some fun." He answered.

We had been becalmed between two rows of crayfish pots for the whole time, and we hadn't moved at all, then as the breeze picked up, although still ever so slight, we all began to hook up on Dhufish, and other species and we were soon working our butts off as we pulled up one after another.

By nightfall we had had enough for one day and we set off for Rottnest Island with a light breeze and ever so slight sea following us in and still no sign of any adverse weather. In all the times that I had been out at sea I had never encountered anything like these conditions, it was almost magical. Once we were tied up at the wharf and everything shipshape we walked up to the bake house, where we swapped a feed of fish for some freshly baked bread with our old friend Frank Thorson, the baker. After a good old chat we headed back on board to prepare a meal of fresh Dhufish fillets, and the best bread in the whole world. You have to try eating fish still kicking fresh from the sea wrapped in newly baked bread to realise how good it really is. I watch the modern chefs on the television occasionally and I feel sick in my stomach when I see them mucking up fantastic food with barrow loads of garlic, spices, and handfuls of coriander, yuk! I like fish to taste like fish and I can't see the sense of making good steak taste like some crazy Asian or European muck. The evening was calm and balmy as we settled down for the night after a final mug of tea to wash down our meal.

It was still dark on Saturday morning and we were preparing breakfast and checking our gear when I happened to spot a small light approaching along the jetty that could only be a bicycle headlamp. Of course, it was Frank's teenage daughter bringing a freshly baked loaf of bread to see us through the day, and if we were lucky, which we were, one of those delicious iced fruit loaves which Frank baked to perfection. Could life ever get any better than this? Not even if we were very rich. I think not.

Once we had our bellies full of the best food in the world we untied the old girl and headed out to sea again through the passage on the south side of Phillip rock, and with a sharp turn to starboard around the end of Natural Jetty, which is a long, low, flat, shelf of rock, running out from the shore, then out into the ocean deep. It was my turn to take the wheel and the others relaxed until I cut the motor in roughly the same area as yesterday and we settled down to another magic day's fishing and relaxing on the water. Like the day before we never set eyes on a single boat all day long.

We had the whole ocean to ourselves with just a slight breeze and a gentle swell.

Normally we would have stayed out all night as well, but with the weather bureau's threat of heavy weather we decided to return to the island. The sun was slowly settling down into a perfect sea again.

Easter Sunday followed the pattern of the previous days but the wind had a little bite in it now and the swell had increased somewhat, but still there was hardly a cloud in the sky. This must be the most perfect way to soothe out the nerves after a hard weeks work with the sun smiling down on us. God must have a great affection for fishermen to treat us so well, and as the time went by we were able to relax more and more.

We were still a little apprehensive about the storm warnings so we decided to return home to Fremantle and our pen at Aquarama, the marina where the boat was moored, at the end of another perfect day.

We refuelled the diesel tanks and thoroughly checked the motor and all the equipment before settling in for the night. Next morning we were away very early as usual and when we were sailing through the harbour Rod said,

"Look at that guys, they've removed the storm warnings today. They certainly got it badly wrong and spoilt a fantastic weekend for a good many boat lovers.

Art made the comment, "I wonder what it was that made them feel that there was a storm around when in fact the weather was so balmy. I bet there are a few red faces in the bureau when they return on Tuesday morning."

I was walking about on the foredeck with the dogs as we were approaching the heads. It was just breaking day and I was fascinated by the clouds on the far, west, horizon. They were comprised of long 'Mares tails",{long streamers of wispy cloud stretching out ahead of a main cloud front}, when my brain clicked into gear and I realised the significance of this phenomena. I walked back to the wheelhouse and said, "I don't like the look of that sky out to the southwest Rod. Maybe the bureau was correct. There seems to be a storm approaching but it's about four or five days later than they anticipated."

"By heck you might be right and look at all these small boats heading out of the harbour, surely they can see the possibility of danger. What do you guys reckon? Do we carry on or play safe? I can feel a new urgency in the wind as well."

I answered, "Look you guys, I reckon, we've had a fantastic weekend so why don't we pull into the wharf and ring the girls. We can get them to meet us at the Maylands jetty. They've been home all weekend with the kids so that we could have a fun time. We could go for a nice run up the river and have a picnic up near Caversham or the back of Guildford somewhere. The kids will have a lovely time fishing in the river, and it's not often that they get the chance to spend a day with us on the water." Art replied, "Hey that's a smashing idea, mate I'm all for it, what about you Rod?"

Sounds great to me, we have plenty of tucker on board and it'll make a nice change." Rod answered.

We pulled into the wharf to ring Rod's house, where all our families were gathered for the holiday, and they were delighted to meet us at Maylands. The ladies were glad to be relieved of most of the responsibility for the kids who had a fantastic day with us, swimming and fishing and having a lot of fun. We dined on fresh fish and the rest of that fantastic bread from Rottnest bakery.

As usual we had the radio switched on, to pick up weather bulletins and other general news It was about mid afternoon that the radio station broadcast a severe weather warning for the coast from Jurien Bay to Cape Leeuwin. Over on Rottnest Island, the Island authorities broadcast a warning to all small boats around the Island. They were warning them not to attempt the crossing back to the mainland until further notice. In fact it was Wednesday afternoon before they were able to give the "all clear" and allow the boats to return home. They had been stranded on the Island all that time, and also lost two days work.

Chapter 45

COPS AND ROBBERS

As a distributor of dairy products it's my job to deliver to commercial premises, shops cafes etc. as required. One day I was delivering to a BP. petrol station and the manageress told me that a customer was giving the teller a hard time at their other petrol station nearby and she had to go and help out. I dropped off the order and because the other station was my next call I followed her as she took off at a great rate of knots.

I pulled into the driveway to find that the police had arrived and were parked directly behind the manager's car, so I parked my F150 truck, which is fitted with a large, shining white refrigerated box body a couple of metres behind the police van.

Apparently a local man had been giving the

attendant a hard time so she called the police. The officers were inside the shop and when I arrived and were surveying the security camera screen in an attempt to identify the offender.

When the police left the office they walked towards my vehicle to gain access to theirs jumped in and started the motor. Then to my amazement and horror the driver selected reverse revved up the motor and slammed into the front of the F150. There wasn't any damage to either vehicle, although it made a heck of a bang and a very shame-faced copper got back out to survey the damage.

I pointed out to him that he had left the rear step of the paddy wagon in the lowered position and it had sheared under the lower edge of my front bumper like a knife and had anyone been unfortunate enough to be walking through between our vehicles he would surely have cut their legs off and a child would have been cut in half. His partner and I gave the poor devil a heck of a ribbing before he could leave the scene. I even suggested that we call up the traffic branch and have him breathalysed as he would surely have done that to me if I had made a stupid mistake like that. I asked his offsider if I should call the police station and report the accident but he assured me that the whole station would be enjoying the story for morning tea break so I wouldn't need to bother about it. It isn't often I get the chance to get one up on the police so I relished the occasion with glee.

Chapter **46**

MINI TORNADOS

One dark and stormy morning I was out on the streets delivering dairy products to my customers and it was already raining quite heavily as I turned into a main thoroughfare. There was a strong squally wind tearing around the streets making life uncomfortable. As I straightened up into Spencer Street there was a terrific blinding flash and a crash.

There had been no visible fork of lightening, but a huge bolt of lightening hit the top of a nearby power pole with a mighty flash, ran down the pole and shorted out onto the ground throwing the wires onto the wet road. The wires then set up a fireworks display as they arced out on the wet street.

A little further along the now darkened street, there were a series of crashes as the lightening bolts hit one power pole after another. Two blocks down the street I turned into a car park besides a large two-storey motel and stopped alongside the building. As I was getting into the rear of the truck another series of lightening bolts ran across the rear of the motel and the wind suddenly whipped up to gale force and more. I was selecting product for the motel when the truck began to heave and jump around violently so I sat on the floor of the truck and held onto some full crates of milk. I thought that even if the truck crashed over on it's side I was much safer inside than out. I was sure that the wind, which was increasing rapidly, would overturn my vehicle at any moment. I could feel the truck bouncing around as first one side then the other wheel lifted off the ground in a sort of crazy dance movement.

Then there was a tremendous roaring, tearing, crashing of metal as the wind tore much of the roof off the main buildings of the motel and threw it over the building into the swimming pool and car park. The iron railings and brick walls around the pool were torn from the ground and smashed to pieces

Because it was still a few minutes before 6 o'clock and therefore too early for breakfast, the car park was fortunately deserted and amazingly none of the many cars parked there were damaged as the storm rampaged on it's merry way. Had the storm hit only 10 minutes later the car park would have been busy with the occupants of the motel rooms walking across it to the dining room for breakfast.

When most of the crashing and roaring had quietened down I got out to service my client and the wind tore at my clothing, threatening to throw me down the street. As I unloaded the milk a torrent of water fell from the sky and totally saturated me to my skin in spite of my heavy showerproof clothing. It wouldn't be accurate to call it heavy rain because it was over in a few seconds. It felt as though God had picked up a whole lake full of water and dumped it on top of me. I was instantly very cold and shaking like a leaf, wondering what on earth would happen next, but it was all over and calm settled down quite quickly although it was still raining heavily. The weather bureau gave it a name of course.

They called it a mini tornado. Thank God it wasn't a full sized one or else someone other than me would be writing this story.

I walked into the motel wheeling my trolley loaded with milk and the breakfast cook said I looked like I had seen a ghost as I moved down the darkened corridor towards the kitchen. My face was as white as snow, she said and I was shaking like a leaf. I took out my torch and went with the motel manager carefully up the stairs to the upper floor to assess the damage and work out a plan of action to protect as much as possible. I pointed out the large cool-room and suggested that we put as many of the electrical machines in there as was possible to keep them dry as there was little else that could be done

I was afraid that daylight would tell a very sorry tale and that repairs would be lengthy and expensive. Thank goodness for insurance.

There was nothing else that we could do so I set off once more on my rounds. I was totally stunned at the extent of the devastation around the area. Although the storm had only carved a relatively narrow path through the town centre and out into the suburbs the amount and extent of damage was unbelievable. I suppose the fact that it only took a few minutes made it all the more amazing. When I went in to see my next clients they were very worried about me because they said I was as white as a ghost and still shivering, either from the cold or fright or both.

One year later much of the damage around the town had been repaired or the buildings pulled down but there were still plenty of scars on the landscape to commemorate the occasion. Some of the older buildings were considered uneconomical to be repaired and will eventually be redeveloped into the latest style of building to suit modern needs of suitable tenants.

Chapter 47

CYCLONES AND TORNADOS

Storms, cyclones, and tornados seemed to be the bane of my life or is God just wagging his finger at the errant male and warning me to lift my game and toe the line or else!!

You see I had the misfortune to drive right through the eye of the worst cyclone to hit South Western Australia, Cyclone Alby, near Manjimup. On that particular night we not only had to bear the brunt of the cyclonic winds but the absolute terror of massive bushfires that were descending on us from the north.

Nothing more than a miracle saved us that night as the wind slowly turned at the last moment and veered off to the east and away from the town. The full story of that terrible night is told in my earlier story "Cyclone Alby" on page 79. You would think that that was warning enough but then I lived through a mini tornado in the previous story during my duties as a milk vendor.

But, not to worry, God still had more bad news and warnings for me.

You see, whilst I was still in the dairy business there was another bad day looming. Almost a year to the day after the previous story the next terrifying incident occurred and it was in the same area of town. That morning the weather had once again been very inclement with a fair amount of rain and plenty of winds. I had just left the scene of the previous tornado and headed into the milk depot to restock my truck when it happened again.

Unbeknown to me the area that I had just left was about to be devastated again only much worse than before. The mini tornado ran through the previous area then went on a wild rampage along Picton Road and followed me into the depot yard. Yes that's right, the damned thing was chasing after me probably upset at having missed me in Spencer Street. At the depot it took out its spite on all and sundry. I was just getting into the rear door of the truck when it hit. There was a tremendous roaring and crashing as it howled round the corner of the buildings and crashed right into the side of my truck. I could hardly hear myself think because the noise was deafeningly loud. It seesawed the truck up and down lifting the wheels clear of the ground and dancing it sideways towards the much larger truck parked alongside mine. I was very lucky that the truck was still partly loaded with about 1 ton of milk on board. I was afraid that it might end up hard against the other truck leaving us with a monstrous task of getting them apart. However it stopped short of that but it had joggled the truck about a metre sideways.

When it died down somewhat I stuck my head out to see what was happening and the sight was unbelievable. There had been hundreds of empty milk crates stacked neatly on wooden pallets by the fence but now they were flying around like confetti and dropping all over the yard in a sea of plastic. Most of the trees that I could see were either completely flattened or torn to shreds and there was a vehicle parked under some of the debris from the trees.

Once I had my load on I made an attempt to get to Eaton and continue with my days work. One of the depot workers ran towards the truck to tell me that the street leading back towards the highway was completely blocked with fallen trees and live power lines. I realised that I might be able to turn left instead of right as I left the yard then travel around the outer perimeter of the industrial estate and onto the South Western Highway, so I gave it a try. The wind was still howling and gusting and swinging the truck about and the driving rain made hard work of keeping the truck heading in the right direction. By driving on the street lawns and verges and ducking and dodging back and forth around trees and branches I was able to reach the main road without further incident.

A short way along the highway there was a semi trailer belonging to a local transport operator that was in serious trouble. A large branch had broken off a tree beside the road and it had crashed through the windscreen of the truck and frightened hell out of the driver. Fortunately the branch hit the passenger side of the windscreen away from the driver and no one was hurt.

As I left the semi trailer behind I realised that it was all over. There was no more damage, hardly a leaf left lying around and all was calm. When I pulled up in Eaton it was hard to believe that anything unusual had happened that morning. Sure Eaton had had it's share of the heavy rain and a fair amount of wind but not the violent storm that I had just witnessed. Friends of ours were running an electrical and white goods store on Sandridge road near Picton road and their store was severely damaged. When I called in later to see how they were they showed me a hole in the gyprock wall running along the rear of the store. They pointed out an electric iron impaled in the gyprock. They showed me the position on a shelf in the front window where the iron had been on show before the wind picked it up and hurled it across the shop into the rear wall. Thank goodness it was early enough in the day that the shop was empty so no-one was hurt.

After about 18 months there is still lots of damage awaiting repair but most of the worst buildings have been demolished including the Roman Catholic Cathedral. The Cathedral had suffered massive damage and even the bell tower was badly damaged. When the rubble was cleared away the bell from the tower was intact and undamaged beneath it all. Maybe it wasn't god that was after me after all, otherwise I'm sure he would have missed the old Cathedral. As soon as the insurance company finished their assessment tenders were called to build a new cathedral on that same hill. There now stands a brand new cathedral as a memorial to the old one and a magnificent building it is.

Chapter 48

CHANTELLE

My granddaughter is named Chantelle and it will eventually take a few years and a whole new book to tell you all about her, but of course, that's another unfinished scenario, although it's a very important part of my life with plenty of deliriously happy days and a fair amount of pain and sadness. However this story has very little to do with my granddaughter and is the story of a steam tractor and the reason for the title will become clear with time.

After moving to Harvey when I was in my early 50's I became involved with a restoration enterprise at the historic workshops in the small southwest town of Yarloop. The workshops had been, for many years, the nerve centre of a large timber getting outfit scattered throughout the south west of our state of

WA. In the early 1900s the developing world had a great thirst for timber, especially hard wood timber suitable for railway sleepers. The world's railways were expanding rapidly with the introduction of steam driven locomotives. There was no better timber for this purpose than the eucalyptus trees of Australia, and Western Australian Jarrah and white gum were among the best available, and there were large quantities ready to be harvested.

Millars Timber and Trading moved into the south west forests and began to extract timber mainly in the form of railway sleepers and most of these were exported around the developing world on sailing ships initially then moving on to steamships as they became more acceptable.

As Millars moved away from the city to harvest more trees they had to build their own infrastructure to get their equipment out into the forests and recover the timber back to the ports.

One of the problems was that most of the best timber was growing in the forests covering the Darling Scarp, a ridge of fairly high hills of around 1000 feet in height running fairly close to the coast and parallel to it from

Perth right down to Busselton. The hills rose very steeply from the coastal plain and were tough going especially in the days of heavy horse and bullock teams.

Once the government railway system was established along the flat coastal strip south of Perth and became available for public use, Millars interconnected with it. They built a system of narrow gauge railways suitable to negotiate the steep climbs over the ridge. Once over the ridge they set up many small steam powered mills to cut the timber into manageable sizes to facilitate transport to the harbours. These mills used up the waste timber and saw dust to feed the boilers of the steam engines.

The company had to build a large base and repair workshops at Yarloop. They set up foundries and machining shops so that they could be independent of the manufacturers in England because it often took about 6 months to a year to get the parts over by sailing ships.

I don't intend to go into the history of the workshops and timber industry because that's another story but I will mention the sudden closure of the workshops due to a devastating cyclone called Alby, which severely damaged the aging buildings that housed them.

A very dear friend of ours, Collin Pusey, collected many steam engines and pumps from around the state and set them up for public display in a shed at the now partly renovated workshops. I worked with Collin and a dedicated band of volunteer steam fanatics to rebuild and run these huge steam engines. The steam house is open and running on a number of Sundays throughout the year and we attempt to teach the general public about steam power and its great significance to the timber industry and other power needs of industry in general.

One day, Collin was approached and asked to provide a home for a half sized replica steam tractor which was in very poor condition having been neglected for many years. Collin, knowing of my involvement with real, full sized steam tractors in England offered the tractor to me to undertake it's restoration and hopefully it's operation at Yarloop and elsewhere in the future. Without hesitation I jumped at the chance and set to work re-engineering some of it's features. Then stripping, cleaning and repainting the rest. I designed and built a steam whistle for it and obtained a couple of passenger trailers to tow behind it and give the kids a ride. The restoration was a great success and gave me, and the visiting kids many days of pleasure.

At last we get to the story of Chantelle. I decided to call the little tractor Chantelle because it reminded me of my granddaughter of the same name. Like the little girl, the tractor needed constant supervision once the fire was lit and like the little girl she was always dirty. Due to the wood fire generating heaps of smoke and soot that poured out of her and the fact that it had, like it's real ancestors, a total loss oiling system. This meant that all the oil that it needed to run and lubricate the moving parts ended up liberally spread over her and the driver, in spite of which I loved her dearly, The girl and tractor alike, I found impossible to keep clean and no sooner had I finished one end than the other end would need my attention again.

One memorable Sunday afternoon I was wiping the oil off the tractor which was standing close to the steam house doorway whilst waiting for more kids to fill the trailers when a tall, thickset gentleman walked over to have a good look at the engine. He stood in front of the tractor and called out to someone behind him.

He called out "Look, Look, come here love. Here's 'Thomas'. Come and see."

A little girl who was probable close to three years old walked around him and into view. She smiled at me with a look of intense anticipation because, apparently she was an ardent fan of 'Thomas the tank Engine' then as she turned to look at the tractor and her face slipped off and turned to great scorn and utter disgust. She stood akimbo with her feet widely spread apart, then put her little hands firmly on her waist with elbows outstretched and looked upwards into the face of this giant of a man who was apparently her dad and spat out with much vehemence;

"Don't you know?" (huge breath) "That's not Thomas." (huge breath) "Thomas is a train."

(huge breath) "Thomas goes on the rails."

Another huge scornful breath, then "That's Terence" (huge breath) "Terence is a tractor". (huge breath) "Terence goes on the road".

With that pronouncement she stumped off in disgust and went into the steam house. She was so disgusted that she steadfastly refused a ride in the trailer. Her dad appealed to me for support but I was only able to agree with his daughter whilst doing my best not to laugh in his face.

Afterwards I said to Collin after recounting the incident, "Poor little girl, fancy going through the rest of her life with a dad as thick as that".

Not really part of this story but I feel compelled to mention that a huge bush fire ignited by lightening strike on the darling scarp rampaged through the area around Waroona and on to Yarloop. Sadly most of the town was totally destroyed and the historic workshops completely consumed along with much of the areas history. Lots of historic wooden houses were razed to the ground along with the hotel and post office. In spite of the savage nature and speed of the devastation only two elderly gentlemen were killed and later a western power worker repairing the damage died of a possible heart attack. The year was 2016.

Chapter 49

GRANDMOTHER'S VISIT

Well here we go again. I have many doubts about my ability to write my next story because it's too close to home. Some of my previous stories still upset me greatly whenever I read through them and I have been putting off writing this story for a very long time. It was always going to be difficult to get all the details and inferences in the correct order so that they make some sort of sense to other people but I owe it to my son David as this is his story. As you will remember if you have read my previous stories and especially 'A Ghost in The Bedroom' David is, like me quite psychic and extra sensitive to unusual phenomena and close personal scenarios. Small incidents that would normally be put aside, upset and affect us both very deeply. Even listening to and singing along with our National Anthem often brings tears to my eyes and I often cry at funerals and weddings so I know this is going to hurt.

It reminds me of our little farm at Busselton where we had a mob of sows and their babies running loose in a grass paddock. We used a low electric wire to prevent the sows digging all the grass up and it was supposed to also limit the movement of the piglets. One day I wandered up the paddock to check that all was well with them. At the time there were about thirty piglets running around but this day something was a bit odd. As I approached them I noticed that they were charging round and round in a tight circle near the 'hot' wire. It seemed as though they were playing a game of follow the leader at top speed when, suddenly, one of the larger piglets peeled off the circle and headed straight for the 'hot' wire going flat out and squealing like mad. All the other piglets peeled off the circle and followed at full speed like a big spring uncoiling. They knew that it was going to hurt like heck but they felt a terrible urge to fossick around at the other side of that dreaded wire and nothing was going to stop them The first one hit the wire at full speed, let out an agonised squeal and the others all followed suit landing in a heap at the other side. They picked themselves up, collected their wits and headed out across the paddock to see what they could find to eat.

At the age of sixteen my youngest son, David left home to join the Australian Navy. We were not at all happy about his choice of careers because David has such an active mind and a determined nature that I couldn't see how he would fit in and cope with all the hierarchy and rigmarole of navy life. He has too much of an independent spirit to tolerate all the 'bull-dust' of military regulations. He had always shown a determination to progress and succeed, that he would and did become a square peg in a round hole. He wanted to advance much faster than his peers or than the navy would allow. He didn't have time to wait for someone to die or retire to make room for him to progress.

David had a great knowledge and understanding of computers and electronics even before going into the navy so he was selected for 'electronic technical weapons' training. David excelled at his trade over the first two years and was selected to join the crew of a new submarine to be commissioned in the USA. However a particular Lieutenant in the training camp took a sudden dislike to him. This was probably due to the fact that he and some of his fellow seamen had caught the lieutenant in a very compromising situation with a fellow officer (female). Both of the officers were married but not to one another and the Lieutenants wife was in bed and dying from cancer. This incident combined with some personal problems, as this story tells, caused David to take a good look at navy life and he decided to resign and return to civilian life.

From the age of sixteen my son and all the other navy apprentices were encouraged to drink alcohol, and 'spirits' were very cheap and available through the officers mess. Some of his shipmates became serious alcoholics before they were legally allowed to drink at all and this, after the navy promised to look after my boy until he became of age. In recent times the media has highlighted this and other behavioural problems within the military and one often wonders how these people could ever defend our great country in times of severe strife. It was a very disappointed and disillusioned boy who walked out of the base at HMAS Nirimba and set about building a successful career in civilian life.

At this point David takes up the narrative and I will attempt to join it all together for you.

Whilst in the Navy I was stationed at the training base in the Blacktown area of Western Sydney and all the recruits were in the habit of socialising in the local communities. We were well respected by some and hated and despised by others. I suppose, due to our transient nature some parents weren't happy to allow their daughters to fraternise with us, although some of them were very willing to do so.

I became friendly with and set up a serious relationship with the daughter of a local milk vendor. Both the navy and the girl's mother were dead set against our relationship but we were deeply in love and continued to see each other. The girl's mother was particularly obnoxious and went to great efforts to keep us apart. When I was still only 17 and my girl only sixteen she became pregnant.

Despite our relatively youthful years we attempted to set up a life together to make the best of what was always going to be a difficult situation. Unfortunately forces within the navy and my girl's family forced us apart and I wasn't allowed to see out the pregnancy and enjoy fatherhood as a result and the navy made arrangements to send me to America to commission a new submarine.

I wasn't told of my girl's confinement. I wasn't able to attend the birth of my child, nor was I allowed any contact with them afterwards. The navy eventually informed me of the birth and told me that I had a son but no other information about the event was relayed to me at any time.

As a result of all this and the severe persecution from one of the navy Lieutenants I contacted my family in WA. and my parents hot footed it to Sydney to try and sort things out. The Lieutenant told my father over the phone before he left home that he was going to get me chucked out of the navy no matter how long it took.

The Lieutenant used one of his mistress's, a lowly midshipman, to set up a scenario so that he could have me charged and disciplined and maybe expelled. Unfortunately for them they miss timed their little scheme because I was due for extra leave because of my voluntary association with the navy field gun brigade. This association was unpaid but extra leave entitlement was tacked onto each segment of normal leave. This allowed me to leave the base one day early as a reward for services rendered. I was on a plane to visit my parents in WA. at the time that the alleged incident was supposed the have occurred.

My dad can be very difficult to deal with when he gets his back up and is extremely dogmatic when he believes in something. By the time he and mum arrived at the base dad was furious and ready to take someone apart. In spite of their professional training and experience Captain Swan and Commander Short were no match for my dad in his present mood and it only took a couple of days to convince them and the 'Big brass' in Canberra that my naval career was over. I was issued with an HONOURABLE discharge from the navy stating, "Not Required for Further Naval

Service" and I was released from duty.

I continued to live in the Sydney area for a while before returning home to WA.

Before I continue with the story I must point out that I was born and reared in Western Australia after my parents immigrated here in the 1960s and I had only very brief contact with my grand parents when I was very young. They were still living in England and had I passed them in the street I probably wouldn't have recognised them.

About the time that my baby son was probably entering this world I stayed off base with a friend who lived in Dural, north of Sydney.

I was visited one night by an 'entity' who left me feeling very strange and totally disoriented. There seemed to be no rhyme reason or logic to that visit and it was several years later that I received enough information to make any sense of it.

As I said I was staying overnight with a navy friend at the home of his father at Dural. It was somewhere about the middle of July when I woke up in the early hours of the morning and it was still pitch dark. Out of the darkness a figure of a woman materialised. She was sitting in a chair close to my bed-head. It was the figure of an elderly lady who was surrounded by a bluish-white light. She was holding something to her breast in the crook of her left arm. It had the appearance of a cocoon or baby all swaddled in soft wrappings.

I sat up in the bed; actually I felt that I had been 'forced' to sit up and take notice. Once I was sitting up, the figure reached out with her free hand and I held my breath as I watched it slide through my breast and into my chest and stopped my heart! I remember her smiling at me as she withdrew her hand and faded away from sight. She left me with the distinct impression that she had been trying to show me something but I couldn't for the life of me work out what it was but it was obviously something very important.

As I was recovering from the shock and getting back my equilibrium I looked up and noticed that my friends father, Ian, was standing in the doorway looking as though he had seen something very unusual, like; maybe a ghost or something similar, and I suppose he actually had done just that.

"Am I going mad or was that what I'm thinking it was, David?" He asked me.

"I really don't know" I replied "But it was a bit scary and a bit odd to say the least."

We chatted about this unusual scenario for a while then Ian went back to bed. By the hard light of the next morning it all seemed too crazy to mention and we left it at that. It was a few years before it came back to mind with another shock appearance, but this time it was only a photograph that triggered it off.

When I was only fifteen we received news that my paternal grand mother had passed away in England and her ashes had been interred in the churchyard, which is situated right across the street from her home. The news of her demise had an unusual effect on me. It seemed impossible to grieve for someone who was in fact a stranger to me because I have no attachment to them and this is how I felt for my gran, sad though it may seem. I was very sad to hear of her death but real grief just wouldn't come, however, what did upset me greatly was the effect that it had on my dad. For the first time in my life I saw dad cry and that illusion of indestructibility that I always carried of him was shattered in an instant. He was human after all, and what an amazing and frightening discovery that was after 15 years of total ignorance. I always realised that there was nothing wrong with all this, but at the time the effect that it had on me was a little hard to encompass. The fact that I couldn't grieve for my grandma but I could grieve for my father's loss was something that I found hard to deal with at the time.

It was shortly after my grandmother's death that I decided to join the Australian Navy after a visit to our school of the navy careers and recruiting officers. I was offered an apprenticeship as an Electronic Technical weapons engineer and I decided to enlist.

The naval training base was at HMAS Nirimba near Sydney so that meant a heck of a wrench at moving so far away from family and friends. It was because of this decision that I eventually met the girl who was to be, not only the mother of my children but later my wife , then ex-wife.

After leaving the navy I worked in Sydney prior to my return to Perth where another psychic occurrence visited me at Victoria Park, as my earlier story on page 119 "A ghost In The Bedroom" tells all.

Several years later due to the dogged persistence of my ex-girlfriend and a few weird events I became reunited with my early love and our son James. It was the first time that I had seen James and what a fine lad he was and a credit to his upbringing by his mum Robie-Lei. James was four years old by then and ready for the world. A few nights after our reunion in Albany I walked into our bedroom and found Robie-Lei in tears on the bed where she was sitting looking at a photograph. I asked her, "What on earth is making you cry, you should very happy my love."

In reply she showed me the photograph that had upset her and it was a snapshot of a gravesite and headstone.

I asked her "What has that got to do with you and how come it's so upsetting to you?" And I pulled her into my arms.

When Robie-Lei calmed down somewhat she said "That is the grave of our daughter Kirrilee. We had her interred with her grandparents in the

"Field of Mars" cemetery in Ryde near Sydney."

"That's impossible" I said. "I've only had one child and James is still with us here, so where does Kirrilee fit in?"

Robie-Lei then told me, "I was pregnant with twins but only James survived because Kirrilee was stillborn."

Then we both had a good cry whilst holding on to one another in mutual comfort before going in to look at James who was sound asleep, and thanked our good luck that at least we still had him.

After working through this momentous piece of information I suddenly remembered the vision that I had witnessed in Dural. Oh my God!! That lady was holding my baby Kirrilee and telling me that she was in safe hands. That she would look after her. But who was the elderly lady and where did she fit into the equation?

Some months later, after my marriage to Robie-Lei we were visiting mum and dad in Harvey when I spotted a photograph of an elderly lady on the table besides dads chair. She must be someone important in my dad's life to be sitting there. Then with a sudden jolt I realised that she was the lady holding Kirrilee in the vision.

I asked. "Hey dad, who the heck is that lady in your photograph?"

"Why? Don't you remember her? That's my dear old mum. She's your granny." Dad answered.

"Oh heck dad that explains a lot." He said.

We sat around and had a good old natter about family and family names. That's when we realised that James had been accidentally named after his uncle, mum and dad's first born baby who only survived only for a couple of days.

Later on we had another baby a lovely girl whom I named Chantelle and we inadvertently added Elizabeth as a second Christian name. Unbeknown to us my grandmother, who was always called Betty, had been christened Elizabeth Jean.

50

HYDEN PRE-SCHOOL CENTRE

Hillary Millar who is a farmer's wife with a farm some 20 miles or so east of the Hyden township decided that it was time that there was a preschool centre in our remote country town. There already was a preschool centre in our shire in the main town of Kondinin, but as Kondinin is 40 miles west of Hyden their centre, which we had to pay a share of in our rates was out of reach of the Hyden residents. Not to put too fine a point on it, most of our residents lived in a farming area to the east of the town and were spread over about 35miles in that direction.

Because our oldest son, Rodney, was old enough to need pre-school, education I agreed to attend a meeting, arranged by Hillary Millar and Monica Lynch, at which they hoped to set up a working committee to investigate the possibility of starting a play group centre or better still a real kindergarten. On the appointed evening I turned up and was in fact the only father who bothered to attend.

If nothing else was possible we needed to have a play group so that the children of the district could get to know each other and learn to play together away from their parents as a group in readiness for school. We were sure that it would ease and maybe even eliminate the first day blues when school started and they were faced with spending their first day away from their mothers. Also We hoped that they would look forward to that first day at school where they would be with the friends that they already were familiar with.

The ladies felt that they needed a strong (minded) man, preferable someone in business, who would be able to stand up to the authorities and know their way around the rigmarole of business meetings and other formalities. Someone in fact who may be able to kick around their counterparts to get things moving as quickly as possible.

The ladies had a vote and the result was that I was pressed into service as the inaugural, and, as it turned out 3 years president.

I believe that Monica Lynch was vice president and Hillary Millar secretary/treasurer.

Our first concern was to raise enough funds to buy the basic equipment to start the ball rolling.

Then the next requirement was a safe and suitable building in which to operate along with a volunteer or two to run the sessions.

The following day after a few phone calls I started to amass heaps of books and other literature which laid out the many rules and regulations that were apparently necessary for the safe operation of a set up like the one that we had in mind. There seemed to be an endless supply of this material and it appeared that the boffins in the education department had little else to do other than churning out all this guff to bamboozle would be aspirants. Some of these rules proved necessary but others seemed totally irrelevant to our situation in Hyden and in fact seemed to have been thought out in such a way as to make life difficult, bordering on impossible. As a result we selected a few basic rules and went to work.

Fund raising was our first priority and many suggestions were made and discussed at length. Cake stalls are always useful but only provide a trickle of money and we were in a hurry. Most of us felt that walkathons had been done to death so we settled on a "Bike-athon", whatever that was.

This momentous event was to be held around the town football oval, with a barbeque to follow.

No-one had heard of public liability in those days but we insured the event against rain. Having picked a weekend that the statistics declared as, "unlikely for rain", we got a very low rate of premium.

The local school children rounded up any machine that could be called a bicycle and worked like mad to sign up sponsors, at a fee for every circum-navigation of the oval.

The eventful day dawned as members of the Buffalo Lodge, of which Sandy Forbes comes to mind was one, donated sheep which were cut up into chops and steaks for the barbeque.

The weather was perfect and the starter set the kids off on their marathon.

Those rotten kids almost bankrupt every one in the district, because none of us thought that it would be necessary to set a maximum number of revolutions.

Those Kids, bless them, rode round and round and round until they virtually fell of their machines.

We were in business, we had enough to get started, even without the proceeds of the barbeque to follow.

As we were settling down to enjoy our meal, a sudden sharp thunderstorm hit the oval and soaked the area. Thank goodness we were finished cycling and could sit in the sports pavilion and watch the rain cascading down. It turned out to be only a sharp and sweet but very heavy shower, made all the sweeter than we thought initially, because there was enough rain water in the gauge to amply qualify the event for the insurance money as well.

The next day I contacted a Miss Mitchell, who was Senior Supervisor, of preschools, at the WA.

education department in Perth, and she was very helpful at first. She sent us a list of basic equipment, such as wooden blocks etc. that we needed and details of suitable suppliers.

We ordered the equipment which arrived in due course and we had decided to use the football pavilion because it was a long way from roads and traffic, where-as the hall and C.W.A. rooms were on the main street and not suitable for safe secure fencing.

The wooden blocks, hundreds of them, were untreated and needed a coat or two of varnish before they could be used. I called for help to paint the blocks and I set up "clothes lines" across the rear of my workshop.

I had bought heaps of small screw-in hooks so that the blocks could be hung up to dry after varnishing.

One Sunday morning, Laura and George Green, who had no children at all turned out to help me install the hooks and paint the blocks and hang them to dry. Not another person turned up to help, not even the two ladies who were tormenting me to set up the preschool centre nor their husbands Once all the hooks were installed we held onto the hooks whilst we painted each block.

A suitable day was arranged for open day, a Tuesday, if my memory serves me well, because it was one of our mail days, and most of the farmers wives would be in town with their kids in tow anyway, to collect their mail and papers. Whilst the mothers were buying their weekly stores we were able to start our play group.

Mrs. Irene Powell, who lived at north Hyden, took on the supervisor's job and was ably assisted by Linda Christian, whose family were running a farming property about 10 miles east of the town.

Actual numbers elude me but I am sure that we had around 20 youngsters from day one and everything went well. All looked rosy, until out of the blue, disaster struck.

Miss Mitchell, the Senior Advisory Teacher, paid us a visit and I escorted her proudly to our ever so humble pre-school centre. The outside of the pavilion did not sit well with her because it was only corrugated iron. Due to the remote location, she was prepared to let it run, provided that we raise funds to suitably fence the area with child proof fencing and line the walls with suitable sheets.

When Miss Mitchell stepped inside the hall she gave a gasp of dismay and disappointment, then utter disgust. I don't think that she had ever been inside a tin shed and she was appalled to see that it was not lined at all. I hated to point out that a number of families in our area were living in similar buildings. Furthermore the windows were too high to see out into the play area without standing close to them. Also in our ignorance, we had put the sand pit at the end of the building where there was no window at all.

Pulling herself up to her full height she announced that this would not do. We must close the facility at once until a suitable venue could be found.

I showed her around all the buildings in the town and she admitted that, maybe, we had picked the best of a bad lot, but that was no excuse, we had to shut up shop immediately and that was final.

I told her that she would have to stay on in Hyden indefinitely if that was her decision.

She stated that was final her decision and

she was not prepared to discuss it any further. Then she asked why I felt that she would need to stay in town.

I told her, in no uncertain terms, that as soon as she crested the hill on her way out of town, we would re-open and stay open.

She then informed me that it would be illegal to do so and I would face prosecution if it stayed open. Now I knew why our committee ladies wanted a strong personality like me to stand in the firing line and cop all the flack.

I had a minor brainwave at that point and told her that she should call in at the shire offices as she went through Kondinin to explain our dire circumstances to the shire clerk, Mr Brian Baker, then she could negotiate with the council for a suitable building to be erected.

A couple of hours later my phone rang and it was the shire clerk, Mr Brian Baker on the other end demanding to know what it was that he had ever done to offend and upset me.

I said, "I'll take a bet that you've just had a visit from a Miss Mitchell of the education department."

This proved to be correct and apparently she

had really laid it out for him. She had got right up his nose and she would not leave without his promise to do something to help us and soon.

I was invited to the next meeting of the Kondinin Shire Council to submit a proposal to finance a pre-school centre in Hyden.

I arranged an urgent meeting with Mrs. Lynch and Mrs. Millar to thrash out a plan of attack.

We decided that all three of us would attend the meeting and organised who would say exactly what, so that we covered all the relevant points without doubling up or all trying to speak at once.

I was to give a lead in and a general overview of our activities to date.

One of my committee Mrs Millar had studied the district stud book, which is a local register of all the kids in the district and I asked her to run through current numbers and forecast of numbers to come, even the ones expected in the future but, as yet, not arrived. Some were little more than baby bumps at that time.

Finally, the finale was a round up of Miss Mitchell's visit, her rulings and our solutions, i.e. a new building on vacant land in Clayton street.

Herb Rae, the shire president, asked me if, myself and my committee, were prepared to service (pay off) a loan if council was able to raise one on our behalf.

I told him that we certainly were, and that we would gladly be able to repay council by an amount equal to that paid by the committee of the Kondinin pre- school centre which was already in existence. We assured the councillors that once we sited their receipt for the Kondinin payment to be made each term we would match it.

This brought a laugh from the councillors, as they knew, and a little bird had told me so that I knew that Kondinin had never kept up to their obligation and steadfastly refused to make a single payment.

Our local representative on the council, told me, later, that the councillors reckoned that ours was the best deputation ever to be received by council and they quickly raised the loan so that building could start as soon as possible, which it did.

Graham Smead of the Kondinin building Company was awarded the contract to erect the building to a design submitted by Miss Mitchell.

The building was to be next door to my own home so I was able to be of great help to speed up proceedings. I provided a power outlet and a water supply free of cost to get things started. Once the brick footings were completed I called for help to cart enough sand to fill the footings to floor height and compact it to the builders specifications.

As no-one came forward to offer assistance, I borrowed Brian Duane's ford tip truck, and John Lynch's front end loader to dig the sand from a pit near John's boundary, cart it into town, and load it into the walled area of the foundation.

With a shovel and rake I piled up the sand to excess before watering it down over the next two days. We didn't have any compacting machines in the district, so I made a ramp to get my Valiant stn. wagon onto the sand to roll it down each evening, after work, until it was solid.

We had contracted with the builder that we would do this to save a lot of money and he made it quite clear that it would have to meet his specifications, before he would lay the concrete.

I was worried that the bed would not be full enough or hard enough, but all was well in the end and we only had to remove a little excess sand.

If I had known how little help I would get, or how much work was involved, I would have made the council pay the extra money. It appeared that the fathers of our kids would rather help at a busy bee for a sporting club to provide for their pleasure, than do anything for the education of their kids. This was to be how it turned out right to the bitter end.

I was led to believe that our builder was a difficult man to work with and that he would mess us around for months. None of this was true as I built up a great rapport with Graham, and we had no problems, not even when the roof tiling company let us down and we had to switch to metal tiles, almost overnight which saved a lot of money and time as it turned out.

Eventually it all drew to a close and opening day drew near. Because of their involvement I invited the shire president to open the building and Miss Mitchell was also invited, of course.

We had a rush to erect a super six fence ready for the great day but only one man, Roger Stuart, turned up in the morning to help to dig the ditches and set up the sheets. After lunch, Wes Smith turned up for a while and Keith Billingham arrived in time to help with the last few sheets.

When Miss Mitchell arrived for the opening she kicked up a storm because she reckoned that the building was the wrong way round and needed to be turned at right angles. When I asked her why, she said to shelter the play ground from the cold east winds in winter. I pointed out to her that this was Hyden, not Perth and we had erected it this way round to minimise the effects of the severe heat in summer. and the only times that we got east winds were in summer not winter. I then showed her my house next door which is situated the way she wanted the kindergarten and pointed out that we had got it all wrong and I would gladly rotate my home if I could, to line up with the pre-school centre.

When all was ready I asked the Shire President

to have his say on behalf of the council since it was their money that built it, but he said, "No mate, this is all your doing and you should have the honour of opening it."

Near the end of my third year in office I handed over to my vice president, Monica Lynch. This move allowed the ladies to hold meetings in the afternoons when they came in to collect the little ones and therefore, save an extra trip in the evenings.

Chapter 51

CANCERS AND TSUNAMIS

As I stepped out of the front door of our home this morning the East wind grabbed me and tugged viciously at my clothing. I headed out to my milk truck ready for the days events. It was very dark since it was only 2.00 am, but I stopped for a moment and waved to my neighbours across the road, just as I do each and every morning.

Not a single one of my neighbours ever makes the effort to return my friendly gesture but I still do it gladly, each and every day.

Occasionally we receive bunches of flowers from them, but that only happens when the East wind is blowing a gale, as it does most days and nights in the summer. The flowers are mainly artificial and the wind roughly uproots them from their vases and blows them over the road into our garden. I would love to return the flowers to their rightful owners, but I have no way of telling which of my neighbours graves they have come from.

There are more than a hundred souls over the road and the reason that I like to wave to them is that 3 years ago I found out that I had a CANCER.

"You have a Testicular Seminoma." doctor Chapman pronounced as she made arrangements for my operation.

"You must realise that it will have to come out immediately and hopefully we get there early enough before there are any secondaries to worry about."

Where do they find the names for these insidious growths? Seminoma is a nice soft sounding word, like Semolina, and should never have been used to describe a deadly disease such as cancer.

Due to my diligence and early self-examination, I had found the brute very early in it's life. My doctors are quite sure that they have removed all traces of the tumour. Subsequent tests reassured them that there are no signs of any secondary infections. However, they have warned me that it may show it's ugly head again within the next 10 years or so, but probably in a different location.

The reason for my friendly waves is that my neighbours, just like many of the recent Tsunami victims around the Indian Ocean, are all deceased. I only ever got to know one of them, a lovely young man in his teenage years whose father worked with me on a large farm at Myalup.

Michael was killed in the prime of his life as the result of a road accident a few years ago, and is buried in the cemetery right across the street from my home. Every day I thank God for the sixty odd years of my wonderful life and hope that it will continue on for a long time to come. I have long passed the 10 year danger period so hopefully the brute is now deceased.

I like to tell this story to encourage all men to self examine their bodies and then rush off to their doctor at the first signs of trouble because speed is the essence of success when dealing with cancer. Don't ever think that it can't happen to you because it surely can.

We are all vulnerable to cancers, diabetes and other serious diseases. Early diagnosis and treatment can make the difference between life and death. Last year out of the blue I was hit with a very savage dose of diabetes, which nearly ended it all. A quick trip to the local hospital, then two days on saline drips to clean up my blood and I started to recover. We are now on watch and wait and hope that I can keep it in check using insulin injections, every day, which are a pain in the arse. However, I seem to be winning now and at 75 its not as big a deal as it would be at 25. I have always been careful with my diet, never smoked, don't drink alcohol or coke etc.

Chapter 52

OF COWS AND CARS

Funny title, funny yarn but true indeed.

A friend of ours and a fellow mechanic ran a workshop in a small country town in the wheat belt. A rich local farmer called in one day with a mechanical problem of some sort and after sorting out his problem he stopped for a bit of a yarn. He was a bit dagged off because of a minor accident to his new car. The car was a top of the range Holden Statesman Deville with metallic paintwork.

The farmer also had a Hereford cattle stud and one day some of his pedigree bulls were milling around in the yard and the car was parked nearby. One of the bulls got a little too close to the car and when it turned suddenly it's backside bumped the door panel of the car.

As you would expect the owner was

somewhat miffed about the damage and at the insistence of his insurers he went around the district to get three quotes for the repair.

Because the car had metallic paint, which is unmatchable for touch ups etc. the quotes were sky high even though the dent was only quite small. The repairers all said that they would have to respray the whole car to get the paint looking the same colour all over.

After listening to his tale of woe Frank went out and had a good look at the damage. He then offered to repair the damage for a mere 100 dollars, less than the loss of no claim bonus in fact and far less than the 1200 dollars or so as quoted

The owner thought about the deal for sometime and finally decided that it was worth a try.

Frank walked up to his house behind the workshop and collected the necessary tools to tackle the job. He returned with a bucket of water and a suction tool that plumbers use to clear out household drains.

With great gusto Frank tossed the water at the dented door and carefully fitted the suction cup in the centre of the dent. Then with a sharp yank on the handle he popped out the dent before picking up a tin of polish and completing the job with a little elbow grease.

The farmer was quite vocal when Frank demanded the 100 dollar payment as per the quote. After some serious discussion the farmer said.

"Frank, if you can give me an invoice good enough to describe what you did and justify the payment I'll write you a cheque for 100 dollars."

Frank picked up an invoice book and wrote the following, *For repairing door on statesman motor car and repolishing the paint time taken ¼hr cost 5 dollars*

For years of training, and the knowledge and the skill to carry out the repair 95 dollars

Total 100 dollars

The farmer had a wry smile on his weathered old face as he opened the glove box, took out his cheque book and wrote out the cheque as agreed.

The farmer said, "Ok. Young man, you win this time but I'll be keeping a wary eye out for you in the future."

Chapter 53

STRAINER POSTS

I spent a good few years working for a cantankerous old farmer near the coast, south of Perth. He knew that he was the only intelligent guy in the whole world and he was so arrogant as well. He was sure that everyone else was a total loser and close to being a complete idiot. He treated us all as though we were too stupid to know what day it was and often found it necessary to tell us so.

If there were more than one way to do a job his way was always right and other's always wrong. He would send the men off to do a job after giving them only minimal instructions then catch up with them later in the day and berate them because he didn't like the way it had been done. Once he had observed how the job had been tackled he would work out a possible alternative method and complain that it had been done inappropriately.

He often made them start again and do it his way. Often his way was no better and sometimes it was worse, much worse or didn't work at all. It appeared that he always found an alternate way so that he could belittle the guys and make them look stupid. He never gave anyone praise for a job well done nor did he give them any credit for using their brain and solving a problem on their own.

It would never do for anyone of us to even suspect that we were as clever as him. He had one other interesting trait. He thought that he knew everything and liked to show off his prowess by using unnecessarily large words which, quite often he didn't actually know the true meaning of and got badly wrong at times which made him look like a total fool.

I was inclined to tackle him head on and argue the point because I was just as stubborn as he was. I never managed to get him to see my point of view and agree with me even though I was able to put up a very sound argument. I found that the only way to get along was to wait until he had gone off to annoy one of the others then do the job my way. Some of the older hands however, had a different approach. They worked out various devious little tricks to win the day, as you will see.

Eric had been with him for many years and had a solid farming background covering most of his life. He had worked out a way of dealing with the boss's obstinacy in many different ways as the situation occurred.

One day Eric was sent out to the back of the farm with a young helper called Bob to erect a new fence.

The boss said in his effected "upper class English" mode of speech "Eric, I want you to go out to the centre paddock next to the lake and erect a jolly fence running north to south about the middle of the paddock. You'll notice that the east side has much better soil types than the west side so I'd jolly well like you to adjust the fence line as you find appropriate. I want you to include all the better soil types to the east of the fence whilst keeping the fence in line with the others.

Eric collected his offsider, Bob, and the

necessary gear. There was only a thin layer of surface soil across the farm beneath which there was a solid layer of limestone. In some places the underlying rock was 'limestone cap rock' which was extremely hard and needed much work with a heavy crowbar to batter a hole through to the softer dirt below.

After a very tough mornings work Eric and the Bob had managed to erect a strainer assembly at both ends of the paddock. The strainer assembly, as you might expect was set firmly in the ground at each end to take the weight or stain of the wire and hold the fence firm.

Just as Eric was about to relax and enjoy his lunch the boss arrived to see how they were progressing. The boss checked the engineering strength of the strainers and could find no fault with it. He then studied the alignment of the fence, noticing that Eric had aligned it parallel with the east and west fences as he expected it would be.

The boss then decided that there was, maybe, more of the better dirt still left outside the fence to the west.

"Eric, I feel that you may have erred somewhat.

I feel that the fence needs to be about 10 feet further west so as to include all that better soil that you have missed.

Eric replied, "You're kidding boss. Do you mean that we have to move it just for 10 feet."

"Quite So Eric, 10 feet should do it." The boss answered.

With much scorn in his voice Eric replied, "What about the other end. Do we need to move that as well."

Realising that he wasn't in a position to make a fair judgement on the other end without driving down there the boss said, "No, no Eric I feel that the other end will suffice. Just shift this end".

Once the boss was out of earshot young Bob said, "He's kidding isn't he Eric?"

"I wish he was, but no, we have to shift it. He'll come back later and check it so get the tractor going and drill the two holes as far as the auger will go down. I'll mark out the positions ready for you."

Bob then said, "Oh yea that's great then we have to spend the rest of the day with the crowbar to get them deep enough. That rotten old sod should take a good look at himself."

"Don't worry mate it wont be that bad this time so get cracking". Was Eric's final remark on the subject.

Bob hopped onto the tractor, fired up the motor and set about positioning it on the west side of the new strainer assembly and about 10 feet away from it ready to start boring the holes.

"No, mate not that side. Bring it over here where I've marked these holes." Eric called out to Bob.

"That can't be right Eric," Bob replied. "The boss said there was more good dirt outside the strainer so we need to move it over that way to get it all in."

"Please, don't start arguing with me Bob, bring the bloody tractor over here and drill these two holes and look sharp about it." Eric retorted.

"I hope you know what you're doing mate, 'cause I don't want to do it all again." Bob shouted as he revved up the tractor and moved it over to Eric.

Once the holes were drilled, Eric quickly pushed the dirt back in again, stamped it down and went back to the original strainer to begin tying on the wire.

Bob was still bamboozled about the holes and said, "Eric, I just don't get it. How does that fix the problem?"

Eric in reply said, "He won't know the difference, mate. Once he sees that we've moved it like 'he' said he'll be happy. Trust me mate I've been here a long time. He can't tell us to move it further west again because that would mean that he got it wrong since he should have told us to move it 20 feet not 10 feet."

Poor Bob, all this political business was way above him, so he went over to help Eric but he was quietly dreading the return of the boss.

It was almost time to knock off and go home before the boss came back. After taking a good look around and checking out the work he stated.

"There you are, Eric, you can now see how much better that is. If you take a little more care you should be able to get it correct the first time in future and save a lot of time and my money." With those words of wisdom he drove away.

Bob said, "I still don't get it Eric. "How could it be any better when we didn't do anything at all?"

"Well it's quite simple really. You just need to understand how the boss's mixed up brain works. He can't help himself. He's just a cantankerous old fart who likes to have his own way. He loves to take every body down a peg or two just in case they manage to look better than him. He hates to give any of us credit for a job well done in case we get big headed about it. Anyway, come on and get that gear packed up. I'm going home I've had enough politics for one day."

Chapter 54

A MINI OR A MERCEDES

Life in a small rural community has many unexpected rewards that seldom, if ever, occur in the bustling existence of life in a city. If someone has the time and keen interest in the people around them there are many little incidents that crop up, which provide a good measure of entertainment even in the middle of a busy working day.

It was mid-morning in a little country town in the wheat belt when a very affluent farmer drove into the main street and stopped outside the local machinery dealer's premises.

Bonzer, the farmer in question, may have been ultra rich but he was driving an old second-hand, red, Morris, mini-minor which he had bought sometime ago for his daughter who had just passed her driving test and received her first driving licence. As his daughter was in the armed forces the mini spent most of it's time at home on the family farm.

The bright red car stood out like a dunny in the desert for all to see. It was the only car of it's type around the district where the big three, Holden, Falcon, and Valiant, ruled supreme. Parked in the garage at home on the family farm was a near new Mercedes 280SE motor car which he traded in every 2 years or so to upgrade with the latest technology.

The Mercedes had not been seen much around the town, or the district for many months as the owner seemed to prefer to drive the sporty little mini instead of the large lumbering Mercedes.

The locals thought that the sheer exuberance of driving the mini in contrast to the staid and steady Mercedes was the main reason for the absence of the Mercedes around town. However, I was more inclined to the theory put about by one of his near neighbours who seemed to know him better than most.

She reckoned that, because the mini was far cheaper to run than the Mercedes, and Bonzer being a bit on the mean side preferred the cheaper option, and my business dealings with him seemed to support that theory.

Also, the fact that the resale value of the Mercedes would be greatly enhanced if he could keep the mileage down below a certain level, was all the reason he needed to drive the humble mini because he was a mean old fart.

However, I digress somewhat from the main point of the story. As the farmer climbed out of the little car outside of a tractor dealership in the main street of town, a farmer's wife and near neighbour of his stepped out of the general store at the other end of the street.

This particular lady was a character in her own right. Jaye never called a spade, a spade, she referred to it as a bloody shovel. She was always dressed in men's working trousers and wore a dusty, broad brimmed, mans working hat. She always looked as though she had just stepped out of the shearing shed.

Even in the days when women were not accepted in the public bar of the pubs, Jaye could often be seen enjoying a welcome beer with her husband and the other men of the district, and God help anyone who was brave or silly enough to make comment of the fact.

In spite of all this, Jaye was a lovely lady with a heart of gold and was loved by all who knew her.

As Jaye stepped onto the pavement she looked along the street and spotted the mini just as Bonzer stepped out onto the road beside it.

"Gooday Bonzer you old fart," she called out loudly, "How the hell are you today?"

"I'm great Jaye," he replied, "And how the hell are you on this lovely day."

"I'm great Bonzer, on top of the world in fact and even better now that I've seen you. I see you're in the mini. I heard that they repossessed the Mercedes. Is that true mate? Times are pretty hard these days and a drop of rain would help"

Bonzer looked as though he had just been hit with that bloody shovel. His face went every colour of the rainbow, but mostly bright red then as white as a sheet as he jumped back into the mini and roared off out of town with the tyres squealing on the bitumen as he gave the mini hell.

Jaye looked at me with a puzzled frown and said. "Was it something I said or has he forgotten something more important, Brian?"

I replied, "It's OK Jaye, you've finally managed to make a hole in that thick skin of his and it must have hurt a bit."

The rich farmer only lived about 12 miles from town and after about half an hour or so he returned to town driving the Mercedes very stately into the main street. He then drove two complete circuits of the residential streets of our little town and headed out towards his farm again without stopping.

About lunchtime I happened to spot the Mercedes perambulate sedately into the main street again then circum-navigate the houses once more before heading back up the hill and out to the farm again.

It was about 5 p.m. when the Mercedes again hit town and once more made a couple of circuits of the streets before parking diagonally across the front corner of the car park at the pub, which was situated on a major intersection and was visible from most of the main street and the main road into, and through the town.

Bonzer walked quietly into the bar, looking over his shoulder as he went to see if anyone was watching. He ordered, and drank a couple of beers before returning home once more, hopefully, having convinced all and sundry, that he was still solvent after all.

HOPETOUN HOLIDAY

Neither A Mini Nor A Mercedes, Just My Service Vehicle And Family Limousine.

(note the telephone number)